HER LIPS WERE BUT A BREATH AWAY . . .

"Lady," he said softly, "you are my wife. And though I've no wish to cause you harm, by God, through violence or tenderness, you will be so tonight."

Her eyes were on his. Her lips were parted and dry.

"No," she whispered.

But he was done talking, she realized.

He lowered his head and though she thrashed aside, his mouth covered and claimed hers. His tongue parted her lips and thrust hot and deeply into her mouth. It seemed he entered more and more deeply inside her with the melding of their lips.

In the flickering candlelight he seemed to steal away her very heart and soul and give them back, and take them once again . . .

QUANTITY SALES

Most Dell books are available at special quantity discounts when purchased in bulk by corporations, organizations, and special-interest groups. Custom imprinting or excerpting can also be done to fit special needs. For details write: Dell Publishing, 666 Fifth Avenue, New York, NY 10103. Attn.: Special Sales Department.

INDIVIDUAL SALES

Are there any Dell books you want but cannot find in your local stores? If so, you can order them directly from us. You can get any Dell book in print. Simply include the book's title, author, and ISBN number if you have it, along with a check or money order (no cash can be accepted) for the full retail price plus $2.00 to cover shipping and handling. Mail to: Dell Readers Service, P.O. Box 5057, Des Plaines, IL 60017.

HE WOULD CLAIM HER.
HE WOULD TAME HER,
UNTIL SHE YEARNED
TO BE HIS.

THE VIKING'S WOMAN

Heather Graham

A DELL BOOK

Published by
Dell Publishing
A division of
Bantam Doubleday Dell
Publishing Group, Inc.
666 Fifth Avenue
New York, New York 10103

The trademark Dell® is registered in the U.S. Patent and Trademark Office.

ISBN: 0-440-20670-7

Printed in the United States of America

Published simultaneously in Canada

July 1990

10 9 8 7 6 5 4 3 2 1

RAD

This book is a sequel to *Golden Surrender*, my first historical novel, and therefore very close to my heart. It was inspired by and dedicated to my mother's family, who emigrated from Dublin to the United States, and so I feel this, too, must be for them.

First, for my mother, Violet, with all of my love. And in memory of Granny Browne, for all the wonderful tales she could tell about leprechauns and banshees in her thick, rich brogue. It is dedicated in memory of Granda, and all of their children, and especially for Aunt Amy, for always being so sweet.

Most of all, this particular book is for Kathleen Browne DeVouno. Neither time nor distance ever dampens the warmth of her heart or spirit, and I am incredibly proud to be related to her.

Love you, Katie.

PROLOGUE

He had been conceived during a tempest, on a night when anger and passion had reigned.

And he was born in the midst of lightning, and it seemed that storms would be destined to rule his life.

A terrible slash of lightning tore across the sky, and Erin, Queen of Dubhlain, gasped out and screamed. Pain, swift and merciless, seized her. She bit her lip, for she was certain that the birth would go well, and she did not want to frighten those around her, or her lord and husband, the king. The pain intensified and peaked and slowly began to ebb, and she breathed deeply. She closed her eyes and managed to smile, recalling the night in which she was certain the child had been conceived. They had ridden too far and had been caught out far from the walls of the town, out by the caves, when the storm had come. She had been furious with Olaf—over what, she could not remember now. But fury had never been a deterrent to them, nor was it that night. Breathless, heated words had merely quickened the ardor that inflamed their passion.

She could remember it all so well. He had shouted something, then laughed and swept her into his arms. She had shouted back, but then forgot the argument in the sweet and savage onslaught of his kiss. In the fury of the storm he swept her down to the ground, above the wild, treacherous shore beneath them, and together, while thunder raged, they had created the life that moved within her now. Beloved life, for she loved her lord well. She could remember her Norse husband that day so clearly. His cobalt eyes, ever tender yet ablaze with his desire. Aye, she could remember well and sweetly the power of his arms, the fever of his kiss, the touch of his hands. She had felt the blaze of his body, like the lightning, deep, deep within her.

She loved him so. They were ever swift to anger and swifter still to passion, but always the love was there.

"Oh, dear God!" she screamed again as another pain seized her, followed by fear. It had been so hard for her to have Leith. She had prayed that this second child would come more easily. But now she burned again, the pain feeling as if it would cut her in two.

She felt her mother's gentle touch upon her brow. "Why, Mother?" she whispered. "Why must it be so hard?"

Maeve smiled at her tenderly and tried not to appear too worried. " 'Tis not easy, love, to give birth to the cubs of the Wolf." Maeve looked up. He was there, in the doorway, the Wolf of Norway, the King of Dubhlain. He glanced at her and at Erin, and then the great, towering blond king made his way to his wife's side.

"I am here, Princess. Fight for me, fight for me again. Give me my second son."

She smiled. He thought of her fragile beauty and of

the strength beneath it. Her eyes were a deep emerald, as boundlessly rich as the strength inside her, the strength that had entrapped his heart. That strength would belong to all their children. It was the passion that belonged to those of the Emerald Isle, and it was the power of the North Sea raiders.

She held tightly to his hand, glad that he had come. "A girl this time!" She managed to laugh.

He shook his head gravely. "Nay, a son."

"A son?"

"Aye, for Mergwin told me so."

"Oh!" She gasped, but he was beside her and she didn't scream again. She locked her fingers with his and drew her strength from him. A new pain seized her like a heated brand, and she gasped with relief, for the babe had fought his way near birth. "He comes!" she cried.

Olaf had been with her at their first child's birth, and he knew to hold her tightly, once, and then again. And then she laughed and cried and he kissed her, for she had expelled the babe, and Maeve assured her that it was indeed another boy.

"And is he beautiful?" she demanded.

"Beautiful beyond belief," Olaf assured her. Erin's woman quickly wiped the babe and handed him to his mother. Erin's eyes widened at the sheer size of the infant. "More blond hair!" she murmured, and Olaf laughed, kissing her damp ebony locks. "I fear you'll have to wait for a daughter, love, and maybe she will have midnight hair," he teased her.

She groaned in mock protest. "You speak to me at this moment of more children?"

"As soon as it's physically possible," he whispered

back, laughing, and they both felt warm. He thought that their love was so good, it was everything in life.

"And his eyes—"

"Blue, too, like his sire's," Maeve said with a sigh. She winked at Olaf, and they continued to stare at the babe.

"They can change," Erin said.

"Leith has Irish eyes," he reminded her.

"Surely eyes may change their color," Maeve agreed.

"Ah, but these won't!" Olaf was certain.

The babe lay on the bed between his mother and father, his grandmother looking on. His eyes were alert, his fists pounded against the sheets, his mouth was open, and his voice was in high command. "Ah, this one is demanding," Olaf said.

"Like his sire," Erin agreed. She was already in love with her infant son. She settled back and guided his puckered mouth to her breast. The babe took root and held fast, sucking instantly with assurance and a power that caused her to gasp and laugh. Olaf stroked her hair as they lay together, and it was a moment of sweet and supreme peace. They had earned it, Olaf thought. They had come through much.

He noted that Erin's eyelashes were drooping, thick black crescents against her cheeks. Maeve glanced his way and he nodded. He started to take the babe from his wife, but Erin awoke quickly, her lashes flying upward in alarm. She held fast to the babe. "Nay, don't take him!" she whispered, and he knew that she was afraid. Not so long ago their first-born child, Leith, had been kidnapped by Olaf's enemy, Friggid the Dane. Friggid was dead now—Olaf had slain him—but Erin had never gotten over the fear that Leith, and now this new son, might be snatched from her again.

" 'Tis I, love," he assured her. " 'Tis I. Let me take him, that your women might give you clean linen and your mother might bathe you. 'Tis I, Erin."

Her dazzling emerald eyes closed again. The smile she offered him was beautiful and peaceful. "Eric," she murmured. "He is to be Eric. Leith, for my brother. Eric, for yours."

Olaf was pleased. "Eric," he agreed softly.

He carried his newborn babe to the window and stared down upon his son. The infant's hair was thick and nearly white, and his eyes, still wide open, were indeed a Nordic blue. The boy was large, very large.

"You'll be one to please," Olaf murmured.

"A fine Viking" came a new voice.

Olaf started and stared hard at the ancient old man who had entered the room. Mergwin. A man both ancient and ageless, Viking and Druid, the child of a Norse rune master and a legendary Irish priestess from an old Druid cult. He had served the Ard-Ri, the High King of Ireland, Erin's father, and though he still served the Ard-Ri, he was most often with his favorite of Aed Finnlaith's children, Erin of Dubhlain. He was her loyal man and therefore Olaf's too.

Even if they did still have their occasional differences.

Mergwin could move like smoke through time and space, it seemed. He had come from his home in the forest, though no one had sent for him. He had known that the child would come this day.

The lightning rent the heavens again. It cast a curious glow upon Mergwin's face and floor-length beard. Its light fell upon the babe, and he seemed to glow in his father's arms.

"A Viking?" Olaf grinned and shook his head, indicating his sleeping wife upon the bed. The women moved carefully and silently to change her sheets and bathe her face. "Don't say that too loudly," Olaf warned Mergwin. "His mother would not like it."

Mergwin touched the boy's face. The baby grabbed the Druid's finger and squeezed hard.

"Leith is Irish, like his mother. Through and through. One day, Lord of the Wolves, he will follow his sire and make a fine king of Dubhlain. But this one, this Eric—you have given him a Viking name, my lord."

Olaf frowned. He sensed some warning from the Druid, and he held his son more tightly against the expanse of his body, as if he could protect the boy from the future.

"Speak up, you old fraud!"

"The Wolf knows better than to growl at me!" Mergwin said calmly. He paused, taking in a long, slow breath. "This child, Lord Wolf, is yours. A Viking. And like his sire, he will ride the seas of the world. He will often know battle, and his sword will learn well to parry any assault of steel. Yet with the power of his skill of his mind and that of his sword arm, he will rule many. He—"

"He what?" Olaf's voice was tight, for though he already loved the child in his arms, Eric was a second son. For him to rule Dubhlain meant danger to his brother, Leith.

Mergwin, sensing Olaf's anxiety, shook his head.

"His destiny lies in other lands. He will face very grave dangers."

"But he will overcome those dangers!" Olaf insisted.

Mergwin stared at Olaf. They did not lie to each other.

"He is ruled by Odin. He will ride the sea to great thunder and storms, and so will the tempest enter into his heart and into the world where he will seek his destiny. When he is grown, there will be darkness . . . but—"

"Speak out!"

"There will be light too." Mergwin's face was grave, and Olaf, Lord of the Wolves, did not know whether to pray for his son to the Christian God he had adopted for his wife's sake, or to Loki and Odin and Thor, the gods of his past.

He would pray to them all. His jaw tightened and he flexed his muscles. Mergwin feared that the great warrior would crush his son.

Mergwin rescued the boy from Olaf. The babe's heat seeped into him and he closed his eyes. "Aye, he will be much like his sire. Danger will follow him, for the passion of his nature, but . . ."

"But what!" Olaf roared.

Mergwin grinned at last, though his eyes remained solemn. "Train him well, Lord Wolf. Train him to battle, train him to cunning. Make his sword arm strong and his hearing keen. He will go a-Viking, and he will meet a terrible, treacherous foe."

Mergwin paused. The baby was looking at him with his sire's ice-and-fire eyes. Watching him, as if he understood the fortune the Druid cast for him. Mergwin's smile deepened.

"He has been born with courage. With pride. With the indomitable spirit of his mother and the power and will of his father. Give him wisdom, Olaf. Then set him free, for he must, like his father, find his own heart."

Olaf was frowning. "No riddles, Druid."

"I don't speak in riddles, I give you what I can. Set him free and he will fight his dragons, his demons. And then . . ."

"Then?"

"Well, then, my lord, he may prevail. For like his father he, too, will meet a woman with Odin's power. Storm power, the power of lightning, the power of thunder. Her will shall challenge his at every turn. She will bring danger, and yet she will also bring salvation. She will be a tempestuous vixen. Her beauty will be unforgettable but her hatred deeper than the sea that separates their homelands. Triumph will fall well within their grasp. Aye, Lord Olaf, triumph will be theirs, if the wolf can tame the vixen."

"Or," Mergwin added pensively, with a subtle grin that he hid from his Viking lord, "if the vixen can tame the wolf!"

1

The first dragon's prow appeared upon the horizon at the same time that the first stroke of lightning sizzled across the sky and the first mighty crack of thunder drummed throughout the heavens.

And then there was a sea of dragon prows, striking new terror into weary hearts. Tall and savage upon the water, like mythical beasts, they sailed in, raining devastation and slaughter.

The fury of the Norseman was well-known along the Saxon coastlines of England. The Danes had wreaked havoc upon the land for years, and all Christendom had learned to stand and tremble at the sight of the swift dragon ships, the scourge of land and sea.

The ships came from the east that day, but no man or woman viewing the host of Viking ships that caught a wind that threatened sails, dared pause to ponder that fact. They saw the endless shields that lined the ships, prow and aft, and they saw that the wind, not the oarsmen, advanced the ships like the wrath of God.

Lightning sizzled and snapped and lit up the gray, swirling sky. The wind whistled and roared, and then screamed, as if to portend the blood and violence to come. Red and white, the Viking sails slashed across the dark and deadly gunmetal sky, defying the vicious wind.

Rhiannon was in her chapel when the first alarm was shouted. She prayed for the men who would do battle against the Danes at Rochester. She prayed for Alfred, her cousin and her king, and she prayed for Rowan, whom she loved.

She had not expected danger to darken her coast. Most of her men were gone to serve with the king as the Danes were amassing to the south. She was without help.

"My lady!" Egmund, her most loyal, aging warrior, long of service to her family, found her in the chapel upon her knees. "My lady! Dragon prows!"

For a moment she thought he had lost his mind. "Dragon prows?" she repeated.

"On the horizon. Coming for us!"

"From the east?"

"Aye, from the east!"

Rhiannon leapt to her feet and raced from the chapel, finding the stairs to the wooden walls that surrounded her manor house. She hurried along the parapets, staring out to sea.

They were coming. Just as Egmund had warned her.

She felt sick to her stomach. She almost screamed in fear and agony. All of her life she had been fighting. The Danes had descended upon England like a swarm of locusts, and they had brought with them bloodshed and terror. They had killed her father. She would never forget holding him and willing him to breathe again. Alfred fought the Danes and defeated them often.

Now they were descending upon her home, and she had no one left to defend it because her people had gone to Alfred. "My God," she breathed aloud.

"Lady, run!" Egmund said. "Take a mount and ride hard to the king. You can reach him by tomorrow if you ride hard. Take your arrows and an escort, and I will surrender this fortress."

She stared at him and then smiled slowly. "Egmund, I cannot run. You know that."

"You cannot stay!"

"We will not surrender. Surrender means nothing to them—they perform the same atrocities whether men give battle or not. I will stay and fight from here."

"My lady—"

"I may kill or wound many of them, Egmund. You know that."

He did; she could see it in his eyes. She was an amazing markswoman. But she knew, too, as he looked at her, that he was still seeing her as the little girl he had protected for years.

Old Egmund wasn't seeing her as a child at all but as a woman, and he was afraid for her. Rhiannon was beautiful and striking, with a siren's silver-blue eyes and golden-sunset hair. She was Alfred's cousin as well as his godchild, and at his command she had been well educated. She could be softspoken and as gentle as a kitten, and she could trade quips and laugh with the men and manage the vast estates she had inherited with a charming ease. She would be a worthy prize for some Viking, and Egmund could not bear the thought that she might fall prey to such a man.

"Rhiannon, I beg of you! As I served your father—"

Two steps brought her to him, and she flashed him a warm, beautiful smile, taking both of his gnarled hands into her own. "Dearest Egmund! For the love of God, I cannot fathom this attack from the east. I cannot! But I will not surrender, and I will not leave you here to die for me! I will flee when there is nothing more that can be done. But now, you must know that as my father's daughter I cannot leave until we have sent some of those heathens straight to hell! Call Thomas and order out what guard we have left, Egmund. Warn the serfs and the tenants. Hurry!"

"Rhiannon, you must stay safe!"

"Have my bow and a quiver of arrows sent to me. I shall not leave the parapet, I swear it!" she promised him.

Knowing further words would be useless, Egmund hurried down the wooden steps, shouting out orders. The huge gates were ordered shut, the few remaining warriors mounted their horses, and the simple farmers rushed about to find pitchforks and staffs. All looked terrified.

The brutality of the Vikings was well known.

A boy brought Rhiannon her quiver and arrows. She stared across the sea. The sky had grown gray and the wind was whipping fiercely, as if the elements were forecasting the horror soon to come. She saw the ships and trembled. Closing her eyes, she tried very hard not to remember the Viking raids of the past. She had lost so much to the Danes, as had England. She, too, was terrified, and yet she had to fight. To be taken or slain without fighting was not conceivable to her.

The attack made no sense at all. Alfred should have known something of the Danish movements. She should have been warned.

The ships moved closer and closer. The sky and sea seemed not to have the power to stop them.

Rhiannon nearly sank to her knees in fear. The ships were almost at the shore. The prows alone, with their hideously carved dragon faces, were enough to strike terror into most hearts. And still the sailors had not taken aim. Rhiannon prayed that her soldiers would let fly the first volley of arrows. Perhaps they could kill some of the invaders before the Vikings reached them. She closed her eyes in a brief prayer. *Dear God, I am scared, please be with me.*

She opened her eyes. She could see a man riding the lead ship. He was tall and blond and rode the tempest of the waves without losing his balance, his arms crossed over his chest. Certainly he was one of the commanders, towering in height, broad in the shoulders, lean in the hips, a strongly muscled warrior of Valhalla. She shivered anew and pulled out an arrow. Resolutely she stretched out her bow.

Her fingers trembled. She had never tried to kill a man before. Now she had to. She knew what Vikings did to men and women when they raided.

Her fingers slipped and a new trembling assailed her. Her mouth went dry and a frightening warmth overcame her. She closed her eyes and inhaled deeply, and when she opened them again, she didn't understand what had seized her. The wind seemed to be whispering to her that the golden-blond Viking was going to be part of her fate.

Impatiently she shook off the feeling and swore she

would not tremble again. If it was difficult to aim at a man in order to kill him, she need only remember her father's death.

She tested her bow again, and her fingers were remarkably steady. Kill the leader, her father and Alfred had said often enough, and the men beneath him will scatter. This blond giant was one of their leaders. She had to kill him. And that was what the whisper of fate had been. She had to kill him, even if he seemed to defy the wind, the sea, and the gods, both Norse and Christian.

Eric of Dubhlain had no idea at that moment that his life might be in danger from anyone. He had not come to make war but at the invitation of Alfred of Wessex.

The sea was fierce, but he knew the sea and did not fear it.

The sky went black, and then the lightning came again, a startling streak of gold, as if God Himself had cast down a bolt of fire to light up the doom that approached. God or Odin, the Lord of the Viking horde, of his father's people, was at work. Odin was casting lightning bolts as he raced his black stallion, Sephyr, and his chariot across the heavens. Odin, god of the pagans, was creating the storm, turning the sky to pitch, lighting it up again with blazes of sheer fire.

Eric stood tall and towering and powerful, like a golden god against the wind, a booted foot braced hard against the prow. The wind played against his hair, and it was as golden as the lightning, his eyes a blazing cobalt blue. His features were strongly chiseled, ruggedly, implacably handsome. His cheekbones were high and wide, his eyebrows set well upon his brow and cleanly arched, his jaw firm. His mouth, wide and sensual, was set in a straight line as he watched the shore. His beard and mustache were clipped and clean, redder than the hair upon his head, and his flesh was handsomely bronzed. He wore a crimson mantle, drawn closed with a sapphire brooch. He needed no fine garments to display his nobility, for his stature and the confidence of his stance made men tremble. The very air about him seemed charged, revealing his vitality. To maids of any race or creed he created a startling, arresting appearance. He was graced with extraordinary power in his muscles, in the breadth of his shoulders, in the width of his chest, and in the strength of his thighs. His belly was whipcord lean. His legs, hugging the tempest-tossed ship with ease, were as strong as steel from years upon the sea and years riding, running, fighting, and coming a-Viking.

Yet he was not the customary Viking, for he was the son of two races, the Irish and the Norse. His father, the great Lord of the Wolves, ruled as king in the Irish city of Dubhlain. Olaf, King of Dubhlain, had gone a-Viking in his time too. But he had fallen in love with the land and with his Irish wife, and he had brought about a curious peace with Eric's grandfather, the great Ard-Ri, or High King, of all Ireland. Eric's maternal grandfather, Aed Finnlaith, still ruled over all the Irish kings at Tara, and far away in the Norwegian icelands, Eric's father's father ruled as a great jarl of the Norse. His education had been well rounded. He had studied in great monasteries of learning with Irish monks, and he had learned about the Christian

God and Christ, about writing, and about literature. At his father's court he had met many foreign men, masters and teachers. He had been taught to listen to the trees and the forest and the wind by Mergwin, the Druid. He had learned to reap, to harvest.

But he was a second son. He had gone to battle with his father and his elder brother, and he loved his Irish kin, but he had equally honored his Norse brethren. His Norse uncles, too, had taken him on many journeys for another kind of education.

A-Viking.

He had been bred to civilization, for men already proclaimed this time a "golden" age for Ireland.

He had also been bred to the raids that had made the savage quests of the Vikings famous throughout Europe and Asia and even the Russias. There were no finer navigators living than the Norsemen. There were no more furious fighters. And there were no men more brutal.

But he did not sail today to do battle. Though he had gone a-Viking with the best fighters in his younger days, he had also learned about a better quest, the one for land.

Eric had been sent to sea for the first time when he was just a lad, in the company of his uncle for whom he had been named. With his paternal grandfather's finest men, he had crossed endless seas and rivers and vast lands. He had sailed the Dnieper, entered into the gates of Constantinople, and learned the ways of the Moslem princes. He had come to know different cultures and peoples, and countless women, by conquest and by barter. A-Viking had been a way of life. It was what he did and what he was.

As the lightning lit up the heavens and the sea churned beneath him, as England's shore loomed ever closer, he wondered vaguely what had changed him. Not that the change had come quickly or easily. It had been like the slow melting of snows in the spring, entering into his heart and his being.

It had begun far, far from the northern icelands that were home to the Viking spirit. It had happened on the coast of Africa, when they had battled the caliph of Alexandria, and the people had come forward to pay with gold for their lives and their freedom.

She had been a gift to him.

Her name had been Emenia, and she knew nothing of rancor and hatred. She had taught him everything about peace. He had known only violence and she taught him tenderness. She had been taught the most exotic arts of lovemaking in the finest harem in the land, but it had been the sweet beauty in her heart, in her unquestioning devotion to him, that had lured him into love. She had enormous almond-shaped eyes, and hair as black as night, all the way down her back. Her skin was the color of honey, and she had tasted of it, and other sweet spices, and had smelled of jasmine.

She had died for him.

The caliph had been determined on treachery. Emenia had heard of it and had tried to come to warn him. He had heard later that the caliph's men had caught her by her glorious dark hair as she ran along the halls of the palace.

They had slain her to keep her silent, slitting her throat.

He had never been what the Vikings called a berserker—a fighter to lose all thought and reason and battle with nothing more than savage intent. Eric believed in a cool head in battle and had never relished needless death.

But that night he had become a berserker.

He had gone after her murderers, alone, enraged, and he had slain half of the caliph's guard before the ruler had thrown himself upon his knees, swearing that he had not ordered Emenia's death, only his own. Somehow, remembering her love of life and peace, he had stayed his sword from slitting the caliph's throat. He had plundered his palace anew and had sat vigil over his beloved's body; then he had turned his back on the hot, harsh land.

It had been so long ago. Many cold winters and many new summers had since passed, and through the seasons, violence had guided him again. But through it all he discovered that Emenia had given him something of a lasting thirst for peace, and she had also taught him something of women.

He was Irish as well as Viking. And just as his father had carved his place from the land, Eric had determined to do the same. His brother, Leith, ruled Dubhlain. Eric was ever Leith's right-hand man, as he was his father's. Land could be given to him, he knew.

But his pride was as savage as his heart, and so was his determination. He would make his own way, as the Wolf had done. They were all fighters. Even his gentle, beautiful Irish mother had an unquenchable pride. She had dared to take steel against the Wolf. She laughed at it now, but Mergwin never tired of telling the story. Or the tale of the Danes who had challenged the Norse Wolf and his Irish bride.

Olaf of Norway had sailed to Ireland seeking conquest. He had been an unusual invader to the Irish—and to their Ard-Ri, seizing land but minimizing loss of life, rebuilding anew as soon as he had secured the land he had taken. There came a stalemate between the Norse invader and the high Irish King—and Erin—and Dubhlain—had been his father's price for peace. Eric's mother, who once had tried to capture Olaf when he had been wounded, had been horrified. She had escaped the Wolf when the tables had turned on her, but she had not been able to escape her father's will.

Eric smiled, thinking of his father.

Olaf had given far more to Ireland than he had taken. He had served Aed Finnlaith, battling with him against the fierce Danish invader, Friggid. And in the fighting he had become Irish himself. In the joint quest to preserve their home and family Olaf and his Irish bride had discovered a love that burned as deeply as their passion. Mergwin had witnessed it all and, for reasons of which Eric was not entirely sure himself, prided himself that everything should have turned out so very well.

Eric's smile turned grim as the wind rushed to meet him and the salt spray of the sea dampened his face. The Danes who continued to harry the Irish coastline already called him the Spawn of the Wolf, or sometimes the Lord of Thunder, for where he battled, steel clashed and the ground trembled.

This ground would tremble! he silently swore. His

hatred for the Danes was innate, he was certain. And he had been asked here to battle them.

Asked by Alfred, the Saxon King of the English. Alfred, who had managed to draw his nobles together at long last against the devasting surge of Danes to hold tenaciously to the kingdoms of Wessex and Sussex and the south of Britain.

Rollo, Eric's companion and right-hand man, spoke suddenly from behind him. "Eric, this is a strange welcoming." As massive as an ancient oak, Rollo pointed past Eric's shoulder to the land. Eric frowned. If a welcome awaited them, it was a most curious one. The great wooden gates were being drawn about the harbor town. Atop the palisade, armed men were taking position.

A coldness seized Eric, and his eyes glittered with pale blue depths of fury. " 'Tis a trap!" he muttered softly.

And indeed, so it appeared to be, for as his ships came into the harbor he could smell the oil being heated that would be poured down upon them from the walls of the village.

"Odin's blood!" he roared at the treachery, and his fury nearly blinded him. Alfred had sent messengers to his father's house. The English king had begged him to come, and now this. "He has betrayed me. The King of Wessex has betrayed me."

Archers ran upon the parapets. Aim was being taken upon the seafarers. Eric swore again, and then he paused, narrowing his eyes.

Something was catching the light from the lightning. A sheath of it, long and radiant. He realized that a woman stood upon the parapet and that the sheath of gold was her hair, neither blond nor red nor chestnut but some shade of fire that was a combination of the three.

She stood among the archers and called out orders.

"By Odin! And by Christ and all the saints!" Eric swore.

A volley of arrows was set loose. Eric barely dodged the woman's shaft as it sped toward him. He ducked. The arrow landed harmlessly against the prow. Screams went up from the wounded men. Eric tightened his jaw in fury, sick at the treachery.

"We're coming fast upon the shore," Rollo warned him.

"Then so be it!"

Eric turned to his men, the ice-blue mist of Artic rage in his eyes and in his stance. He had learned to fight with control and thus to win, and he never gave away emotion, except through the terror evoking chill in his eyes and the clenching of his teeth.

"We were asked here to do battle! Begged to assist a rightful king!" he shouted to his men. He didn't know if his words would carry to the other ships, but his wrath would. "We are betrayed!" He stood still, then raised his sword. "By Odin's teeth, by Christ's blood! By my father's house, we will not be betrayed!"

He paused.

"A-Viking!"

The word went up on the air and screamed upon the wind.

The ships came to shore. Rollo brought out his double-headed ax, the Viking's most heinous weapon. Eric preferred his sword. He called it Vengeance, and that was what he offered.

They came in upon the sand and the shoals, and the Viking ships scraped bottom. In their fur-lined boots, Eric and his men splashed into the shallows. A horn sounded, and a battle cry began as a chant and rose to a chilling crescendo. The Vikings had come.

The gates to the fortress opened suddenly. Horsemen appeared, armed, like Eric's Irish and Norse crew, with two-headed battle-axes, the kiss of death, and pikes and swords and maces, but they were no match for the ferocity of the Vikings and the depths of Eric's rage.

Eric never fought as a berserker. His father had taught him long ago that anger must be controlled and turned to ice. He never let his temper carry his sword arm too far, to drive him too recklessly. He fought coldly and ruthlessly, slaying his first challenger and dragging the man from his horse. The challengers fought bravely, and in the midst of the carnage Eric thought that it was a pathetic waste of life and limb. There were a few professional fighters here, surely men of the king's fryd, "carls" who spent their days in his defense.

But mostly they were simple farmers, freemen, and serfs who fought with picks and hoes and whatever else they could find.

They died quickly and their blood fed the earth. More and more of the Vikings were mounted. More and more of the men of Wessex lay dead upon the dirt.

More cries went up. Mounted upon a chestnut horse seized from a fallen man, Eric lifted his sword, Vengeance. He cast his head back and raised the bloodcurdling battle cry of the Royal House of Vestfald.

Lightning tore across the sky and the rain began.

Men slipped and slid in the mud, and still the fight went on. Eric urged his mount toward the gates. He knew that Rollo and a horde of others followed him toward the gates. Archers remained above them. Impervious to the flying death, Eric ordered that a ram be dragged from the ships. Despite the arrows that flew and the oil that was cast down upon them, the barriers were quickly breached. The Vikings burst into the fortress town. Hand-to-hand combat followed, and with every moment that passed, victory came to Eric's men. He shouted in English that the men should lay down their arms. The pillage had begun—one did not bring a host of such raiders across the sea, set them to battle, and not expect that they would demand reward. But his fury had begun to ebb, and the blood lust was leaving his veins. He could not understand why Alfred, known far and wide to be a fierce fighter and a wise king, should have betrayed him so. It made no sense.

More and more men began to lay down their arms. Many of the buildings were afire. The parapets were falling down, and the fortress town was nearly a ruin of earthworks. Terrified squealing pigs and mewling cattle ran through the debris. Those men still alive were gathered together in a corner of the stockade before the gates that led out to the fields. Eric told Rollo to take charge of them. These men would become his serfs. He spun his mount around as he heard screams, and he knew that his men had come upon the town's maidens.

He raced to the center of the earthworks. A group of his men encircled a dark-haired girl who was no more than sixteen years old. Her tunic was torn, and she cried and screamed in a harried panic.

"Cease!" Eric demanded. He sat upon the great bay and stared down at the scene. His tone was quiet but harsh, and his command was met by silence. When all was still, except for the sobbing girl, he swept his icy gaze around all of them, and then spoke again. "We were betrayed here, but I've yet to comprehend why. You'll not abuse these people, man or maid, for I have claimed them and this place. We will take the riches of the town and divide them to a man. But the livestock will live, and the fields we will keep fertile, for this will be our land upon this Wessex shore."

The girl did not understand the Norse he spoke, but she seemed to realize that she had been granted a reprieve. Slipping and sliding in the rain and the mud, tears still stinging her eyes, she ran to him where he remained mounted atop the bay and kissed his booted foot.

"Nay, girl—"

He caught her hands impatiently and spoke in English. She looked up at him with dark eyes, and he shook his head again. He beckoned to Hadraic, one of his captains, to come for her.

Even as the Viking lord obeyed his command there was a whistling in the air. The bay screamed and fell, and Eric realized that an arrow meant for him had caught his mount instead. The horse fell, thrashing and screaming. Swiftly Eric leapt from it and stared about at the buildings, those burning and those still standing. A cry of fury went up among his men. A second arrow flew. Pain like fire tore into Eric's thigh where the arrow struck. He threw back his head and clenched his teeth, reaching for the shaft. His men raced forward. Taking cover behind the dying horse, he held up a hand, stopping them. Sweating and convulsing, he grasped the shaft and pulled. A cry of sheer agony tore from his lips, but the arrow came free. Blood flowed over his hands, and blackness spun before his eyes. He sat in the mud with the rain still pouring down upon him. For many seconds he feared that he would fall flat upon the earth, unconscious.

Fury revived him. He ripped off a piece of his mantle, tying the wound, and staggered to his feet. His jaw tightened and his eyes were like frost as they swept the area. A two-story lodging lay far to his back. It wasn't burning and there was a window on the second floor where an assassin might well have taken aim upon him.

"Hold, Eric—" Rollo called to him. But Eric lifted a hand and shook his head. "Nay, I will find this treacherous assassin and I will deal with him." He paused only a second longer, indicating the fallen horse. "Have mercy on this beast and set him free from his misery."

He strode toward the building, heedless of the danger that another arrow might fly. Rage blackened his vision now, but he knew that no one lurked in the window. Whoever had attacked him surely meant to run now, but there would be no escape.

He burst into the building. It was a fine manor home with a great hall and a line of shields upon the wall. There was a great fire in the center of the room, with an open shaft to the sky above it. Trickles of rain came through the flume of the shaft and hissed and steamed on the rocks that surrounded the fire.

Eric turned from it and looked to the stairs.

His attacker surely was waiting for him to take to the stairs. The man had doubtless come down there already and waited to attack his back as soon as it was turned.

He did not walk toward the stairs.

He looked about the room and saw a fine table set with plates and cups and ewers of ale and mead. Limping, he dragged his injured leg with him and poured out a long draught of mead.

He waited and in time was rewarded. Staring across the hall to a storeroom, he saw the slightest movement beneath a covered table. Casually he leaned down to slip out his knife from the sheath at his calf. Slowly he approached the storeroom. He moved as if he had no purpose. Then he swept up the linen that covered the table, and prepared to seize the man beneath it.

He swore as a cloud of flour hit him in the face, blinding him. A scurrying sound assured him that the man was trying to escape. Ignoring the pain in his eyes and in his leg, Eric lunged at the fleeing assassin. His hands curled around an arm, and he dragged the man down easily. He fell hard upon his attacker and swiftly brought up his knife, ready to deal out death.

Then he heard a woman scream, and he saw that he had caught the woman from the parapets, the creature with the fiery hair and the deadly arrows. He stayed his hand.

She trembled beneath him but swallowed her

scream, angry that she had already released it. Her
eyes were glazed with tears that she would not allow
to spill. Her irises were blue gray, almost silver, and
though her hair was that curious color of sun and fire,
her eyes were fringed by midnight-black lashes. They
were both startling and beautiful. Her skin was fair, a
creamy ivory, and as soft as a rose petal. She lay beneath him, gasping for breath, her breasts rising and
falling, their firm mounds apparent beneath the soft,
taut wool of her fur-trimmed tunic. He was assessing
the fine curves of her mouth when suddenly she
pursed her lips and spat at him.

He sat back, his thighs hard around her hips, and
with a flick of motion brought his blade to her throat.
He saw her pulse race there, and then she gulped.
The long, brilliant length of her hair was tangled beneath her to her buttocks, and he knew that his knees
pulled it where it fell beneath them. He offered her
no mercy. A man would not spit at him and live. But a
woman . . .

He wiped the spittle from his face, then dried his
hand upon her breast. He felt her flinch and felt the
full, evocative softness of the woman beneath the
gown.

"You've hurt me gravely, madam," he told her in
her own language. His tone was low. She seemed to
sense its deadliness, and yet she seemed not to care.

"I meant to *kill* you, Viking!" she retorted vehemently.

" 'Tis a pity then that you failed," he warned her.
He moved his blade against her cheek, and let it fall,
ice cold, against her throat again. He felt her shiver
and drew the knife away. He stood, yanking her to

her feet. With the effort he felt fresh blood surge from
the wound in his thigh. Blackness spun before him.
He should have had his physician cleanse and bind
the wound before coming against an enemy—any enemy—whether ten men with swords and maces or
this fire-haired young bitch. She knew how to aim an
arrow, and one look at her silvery eyes assured him
that she was watching for his every weakness. She
trembled, but her eyes emanated hatred.

Suddenly, fiercely, viciously, she brought her knee
up against his groin. He caught his breath at the raw
agony, doubling over as everything went black on
him again. He did not release her, though. He kept
his fingers wound around her wrist, and as he staggered back, seeking a chair at the banqueting table,
he dragged her with him. He fell backward, dragging
her down to her knees before him. He wanted to kill
her at that moment. He wanted to strike her so hard
with his powerful hand that her neck would snap. He
gasped for breath and forced himself to open his eyes.
For a moment, a moment so brief that he was certain
he imagined it, he saw pure, wild terror in her gaze,
like a pheasant caught in a snare. But the look was
quickly gone, and though he tempered his anger so
he would not strike, he was certain she knew the
extent of his wrath, for, upon her knees now, she
desperately began to fight for her freedom. He almost
forgot the fight as he found himself watching her,
studying her. She was an uncommon beauty, with
fine, beautifully chiseled features; a long, stunning
neck; and the startling crowning glory of her shimmering hair. Evidently she was of noble birth: The

fine linen, wool, and fur she wore were testaments to a high station in life.

He watched her too long. She was quick to assess the slight easing of his hold. She bit into his hand; he released her wrist, grabbed her hair, and smiled grimly as she cried out in pain. She might be beautiful, but she was also quick and cunning—and decidedly his enemy. He pulled her very close to his face, his eyes were merciless daggers as they bore into hers. "What happened here?" he demanded.

"What happened?" she repeated. "A scourge of bloodthirsty crows sailed in from the sea!"

He tightened his grip, dragged her closer. "I repeat, lady, what happened here?"

Tears hovered on her eyelids. She clawed at his fingers and her hand slipped. Unwittingly she had found his weakness, striking his thigh.

Stars burst before his head. His grasp eased. He was going to black out; he knew it. He forced himself to fall forward, catching her beneath him. He fought for consciousness and they rolled together. The mud and flour that covered him covered her. Their legs intertwined, and the movement of his thigh pulled up the length of her tunic. She cried out again in fear and fury. Ambushed by unexpected desires he let his rough warrior's hands slide over her naked flesh, finding it soft and silky smooth. She coughed and choked and fought more madly, and curiously he felt the fever within him burn, for her thighs were warm and supple. He hadn't thought previously of carnal pleasure, not even as he noted the beauty of her eyes or felt the erotic tangle of her hair about him. But then, with her breasts crushed beneath the chain mail on his chest and his hand against the soft inner flesh of her leg, he felt a surge of desire spill hotly through his loins.

He clenched his teeth and saw that her eyes widened with alarm. She tried to roll and further wedged him on top of her. She swore, struggling fiercely. Her nails raked him, and he caught her wrists and dragged them high above her head, his eyes ice blue and frigid as they gazed upon her.

He had ordered Rollo to stay behind, but where in Valhalla was the man now? Eric needed him. His strength failed more completely with each second that passed, and he had lost a tremendous amount of blood. He had battled countless men and not received a scratch, but this bitch with her silvery blue eyes had nearly brought him down. A small sound escaped her. She twisted her eyes not to stare at him, and he saw that she bit into her lower lip.

"You will die for this!" she cried out suddenly, passionately.

"For this? For what, my lady, precisely? For coming to your coast or for refusing to die despite your talented aim? Ah, or for touching you so . . . ?" He shifted his weight, fighting the darkness that threatened and softly sliding his fingers along the bare length of her inner thigh.

Her face flushed with anger, and perhaps other emotion, and he laughed. But then pain streaked through him again. She'd shot him with her damn arrow, had kicked, bitten, and clawed him; and he was a fool if he didn't realize that a beautiful enemy was a deadly one indeed. He hardened himself against her beauty, as well as against the raw desire that the bitter fight and the brush with her soft, naked flesh had ignited.

"Don't fear, English witch," he taunted, and he ran his hand freely along her thigh, dangerously near the apex of her limbs. "You are neither gentle, nor tender, nor appealing, milady. My options are to slay you or enslave you, and that is all. When I take a woman, she is just that—all woman, evocative and enticing. Don't provoke me, madam, for if I were to touch you, it would indeed be mindless savagery."

"What else can be expected from a Viking other than savagery and death?" she charged him.

He gritted his teeth, fighting the temptation to strike her again. He forced himself to smile slowly. God, where was Rollo? He saw everything through a red haze, but even through that haze she was beautiful . . . and deadly. Skeins of fiery gold hair entangled them, hair as fragrant as the spring flowers, as soft as swaths of the finest silk. Her blue-gray eyes were wide set and lovely, except for their expression of pure hatred.

Her breasts rose and fell, nearing spilling from the confines of her tunic. "Perhaps I should take you," he whispered. He touched her cheek with his knuckles, and she twisted her head violently. His fingers trailed over her throat and cupped over her breast, caressing the soft mound. His thumb moved in a rhythmic circle over the crest that hardened to his touch. She inhaled sharply, tossing her head again; her eyes glittering and wide as they touched his.

"No . . . Viking!" she swore.

He frowned, wondering why she insisted upon harping on his Viking lineage when he had come from Ireland. Not that he would bear the insult, or any insult, against his father or his father's race. But he had come from his mother's country.

He ceased to torment her, his anger taking precedence. He hadn't much time, he knew. "I want to know what happened!" he thundered at her.

She stared at him in absolute silence for a moment. He released her wrists and reached for his dagger where it had fallen from his grasp, away from them. He started to sheath it at his calf when suddenly he was seized with weakness. Blood was pouring from his thigh again.

He fought to stay conscious. To clear his head. "Nay, milady," he began, "you'll tell me who is the lord of this place, and why—" He broke off. He was falling again. He leaned forward, fighting darkness.

He was going to die. The great warrior, the Spawn of the Wolf, was about to die because this chit of a girl would slay him when he lay down and closed his eyes.

"Oh!" He felt her move beneath him. She shoved him, and an awful lethargy swept over him. She was up upon her knees, staring down at him, meeting the blue ice in his eyes. She reached for the knife. His fingers closed around it but he was fading fast. She dug at his hand where he held the blade. He heard her sobs, coming hard and fast and desperate. She intended to slay him. She needed the weapon.

"My lord! Where are you?"

Rollo was coming at last. Horses' hooves pounded against the earth and then ceased, and Eric knew that help had come. He held fast to the knife.

The girl rose to her feet. Her pulse palpitated furiously in her throat. She turned to run.

Eric pushed himself up, holding the knife. She made it to the hall and turned around.

He had a vision of her for a moment in the haze of his mind, caught in the dying light of the day. Tall and slim and regal, her radiant hair flowing out around her like a glorious golden cloud.

She saw the dagger and his icy gaze, and she gasped, her back against the wall. He held her life in his hands.

He could have slain her then and there, and they both knew it. Instead he took careful aim and threw the knife, catching her sleeve, pinning her to the wall. He caught the material of her gown, just to the left of her heart.

He smiled at her with deadly, chilling intent. "I am a Viking, as you say, and you live. Pray, lady. Pray to your God with all your heart that we do not meet again."

Her thickly lashed eyes betrayed her terror and her hatred. She stared at him, cried out, and spun around, tearing her tunic free from the blade and the wall, and ran again.

Then she was gone.

Rollo burst through the doorway. "Eric!"

"Here!" Eric called. Rollo reached him, came down to the floor, and helped his leader to his feet.

"Get me to a bed," Eric breathed. "Get my physician and an ample supply of ale or mead."

"The blood!" Rollo moaned. "Hurry, we must get your wound bound. My prince, you must not die!"

He smiled at Rollo with grim determination.

"I'll not die. I swear it, I'll not die. I'll live to find vengeance for this day. I will know what happened here, else Alfred of Wessex will soon find himself battling the Norse and the Irish, as well as the Danes."

High atop a white-cliffed hill, overlooking the destruction of the Wessex town, a slim youth pushed to his feet from the dirt, backed his way into the foliage, and then ran. His fleet young legs carried him swiftly into the forest on an old Roman trail. His heart pounded, his legs were raw with pain, but he kept on moving until he entered into a copse and there found two mounted English noblemen from Wessex. They were fine lords of the realm, the elder in blue wool and stoat, the younger in forest green trimmed with white fox.

"Well, boy, tell me of it," said the elder nobleman.

The boy panted and was urged, none too gently, to speak up. "It went as you wished. Lord Wilton of Sussex led the battle and fell to the Viking blade immediately. None knew of the king's invitation or that the Viking ships carried Irishmen as well. Wilton and Egmund are assuredly dead and may well be fingered as the traitors. The townspeople met the Vikings as invaders. The town burns. The men not slain are caught. They will be slaves, and the women concubines."

The elder man smiled, a cruel twist to his lip, and the younger of the two noblemen spoke up more anxiously. "What of the ladies Adela and Rhiannon?"

"Adela escaped as was planned." The boy paused, fearing the men's wrath. "The Lady Rhiannon would not leave men loyal to her since birth; she stayed to join in the fight."

The younger man began to swear viciously. The serf continued hurriedly.

"She was caught in the manor by one of them, but in time I saw her escape into the woods by the rear of the manor."

"She was caught by a Viking, you say?"

The youth nodded. "But she escaped."

"Aye . . . but in time?" The nobleman pondered. He gazed at his companion, who appeared miserable.

"Why do you fret? I pray that the Viking had her, and had her without mercy! 'Twill speed my suit, for she will not be so hasty to spurn my offer now. Used and discarded by such an enemy! She will be grateful for the crumbs that I offer."

The younger man did not look at the elder. "You could be wrong," he said. "She is in love with Rowan, and Rowan with her. She will accept no other."

"She will do as she is told."

"Only the king can command her."

Laughter, harsh and jarring, followed the words. "After this day I am certain that the king *will* command her. And he will not let her have her penniless young lover, of that I am certain. Come, the deed is done and the day is ours. We must ride to the king with the dire news of what has happened."

"My lords!" the youth, their spy, called to them.

The elder looked at the boy, his cunning eyes narrowing. "What is it?"

"My reward! You promised me payment in silver."

"So I did," the elder of the men said.

He nudged his horse forward, closer to the youth. "You are certain that all who could name me are dead?"

"I am certain. I have done well. You promised me reward."

"Aye."

He smiled. The youth's startled eyes grew large as he watched the nobleman reach for his sword. He did not have time to cry out; his life was too quickly sliced away. He sank to the ground in a pool of blood.

The younger lord protested with a choking sound. "Was that—God, was that brutality necessary?"

"Aye." Calmly the elder cleaned the blood from his sword. "Aye, completely necessary. Mind my words. If you would commit treason, friend, leave no clues."

Ruthlessly he led his horse to step over the body. "Come. We ride to the king."

2

Rhiannon's heart hammered, her legs ached, and her lungs were in agony, but still she ran, tearing more and more deeply into the forest, farther and farther away from the town that had been her homeland, her birthright. For all of her life she had been fighting, but she had never come so close to sheer terror and despair as this.

At last she paused, having entered into the forest, which was a sea of green darkness. She knew the area well and welcomed the night. She found a lichen-covered rock and paused, gasping desperately for breath and listening lest the Viking horde be coming at her heels. At last she began to breathe more easily. They did not seem to be coming after her. She was not worth their effort. Perhaps they did not know who she was; perhaps they did not care.

She started to shiver.

He could have killed her. And if he weren't so grievously wounded, he would have come after her.

A trembling started up inside of her, and she closed her eyes, fighting it. But she could not close her eyes to memory, and she saw the Viking in her mind, blond and powerful, and it seemed that she still breathed in the subtle masculine scent of him, still felt his hands as he touched her. . . .

She took a ragged breath. He could have killed her. He could have aimed his knife at her heart, but he had not done so. He must have known that she would run, that she would bring a warning to the king. And still he had spared her.

'Twas hardly mercy, she thought. He had been ruthless enough. But what had he meant when he demanded to know what had happened? She swept her arms around herself, wishing that she dared scream aloud with fear and fury and frustration. What had happened? A horde of Vikings had descended and destroyed her home!

She had to keep moving. She had to reach the king.

Rhiannon rose and stumbled onward until she came to the bubbling little brook that crossed through the forestland at this point. She wondered if the Vikings would raze the town. So many were dead. Nobles, carls, and serfs had died alike, with pride, with courage.

Tears welled up in her eyes. Egmund was dead. Dear, loyal Egmund with his drooping mustache and sad brown eyes. She could not bear it. He had been with the Welsh Prince Garth, her father, when he had rescued her mother from the Danes who had sacked the Cornish coast. Garth had been honored by Alfred's father for the deed, given the fair Allyce as his wife, as well as many shires and fertile lands. Egmund had held Rhiannon as a babe, bounced her upon her knee. And like Rhiannon he had spent his life fighting. Fighting the Vikings, the heinous horde of death.

Kneeling, she dipped her face into the cool, bubbling water. She let it wash over her and cleanse away the mud—and the touch of the Viking. She began to shiver all over again and pushed herself away from the water, forcing herself back to her feet. The rain had stopped at last. Lightning no longer lit up the sky. She had to go on. She had to walk until she could reach Alfred.

She trembled again, so eager was she to reach the king. She could not wait to cast her weary self upon his care and tell him her tale. She did not wish to burden him further, but Alfred was the only one who could exact revenge on the Vikings.

Alfred had been born to the battle with the Norse invader. Even before his birth the Vikings had invaded with deadly menace, besting the men of Dorset, Lincolnshire, East Anglia, Kent, London, Rochester, and Southampton. There had been battles fought against them, and battles won, yet it seemed that the invader had an ever firmer foot upon the ground. Alfred had been the youngest of his father's sons and had lost three warrior-king brothers before becoming the king himself. He had, upon occasion, paid the Vikings their price for peace, but they were treacherous and broke their truces. Alfred had no recourse but to fight. When the Danish host left Wessex, they went on to Mercia and camped in London. Burhred, the king of Mercia, married to Alfred's sister, at last gave up the long fight and departed. There was an Englishman—one of the true king's nobles—on the throne in his place. But in East Anglia, King Edmund had died at the hands of the Danes. In the north they were ruling supreme. Alfred could not fight their numbers in the north. He was determined to keep

Wessex, and perhaps from there they could some day fight further.

He fought well, Rhiannon knew. More men had gathered to fight beneath his banner than under that of any other king. He was brave and wise and passionate, and she loved him dearly. Now an army of Danes laid siege to Rochester. Alfred was gathering his forces and preparing to strike, offering aid and succor to the men within the walls of the town who had so bravely held off the enemy throughout the long winter.

We did not hold on at all, she thought. They had fallen within a day. And they'd had no defenses set; the men trained to battle were all with Alfred, for there had been no warning of an attack.

Once again she began to shiver. Rowan was with the king. Thank God he had not been with her, for he would never have surrendered to the invaders and he would have died. Too many others had been taken from her. Her father had died in battle with Alfred against Gunthrum; her mother had soon followed him to the grave. So many of her people fell to the Viking blade, or so it seemed, and she could not bear it if Rowan were to die too.

Rhiannon began to walk more swiftly. On foot, it would take her days to reach the king, she realized. She had meant to escape on horseback, but the Viking lord had caused her to change her plans. She'd had no chance to do anything but flee. She had no horse and was weary and sad, but she had to stumble onward. She didn't dare stay near the Vikings.

She started walking, hugging her arms about her as she trembled anew. She didn't want to be caught by the towering blond invader. His face was still too clear in her memory, the rugged face with the ice-cold, savage blue eyes. His words of warning echoed in her mind and caused her to quicken her pace. She did pray earnestly that she would never meet him again.

She remembered him then as she had seen him first from the parapets, even as the host of death had borne down upon them. She had seen him standing there, as if not even nature's fiercest bolt of lightning could strike him down. Insolent, arrogant, he brought destruction to those she cared for. She had wanted so desperately for him to die; she had sensed that without him his men would falter.

He had even stood still while her arrow had aimed for his heart, but at the last second he had stepped aside and thus lived. She despised his pride and his supreme confidence, and the bloodshed he had brought to her home. She should have run more quickly, but she had seen him in the yard and the horror of death had been with her; she had wanted, desperately, to kill him.

She had come so close to death herself!

A heated trembling swept through her, and she remembered the sheer towering size and fury of the Norseman. His hand upon her had been like a manacle, his muscle had burned against her and into her, and she had never known such vehement hatred or such terror. She would never forget those eyes. Ice and fire, they seared and they scorched, seemed to rape her very soul. Because of him, a town lay in ruin, people made slaves. Egmund lay in a pool of blood, along with dear Lord Wilton—her champion, like

Egmund, for years. Brave Thomas was dead too. And so many others.

She paused again, clutching her stomach, fighting the pain that seized her. She gazed up at the smoldering heavens and prayed that Adela had escaped inland. Adela was her cousin, the widow of a noble thane of Wessex and ever with her now—her servant, her friend. Adela could not have survived the cruelty of the Norsemen, Rhiannon was certain.

"By all the saints and Father in Heaven," Rhiannon prayed, "see her safe!"

She paused in sudden panic, hearing a rustling from the brush ahead, to her left. Her heart raced and she dropped down upon her knee, seeking shelter behind an oak. Fear seized her, and all that she could see before her was his face . . . muddied and covered with the coarse flour but hard and chilling and striking still. She felt the sheer power of his touch, the vibrancy of his barbarously muscled form. "Pray," he had told her. "Pray that we do not meet again. . . ."

A scream played against her throat as a mad thrashing sounded. Hell had come alive in those bushes. Her breath faltered.

Then a sad-looking roan horse tripped its way out of the bushes.

Rhiannon burst into laughter. Her laughter came more quickly, and then she burst into tears.

So many were dead! The Viking had cost her everything, and she could not even go back, could not offer her good friends and companions and champions a Christian burial. The vultures and wolves would come to feast upon them.

The roan stared at her as if she had gone mad, and

she did indeed wonder if the Danes had not at last made her insane. She staggered back to her feet and realized that she needed the roan. With the horse, possibly she could reach Alfred by morning.

She called out to the animal. It had no intention of bolting. It had come from the battle and its reins trailed upon the ground.

Rhiannon wondered who had ridden the horse and had died. The saddle was slashed and torn. Gritting her teeth lest she start crying again, Rhiannon freed the cinch and cast the saddle into the bushes, then lifted the hem of her tunic and vaulted onto the roan's back. Night was falling, and yet it mattered little. She would have to pray that the moon would guide her, for she could not stop.

As the roan moved contentedly along, Rhiannon thought of the years gone by. She'd had to flee London once when her mother and father still lived, for the Danes had been close. She'd been sent from Alfred's manor and Waringham, and she had run once before from the coast, but that time the invaders had been a small party of foragers in three ships, and her father and Egmund and Wilton had slain them all and sent their boats back to sea, afire. She had known fear before. And there had always been danger, enough that her father had determined she should learn something of archery and swordplay. With him she had always hunted boar and deer in the forest, with falcons and hawks. But it was at archery that she excelled. Her father had boasted that she could thread a sewing needle from a hundred paces, and though his men had laughed, they had all known that it was not far from the truth. She could hit almost any target.

Until today, when it had mattered so desperately.

She wondered then, bitterly, why her arrows had not hit home.

Or why the Viking had thrown his dagger so as not to slay her. She knew instinctively that if he had wanted to kill her, she would be dead.

She gave a deep sigh. Night was falling. She did not want to think about the fair-haired giant anymore, and she would not. She would not tremble, and she would not remember the heat or the strength of him, or the danger in his ice-blue eyes.

Pray, milady . . . that we do not meet again. . . .

An owl shrieked in the night. Rhiannon nearly fell from the horse, then she caught her seat again. The moon was rising. It would light her way and she would not stop.

But she was exhausted and heart-weary, and she suddenly felt terribly, terribly alone. She could not help but remember when they had brought her father's body to her mother. Rhiannon had seen his face, his handsome, proud face, reduced to the ashen pallor of death. She had seen the blood dried upon his temple, and the massive gash from the Danish battle-ax that had split his skull in two. She had screamed, held his bloody head, and crooned to him as though to revive him. Then her mother had pulled her away at last, and she had nearly ceased to believe that there could be a God in heaven.

And now Egmund, Wilton, and Thomas. And so many others.

Rhiannon threw back her head and screamed, and

the heartbreaking sound was terrible. They would take no more from her. She swore it. They would take no more from her—ever again. She would die first.

Alfred, King of Wessex, paused as he walked from the chapel to the manor. He stared up at the morning sky. The rain had stopped, and it seemed that the crimson streaks of morning painting the sky were like a portent of blood. He was a pious man, a great believer in the one and only Catholic church of Christ, but this morning the sky seemed an ancient, pagan warning.

He sighed. He was not ready to return to the house. To see his wife's face, to listen to the children. To have the children see him and stop their laughter and grow tense.

He wound his fingers tightly into his fists. *God in Heaven, in Your infinite mercy, let this battle that comes be the one to tame the beast that plagues.*

He could not remember when the Danes did not control his life. His earliest memory of childhood was his pilgrimage to Rome, a journey taken by a four-year-old because his father and brothers could not be spared from battle. And now they were gone. All gone. His father, three older brothers. None had had the opportunity to grow old.

There was a natural seat, formed from ancient rock, between the wooden chapel and the long manor house. Alfred sat there and realized that his fingers were still clenched into fists.

He had battled the Danes first with his brother, and when he had died, Alfred had been twenty-one. A young man, with a young wife and a child due. Now that child was nearly fifteen, and Alfred was grateful that his firstborn had been a girl and that her coming of age would not prepare her for this endless war and for death. But a son had followed his daughter, and he would come of age soon enough.

He stared up at the sky and wondered at the message in the bloody-looking streaks. What had happened, or what was to come? Though he hadn't the fey instincts of the Celtish folk, he knew that England herself still hovered sometimes on the verge of paganism and that the first coming of the Viking had been foretold in omens of doom. Druids still roamed the forests, and despite their Christianity, most of his people were as superstitious as the pagan Danes. Something was to come.

He prayed again. He prayed that the sign meant victory at last. God had granted him many victories. Alfred knew that men hailed him as the greatest king since the legendary Arthur; he had bested his enemy in skirmishes many times. He was king, and men bowed down to him and fought for his honor. He wanted more. He wanted peace. He wanted England to be a place of learning, and he wanted his children to read and to write, and to study with scholars from all over the world. He had not read himself until he was twelve years old, and though he had been very young when his mother had died, he had never forgotten how she had read to him, how her voice had been a melody, laughing and tripping over the words in a poem. Time had hampered his study, but he had learned to read before his brothers. He had loved learning and craved it for Wessex. He needed peace to achieve his goal. He was thirty-six. Not a young man anymore. But not an old one. There could be long years ahead of him. Time to do so many things. English craftsmen were known for their work in metal and stone; beautiful jewelry was made here. Once English monks had toiled in the monasteries, creating works of grace and beauty. Now the monasteries were plundered, and all too often precious metals and stones were taken, along with anything else of value. An Englishman was lucky to hold to his piece of earth.

Before the stone Alfred fell down upon his knees again, though he had just come from Mass. He picked up a handful of dirt and stared at it. "God of my fathers, let me tear the Dane down this time! Let me strike him from my land and force him to see the true way of Thy light!"

Even as he spoke, he heard the earth tremble. Allen of Kent, one of his most entrusted retainers, was racing toward him. Alfred came quickly to his feet, and Allen dismounted from his horse and dropped down before the warrior king. Alfred knew it to be bad tidings.

"Get up, Allen, and tell me. What is it? Did the Irish prince change his mind and refuse to come?" The sky had warned him. He waited for what would come.

"Oh, no, my king. He came, and 'tis disaster that he did. No message reached the coast. The people thought themselves under siege and tried to strike the first blows. The Lady Rhiannon ordered an attack. The Irish prince received no welcome but a barrage of arrows."

Pain searing his heart, Alfred took Allen fiercely by the shoulders. "How do you know this?"

"I was riding to the Lady Rhiannon's and met a survivor on the way, trying to make his way here to you." Allen's eyes would not remain on the king. Alfred wondered what the man was hiding, then he thought that Allen lowered his gaze with misery and with fear for Rhiannon.

"And it is true, you are certain?"

"Aye, I am certain. The town is nearly razed."

"It would be no less," the king said. He had taken a beast by the tail—a civilized beast, he had believed. But he knew the reputation of the man, and he prayed that the repercussions could be limited to what had already occurred. Eric of Dubhlain could well be marching on Wessex right now, his battle cry for vengeance. The Irish prince would assume that the King of Wessex had betrayed him. Had Rhiannon betrayed Alfred? Impossible! Alfred wondered in his heart about Rhiannon, worrying about what *had* happened, but he spoke to Allen with expediency as the king. He had no choice. He was a king before all else. There was only one way to hold some part of Britain for the Saxon people.

"Where is Eric now?"

"Taken over the town."

"He has not moved inland? How can you know?"

"An ominous silence comes from the town. I know, sire, for I rode toward the coast to see for myself what had happened before riding swiftly to you."

Alfred briefly thanked God that the Irish Viking was not set upon instant retribution. Then he asked about Rhiannon. "My cousin?"

Allen shook his head sorrowfully. "She has not been seen. But the man I met was certain she escaped."

Alfred tossed back his mantle and stared up at the spring sky once again. "Allen, find Rowan and have him take his men to search the way for Lady Rhiannon. If she lives, and if she can be found, his love will guide the way."

"And you, sire?"

Alfred looked at his man and hesitated. He and Allen were of an age. They were both fit from the eternal practice for war. Allen was dark, with sharp gray eyes and a mouth that could slant to cruelty. They had all become hard as granite, the king thought.

"I will go to Eric of Dubhlain. I will seek to rectify this wrong." He turned and started for the manor, his mantle sweeping behind him. He paused, looking back to Allen. "How could this have happened? The message was delivered?"

"Sire, I know that the messenger was sent. The man I spoke with knew nothing of it, though. He said that perhaps old Egmund refused to tell his lady, his hatred for all Norsemen is so great. He died upon the field, so we shall never know."

The king smiled grimly. "Oh, we shall know, Allen. We shall discover the cause as soon as possible."

"Sire!"

The cry was shrill and feminine. It brought Alfred swinging around to face the dense forest to the east. He knew the sound of the voice, and relief swept through him.

He saw Rhiannon. She was racing toward him on a roan, coming across the meadow and the clearing. Torn and disheveled and wild and beautiful still.

"My God," Alfred whispered. Then he started to

run toward her. Earth flew as the roan churned up clumps of mud, then she reined in, and in a new flurry of exhausted tears she collapsed into his arms.

He held her, smoothed back her hair, lifted her into his arms, and his heart thundered with sweet relief. Silently he thanked his god for returning her to him.

He didn't know why he loved her so much—like one of his own children. Perhaps it was because he had once loved and admired her mother. Perhaps it was the fact that he was her godfather, having stood sponsor to her at her baptism. He didn't know the reasoning of the heart but he did love her as one of his own, and he held her, cherishing her. She was fairly tall for a woman but as slim and shapely as a sprite, easy to sweep up into his arms. Forgetting Allen, he hurried toward the manor, calling to his wife.

Rhiannon held to him tightly, trusting in him like a child. Her eyes, so incredibly blue, met his.

"Danes attacked, my lord. Dragon ships. They sailed down upon us and butchered us."

Her eyes closed. She was cold, exhausted, and wet through and through. She had ridden all night in the rain.

Suddenly fury at the savagery, at the waste of life, cut into Alfred like a blade. He shook as he held her. "Those were no Danes."

She stared at him. "My lord cousin! I was there. They came like hungry wolves, they—"

"A message was sent to you, Rhiannon. I called for help across the sea. To an Irish prince of Dubhlain, a man who hates the Danes as fiercely as we do."

She shook her head. He didn't understand.

"I saw no Irishmen!" Rhiannon assured the king.

She clenched her teeth tightly. She could not forget the Viking she had almost killed—golden blond and as wintry cold as his homeland. "Dragon ships came!" she whispered. She could not tell Alfred about her encounter with the man. He would be furious with her that she had not fled immediately.

"The prince's shipbuilders would be Norse, Rhiannon, as would many of his men."

Again she shook her head. She was so tired, and she couldn't make the king understand the danger. "My lord, perhaps I am not being clear, maybe I am incoherent—"

"Nay!" he told her firmly. His temper was rising. He was ill for those who had suffered so needlessly and was very afraid that some treachery had perhaps cost him the assistance of the Irish prince when he needed it most. He held Rhiannon too tightly. He did not blame her, but he was shaking with emotion and anger. "Nay, you are clear, but you do not understand my words! I have been betrayed. You set your men to attack a man I asked here in friendship. You set your hand against me."

Rhiannon gasped, horrified. "I would never betray you, Alfred. How can you accuse me so? I fought the enemy! We have always fought the enemy."

"I do not accuse you, but I tell you that you were to have welcomed the man but you fought him instead."

"I swear I did not know!"

He loved her; suddenly he could not look at her. He could not lose the manpower he needed now. Victory was too close; it was sweet on his tongue. He could not bear that it could be seized from his grasp. He needed the prince of Eire, and if the Irish prince demanded some punishment, he might be forced to fulfill the price.

He raised his voice as he entered the manor house. He carried Rhiannon before the fire and set her there. "Alswitha!" he called to his wife, and she was there, his bride of Mercia, with his young daughter, Althrife, in her arms. She quickly set the child down and gasped, staring at him reproachfully as she greeted Rhiannon, embracing her. "What has happened to her?" she demanded, dismayed at Rhiannon's dishevelment.

Alfred could not dispel the rage that had settled over him. "Someone within her household chose not to honor the order of the king; that is what has occurred."

"Nay, that cannot be true!" Rhiannon protested.

Alfred was trembling. She didn't understand the depths of his emotion, and she was stunned that he would be so furious with her when she had come to him for succor.

"I accuse *you* of nothing, Rhiannon, yet someone did betray me—and you. And what has happened could have dire consequences, far more deadly to our cause than what has already occurred."

Rhiannon disengaged herself from the queen's embrace and stood, shaking, to challenge the king. "More dire than the sea of blood before my town? Have you forgotten, Alfred? Men, good men, my dear friends, lie dead—"

"Have you forgotten, lady, that I am the king?" he thundered in return. "And, Rhiannon, it might well be your dear and loyal friends who turned traitor, for the message was sent that the prince of Eire sailed, that he was to be greeted with all courtesy and escorted here."

"No message came, my lord!" she cried. "And believe me, sire, I saw no Irish prince, just a horde of Viking raiders."

He spun around, ignoring her.

"By the saints, Alfred!" Alswitha called after him. "How can you be so cruel as to doubt the girl!"

He turned back to them both and his gaze seemed empty. "Because all Wessex could depend upon this. Because peace could depend upon the whim and fury of a foreign prince." He swept his mantle around him, buttoning it high. "I ride, my lady," he told his wife, "to the coast. Rhiannon has survived, and she is, I trust, safe in your keeping."

He left them, staring after him. Alswitha seemed even more distraught than she.

"He does love you. Dearly," Alswitha said.

Rhiannon turned to her and tried to smile. The effort failed. "Aye, he loves me. But not as much as he loves Wessex."

"He does not love *me* as much as he loves Wessex," Alswitha said dryly. She noticed that Rhiannon was shivering, and she called to her women, who came scurrying into the hall. "Quick, we must have warm water and give the lady Rhiannon a bath before the fire and warm her, lest she be ill."

Beyond the walls of the manor they could hear the sounds of hoofbeats and the jangling of the horses' trappings as men mounted to ride. Alswitha put an arm around Rhiannon's shoulders and led her toward the easterly side of the hall, the women's solar. There her bath was brought. Alswitha did not leave her. She washed out Rhiannon's tresses herself and tried to talk idly—of folklore, of the hearth, of the home. But when Rhiannon was done, wrapped in a linen towel, and sat huddled before the center fire, she started to shiver again.

Alswitha, still beautiful with her honey-colored eyes and delicate features, sat by Rhiannon to reassure her again.

"We'll have Masses said for your people. We shall pray for them this very evening."

Rhiannon nodded. She swallowed. "Alswitha, you must believe me. They were not Irishmen—I saw them. They were Vikings."

"Rhiannon, I do believe that you are telling me what you saw. I think that you are not understanding that this Irish prince has a Norwegian father and may appear very much the Viking. Don't you see? Viking shipbuilding is the best, so the ships would be dragon prows. And perhaps many of his men fight like berserkers. Alfred needs such men to go against the Danish madmen. The Irish prince Alfred seeks to please is from the stronghold of Dubhlain but Norse in his paternal heritage."

Huddled in her towel, Rhiannon shivered. "I tell you, Alswitha, that Alfred has entered into a pact with demons! I saw them, and they were not Irish Christians but heathens!"

Heathens with the golden hair of the north sun, and blue eyes of crystal coldness. Alfred had entered into a pact with them. She might very well see the prince's Viking captain once again.

"Oh, God!" she whispered, and she felt ill. The blond Viking surely would have told the Irish prince about the Saxon wench who had tried to skewer him with arrows. Alfred was already furious with her. He would be doubly so once he had been to the coast.

"How can he care so little for me, for my people, for what has happened?" she cried to Alswitha. "I am his blood and he is my guardian, and he rails against me for defending what is mine!"

Alswitha was very quiet for a long moment. Then she spoke quietly. "Nay, you forget the King. Wessex, Rhiannon—all of Wessex—is his."

"He is cruel!"

"He is harsh and can be unforgiving. Fate has made him so, for he must be strong. Remember, he is your guardian and your king and your protector. And he does love you." Alswitha pulled the drying strands of her hair from her towel and smiled gently. "He is concerned for your welfare. He did not mean to hurt you and would never try."

Rhiannon wanted to believe it. She loved the king. Alfred and Alswitha and the children were her family. They were all that she had left. She curled her toes beneath her and hugged the linen towel, staring at the fire. Silent tears slid from her lashes.

"It was horrible!" she whispered. "So much death, so much blood. I loved dear Egmund so very much. And Wilton too. Think of the wives who will never love again, think of the orphans." She looked up suddenly. "And Adela! I didn't see her when I escaped. She must be missing, Alswitha. I know not whether she was captured, or she if runs terrified in the forest even now."

"Alfred will find her," Alswitha said with confidence.

"Oh! I was so selfish! I did not tell Alfred about her."

"She will be all right, I am certain. Alfred's men will find her."

"What if the Vikings find her?"

"If she escaped to the forest, why would they pursue a woman they did not know existed?"

Rhiannon was silent. They would not pursue Adela, but the Norseman she had so grievously injured might send someone out after her and Adela might be found instead.

She did not tell Alswitha so. She could not tell Alswitha about her encounter with the Viking. She did not dare. Alswitha was Alfred's wife, and she might think it necessary to find him and tell him.

"Come, Rhiannon," Alswitha said, urging her gently. "You must eat, and then you must try to sleep." She hesitated, studying Rhiannon. "What is it that you're still so afraid of?"

"What?" Rhiannon looked at her with wide, frightened eyes.

"What is it? Why are you still so afraid?"

She shook her head. "I—I am not. Not now. I am here with you. I am safe."

But she didn't know if she was safe or not, or if she could ever be safe again. She could not forget the Viking. She could not forget the fires of his body, or the ice of his eyes, or the husky timbre of his voice when had spoken to her in warning.

Pray, lady . . . that we do not meet again.

And she would not meet him again, ever. She would stay with Alswitha and the children, and Alfred would ride forth with his mercenary army and meet the Danes at Rochester. She would never, never see him again.

Her teeth began to chatter. She was praying—just as he had suggested. She prayed, too, that Alfred would not know just how involved she had been in the fight.

Alswitha, concerned, patted Rhiannon's shoulders. "Come. You must sleep. There is someone else here who loves you, you know."

"Rowan!" Rhiannon cried suddenly, leaping up. She had nearly forgotten him—her very love!—in the trembling aftermath of all that had happened.

"Aye, Rowan. Except that I am sure that he rode with the king and most probably will not return until tomorrow. So you must eat now, and then you have a night's lost sleep to regain. You would not have him see you in such distress, would you?"

"Nay, nay, I would not!" she agreed quickly. She could not let Rowan know of anything that had happened. He was not in love with Wessex, he was in love with her, and surely he might want to avenge her honor against the Norseman in the so-called Irish prince's party who had so abused her.

But when Rhiannon was at last put to bed in a long linen gown between clean sheets and covered by a warm woolen blanket, she did not dream of Rowan as she had assumed she would. Nay, she did not see the man she loved in her dreams, the young Saxon with laughing green eyes and tawny hair.

She saw instead a towering Viking with golden hair, and golden beard, broad shoulders as hard as steel, and eyes as hard and wintry cold as a glacier that cut into her heart.

She heard his laughter, remembered the strength of his touch, and felt the sudden, startling burning deep within her when his hands had roamed so freely and intimately upon her flesh—against her breast, upon her thigh. So tauntingly gentle in contrast to the fury of his eyes, the violence of the fight.

She heard his whispered words, haunting her dreams, over and over. *Pray, lady . . . that we do not meet again.*

The memories would not leave her, and she lay awake for long hours, trembling. She had felt that strange shiver of apprehension when she had first seen him. And then she felt his eyes upon her, felt his touch. She had thought that he might fall in battle.

He had not fallen. He lived, she was certain.

And they would meet again.

No . . .

Yet she felt sure of it. He had come with the storm and the savage waves in the sea. He was destined to rock her life with tempests.

3

His sleep had been uneasy. Scattered dreams danced through his mind, and snatches of the past came before him. He saw the curious mosques of the Arab traders, and the grand palaces of the black-skinned Moors. He saw a sea on the day when Odin had thundered and sworn and cast men to death with heady abandon. He remembered traveling down the Seine to Paris, and even farther back in time he could remember the schoolroom in his father's fine stone castle in Dubhlain. Leith was ever the scholar and ever the peacemaker, and Leith was their father's heir. Leith had known their Irish history like a born seneschal, and Eric, often in jealousy, would leap atop a study table, wave an imaginary sword, and swear that he would conquer the world.

Then his mother's voice would come to reprimand him—soft, strong, and melodic. And his dreams of conquest would subside as she gathered her brood around her: Leith, Eric, Bryan, Bryce, Conan, and Conar; and the girls, Elizabeth, Megan, and Daria. She would speak to him of the Tuath De Danaan, the ancient tribes, the honor of Irish hospitality, and the pride of their race. They might well travel far and wide, she assured them, but they could never forget that they were Irish. Their race was in their blood, a part of them, and it would be ever with them. The sound of the pipes would always tug upon their hearts, just as they would sense the banshee, the death ghost, in the wind. And in the forest, if they listened, they would know that the wee people played their games and tricks and that in the end it was the land that was sacred. Erin would spin her tales and legends, and the whole quarrelsome lot of them would be silent at her feet. Then Olaf would appear in the doorway and would seek to best her with sagas of Odin, Thor, Loki, and the rest. There had always been warmth in the castle at Dubhlain. Warmth and love.

Those scenes stayed with him as he tossed in his sleep. The great hearth, the hounds, and the land. Days when they rode to Tara to sit with the kings of all the land, days when his grandfather, Aed Finn-laith, ruled with justice and wisdom over the Irish. And days, too, when he had been sent into the woods. Sent to study with the colossally old Druid, Mergwin. Days when the wind had whipped and the thunder had roared and the old fool had stood out in the rain, lifting his arms to the heavens. "Feel it, boy! Feel the wind! Feel the hawk as it flies, and feel the earth as she lies beneath you. And remember, remember always, that answers lie not with other men but always within your own soul—you and the earth are as one."

Mergwin had forced him to read. To study his scripts in Latin, Frankish, Norse, Irish, and English. Mergwin had dragged him through the rotting bogs and taught him which herbs drew poisons from the body, what mold could create a poultice to stop a man's life-blood from flowing away. The Druid had driven him hard, far harder than his brothers and sisters, and once he had protested, drawing himself up and telling Mergwin, "Cease, old man! I am a prince! I am the Spawn of the Wolf, grandson of the great Ard-Ri!"

Mergwin had surveyed him from head to toe and then had tossed the boy an ax. "Aye, Eric, you are all that you say. Therefore let the strength of your body match that of your conceit. Chop these trees, and don't cease till the pile is high, for it promises to be a cold winter."

He never knew quite why he obeyed the old buzzard, except that his mother loved Mergwin, and even his father sought out his advice.

The Druid was never wrong.

He had known when Emenia would die.

Upon his new-won bed in the seized manor house, Eric groaned and twisted around again. The Druid had tried to stop him when he was to sail away with his uncle. The days of his youth were past then, but Mergwin had come to the shore. His beard and his hair and his robes had flapped around him, and he had appeared much like a giant crow. But he had stood tall against the wind and had waited until he could speak with Eric alone.

"Don't go," he had warned him.

"Mergwin, I must. I have promised my uncle."

"You are in peril. And I cannot warn you from where, or from what. Your heart, your soul, and your life are in grave peril."

He remembered feeling a grave affection for his old tutor that day, and he had set his arm around the

Druid's scrawny shoulders. "I am a prince of Eire, Mergwin. I do not recant my word and, as my father before me, I must live in danger."

Mergwin had argued no further.

And he had gone, and he had met Emenia, and his heart and soul had indeed been in peril. In his dreams he saw her beauty. He saw the supple, naked beauty of her flesh, her smile as she straddled over him. He felt anew the silken brush of her hair over his shoulders, sleek as midnight, shining. She knew where to touch a man, as if she were inside him, as if she knew just what he needed when and where and how. He saw the honey of her body, shimmering with a glaze of sweat from the sweet tempest between them, the shape of her breasts, the darkness of her nipples. He could see the scent of her.

He had slain so many men that night. Sent them to rest with their Allah, sent them to heaven, Valhalla, or hell, he knew not which. But no amount of death and no spillage of blood could have stilled the pain that assaulted him and became one with him, one with living. It would not end. It would not cease to enter into him; would not cease to plague his dreams.

He groaned again. His leg pained him, and that pain seared into his subconscious. Mergwin—the old Druid—with his haggard, lean, eternally wrinkled face—was haunting his dreams again. Eric smiled ruefully. "Begone, Druid! Leave my dreams to peace!"

"You're not dreaming," Eric heard. He blinked and shook his head, but the face remained. Eric jerked up. Dizziness swept through him and he almost fell back.

He fought the sensation and the room slowly ceased to spin.

The Druid was indeed before him.

Eric scowled fiercely. "You old bat from hell! What in Odin's name are you doing here?"

Mergwin sat by his side on the bed. Eric winced, gritted his teeth, and realized that the Druid was treating the arrow wound in his thigh. "Christ's blood, but that hurts!" Eric swore.

The Druid shook his head sorrowfully. "Eric, you have spoken of Christ and Odin and hell, and all within but a few breaths. Decide upon your gods, Young Wolf, and pray to them properly, if you would."

"How did you come here?" Eric demanded.

Mergwin tied the poultice in place with a linen bandage. Eric was startled to feel the pain lessen almost instantly, as if there were truly magic in the old man's touch. The Druid observed him pensively without answering.

"I spoke to you!" Eric reminded him.

He had his father's temper, this one, Mergwin thought. Nay, more. Of all the brood of the Wolf and his princess, this one was truly the most like the sire. He possessed his own code of honor, and none could break it. But he would be demanding of all those who crossed him in life, just as he would be ruthless when brought to battle, any battle. He was as tall as his father and as golden a warrior, broader in the shoulders, heavily muscled, and still trim and lithe and agile. He could walk silently on leaves—Mergwin had seen to that himself—and yet he walked in power. He asked of his men no more than he gave. He dealt honestly, and men were quick to follow him. His justice was swift, and though his sword could be merciless, his judgment was ever fair and wise. His fault, Mergwin thought grimly, was a stubborn streak that ran wide and strong.

"I cast your runes," Mergwin said at last.

Eric's blond brow shot upward. "You cast my runes?" he repeated. Like himself, Mergwin had been born of an Irish mother—a witch, so many said —and a Norse rune master. The runes were symbolic stones; they could foretell the future—if a man believed in their power. Many of his men would not sail if the cast of the runes did not prophesy a good voyage.

"I sought to find you ere you sailed," Mergwin said. He checked the leg he had administered to so carefully. "Your ships had gone, and still I followed as swiftly as I could."

"Why?"

The Druid stood. He stretched out his arms, indicating the manor and the land around them. "This! This is some treachery."

Eric scowled and tossed his blankets aside, determined to rise.

"You should lie still. You will bleed again," Mergwin warned him.

"I cannot lie still." Eric walked for the bowl and pitcher of water that awaited him on a side table. His leg blazed, but he did not let the Druid see his pain. He ducked his face into the water and the coldness of it awoke him.

"It might have cured more easily," the Druid told him caustically, "had you allowed the shaft to be properly removed. But nay, the prince of fools must rip muscle and skin to rid himself quickly of the missile!"

Eric cast Mergwin a scowl and dried his face on a linen towel. "You have tended to my leg, and your warning of treachery is too late. Perhaps, Druid, you could sail back across the sea whence you came and plague my brother, who surely needs assistance with some project."

Mergwin ignored him and pulled a wooden chair before the low-burning fire. The flames reflected on the incredible length of his beard, a beard that never tangled but rather seemed part of the steel-gray hair that flowed from his head and down his back. Eric, in turn, ignored Mergwin and went to the bedroom door, throwing it open. He was on the second floor of the wooden manor house, and where he had lain had surely been the lord's room once, for the beautiful bed where he had slept was raised high on a pedestal, and the mattress upon it had been filled with down. Then there were the chairs; the beautifully, elaborately carved fireplace; the mantel, majestically adorned with both saints and gargoyles. Tapestries warmed the walls, and the pitcher and basin on top of the table were finely crafted, the handle of the latter set with jewels.

Aye, the room had belonged to the lord of the place —shared with his lady, perhaps. Or possibly it had belonged to the wicked little minx who had cast him into his present sorry state.

"Rollo!" he called, but even as he called, he saw the young dark-haired girl whom he had rescued from the overeager advances of his men the afternoon before. She was cleaned and neat; her dark hair was tied back in a knot; her tunic was long and demure; and her face, with its wide, adoring eyes, was scrubbed and fresh.

She curtsied to him quickly. "My lord, I've been awaiting your pleasure." She presented him with a tray. The aroma was enticing. The plate was filled with a roasted fowl, fresh bread, and a pitcher of ale. He stared at her and nodded. "Tell me, what is your name?"

"Judith, my lord."

"Judith, have you lived here always?"

"Always, my lord."

"Tell me, where is your master? Was he killed in the fray yesterday? Why would he seek to attack me? Do you know?"

The girl shook her head, confused. "There is no master here, not since Prince Garth died many years ago."

"No master?" Eric said.

Mergwin, his back toward Eric, his face toward the fire, spoke up. "Ask her of her mistress, my prince."

"The Lady Rhiannon," the girl said.

"Ah, the Lady Rhiannon," Eric repeated. "A slender nymph with golden-red hair that falls well past her hip?" And with a wicked ability to send arrows flying, he added silently.

"Aye, that's my lady."

How dearly he would love to have his hands upon her again. He smiled casually. "Well, then, what of the Lady Rhiannon? Why did she seek to attack me? I came here at the invitation of the king."

The girl shook her head. "You came in a dragon prow, milord. You came in a dragon prow."

"Yes, we build dragon prows; they are fine ships," he said. "But still I should have been welcomed here, unless there has been some treachery against me or the king."

The girl shook her head. "I know nothing of it!"

He eyed her carefully. She was a pretty thing but a mere serving girl. She could not help him.

"Thank you, Judith," he told her, dismissing her.

She colored greatly, offered him another little curtsy, and lowered her lashes. "May I serve you in any other way?"

"Aye. Find Rollo for me—the big redheaded man. Send him to me."

She bowed to him again. "He has been waiting for you. . . ." The girl paused.

Eric frowned. "Go on, girl, send him to me."

She fell before him, kissing his hand quickly, then she was up and scampering away. Eric stared after her, then shook his head and came back into the room. He sat down at the table and discovered that he was ravenous. He bit heartily into the fowl and found it very palatable. He stared over at Mergwin, who was watching the flame. "So tell me, Mergwin, you who knew of this danger, what was the cause of this wasteful bloodshed?"

Mergwin shrugged, then stared very intently into the flames. "I cannot tell you the cause. I am not a seer."

"Oh, you're not," Eric said dryly. He lifted the ale to his lips. He was very thirsty and downed it quickly. There was a knock at his door. He called out and Rollo entered. He was anxious and dragged a lean priest before him, pressing the nervous man toward Eric.

Eric arched a brow at Rollo. "What is this?" he asked in Norse.

"Speak up, Father, and quickly," Rollo urged the monk.

The little man wet his lips, and his eyes seem to grow wider as he stared at the blond giant seated before him. He was clad only in a short leather tunic; his shoulders were bare, the muscles of his arms massive and sleek and taut. Eric rose, towering above the monk. The priest crossed himself, then tried to step forward; he stammered out some words. Eric crossed his arms over his chest, annoyed and amused. "Come, good father, speak up. We are not barbarians here."

The monk seemed to doubt those words sincerely, but he found his tongue. "I am Father Paul, of the old order of Saint Bede. I have come from the king, Alfred of Wessex."

"Have you?" Eric said sharply. He tensed. The feeling of betrayal scratched along his spine.

"Please, dear Prince! The king is distressed and knows no more of this treachery than you, but he swears that he will discover it. He has sent you mead and wool and furs and jewels created by his finest goldsmiths and silversmiths."

"The king would give me what he fears I might take," Eric said.

The monk drew himself up with impressive dignity. "Alfred is a great king. He is a man of his word and afraid of no fight."

"Well said," Eric murmured.

"And true," Mergwin added quietly. The monk

stared at the Druid's back with some fascination. Eric walked over and leaned against the mantel. Mergwin's poultice was at work on his leg, and he felt as if new strength and vigor had worked themselves into his limbs. He rubbed his bearded chin with his fingers, eyeing the monk, who continued to seem fascinated with Mergwin's back.

"What does the king wish?"

"He would—uh—er, that is, the king would meet with you here. He awaits you beyond in the wood and would take a hostage first, for he expects your anger."

"I'll give no hostage," Eric began, but Mergwin, tall and lean and ever like the crow, stood. "Aye, my prince. I will go, as the English king bids."

Eric frowned. The Druid was oft a thorn in his side, but he was also as dear as any blood relative, and Eric was loath to risk the man. "Nay, you should not."

"And why not?"

"You are too old for this game."

"When I am too old, I will die." Mergwin bowed low and respectfully to Eric, then he turned to the monk and smiled at the gaping man. "Shall we go?"

The monk stared at Eric. Rollo laughed. "He is no black magician, Father. Merely my lord's hermit. Mergwin will not turn you into a blackbird." He paused and gazed at Mergwin. "Will you, Druid?"

Mergwin shrugged. "Nay, not this day."

"I don't know if a madman will suffice—"

Eric cut him off. "Tell your king that he holds someone precious, my mentor, a man who is oft my strength, in his hands. Tell him that he holds a treasure, and if there is treachery now, all England will pay. Then you may tell him that I await his leisure. We will talk in this fine hall."

The men left him, the monk more nervous than when he had come, Mergwin stoic. Rollo awaited their departure and left himself, amused. When they had gone, Eric finished his meal, then he set to dress. Sometime during the night Rollo had brought his trunk, and he determined that since he would meet a king, he would dress as the son of one and the grandson of two. He chose Irish dress, warm woolen hose, a soft blue fur-trimmed tunic, and a belt that buckled with a finely crafted Celtic cross. At his shoulder he held his regal crimson mantle in place with the crest of his father's house, the wolf and the crown.

When he was done, he glanced around the room. Rollo would have had him brought to the best in the manor, so if it was not the lord's room, then it was the lady's. Curious, he went to the trunk at the foot of the bed and opened it. The trunk was filled with women's wear, long tunics in fine materials trimmed with fur and with jewelry.

So the Lady Rhiannon had ruled here. This had been her room. He had cast her from her place, or so it seemed. Tension filled him, tightening his jaw, constricting his muscles. There had been treachery here, and this Rhiannon had surely been the cause of it. It was her land, so said her servant. She had been the one to order the battle and to see it to its bloody end.

She had sent her rain of arrows descending upon him. She had struck him. She had heartily desired to slay him. "Witch!" he muttered, and that she was, with her silvery-blue eyes, her hair of pure fire, and her sizzling hatred. He picked up a jeweled dagger, pondering all that had happened. Perhaps he should have thrown his knife at her heart. If the treachery had been hers, it had cost many, many lives. And if she had the chance again, Eric thought, she would gladly slay him. She had come closer than any man to ending his life. She was no gentle, demure lass. She had fought like a vixen and cut him; she knew where to aim against a man.

"Well, my proud one," he muttered aloud, turning her jeweled dagger over in his hands, "you will pay in part, for you will give up this land and these clothes and all that I hold. You will never regain them—that I swear. Perhaps you will learn humility. If ever I am given the chance, lady, I will see that you learn it well." He still could not forget the rage she had instilled in him. Nor in honesty could he forget the woman herself. Even shimmering with the passion of her hatred, her eyes were beautiful, with their ambient gray-blue irises and thick fringe of dark lashes. She did not elicit his tenderness but had touched a haunting cord of desire within him. He smiled. 'Twas a pity she was a lady born. To be given to a man she deemed a Viking, as his concubine, surely would be a difficult cross for her to bear.

He cast the dagger back into the trunk and closed it. No woman, no matter how beautiful, was worth as much to him as the land. And though the taste of revenge lay sweet within his mouth, he wanted this piece of earth and the surrounding coves with a passion. If the king was not behind this, Eric would demand the *land* of him in retribution. As a Christian prince, he couldn't demand a lady as a passing diversion, a concubine.

He came downstairs, where certain of his men sat around the great fire. Mastiffs roamed the great hall now, and it seemed that the serfs were back at their work. The blessing of being a slave! Eric thought wryly. For if a master was a decent one, a serf did not change his or her position much in life—no matter who triumphed, no matter who ruled.

Hadraic, Rollo, and Michael of Armagh ringed the fire, drinking ale. Hadraic was the son of one of his father's men and an Irish maid. Rollo was a Norseman through and through, and Michael was as Irish as Queen Erin. Watching them, Eric thought that his father's alliance with his grandfather had been a good one. They had learned friendship and had prospered. These three men were important to him. They fought together, cared greatly for one another, and were fiercely loyal.

Yet, like him, they were seeking . . . something. Conquest, perhaps, of their own.

Rollo gazed up at Eric as he came down the stairs. "We've ordered a feast prepared for the King of Wessex. He has sent us a young noble of East Anglia as hostage, and we have now sent an escort to meet with his party. I was thinking that we should now ride out and meet the King of Wessex at the gates."

"Fine, we shall ride." Eric came before the fire and warmed his hands. Then he gazed sharply at Hadraic. "Have we taken any prisoners during the night?"

"Nay, Eric. We've taken the men at the battle's end, and the women, but none is of the manor. We've got farmers, serfs, and craftsmen. They have all taken their oath to you."

Eric nodded. "Good." There would have to be a

renegotiation with the English king, but he would not relinquish this place.

Still, he wished that he had the girl. He would like to take her bow and arrows and crack them over her backside.

Or perhaps she needed a few nights in solitude with nothing but bread and water. . . .

He stepped away from the fire and looked at his three men. "Shall we go?"

Michael, Hadraic, and Rollo nodded. Eric led the way out into the courtyard. It was another day already, he saw. Pigs and chickens were moving around; farther out he could see a boy urging his oxen forward. His own men were up and about. Some leaned against the barn and whittled, as was the Scandinavian way. Some were wary, their hands on their weapons, their gazes ever sharp.

Denis of Cork came forward at the sight of Eric, leading a massive white stallion. He grinned from ear to ear. "He's a beauty, my lord Eric! Finely bred, finely built, fast and strong. I was pleased when I saw him here, and I knew he could go to none but you."

"Aye, he's a fine one," Eric agreed. He moved his hand in a caress over the animal's soft muzzle. The stallion snorted and pranced, and Eric felt his great power. He smiled back at Denis. "Aye, Denis, you serve me well."

He mounted quickly, then lifted a hand to his men. Their cry went up and he lifted the stallion's reins. With his captains behind him, he rode for the gate.

High upon the hill overlooking the town, Alfred watched as the dangerous prince he had asked onto his land galloped forward. Eric of Dubhlain was unmistakable; his stature surpassed all rumor. He rode the great horse with a warrior's ease, tall in the saddle, a forbidding sight with his towering size and burnished mane. The horse's hooves pounded the earth, fresh and fragrant from the storm.

The king assessed the Irish prince carefully, looking for some fault. There was none. The blue eyes that assessed him in return were unblinking, hard—ruthless, perhaps. They met his with a demanding look, a certain wariness, and an undisputable honesty.

"Alfred of Wessex?" the formidable warrior demanded.

The king nodded. "Eric of Dubhlain?"

Eric nodded in turn. For several moments tension lay heavily on the air; suspicion was rife. Alfred was attended by several horsemen—noblemen, by their dress. In those initial moments, though, neither the king nor the prince noted those around them. The import of the meeting lay in their impressions of one another, and in whatever faith they could find to give one another.

Alfred nudged his mount forward and offered his gloved hand to Eric. Eric barely paused before accepting the proffered handshake. The man had courage to meet him so, or he believed in Eric's reputation for honesty, or so hated the Danes that he would take any risk against them. Gazing at the king, Eric liked what he saw. Alfred was a man of medium build, with sharp hazel eyes and brown hair and beard. He would miss little, Eric thought. He appeared wise and weary. Intelligence rested in the depths of his eyes.

And Mergwin had believed in him, Eric remembered as he felt the firmness of Alfred's hand in his.

"We'll move back to the town," Eric said. "The women are busy at the fire, creating a feast of welcome for the great Alfred of Wessex."

The king nodded, watching him, and Eric was aware that Alfred knew he had laid claim to the town and had determined not to dispute him. He noted that the king was an excellent horseman, and he realized that they had both been fighting the Danish enemy since their births, though it seemed that the king was perhaps five years or so older than he was.

They came back through the gates, Eric and King Alfred and their retinues. It seemed that both parties were loath to leave their leaders alone—trust came more slowly to their followers. But when they had reached the Great Hall, the king ordered his men to wait outside, and Eric nodded to Rollo and the others. They were alone then in the manor's vast hall. Eric commanded that mead be brought to them and then he and the king sat in facing chairs, and openly surveyed each other again.

Eric waited for the king to speak, for he was the one with an explanation to give. Gravely he watched Alfred.

The king leaned across the table. "I cannot tell you what our life has been—nay, I suppose that I need not imagine you do not know, for the Danes have harried the Irish coast forever."

"My father fought the Danes, and my grandfather fought the Danes, and I fight them too."

"As do I."

Eric sipped his mead, sitting back. He eyed the

king over his chalice. "Then tell me, Alfred of Wessex, why were my ships attacked when I came in answer to your plea for assistance?"

Alfred shook his head and slumped back in his chair. Eric was convinced of his sincerity. "There is some treachery here, but from where I know not. I swear, though, that I will not rest until all is discovered. Many believe that one of the men slain by your troops was the traitor, preferring to fight you rather than welcome you."

"What of the girl?"

"The girl?" the king said.

"The Lady Rhiannon. It was her land. Did she betray you?"

"Nay, nay!" Alfred assured him hastily.

"How can you be so certain?"

"She is my godchild. And my kin."

Eric did not believe that the girl could be found innocent so easily, but he chose to say nothing more of the matter at the moment.

"I take this hall and this land," he told Alfred.

"You have already done so," Alfred admitted with dry—perhaps bitter—humor.

"There has been much ill will created," Eric said.

"Aye," Alfred agreed. Again he leaned toward Eric, and the fever of his quest burned in his eyes. "But you came to fight the Dane. It is not your native soil you seek to defend, but I will make sure that your rewards are great."

Eric rose, swallowed down his drink, and wandered over toward the great fire, resting against the mantel to look back at the king. "What rewards?"

Alfred started. He, too, rose and came to the fire. It

blazed between them like the passionate hatred they shared for their enemy. "What would you have?" the king demanded.

"More land," Eric replied flatly. "I want the surrounding coves and some coastal land north of here that borders the sea. There is a protected bay and, around it, high-rising cliffs. No one could take that land were it protected. The valley there is fertile. It grows rich and green. It is a natural harbor; I saw that from the sea."

Alfred hesitated.

Eric coolly lifted a brow, and the king saw that the man's eyes could quickly turn to ice. "Is that too much to ask for the blood you ask of me?"

"Nay, it is not that. I would freely give you the land, but it is not mine."

"Then tell your lord, your alderman, that he must take another parcel. We will wrest one from the Danes."

" 'Tis no lord that owns it," Alfred muttered. Eric frowned. "It, too, belongs to my goddaughter, the Lady Rhiannon."

Eric nodded slightly in acknowledgment. "Then she should be very willing to give to your cause."

"She has already given," the king said with some humor. "This was her town, won by her father."

A picture of the fire-haired maiden with blood lust in her heart flashed through his mind, and Eric smiled with a certain malice. "So this, too, I would take from the Lady Rhiannon?"

"Aye," the king murmured. He walked back to the table. "Rhiannon is lady of this coast, all of it. Her father, Garth, was a fine warrior. He fought long and with great loyalty, and the people remember his name. To dishonor his daughter I will have to fight my own people."

"I will not give up this land," Eric said flatly. And, he would not. The blood of his men lay upon it. Nor would he ever return a handful of dirt to the Lady Rhiannon.

Alfred frowned. He was angry with the implacable prince, and angrier still with Rhiannon. Eric of Dubhlain would not change his mind; the king saw it in his glacial eyes and in the unrelenting set of the man's jaw. And Alfred saw his dream of peace within Wessex fading before him. He could fight and he would, and by all that was holy, he would win. He was a great king.

But he could not go to battle without more men. Englishmen had sprung to his aide. Untrained warriors had died for him. And now a great reckoning was upon him. He wanted these fighting Irish-Vikings with him. He wanted these warriors with their fearlessness and their courage and pride and sheer strength and training. He wanted the power to *win*.

"We could do fierce battle here again—my forces, your forces—were I to strip Rhiannon of all that is hers," Alfred said.

"Ah, well, then, I wonder if we can come to terms at all, for I feel that there are things I also need to settle with the lady," Eric said softly.

"With Rhiannon?"

"She ordered my ships attacked," Eric said. He wondered why he chose not to tell the king about their more intimate meeting.

Alfred moistened his lips. "All right. I will give you

the Lady Rhiannon as your wife, and therefore all of her land—more than you have requested—shall be yours."

"What?" the Irish prince said, startled.

"I will give you the Lady Rhiannon to take as wife, and therefore you will be lord of all her lands. The people will accept a marriage in Christ, and they will see that we are bound together by these ties. And when I give you my own goddaughter, your men will know that treachery did not come by my hand."

Alfred was surprised to see the look of pure amusement that came to the Irish prince's ruggedly handsome face. "But, Sire," Eric of Dubhlain protested, "I do not wish a wife."

The king drew back, offended. Every noble in his court and from far abroad had vied for Rhiannon. God had created no angel more beautiful, nor had he ever granted a woman such grace.

Or given her such fine lands to boot.

"Eric of Dubhlain," he said sharply, and his fingers drummed against the table. "We speak of a woman of my own blood, a child of the Royal House of Wessex and a descendant of two of the royal houses of Wales. And We give you land that far surpasses a dream of conquest, for it is exceptionally fine land, land that you, yourself, crave."

Eric gritted his teeth. He wanted vengeance; he did not want a wife. He had learned what it was to love once and had lost that love. He'd never been able to call Emenia wife, and now he wanted no other. His heart had hardened. It was one thing to find pleasure in the company of a talented whore, quite another to take a wife. Even the thought of it repelled him.

And Alfred spoke of not just any wife. He would wed Eric to the girl with the fire in her hair and the rage in her heart.

Eric almost laughed aloud. That would truly be a match made in hell!

"Alfred, I do not mean to offend you. First, I remind you, I am the son of a king, the grandson of the Ard-Ri of all Ireland, and also the grandson of a very powerful Norwegian jarl. I do not offer myself lightly at any bargaining table."

"I would not take you lightly, sir. I offer you my own blood."

"I doubt that the lady would be amenable to such a betrothal."

"She will do as she is told. I am her guardian and her king."

Eric shrugged. He almost smiled. It did have its ironies. He had warned her that she should pray that they not meet again. Surely her prayers were going quite unheeded. The king, in his passion, was determined.

Suddenly Eric felt a cool draft. He looked to the doorway and saw that the door had opened. The king's men, as well as his own, stared in upon them expectantly. They were all hopeful of an alliance, that the treachery and the battle and the blood between them could be put aside.

He did not want to marry her! He despised her and her ignorance, which caused her to abhor all things Norse with no understanding. She was spoiled and willful and arrogant, and he wanted to wreak vengeance on her. He did not want to honor her as his wife.

"Damn you, man!" the king swore. "There is no more beautiful woman in the world. I tear out a piece of my heart to offer her to you!"

Eric arched a brow slightly, watching the king. "Alfred, the lady will not agree to this marriage."

"She will," Alfred said. He was the king; his word was law.

He clamped his jaw down hard. It had taken all of his willpower to offer her to another man when he knew that she was in love with Rowan, when he had allowed her to believe that she and Rowan would be given his blessing to wed. But now he could not afford to remember that she loved Rowan and that Rowan loved her. The battle against the Danes was more important than Rhiannon or Rowan—or love.

"It is the only way!" Alfred said harshly.

The only way, Eric thought. Alfred wanted him there and was willing to compensate him handsomely. But he could not give him the land without a battle—unless Eric took the girl as his wife.

What did it matter? Eric wondered, a coldness settling over him. Marriage was a contract, and he would enter into a contract—nothing more. She would be his to command till death did them part, and perhaps that was the greatest payment she could ever make.

He was being offered his place at last. His own land —good land, rich and verdant, with a fine harbor. Not inherited or granted but earned.

He had to have the land. He could taste it, he could feel it. Excitement ripped through him. He wanted it; he wanted to be the lord of this coast. He would tame her. One way or another he would tame her. If she could not reconcile herself to life in her own home, all the better. He would send her to Ireland and be free of her.

Marriage was a matter of convenience. It was the very substance of pacts and lands and alliances.

For a swift, shattering moment he remembered the feel of her beneath him. Remembered the feel of her flesh, the rage and passion in her eyes and their startling cerulean color. He remembered the violent surge of desire that had seized him and that in those seconds he could have taken her—like a Viking, like the barbarian she called him.

This had been her land! She had sent arrows flying against him. There had been a traitor here. . . .

If she had played treacherously against him, against the King of Wessex, if all that blood of the Irish, the Norse, and the English that so wastefully drenched the coast was her doing, she would pay—dearly, for every day of her life to come. If the king would not see to it, then Eric, himself, would.

And he would have the freedom to do so. He would wed her, as the king demanded.

None of his emotion and none of his thoughts were betrayed in Eric's features. Alfred knew that the Irish prince was thinking, but his thoughts were a mystery, hidden in the swirling arctic mists of his eyes.

Eric walked back to the table. He poured more mead into their two handsomely appointed chalices.

"To a long and lasting friendship," he said, offering one chalice to the king.

"To the death of the Danes," the king pledged.

"To their destruction."

The king swallowed his mead, staring at Eric. He was quiet for a moment, watching the foreign prince.

Any maid would want this man! he thought, trying to assure himself. Once the girl had seen him she would not be so displeased. Within him ran the blood of kings, the strengths of two warrior nations. He was noble in appearance and in bearing. He was as honed and muscled and sleek as the finest-bred war-horse, and his features were startling, strong, and handsome, his eyes mesmerizing. . . .

And as chilling as ice at times.

Nay, any maid would want him. He was cultured and fair. He spoke many languages and had learned wisdom as well as warfare.

Any maid . . .

Except Rhiannon.

He shoved such thoughts from his mind. He was the king and had learned wisdom as well as warfare himself. Like the hard blond warrior before him, he had learned a certain amount of necessary ruthlessness.

Alfred lifted his chalice once again. "To your marriage, Eric of Dubhlain. Come, we'll call our scribes and cast our seals upon this pact, and it will be as we have said."

4

Though the king was gone from Wareham, the meadow was filled with his men.

Men who prepared for war.

Throughout the day the sounds of it could be heard. The shouts, the orders, the commands.

And always the clash of steel.

Rhiannon didn't think she would ever be able to hear that sound without reliving the horror of what had happened on the coast, without seeing the bloodshed and the death. All through the hours of light it went on, and with each clang and clamor she winced anew, envisioning the deadly yield of the mace and the ax and the sword.

In the king's household she spent her time with the children. Alfred was deeply dedicated to learning. She knew that he regretted the interruption of his own education, which he longed to resume, and had determined that it should not be the same for his sons and daughters. He spoke often of the sorry state they had come to, for England had passed a golden age a century ago, Alfred thought, lamentingly. Then the monks had created the finest scripts, and the words of the poets were gifts to less eloquent men. Alfred had tutors for his children to teach them Latin and science and mathematics. Rhiannon spoke Welsh, which Alfred considered an important language for his offspring, since he and the Welsh kings were either making pacts to fight the Danes, their common foe, or making war against each other.

Three days after the battle Rhiannon sat in the king's house with his younger children and spoke to them in her father's language. But her mind wandered, for she could hear that endless clash of steel and could not concentrate on her lessons. She determined that she would take the children into the meadow, then behind the house, still well within the walls of fortification. To feed the geese was their job, for in the king's household everyone worked.

Edmund, the oldest of the children in her charge, raced forward with his handful of barley, and the other children followed happily. Rhiannon let them scamper ahead of her, then she sank down into the spring daffodils and idly chewed upon a blade of grass.

She could not believe that the king had sent for the foreigners to help him fight the Danes. Viking against Viking—it seemed inconceivable! And now, too, while she was here and safe within the king's own compound, it was impossible to believe that the invaders were overrunning her home, the place where she had been born, where her parents had lived and loved.

Alfred would move them with all haste, she assured herself.

But some foreboding filled her heart, and she shivered despite herself. She had never seen the king so enraged as he had been over the battle. Surely he believed her that she had known nothing about his invitation! Dear God, her people had died there; they had lain down in pools of blood and given up their lives. And they hadn't even had a chance, for most of her carls, trained fighting men, were here at the king's disposal.

He would not let the Vikings remain in her home, she promised herself. He could not. He was her cousin—and her protector. By all honor he would see justice done.

It was not so difficult to convince herself then. He claimed that he had called forth an Irish prince, but she had seen a crew of bloody, barbaric Norsemen. She prayed suddenly, hastily, that the king would not live to regret his unholy alliance. Tears stung her eyes suddenly. He did not need these men! All of England loved and respected Alfred. He had pushed back the foe again and again, and men rallied to him. He would ride forth to Rochester and free the besieged town, she was certain.

And yet again her heart seemed to tremble, for she had believed that her father was immortal. He was beautiful and courageous and fine . . . but he was flesh and blood and had died like the next man.

The children were laughing. Spring had come and it was right that they should feel the renewal of life and laughter. She watched as they ran in the tall grass, allowed the tempest in her soul to fade, and then had dared to smile. She loved little Edmund. He had his father's serious eyes and dark crop of hair, but he had something of his mother's features and was a beautiful child.

She wondered what her children would look like

and if they would resemble Rowan or herself. Rowan's coloring was much like the king's; he had wonderful mink-brown hair, a fine mustache and dark beard, and expressive hazel eyes. He was taller than the king, lean but strong, and—Rhiannon decided—was entirely wonderful.

She lay back for a moment in the tall grass, closing her eyes. Rowan was with Alfred now, and she prayed that he would soon return. When he took her into his arms, all would be well. She would forget the nightmares and would cease to fear the ice-eyed stranger.

And when the king had finished with the Danes at Rochester, she would marry Rowan. Alfred had been too preoccupied with war to sanction their union yet, but when the king returned, she would beg him to have the banns called from the church. Alfred was fond of Rowan, she knew. He would not protest. He had always smiled benignly on their love affair.

It was an appealing daydream. The king would give her to her bridegroom, and Alswitha would laugh with her and give her warnings about the night to come. But she was in love and not afraid of the bridal bed. Rather, she had loved the slow, sultry kisses that she and Rowan had exchanged, and she had been sweetly eager to know more. To give herself to Rowan seemed but a natural and beautiful thing to do. She loved to imagine being with him through the night, at his side.

She started, her reverie broken, as she felt a thundering against the earth. Edmund was shouting excitedly and drawing his sisters through the high grass. Rhiannon scrambled to her feet and saw that the gates were opening. The king was returning.

Looking toward the manor, Rhiannon saw Alswitha come from the house. She did not rush to meet her husband but waited. Alfred gave the order that his men were free to engage in leisurely pursuits, then he turned his mount toward the house. He dismounted, and there, as a groom came for his horse, he greeted his wife. Rhiannon watched them for a moment, glad of their love, and then she searched through the crowd of returning horsemen until she saw Rowan. Her heart went out to him, for he appeared tired and very forlorn, and she wondered with a new rush of fury what had happened on the coast for him to appear so pained. Like Alfred and his important aldermen—Allen, Edward of Sussex, William of Northumbria, and Jon of Wincester—Rowan was heading toward the manor, after the king. There was to be some kind of a council meeting, Rhiannon thought. But perhaps Alfred would allow her a moment with Rowan, a quick greeting, before he took sole use of the hall.

"Children, come!" she called to them. "Your father has come home!"

She did not need to tell the little ones, for they were already racing toward the manor. She followed, first at a run, then more discreetly, as befitted her station in life. But when she came to the house, she burst through the door as quickly as the children.

Serfs were already busy supplying the king and his men with ale. Alswitha was greeting them cordially. The children ran to their father, demanding his attention. Alfred's eyes glanced at Rhiannon and slid away, and she was startled, for the king always looked everyone, man or woman, straight in the eyes. Edmund had reached him. He hugged his son and turned his back on Rhiannon. She stiffened. So he was still angry with her. Yet none of it was her fault.

She did not care, she thought, but she did. She did not love him so much because he was the king but because of his value as a man. She loved his quick wit and intuition and loved to listen as he expatiated on his dreams. Alfred saw an England in which learning and culture flourished once again.

Rhiannon bowed her head, acknowledging Allen, Edward, William, and Jon. She was fond of Jon and Edward; they were both men near her own age, quick to laughter and the use of flowery phrases, and ever her defenders. Allen she found too grim, yet she forgave him, for it was easy to understand his ever-serious nature. William sometimes frightened her. He watched her and studied her, twirling his fine, dark mustache as he did so, making her wonder what cunning lurked in his mind. He made her uneasy, but she nodded to him, anyway. Then she realized that they were all three staring at her and that each of them seemed very grave and serious and grim. She couldn't understand it, for they had come back with their full number, so the Irish prince must have negotiated. There couldn't have been another battle.

The king still held little Edmund, so Rhiannon felt that she was free to smile at the others and hurry past them in her efforts to reach Rowan. She quickened her pace as she neared him, casting herself into his arms.

"Rhiannon!" He whispered her name painfully.

Something was wrong. She knew it instantly. She stared into Rowan's eyes and was certain that she saw a glaze of tears there. Nor would he hold her. He caught her arms and held her from him, and the confusion was almost more than she could bear.

"Rowan, what is the matter?"

"I—I've no more right to hold you," he said softly, and only then did she realize that everyone in the room was staring at her—the king harshly and coldly; Alswitha with confusion; and each and every one of the men sorrowfully and with a keen discomfort.

They all knew something she did not.

"What has happened?" she demanded.

Whatever it was had to be awful, she knew. She looked at Rowan again. His features were taut with pain and he held her tightly but away from him. A slow chill swept through her. It took root at the base of her spine; swept upward, catching her nape; then spread to her limbs.

"Rowan—"

"The king must tell you," he said. He set her from him and quickly addressed Alfred in a choking voice. "I would leave now, Sire."

The king nodded. Rhiannon stared at Alfred, demanding an answer with her eyes.

"What is it?" she asked again at last. She tried to keep her voice low. Then she knew. They had not been able to dislodge the Viking from her land. Viking? she thought bitterly. Nay—the Irishman. The king kept insisting that the usurpers were Irish.

"My home," she said. "It is lost."

"All of you, leave us," Alfred said.

"Alfred—" Alswitha began.

"Leave us!" the king repeated to his wife.

She heard the men turn and leave. She didn't see

them; her eyes were locked with the king's. She was dimly aware that Alswitha called to the children, and then Rhiannon was alone with the king, and an awful terror filled her heart.

"Alfred, tell me!" she cried hoarsely.

For a moment she thought that he meant to stall, to speak to her as gently as possible and to try to soften the cruelty of his coming words.

But then he spoke flatly, in a tone of·voice he had never used to her before.

"You are to be married."

Married. She had just been dreaming of such a blissful state. But if she were to marry Rowan, there would not be this awful tension in the room.

"Married?" she repeated, and her tone was as cool as his.

"Immediately."

"To whom, may I ask, my noble king?" The tone of her voice was subtly sarcastic. The inflection was not lost upon Alfred.

"I am sorry to hurt you in any way, Rhiannon, but I am doing what I must. I have betrothed you to Eric of Dubhlain. The wedding will take place here, in two weeks."

She could not believe him. The words washed over her and then seemed to fall at her feet like cold droplets of rain.

She shook her head. "No. This is some jest."

"Nay, Rhiannon, no jest."

The cold seized her. It surged through her. He meant to give her to some unknown prince. To an Irishman, a foreigner with Norse blood. He had used her like some playing piece in a game, as an appeasement for what had happened.

"Alfred, you cannot mean this. You cannot do this to me. I am in love with Rowan and he with me."

"Rhiannon, love is a luxury I cannot allow you at this time. Rowan has understood that I had no choice. You must do the same."

Seconds elapsed. She stared at him, stricken. For the first time in her life she did not know how to deal with the king.

Supplication, she thought swiftly. She had always been one of his favorites. She must plead.

"No. Please!" she whispered, and she hurried to him, falling upon her knees before him. "Alfred, however I have offended you, I beg your pardon! And I beg your mercy! Please—"

"Stop it! Stop it!" he roared at her. "Get off your knees. You have not offended me. This is no punishment. You will do as you are told, for I have commanded that it will be so. I have done you no injury! I have given you to the son of a king, and the grandson of the great king of all Ireland. You will not shame me by protesting this arrangement." He jerked his hand away and turned from her. "Get up."

Stunned, amazed, Rhiannon stared at him. She could not believe that he would turn so callously from her.

She stood slowly, staring at the back he presented to her. Her voice trembled as she spoke. "I cannot. I will not do it. Perhaps your Irish prince never stepped ashore, but his Norse henchmen destroyed my town and my people. I will not marry the man."

He swung around in fury. "You will!"

"No," she said softly, emphatically. She felt so very cold, almost numb. The king was not angry. He was not seeking revenge, and she could not plead her case before him. He was a man obsessed; he had set his mind and issued his command. And he *was* the king.

"You have no choice," he told her flatly. "If you continue to argue with me, I will have you imprisoned until the day of the wedding."

"Do what you will, I will not marry this man!" she vowed.

"You force my hand, Rhiannon."

She remained silent. "Allen!" he called out sharply.

"What are you doing?" she demanded desperately. She hadn't wanted to lose her control, her dignity. Now he was calling upon one of her least favorite of his men to . . . to do something with her.

Her control snapped. He was her cousin, her guardian. Tears formed in her eyes and hovered on her lashes. She sprang to life, her dignity abandoned, and raced toward him. She slammed against him with passion and fury, beating against his chest. He caught her arms and her hands fell futilely against his chest. She met his eyes and thought that he was glad of her wrath, that he welcomed the storm of her fury, for it somehow absolved him.

"Alfred, whom the English hail as great!" she whispered scathingly. "I will never forgive you for this. Nor will I marry this man!" she promised.

For one moment it seemed that he would soften. His lips parted as if he would speak, his hands moving as if he would stroke her hair. He did not. He thrust her from him. "Allen!" he called again.

Allen came at the second call. Rhiannon kept staring at the king. Allen touched her arm, and she jerked free of him, approaching the king heatedly once again. "I'll not do it! You cannot force me! I will run to the holy sisters, I will seek refuge in Paris—I will go to the Danes!"

The last caught the king's attention. He spun around and returned to her.

"Nay, lady, you will not. I will keep you under lock and key until the moment you are wed. And if you persist in this infamy, I will pray that he is more Viking than Irishman and that he will take all necessary measures to silence you! Allen!" he roared. "Take her from my sight!"

Allen grasped her arm hard. She turned to face him and saw that there was a malicious gleam in his eye, as if he enjoyed her discomfort.

"Let go of me, Allen!" she demanded. "I will walk where you so choose. Just keep your hands off me."

His smile straightened, his mustache falling low over his mouth. His gaze upon her darkened. "Lady, I would watch your noble tongue!" he warned her.

"I will watch nothing!" she said. She jerked free and hurried past him, storming out the door. Within seconds he was behind her. He caught hold of her arm just as Edward reached them both. "Please, let me take her!" Edward implored.

She didn't look at Allen; she was too close to tears. It seemed that he acquiesced, for Edward was leading her then. She stumbled, amazed that the sun could still be shining, that the clash of steel could still be heard as men practiced the arts of war.

But now there was no one close to the king's house.

"I'm sorry, Rhiannon," Edward said to her. "So very sorry."

"Where are you taking me?"

"The spring house."

It was a small, unfurnished structure down the slope of the valley, usually used for storage. There was nothing at all within it now. One single high window let in the light.

"Don't bolt me in. Let me escape," she pleaded.

"You know that I cannot," Edward told her sadly.

She managed to square her shoulders and step into the small building. She slammed the door of her prison, and sank down to the dirt floor.

Then she burst into tears, trying to muffle the sound so that no one set to guard her might hear her. She cried in silence until the darkness descended. No one came near her. No one brought so much as a drop of water. She sat through the dark, silent night in abject misery, her resolve stiffening.

She slept, but her dreams were filled with terror. The Irish prince had turned her over to his blond Norse henchman, and the man was stalking her. Her arrow protruded from his thigh, and blood cascaded down his leg as he shouted at her, "Pray, lady. Pray that we do not meet again."

In the morning the queen came to her. Rhiannon was pale and exhausted and bitter.

She told Alswitha that she wanted to see the king.

Alfred had betrayed her. The king had cast her to the enemy, but she would not consent to his decree. Somehow she would elude them all. And they would never suspect.

Alswitha brought her to Alfred. Rhiannon knelt down before him and whispered that she acquiesced to his will.

She could not face him as she lied; yet a lie was her only road to freedom.

He took her into his arms again and held her tightly. He whispered that he was glad and grateful that he loved her and would always be there for her.

I hate you! she cried inwardly.

But she didn't really hate him. She remembered her father and knew that Alfred could die at any time. She held him tightly in return; she could not obey him but she did love him.

She just couldn't forgive what he had done. She could not accept it. There seemed to be a coldness that wound around her heart and turned it to ice. He was unrelenting. She could be the same, Rhiannon knew, yet if she did not pretend to accept his will, then she would have little chance to change her fate.

She had already bought her freedom from the spring house.

The next morning she went out to the stables. She longed to take the roan that had brought her there and fly with the creature, fly into the wind, to the north, to the south, to oblivion. She knew that she had to be patient, though, and cunning. She fervently wished that she had not fought the king so forcefully when he had first brought the news to her, for now she would have to cultivate his trust carefully. Today she would just stay here for the morning and stroke the soft noses of the animals. She would whisper to them and choose her mount. She needed the strongest and swiftest of them. She could not judge them easily here, but she was familiar with horseflesh and breeding and could choose a sound mount to ride when the time to escape rolled around.

She smiled, pausing where the roan was stalled. He was not the finest beast but had delivered her once from imminent danger. She paused to stroke the creature and then heard her name whispered softly, brokenly, and heartrendingly.

"Rhiannon!"

She turned; she knew the voice. Rowan stood there, tall and handsome in his linen chemise, short leather tunic, and sturdy hose. His sword was at his side, his eyes plagued by misery. His face remained ashen, yet she thought that it had taken courage for him to come there after the king had spoken on her fate.

She cried out his name and rushed to him. His arms tightened around her. He swept her from her feet and carried her to a mound of hay, and they fell there together. He held her as if she were a priceless treasure. She reached up and touched the curling locks of his hair that fell to his neck, then moved her palm lovingly over his bearded chin. "Rowan!" she whispered, and sobs bubbled up within her.

He saw the tears in her eyes. He touched her lips with his fingers. And suddenly she remembered everything about him, remembered why she loved him. He had been with the party that had returned her father's body to the coast when Garth had died, and when she had fallen over his form in tears, Rowan had taken her up. When the horror had been too much, he had lifted her into his arms. And in the days that followed, he had spoken of her father's courage and determination. He had given much of Garth back to her, and for that alone she could have adored him.

He held her away and stroked her cheeks, staring at her face as if he could imprint the memory of it forever on his heart. She felt a new surge of fear, for she now realized how fully he had accepted the king's will and realized that she truly had no help for it.

"We should have married before," he said dully. "We should have married ere now and the king could not have done this thing."

"It is not done yet," she murmured.

"Rhiannon . . ." He pressed her back against the hay and moved over her. She suddenly felt keenly aware of the moment, of all sensation. The scent of the hay rose up, and she heard each shuffle of the horses' hooves, felt the very texture of the flesh on his palms. The day was ridiculously beautiful, she knew, beyond the paneling of the barn. It was spring in Wessex; the grass was green and the brooks and streams bubbled and laughed. And she loved the man here beside her.

If they were caught together, though, they would both be condemned as guilty of defying the king's will. Nay, it went further, for she knew that it was not only Alfred's will but his honor, as well, at stake.

Alfred's honor—and perhaps Rowan's life.

She scrambled up upon the hay. "Rowan! If someone saw you come here . . . I am afraid."

"Hush. No one saw me. I would not jeopardize your future so."

"My future!" She reached out again, needing to touch him. He had kissed her before, had held her.

She knew his touch and cherished it. Perhaps she felt no great stirring wonder, but she did feel loved and secure in his embrace.

Suddenly, bitterly, she wished that she had given herself to him before. She could not believe in honor now; she had been sold to a heathen, and so honor could matter little. She might have gone forth from there with one sweet memory of having been loved. She smiled at him tenderly. "Think not of my honor, love, for such a thing is suddenly not my own at all. I fear for you, dear Rowan. The king has spoken."

"Aye, the king has spoken," he agreed tonelessly. "And I am left a fool, bereft."

"I will not marry him," Rhiannon vowed. She came to her knees, and he pressed his face against her chest.

"God, that I could have been your husband!" he breathed.

"I am not going to marry him. I am going to escape. My dear Rowan, Rowan . . ." she murmured. She didn't feel his passion, but she did feel his pain and his emotion, and she gladly would have fallen then and there with him into the hay and defied the very world. But she suddenly heard the sound of laughter, and she realized that men were coming into the stables, seeking their mounts.

"Rowan!" she cried.

"I will not leave you as if we were ashamed of this love—"

"You must!" She shoved him from her. "For the love of God, Rowan! Let not your life be the price of love!" He still did not move. She leapt to her feet, determined to leave the stables. But when she saw the desperate way his eyes followed her, she rushed back to him. "We will be together," she murmured. "And I'll not marry the invader who laid waste to my home!"

Then she ran, quickly escaping the stables and racing out to the meadows.

The sun was high. Newborn lambs brayed in the fields. All of Wessex was redolent with spring. Yet she would escape it, she vowed. When the Irish party was near, and when the king and his household were most preoccupied, then she would fly.

As the days continued to pass, Alfred and Rhiannon waged a cold and silent war. Rhiannon stood still as she was fitted for the splendid garments she would wear for the wedding: a long linen tunic, white for purity, trimmed with dusky ermine; the shift she would wear beneath was exceptionally fine silk, rich and expensive, for it had come all the way from Persia. The bodice would be jeweled, and the king had given her a crown of amethysts to adorn her hair. She had not thanked him for the gift. Nor had she ceased to dream of her departure.

With but three days before the wedding was to take place, Alfred appeared at the doorway to the extension of the women's solar, where the ladies worked diligently sewing jewels into the gown, crafting the soft woolen hose Rhiannon would wear beneath it. The king stared at her, and she returned his gaze coolly. Her heart pounded and she hated this thing that stood between them.

When Alfred entered the room, the women working around Rhiannon backed away. He lifted a hand, indicating that he wished to be alone with her, and they bowed and left them. Rhiannon remained standing there, tall and proud and still somehow fragile in the white gown.

"You have really accepted this?" he asked her.

Again she could not face him. She felt her gaze wavering, and then her lashes fell. She lifted her hands vaguely. "You have commanded it."

"You will obey me."

"I always obey you."

"That's not exactly so. And you do not forgive me."

She lifted her eyes and they were filled with passion. "Nay, I cannot forgive you!"

His fists knotted at his sides, and he ground out a sound of anger and impatience. "Rhiannon, this was not easy for me."

"Ah, but, Sire, you love dirt more than you love people!"

"Aye!" he returned to her angrily. "Aye, I love this dirt, this England!" He caught her hands and pulled her to the window that opened to the east, where the hills sloped away in vernal beauty, covered with yellow daffodils and soft purple violets. "Aye, lady, I love this land, and you love it too! Your father fought and died for this, and deny it or no, you love it too. You have shared the dream with me—of a time when peace will come, when music will float through the forests, when men will read, when artistry will flourish. But first I must expel these Danes, I must cast them from this land. By the dear Lord, Rhiannon!" He spoke out impatiently. "You were raised in a noble household and are aware that marriages are often contracts and seldom matters of love. You were raised to do your duty and to honor your king. You must understand that an alliance rides on this issue, that England's future is at stake here."

She stood still and waited several seconds, watching him gravely. "And you must see," she said at last, "that the land is composed of people. I have shared your dreams and I have had my own. Now you, my king, have cast aside my hopes and dreams and happiness so carelessly, so ruthlessly."

"I have not offered you up to an ancient man but a virile prince of a noble house."

"A Viking."

The king was very still for a moment. She watched his fist clench, then ease.

"An Irishman—but I would have offered you to Satan himself, Rhiannon, had it been necessary. I am sorry for you, and for Rowan. But unfortunately a woman is part of her land, and you, lady, are most certainly part and parcel of yours. I have already appeared a treacherous fool, for your people attacked invited guests—"

"Alfred! I have told you—"

He held up his hand, stopping her. "And I have believed you. Yet I would take grave care, for the man you will marry knows that you were the instigator of that fight."

"I believed that I was attacked! Dragon prows—"

"We'll not speak of it. But you'll not make matters worse or embarrass us further. I have promised you to this man, and you will uphold my promise for me. I do not trust you, Rhiannon. I fear that you will deny him when you stand before God. I have loved you as I have loved my own children. But if you shame me now, if you dishonor me and cause rivers of your countrymen's blood to flow, I will turn my back on you, and from the depths of my heart I will damn you." He held still for a moment, watching the effect of his words on her. "Good day, Rhiannon." He bowed stiffly and left her. Tears rose to her eyes and she almost ran after him. She could not bear the coldness between them; she had lost everything, and now she had lost Alfred too.

She did not sleep that night. She lay awake and remembered the king's words. She had nightmare visions of dragon prows sweeping across the sea and crawling upon the land. The dragons came toward her, breathing fire, and they were like serpents, sliding around her to choke her. She awoke shaking and swore that she would not marry any Viking.

But neither could she be the cause of more bloodshed.

She could not think or feel anymore. In the morning she followed Alswitha to confession and tried to whisper the words that she could not obey her king. Father Geoffrey bade her speak up, but she could not; she ran from the church without seeking absolution.

She had to see Rowan. Alone. Just one more time. She had to taste the love she might have savored for a lifetime. She still hadn't forgiven the king, but she didn't know now whether she could run away. If she did so, the men would have to fight, the Irishman to avenge his honor and the king because he would have no choice.

Often she thought of her father, who had loved her mother beyond life and reason and had ridden to sweep her away and demand her for his own. Rowan could not ride against Alfred, she knew. Yet each day caused a greater pain, and the time came closer and closer. They saw each other every night, from a distance. Their eyes would meet across the banqueting table in the hall, and she would know that the king watched them. Rowan would hang his head miserably.

Sweep me away! she longed to cry to him. *Carry me from here on the king's fastest horse, and we can live forever in the mountains of Wales.* She did not hear the lutists or the pipers who played through the meal, nor did she listen to the seneschals who related tales of courage and grandeur. She watched Rowan and dreamed of a horse that could fly.

Rowan did not come to her to carry her away.

But where he usually avoided her at the evening meal, he came close to her one evening, when the wedding was just two days off. He leaned low, pretending to reach for the delicate meat knife he had dropped, but he whispered to her instead, "I must see you!"

Her heart took flight.

"Meet me with the dawn. At the split oak, by the brook."

She nodded. She went to her room with her nerves aflame and her heart quaking. She did not sleep but lay in torment. She could save her heart and dishonor her king. Or she could bow before honor and duty and cast aside her very soul.

When she dreamed, the dragon prows came alive again. She fell into a deep pit of dragon vipers, and she screamed and screamed, trying to elude them. Around her at the pit stood the king and his liege men, Allen, William, Jon . . . and even Rowan. They watched her struggle and listened to her scream. She reached out, and a powerful hand caught hold of her hand. As she watched, her fingers entwined with more powerful ones, long and rugged and heavily callused.

A pair of sizzling blue eyes captured hers, and she opened up her mouth to scream again. Laughter rang around her, and she was lifted upward, into a swirling mist, into the arms of the Viking with the golden hair and bronze, muscled chest and towering height.

"Pray, lady . . ." he whispered to her, and she started to scream; then she awoke.

She shivered through the end of the night and then rose, still agitated.

Whoever this Irish prince was, he was half heathen at least. Alfred asked too much of her. She could not differentiate the Norwegian menace from the Danish terror. They were all Vikings.

And the man with ice-fire eyes and barbarian build was surely one of the prince's closest captains. She had nearly killed him.

And she was about to be cast on the mercy of a barbaric prince. Nay, she had too much pride! She could not bear it.

She gazed about the room where she had stayed so often, where she had laughed with Alswitha and the children, and where their love had warmed her.

The warmth of the room was gone. Nay, the very warmth of life eluded her.

5

Eric sat upon the beautiful white stallion and stared southward toward the coast, his startling blue gaze assessing and appreciating all that he saw. His mantle lifted and blew behind him in a curious majesty. It fell, delineating the breadth of his shoulders and the tall ease with which he sat his mount.

Behind him, the walls of the town were already rising again. The sea breeze, from the shore ahead, touched his face and dampened his cheeks, and it was good.

The land was like a mistress, his father once told him, achingly demanding and calling to the senses with a seductiveness that couldn't be denied. This land called to him.

A slight smile curved his mouth.

Once he had stood upon the cliffs of Eire as a boy. He had waved a wooden sword in the air; Leith had approached him and they had engaged in mock battle. Leith had dropped his wooden sword, and Eric had stepped forward, claiming himself the victor.

"Nay, you churl!" Leith had protested, a mischievous smile playing upon his lip.

"What? Nay, what is this? I am no churl. Rather, I am the better man, for I have bested you."

"Churl, you have not! For I will be the king, and you, my brother, will be my liege man. You will fight for me and obey me."

"I will obey no man! I will rule my own destiny!"

Erin, who had idled her time upon a blanket with their baby sister while the boys played, leapt to her feet, coming between them. Eric twisted and set his jaw stubbornly.

"Will he be the king, Mother?"

"Aye, he will. But you will both honor your father first—for many years to come, God grant us!"

"I will always honor Father," Eric grumbled.

"And your brother," Erin said softly.

He paused, then he had come down on one knee before his brother. "Leith, I will honor you, as I have honored my father. Aye, I will raise my sword ever in your defense. Until I have my own kingdom, that is." He gazed over to his mother. "I will have my own land?"

She smiled. "Your father is a king. Your grandfather was a great king. You will surely have a place to call your own."

He went to her and placed his hands upon his hips. "They needn't pity me, Mother. I will claim my own land. Like my sire, I will go a-Viking, and I will find the land that is to be my own."

Erin had picked up this stubborn child and held him tightly to her breast. "You are an Irishman, love. We will see that you have a place here—"

"Nay, Mother. I must find my own."

"That is years hence—"

"Father will understand."

And his father *had* understood. They had all grown;

they had all ridden off to war. He had set sail in many a Viking ship, and in time he had created his own army of men and acquired great riches. But the land had eluded him, the land of his dreams.

But now it stretched before him as a great and vast prize. He had to go to war to defend that land, and then it would be his. He had to go to war . . . and accept a fire-haired menace who might very well have betrayed her king, as a wife. That was part of the contract, and it seemed a very small payment when compared with the quickening of his heart and the triumph in his soul.

Seeing the harbor and the meadows and the cliff stretch out in all of spring's sweet majesty, he felt that he could be generous. He would offer her peace. He wondered if a peace between them was possible and remembered the way she had looked at him, silver daggers in her eyes, and then he recalled the way she had spoken so vehemently. Nay, there would surely be no peace.

He shrugged dismissively. He would seldom need to see her. If he could deal gently with her, he would. He would leave her to herself and to her hatred. But they would be united under God, he thought, and the quickening, the love of the land, came to him again. Men sought out land to create great dynasties, and he was no different. He had wandered the earth long enough. He wanted heirs. Certainly she understood her duty there.

Curiously his pulse began to thunder, and a rising heat seized his body. She did not elicit tender emotion within him, but she had reached into the savage recesses of his heart. In anger, in pain, he had felt a blossoming in his loins. He had desired her. Yet he did not like the depth of that desire within himself. He was no barbarian. He had sown his wild oats in his youth. He was as proud of his father's people as he was his mother's, for he knew the civilized side of the Viking—had learned it from his father and had seen the great potential of the sea-roaming race. When they did not engage in warfare, the Norse were great builders. They farmed the land in summer and created beautiful carvings when the north winds blew. They spun sagas of challenges met, of daring. They set down laws and lived by them. They built towns and brought commerce and trade to many peoples.

His jaw tightened. They were not savages.

Not barbarians.

"Eric?"

Rollo rode up behind him. Eric spun the magnificent white horse around. A long trail of his men stretched out behind, awaiting him.

"We ride to Wareham!" he said. He raised his shield, a shield of wolves, and sent forth his battle cry. Answering shouts rose high upon the wind, tossing and echoing from the sea to the land. The white stallion reared and snorted, and his forefeet plunged back to the earth.

Then the ground was a-thunder as the party rode out for Wareham.

Eric, pensive, kept ahead. He observed his journey carefully over the hills and vales and through the Roman roads that marked the way through dense forests. And all the way he felt the land. He raced upon the flowers of spring and sailed through the freshness of the air. Fawns leapt before them, and pheasants set up a mighty whir, rising from the tall grasses to streak upward into the sky.

With the coming of darkness, they neared Wareham. Eric ordered that the party stop and camp for the night. He could see the walls of the king's home before him, but he was not ready to enter those walls. A curious brooding was upon him, and he wanted solitude.

They set up fires and cooked their meals. Eric kept his distance, leaning against a tree, drinking English mead and watching the light in the night that denoted the king's walled manor and surroundings. He admired Alfred greatly. The King of Wessex was a man of action who longed for finer pursuits. A king who shed blood but lamented the deed.

Eric drank deeply of his mead and wondered what would come of the wedding. He feared that there would be battle if the girl chose to dishonor the betrothal. Christian banns had been cried, and the honor of not only himself but his men was at stake. He shrugged, trusting in the king. Alfred would not risk insulting him again.

"Take heed, young lord!"

He turned, aware that Mergwin had followed him. The Druid stood tall. The moon fell upon him, whitening his beard and his hair, until he appeared as a mad magician. His ancient face was weathered, infinitely wrinkled.

"I always take heed, Mergwin. If you followed me across the sea to warn me to watch my back, know it is a lesson I've learned well."

But Mergwin didn't smile, and he didn't turn away. "I cast your runes again today."

Eric lifted his cup vaguely. "And?"

"Hegalez. And then the blank rune."

"Hegalez warns of storms, of tempests and great power, of thunder on the earth. And we know that is destined to come, for we ride to fight the Dane at Rochester."

"I read the same runes for your mother once," Mergwin muttered.

Eric felt that the old man was digressing, that his great age was beginning to tell on him at last. It seemed that he had lived forever, for Mergwin had served Eric's grandfather, Aed Finnlaith, Ard-Ri of all Eire, since he had been a boy.

Eric spoke gently then, because he did love his ancient mentor greatly. "Mergwin, do not fear for me. I face the truth of battle and do not fear death. Nay, rather I fear the life in which a man could forget that death is one day his keeper, whether he is brave or a wretched coward. I will watch my back when we fight the Dane. I will stay in close union with Rollo, and we will be like an impenetrable wall."

Mergwin walked over to him. He leaned his back against the tree and sighed. "There is some darkness closer. Clouds hover and I cannot read them."

"Clouds are a part of life."

The Druid pushed away from the tree. He stared at Eric intently, then he wagged a finger at him. "Take care, for the treachery looks close. It is not the enemy that you see but the enemy that you *cannot* see."

"Mergwin," Eric said wearily, "I will heed all your warnings and take great care. For tonight, though, I am suddenly quite tired." He clapped the old man on the back and turned away.

He did not want to be with his men that night. He sought the earth beneath him, and the moon over his head, and the darkness and solitude of the night.

He carried Vengeance with him, though, for the Druid's words had hit their mark, and Eric was ever wary. He walked until he came to a bubbling brook and sat there, listening to the sound of it. It was a lulling, peaceful melody, and his soul wreaked havoc with him. He laid out his mantle there and slept.

Dawn came.

Rhiannon quietly left the manor. She wore her warm mantle, but she knew that she would have no need for the jewels she had sewn so carefully into the hem of the garment.

She would meet Rowan. She would meet him because she had loved him, because they had dreamed together. She would meet him because they had really been in love and because she had to say good-bye. But she would no longer dream of an escape.

She would not run away with him.

It was not fear of Alfred that had brought her to obedience to his will. It was fear of the bloodshed that could follow if she refused to honor the pledge to the Irish prince. Alfred would be forced to war with the very men he had summoned to be his strength against the Danes. The king, himself, would fight, and endless men might die. She had seen enough bloodshed on the coast.

And if the Norse-Irish and the men of Wessex decimated one another, the Danes would take the victory in the end. She did not think that she could be responsible for such horror.

At the stables she hastily chose a dappled gray mare, saddled her, and rode out. If the grooms were awake, they did not notice her. When the sentry at the gate saw her, he merely waved, and let her pass.

At the oak she waited.

Dawn broke in the east and Rowan didn't come. Heartache seized her, and she grieved for the time that might have been theirs. Rowan was another reason she could not run. If Rowan was caught with her, he could be slain. If war broke out again between the Irish and English troops, that blood would lie at her feet. She had longed for rescue and fought the demons in her heart, but she could not flee.

She heard a rustling in the bush and turned, half expecting that she was to be dragged back to Wareham by the king's men, half praying that her love had come to her at last.

"My heart!"

The urgent whisper filled her with gladness. She pushed away from the tree and ran through the brush to greet him. She cast herself into his arms, forgetting that she was soon to be another man's bride. He did not push her away, and for a moment she forgot that she had come to say good-bye. He held her tight as his mouth found hers and melded to it. He ran his fingers through her hair and gazed into her eyes, then he kissed her again, delicately plunging his tongue into her mouth.

It was just a kiss, she thought. A sweet remembrance to hold her through the aching, empty years. God would understand and forgive her.

She was about to be wed. Legally wed in a binding Christian ceremony.

But her heart was being torn in two, and she could not pull away from the warmth of Rowan's tender kiss.

It was he who pulled away. He drew her to his chest.

"I love you!" she sobbed. "I love you so dearly!"

"And I love you! We will be together."

"Oh, Rowan! We cannot be together—ever again."

He seemed not to hear her. He held her more closely to him, whispering. With his arms around her they fell down gently together into the tall grass. It was barely daylight and they were alone. Rhiannon forgot her fears that someone might come after them. She forgot that she was to become the Viking's bride. She gave way to the beauty of the dawn. Who could they hurt by sharing these last few minutes of words and whispers, and aye, a final kiss or two?

Rowan, dear Rowan, gazed down upon her, caressing her cheek. He sighed. "I linger. We must make haste!" he said.

He hadn't understood yet. He still thought that she had come to run away with him. She shook her head sadly and Rowan frowned. "We must make haste, love, for they will discover us gone. I would lay down my life for you but I would rather be with you."

"Damn the king!" she swore softly.

"Love, suppress such words. They are treasonous." He kissed her fingers, and she stared with love into his eyes, at his manly features.

"Damn him, Rowan," she repeated. "That we have come here now is treasonous—even if just to say good-bye to each other. What greater harm can I do with words?"

"But we will flee—"

"Nay, Rowan, listen to me. We cannot."

It took him time to understand her brokenly stated words.

"He would catch us," she whispered miserably. "He could slay you."

"Ah, love! I cannot watch you go to him!"

"You must. Oh, God, Rowan! I have weighed this so carefully in my mind! I have no choice, except to be the cause of endless death! Would that it could be otherwise. Oh, Rowan, it breaks my heart, shatters it, to cause you pain!"

Indeed it did, for he looked down upon her with such anguish that she could not bear it.

"Oh, Rowan!" she cried. "You will always have my heart, I swear it! I do love you so very much."

"My God, and I love you!" he vowed, and the passion and pain were so intense in his words that she suddenly found herself in his arms again, held tightly and fiercely. And his lips were hot with ardor upon hers. The kiss was sweet, intoxicating.

And then . . . it was more.

She did not know who seduced who, or how things went so very far so very quickly. It was the moment, it was the bitter pain of parting, it was the pain of love. She was touching his shoulders, and they were bare. And his hands were upon her naked flesh, for her mantle and tunic had been swept away. And then she was whispering anew.

"I love you, I love you. I am pledged to a viperous rodent, a vile Viking bastard, but I love you."

Then his whisper caressed her, heated, tender. She realized what they had come to, what she was about to do. It had to be right. She loved him. And words filled with his love were falling passionately from his tongue.

It was not right and she knew it. She was pledged to another man. She would marry him before God.

"Rowan!" Her wrenching cry stopped him. His eyes touched hers and he saw the sadness, the agony.

And the passion between them faded. He held her still but gently.

For these few moments she would feel no guilt. She held tightly to him and heard the song of a bird, thinking that she would cherish those few moments alone with him forever.

She did not know that they were not alone at all.

Eric, Prince of Dubhlain, stood hard and cold not twenty feet away.

In the night he had dreamed of serpents.

Wicked, evil creatures, they had raised their heads around him, and he had risen with Vengeance to fight them. With all his strength and power, he did battle, but they sprang back from the earth. Emenia was beside him, and he knew that she had lain there; he had felt her gentle touch, had known that her hair entangled him, that her limbs had been entwined with his. He fought the serpents and slew them again and again. But when he reached for her, a cry of agony welled within him, rising to the heavens and beyond in endless anguish. The blood was upon her and sprang from her. He took her into his arms and tried to breathe his life into her, but the blood rose around them like a storm, like a tide. And then he knew that it wasn't Emenia at all but another woman who lay with him, another woman whose hair entangled him. He tried to sweep the blood-soaked strands of hair from her face, but she began to sink in the ever-rising red pool. The serpents were dragging her down. He reached for her and she screamed again. . . .

He awoke shaking in the night. He jumped to his feet, Vengeance in his hands.

Slowly he began to breathe evenly again. He mocked himself for fearing a dream when he did not hesitate to meet the whole of a Danish army.

He lay back down. He looked at the moon, and sleep eluded him while memories haunted his mind. At last he slept again, deeply.

He felt the coming of the morning, the kiss of the dawn, the faint touch of the sun. He heard the gentle gurgling of the brook in a pleasant state between wakefulness and sleep. Vaguely he heard rustling in the wood. The sound was furtive, and he knew that it presented to him no danger, so he did not rise. Some maiden came, he realized dimly. She seemed to crave silence and was in no mood for company. Let the girl be. He'd not destroy her solitude by alerting her to his presence.

But then she was joined by a man.

He heard fragments of her whispers. He wanted to leave the lovers together but could not go without being seen.

He saw their garments seem to slide away. He saw the exquisite beauty of her back, naked even of her hair, for it had been bound high and knotted in a braid. She had been achingly beautiful, the curves of her breasts just visible to him, her fine, molded buttocks flaring out from a tiny waist and touched with delicate dimples on either side of the small of her back. Her neck was long and graceful, and her shoulders were beautifully sloped and supple. He caught his breath as he watched her, and then he again longed to be far away, for he did not wish to disturb a pair of star-crossed lovers.

Then he heard their words clearly, and within moments he realized who the woman was.

Rhiannon. His betrothed.

Fury exploded within him.

He could not allow it. He had not wanted to enter her life, but she had been given over to him, and what was his he guarded carefully.

She was to be his wife!

The rage swept through him and he fought to control it.

Perhaps the lovers had met and mated here, in the tall grasses, many times before.

He was not about to let them betray him now, or ever again. He stood hastily, reaching for his sword, lest the foolish young buck think to fight him.

He did not have a chance to reach the lovers, for the quiet clearing by the brook was suddenly shattered by the sounds of hoofbeats. "Find them!" someone shouted. "By the king's honor, find them!"

Rhiannon cried out and jumped to her feet. She hadn't time to dress, but her lover rose with her, casting her mantle about her.

"Run!" he urged her. "Reach the clearing!"

"Nay, the king will not kill me. He could well slay you! Oh, Rowan, if harm comes to you—"

"Go!" the young swain ordered her. He shoved her toward the place where Eric stood.

"Nay, not until you return! You run. If they do not find us together, they cannot charge you with my disappearance, or with—" She broke off, her voice trailing away miserably.

"I will run!" he promised her, and he propelled her onward again.

She came stumbling through the foliage. Eric stood still, fighting his rage. Riders thrashed their way through the grasses, and he knew that she was desperate to elude them. She came crashing through the water of the brook, and she stumbled right before him. She saw the hem of his mantle and grabbed it.

"Sir, kind sir, I beg of you, help me! My guardian is marrying me off to a Viking bastard, and I am desperate to elude pursuit at this moment. Please! My life shall be spent with a viperous rodent, but I—"

Her silvery blue eyes at last rose to his, filling with amazement. She recognized him, but Eric realized then that she didn't know just who he was. Stunned terror followed the amazement, and her ivory skin grew pale and as white as snow.

Rhiannon realized with numbing horror that she had come upon the Viking. There was no help here. Nay, she faced disaster.

"Oh, no!" she gasped. "You!"

She had to elude this man. She rose with lightning-quick speed and spun around. But before she could run, he reached for her. His boot fell upon her mantle, and it tore from her shoulders. He spun her around, and she came, naked, into the brutal grip of his arms.

Maybe he had forgotten her.

No, he had not.

He remembered her—that was all too evident. He remembered her arrows—and her knee, no doubt. She had never seen such a dark fury lay hold upon a man's face before. A weakness filled her. He was surely the Irish prince's bloody henchman. He would return her to Alfred or to his own liege lord. Or perhaps he would slay her and not even the king would protest.

"Have mercy!" she whispered, tossing her head back. Her braid tumbled down. The heavy locks broke free from their twining and came cascading down her back. She longed to sweep it about her to clothe herself.

But he did not look at her nudity; he stared into her eyes and a dark, brooding hatred remained within his own.

"Mercy?" he inquired. It was voiced softly and yet with a deadly menace. "Mercy?"

She cried out as he dragged her closer, slamming her against the heated power of his chest. He gripped her hands so tightly that she feared he would crush her wrists, and she was forced to feel the hard, towering length of him, and the brutal anger that coursed icily from his eyes into her own and onward to her heart.

"I fought you because I thought we were under attack!" she told him swiftly. "I would not have caused you injury had I known that you came at the king's invitation. Please, let me go now! You must have mercy because—"

"No, lady, no. I do not think so."

"But—"

"It has nothing to do with the deadly arrow you meant for my heart, the one that struck my thigh and causes me to limp to this day. Nor does it have to do with your delicate knee slamming against my groin or your elegant fists tearing into my chest. Nay, lady, all of those I could perhaps forgive."

"Then—"

"You shall have no mercy from me because I am, you see, that viperous rodent; the bastard, barbaric Viking to whom you are betrothed."

Her mouth parted and fell into an *O* of horror. And then she cast back her head and screamed in sheer, mad panic, jerking her wrists desperately to free herself. She screamed again and again as horror filled her, cold, icy, seeping throughout her. She was in his power. Naked and vulnerable, crushed against him. She felt acutely the awful strength of his chest, thighs, and arms.

"You!" she breathed.

"Aye, lady, me!"

This could not be the Irish prince!

"Oh, God, no!" she whispered, and she pitted herself against him again, as wild as a tigress. There was nothing left to salvage; she had to escape him and flee.

She could not ease his hold upon her, and she tried to bite his flesh. When that failed, she raised her knee with wicked insinuation against him again.

"Hold!" he raged at her, and swept her up and furiously cast her down upon the earth. Breathless, her hair tumbling all about her like a heavenly fire, she stared up at him. Her breasts lay bare beneath the fall of her hair. She realized her vulnerable state, and a desperate sound escaped her as she tried to rise.

He stepped over her fallen body, placing one booted foot on either side of her hips, catching her hair beneath his tread so that she could not move.

Then he came slowly down himself, straddling her. She lifted her fists to beat against his chest, but his hands seized her wrists and he pressed them hard to the earth on either side of her head. His body was against hers, hard and merciless. Powerful and vibrant, like heated steel.

She could not free herself.

Yet as he stared at her, his mouth a line of fury, his hold a touch of iron, she realized with a searing dread that her dream had been prophetic—her Viking adversary was the prince of Dubhlain.

"We meet again, lady," he said softly. The ice-blue fire of his eyes entered her very soul, searing her. She wondered just what he had seen, what he had heard. Everything . . .

"And under such . . . interesting circumstances. I had nearly determined that there might be a slim chance of peace between us, and yet I come to Wareham for my wedding, and what do I discover? My bride, naked to the core, awaiting me."

He moved away from her at last, still straddling her hips, balancing his weight upon his haunches. The cold morning air swept over her flesh, causing her breasts to swell beneath his gaze, her nipples to harden. He had barely seemed to notice her nakedness before; now he inspected her with brazen disdain, and the touch of his eyes brought fire to her flesh.

Life returned to her. She twisted beneath him, trying to evade the hold of his thighs. "Let me up, free me!" she commanded.

"Nay, lady, nay!" he promised her softly. His Nordic eyes impaled her, striking her heart like a shaft of cold steel. He leaned closer to her once again, his breath touching her lips. "Not until the day you die, my sweet."

A black wave of terror seemed to engulf her. She fought it, determined that she'd never show him fear.

"Tell the king that you don't want me!" she whispered fervently. "Tell him—"

"Would you have a war so fierce that your land would run with rivers of blood?" he demanded harshly.

"But you cannot want me—" Rhiannon broke off as she heard the thunder of hoofbeats again. The king's men were coming close.

The Viking stood and reached down for her wrists, jerking her to her feet and, for a moment, hard against himself. "No, lady, I do not want to wed you!" he assured her quickly. He released her. She stared into his eyes for a brief second and then turned, instinctively, to run. His fingers closed savagely on her hair, and she cried out as she was wrenched back against him. His whisper touched her ear.

"Come now, you mustn't be a coward," he told her harshly. "I had admired your courage, at least."

She faced him again, hatred tripping from her tongue. "Nay, I do not fear you, and I shall never fear you. You've no power to hurt me, ever!"

He smiled at her but it was a grim smile, and his eyes were like frozen fjords in the height of winter's fury. "I do suggest that you learn to fear me, lady. Aye, I do suggest that you learn to fear me—and quickly. There's much you need to fear."

She longed to keep her chin high, but she was naked, and his ice-blue gaze swept dispassionately and with contempt over the length of her.

The horses pounded ever closer. His gaze flickered away and he knelt, picked up her mantle, and drew it around her shoulders. She wanted to bolt, to run, and she could scarcely breathe. She was amazed that he had covered her nakedness. Tears sprang behind her lids, but there was no kindness to the act, she quickly discovered.

"I believe you've exposed enough of what is supposedly mine for this day, don't you, milady?" He arched a brow but did not wait for an answer. He did not expect one.

She found her voice even as he turned from her, whistling for his mount.

"I will never be yours!"

His mount came forward, and she gasped with surprise. Numbness filled her. The horse was hers. It was Alexander, her favorite stallion.

"That's my horse!" she cried.

"*My* horse," he corrected her.

She had forgotten that he held all that had been hers.

His smile, a chilling one, remained in place when he looked at her again. "My horse," he repeated. "And as this animal, lady, is mine, so you shall be. And you, too, will learn to come when I call. If I still choose it to be so. A used horse is one thing, a used wife another."

She gasped. "Vile bastard—" she began, but her words were cut off in a frenzied protest as she felt the biting power of his fingers once again, closing around her arm.

"Nay!" she cried in panic, but he ignored her, sweeping her off her feet and into his arms. In terror she attempted to strike him, to claw him, to free herself. He secured her wrists with one swift measure. His gaze alone stilled her then. "Lady, push me no further!"

He waited. She could not move. She clenched her teeth together and fought the rising panic within her.

He nearly threw her atop the white stallion, then quickly mounted behind her. "Don't fight me," he warned her. "Don't even think of it, for if you attempt to strike me again, I promise that I will strike more swiftly—and with greater effect."

She choked back her rage at his callous words.

"Barbarian!" she accused him, but she did not move. His eyes narrowed.

"Shall I show you?" he inquired.

Rhiannon fell silent. He nudged the horse forward, and her mind began to race even as she shivered against the powerful feel of his arms about her.

The king's men were almost upon them, and suddenly it was too much for her.

She had dishonored Alfred. Alas, when she had meant at last to obey him, she had dishonored him. She had truly meant to go through with her wedding, to create the alliance the king desired.

But it had all gone wrong. And though innocent in truth, she had been caught by the very man to whom she had been promised. A man who had already sworn her vengeance. . . .

There would be no help for her from the king.

Rowan! She thought desperately. This loathsome Viking had seen them together. He would seek out Rowan. He would demand recompense.

Blood would run, and the burden of it would be hers.

Blackness danced before her eyes, and the mercy she had pleaded for came her way at last.

She passed out cold, yet even as consciousness eluded her, she realized that she was being caught by the strong arms of the very man she was so desperate to elude.

Her Viking master . . .

6

Merciful oblivion was not to be hers for long. A sharp tap upon her cheek awoke her. She rested against the crook of the Viking's arm. She would have bolted from him, were he not lifting her already, sliding her to the ground with little care. She could not gain her balance and fell upon the earth. She stared up a tremendous height to meet his unyielding, glacial eyes once again.

"Your clothing, lady," he told her dryly. He had brought her back to where her clothing lay in the grass. She longed to survey him with disdain, pride, and hatred. Her eyes fell and she gazed at the haphazard pile of her belongings: her fine, soft shift; her long tunic; and her hose and leather slippers.

A blush suffused her cheeks. She couldn't expect much courtesy from him after the way he had found her, but she couldn't possibly cast aside her mantle and dress before him. Besides, she was innocent. And Rowan was innocent—even if he probably would never believe her.

She lifted her chin but could not raise her eyes. "If you please—"

"I do not please!" he swore.

"Grant me this courtesy!"

"First it is mercy, and now it is courtesy you want. I am trying hard to grant you life! Dress now, and quickly."

The hell with the bastard, she decided, her emotions simmering hotly inside of her. Courage came to her—a fool's courage, perhaps. She rose slowly, regally, staring at him with open defiance. She held the mantle tightly about her and arched a brow as her lip curled into a scornful smile. "Slay me if you would, lord Viking. It might well be a better fate than being your bride."

The tightening of his jaw was just barely perceptible, and despite herself, Rhiannon felt a chill race down her spine at the sight of his cold control.

"Really?" he murmured politely. "It grieves me that you should feel so, milady." His tone changed abruptly. "Get dressed. Now," he said. His voice was low, deep like the sound of thunder. She braced against the sound of it.

She shook her head, determined.

"Do it," she said.

"What?" he demanded sharply.

She forced herself not to waver as she stared at him, far up where he sat towering atop the stallion, regal and splendid in his dress, for he wore the rich trappings of a prince that day. Norse jewels sparkled from the horse's harness and from the jeweled brooch he wore upon his shoulder to fasten his mantle. She had risen, but she still seemed to be so far below him, encased in the folds of her mantle, disheveled, her hair a wild cascade of flame about her. Her eyes were alive with silver, sparkling and glistening in pride and defiance.

"Do it!" she cried. "Take your pagan sword and skewer me through."

Then she cried out, amazed, for he did draw his sword. The stallion pranced and pawed the earth, and the cold, ruthless Viking upon him leaned forward, casting the tip of his blade against her throat. She could not move then, for it played against the vein where her lifeblood flowed.

"Dress. I have no intention of slaying you, milady. Not when our joyous future lies before us. But I shall come down and perform the task for you."

"How dare you!" she spat out, trembling.

"How dare I?" His voice was low, yet it was laced with fury and tight control. In seconds he had dismounted from the stallion. He stood over her, the blade of his sword still against her throat. Then he sheathed the sword. She was not small, and still he towered over her. "How dare I, milady?" He spoke deceptively softly. Then his hands were upon her, catching her mantle where it closed over her breasts and pulling her by the material until she was flush against him. His breath fanned her cheeks as he spoke. "You dare speak to me so, when I have discovered you here this day as you were? You had best take care, my little Saxon, grave care. Don't forget that I am, in your own words, a barbarian. And we dare anything."

With this last he tugged the mantle from her with a deceptively gentle touch. She was so startled that she remained still for a long moment, staring at him. And when she realized that she did so naked, she nearly spun about in panic. But she held her ground, lifting her chin and her eyes. "Definitely a barbarian," she taunted, and then spun around, fighting the fear that continued to rise within her. What would he do?

She reached beneath the oak for her shift, and all the while she felt the searing chill of his gaze upon her. Her fingers were numb with fear, and she could not pull the soft shift over her head without a struggle. She did not look his way but donned her tunic and tied the belt. He did not move. She felt his ominous gaze all the while, and as silence stretched out between them, her apprehension grew. She could scarce pull on her hose, and she stumbled into her slippers, her back still to him. When she was finished at last, she found her mantle and swept it back around her shoulders with what dignity she could muster. She realized then that shouts still rose around them, that the king's men still sought her. And she wondered desperately if Rowan had made good his escape.

She heard movement and realized that the Viking had mounted Alexander once more. She spun around quickly and warily to watch him. He stared down at her, and she knew that he read her mind, sitting calmly, supremely, upon the stallion. His sword remained sheathed. He reached out a hand to her, betraying no emotion in his features. She sensed the fury that emanated from him in great waves.

"What do you intend?" she said. She had meant it to be a demand. It came as a whisper.

He urged Alexander forward with the press of his knees. She started to back away, but he had too quickly reached her. With little effort he scooped her up, reaching low to sweep his arm about her waist. She was seated before him again on the stallion. She felt the rugged hardness of his thigh and the steellike band of his arm. He nudged the horse and they started forward. His eyes were not upon her, he looked ahead; and when she turned to see where he gazed, she felt the soft friction of his beard against her forehead.

William and Allen were riding toward them but they were still at a distance.

"Were this my mother's country," he murmured, "I'd cast you aside and return you to your father's family dishonored."

She had no father; he would return her to the king. And Alfred would banish her to some distant port. She would be despised here forever, but she would be free. Free from this man. Yet her heart was thundering, and she was afraid that he would do just as he said. As much as she hated him, she loved Alfred and Wessex, no matter what the king had done to her.

"That would suit me well," she told the Viking.

He ignored her, continuing as if she hadn't spoken.

"Were this my father's country," he added with a warning ebb to his tone, "a whore would be sold into slavery. Straightaway to a crew of the filthiest Danes I could find, I believe. In your case I'm sure I could find a berserker who'd take you off my hands."

She stiffened, a furious gasp escaping her, but she could do no more than swear against him, for his arms were suddenly so tight about her that she could not move. Tears pricked her eyes but she refused to shed them. "I have already been given to a Viking. What matters if he invades from Norway or Denmark?"

"Or Ireland."

"Or Ireland!"

"There might be a great deal of difference, my lady. Perhaps you will discover just how much."

Again she trembled despite herself. Alfred would be even more furious with her than this Viking was. She had disobeyed her king, had dishonored him. She had perhaps cost Rowan his life, and her own had become a nightmare.

"I despise you!" she hissed vehemently.

"Cease!" he told her sharply as the riders approached. His arms tightened around her. "Are you truly so selfish that you long to see more Norse and Irish and English blood spilled upon this ground?"

She went still, wondering if there was some way to avoid the bloodshed. Surely the Viking would not accept her as his bride now. Yet if he discarded her, there could be war among the English and the Irish prince's followers.

"This will be our battle," he added softly, brushing her cheek with his whisper and sending a spiraling heat deep within her. "With luck, lady, no other fools will die for your treachery."

"I am guilty of no treachery!" she protested heatedly, swirling to meet his gaze. It was chilling. He would never believe her.

Then his gaze rose from hers. "At last," he said softly, "we are met."

"Eric of Dubhlain!" William cried in greeting, his dark, condemning gaze touching quickly upon Rhiannon. "The king begs pardon again for the way you are met—"

"I will make my own way to the King," Eric said. "The girl will be—"

"I will bring the girl," he said coolly. He urged the

stallion past the two men and then nudged the horse to a smooth lope. The wind, filled with the freshness of spring, rushed upon Rhiannon. The air suddenly seemed unbearably cold as the stallion moved beneath her. She was cast hard against the Viking's arms, and again she shivered at the power in them. His power came from his prowess in battle, his deadly prowess.

She had labeled him a barbarian and he had heard her. He was probably the most capable warrior she had ever encountered. He had seen her with Rowan, and he could kill Rowan easily.

No, she couldn't think such thoughts, or she would give way to a fit of trembling. He could feel her every movement, for with each smooth stride of the stallion she was swept hard against his chest.

They fast approached the gates. Men were emerging from either side of the forest—the king's men, the Irish and Norse contingent. She did not see Rowan among them, and she prayed that he had managed to disappear into the harbor of the trees.

The gates opened. The massive stallion sailed through them, and they came to the manor.

The king himself waited in the courtyard before the manor's longhouse. He watched Eric as the Viking rode to within mere feet of him. Eric lifted Rhiannon from the stallion, setting her upon her feet.

She stood before the king.

She could scarcely stand as she faced Alfred. Her knees trembled and she was afraid. To feel condemnation and hatred from the Viking was one thing, but the fury and hatred of the king's cold gaze was another. He walked toward her, and she realized that he knew she had gone to meet her lover. He couldn't know that she had meant to obey him. She had just wanted to see Rowan alone one more time, to say good-bye.

Alfred thought she had willfully and treacherously betrayed him.

He walked straight to her. He stared at her and then struck her so hard that she cried out and fell to her knees. Behind her, she heard the Viking dismounting. Thunder touched the ground, for the horsemen were all returning, and the massive array of English and Norse and Irish troops was entering into the walls of the manor fortress.

"Eric of Dubhlain," the king said, "I release you from your vows of allegiance and free you from your promises."

She heard the Viking dismount from behind her. He came down beside her, lifting her to her feet by her elbow. A tempest burned and tossed within her. She longed to wrench free from his touch. She did not dare. She bit her lip lest she cry out.

"Alfred, King of Wessex," Eric said, "I bid entry to your manor, and I would speak alone with you so that we may rectify the damage done here."

The king nodded slowly. "Then welcome, Eric of Dubhlain, welcome, indeed, to my home."

Rhiannon couldn't move. Eric's fingers tightened upon her arm until she nearly screamed out with the pain. She gazed up into his Nordic eyes and felt their power. Her chin jutting upward, she returned his stare.

"Milady?" he said, the word polite, his tone anything but. Yet she managed to stand tall and follow Alfred.

The Viking did not release her.

When they came inside the house, the king's servants fell back, awaiting Alfred's orders. Alswitha, smiling nervously, hurried to Alfred's side. She curtsied beautifully before the guest, her eyes darting from Rhiannon's ashen pallor to the cold fury that knit the king's brow. Stuttering, she offered Eric ale and bread and herring. Servants came forward then, and he took a stout leather cup of ale but declined the meal. The king lifted his hand and told Alswitha, "Take Rhiannon."

Dread filled her. The Viking's hand lay heavily upon her shoulder, and he urged her toward one of the chairs before the fire. "The girl stays," he said, pressing her down into the chair. To her great unease he remained behind her.

She swallowed, then turned to Alswitha in desperation, but there was no help to be had there. The queen stepped back and stood demurely behind Alfred.

"I'd not have men go to war over this girl again," Eric said.

Rhiannon started to leap to her feet, to deny her guilt for the previous bloodshed. His fingers clamped down upon her shoulders and she understood the command to be still.

"You've every right to break your vows," Alfred said.

"The right, King of Wessex, but not the desire. I will take the lady and the land, but with these conditions: We go to war against the Dane at Rochester before the nuptials. Rhiannon will be given over to a holy house until such time as it can be determined that she does not bear the seed of another man. If I am killed in the battle, the lands to which I have laid claim will pass to my father, the King of Dubhlain, to distribute among my brothers as he sees fit. And if I am killed, the girl, too, is given over to my family, and they will decide her fate."

"The alliance stands and we ride against the Dane?"

The Viking lifted his cup. "Aye, it stands."

"It will be as you say," Alfred promised. The two men clasped hands firmly. Rhiannon's fingers curled over the carved handles on the chair, and her blood seemed to congeal.

"What has been will not go unpunished," the king continued. He glanced her way briefly, and she had never seen him so cold or cruelly dispassionate. She had heard that he could be ruthless, and he had been brutal to traitors.

He had never been brutal to her. He had loved her. He had been strict but he had loved her.

No more.

He spoke again with a savage anger. "I promise that your bride will be taught humility and that the man who knew my will and my promise but ignored them will pay as is fitting."

"Nay, Alfred," the Viking said. "I will take my own vengeance."

His hands were like fire and steel upon her shoulders, and she felt the determination in his words with every fiber of her being. They were no heated threat but a sure declaration of intent. He would surely beat her within an inch of her life, she thought dully, but then a staggering fear filled her, not for herself but for Rowan.

Suddenly the doors to the manor burst open without the king's leave. Alfred turned in anger but saw that his liegemen, William and Allen, had returned. Between them, held by either arm, was Rowan, bloody and beaten.

She should have remained still. To salvage what remained of her honor she should have remained seated. But she could not bear to see Rowan injured and bleeding.

She forgot everything except for the gentle love she had shared with him. She escaped the Viking's loathed touch and leapt to her feet, a horrified cry upon her lips. She started to race forward, but she barely moved a single step. Strong arms swept around her waist and she was crushed back hard against the Viking, who held her tightly to him.

No wonder he stayed so near her, Rhiannon thought bitterly. He was not going to let her further dishonor him or Alfred.

Rowan, dazed, met her eyes and smiled vaguely, then sagged between the two men. They shoved him forward so that he fell before the king.

"Sire," William said, and his dark gaze took in the room, "we do not know that they were together, but we found him beyond the gates, not far from where the Lady Rhiannon's horse had strayed."

"Go," the king said.

"But, Sire—" William protested.

"She is clean, my liege," Rowan mumbled. Blood gurgled over his lips, and Rhiannon cried out again, hating the arms that restrained her. Rowan spat out a tooth. He gazed up, dazed, from Alfred to the Viking. "She is untouched, I swear it."

The king walked toward him. He bent low, grasping Rowan's tunic and chemise at the neckline. Rowan fell forward, and Rhiannon screamed again, scratching mindlessly at the hands that held her, for she feared that he was dead.

"For the love of God, let me go!" she pleaded.

"Stop it!" the king roared at her. "Have you not shamed us all enough?" He touched the pulse in Rowan's throat. "He lives . . . for now."

Tears flowed down her cheeks. The Viking released her suddenly, and she stumbled forward. She came down beside Rowan and discovered that he did indeed live. She held him in her arms, and silent tears streamed down her face.

The king called for servants to take Rowan. She felt a touch upon her shoulders, and it was not altogether cruel. She was pulled up and held once again. By the Viking.

Rowan was taken away. The king and the Viking continued to talk, but she did not hear their words, for she was numb again and praying fervently and earnestly that she would not be the cause of Rowan's death. What vengeance the Viking might take, she could not determine. She wondered if she might plead for Rowan's life; if she might humble herself and find some mercy.

He had already refused her mercy.

"It shall be done now," the king said. "Now, this very hour." He told a servant to find his physician and a midwife. Then he told Alswitha, "Take Rhiannon to her room."

The Viking released her shoulders. Alswitha reached forward for her hand.

Instinctively Rhiannon backed away, staring at them all and wondering what new horror they had conjured to destroy her.

"Come, Rhiannon!" Alswitha urged her.

She looked at the king, who was grim and pensive. And she stared at the towering Viking, who watched her now with an idle, dispassionate curiosity. He shrugged, as if she were of very little consequence. "I still think that the wedding should wait," he told the king.

"I promised the lady to you, and she was in my care. She is like my own child. It will please me to know the truth of this matter."

"Truly, King of Wessex, I can discover the truth for myself, and I can dictate the ultimatums of my own house."

"But she is still a ward of the house of Wessex, and I would honor my vows."

The door opened again. The king's most trusted physician stood there, his stout servant at his side. The woman gazed at Rhiannon with small, cunning eyes. She smiled furtively, as if anticipating the enjoyment of some cruelty.

Then Rhiannon realized what they meant to do with her, and her eyes widened with shame and horror. "No!" she exclaimed fiercely. She wanted to run madly to freedom but there was nowhere to run. She fought down the fury and the panic and forced herself to walk slowly forward, not to the king but to the

Norse-Irish lord. Alfred had disowned her, as he had sworn he would. Perhaps he ached inside, but he did not betray it. The Viking had already pronounced her a whore. He had claimed his own vengeance; this was not of his choosing.

"Things are not always what they seem, my lord. I was guilty of no treachery against you before, and though it perhaps appeared that I . . ." She paused, seeking dignity and resolve and enough intensity to convince him. "I did not dishonor the king's pledge, though he who swears to love me does not offer his faith. Don't let them do this to me!" she demanded passionately.

She shivered, knowing that his methods of dealing with her could be far more brutal. Then she thought that nothing could be so demeaning as what they planned.

Whatever they did to her now, it would not save her when she was cast into his clutches, anyway.

Yet it seemed that there was a curious spark of admiration in his eyes, even as he denied her. "Milady, this is not something that I am doing to you," he told her.

"It will make me hate you until my dying day," she said, clenching her fingers at her sides. She could not accept the fact that she could not escape the king's intent for her. Nor would she plead again with the Viking.

He sighed softly. "Milady, I admit I have little reason to be overly fond of you, but this is not my doing. Alfred is king here. And he is your guardian. This is not my choice. I have my own ways and means of discovering the truths I seek. Your king has spoken. In his house he is the law. In my house, my lady, I promise you that I will be your law."

His words were not reassuring.

He offered her definite menace, yet it was the king who had decreed this ignominy for her. She swung around, facing Alfred.

"You might consider my word on the truth of this!" she told him.

"I cannot trust your word again, Rhiannon. You have brought us all near the brink of disaster."

Alswitha caught Rhiannon's arm. Rhiannon found the queen's eyes damp with tears and searching out her own. "For Rowan's sake, submit!" she pleaded in a whisper.

"Take her!" the king thundered.

Alswitha was no longer allowed the task. Two hearty women arrived from the kitchen, grabbing Rhiannon's arms. She screamed then, and fought them. To no avail. She was dragged from the hall and into the manor's annex, where her small bedchamber lay. No matter how fiercely she struggled and fought, she was soon pinned down, and her clothing was carelessly torn. Then, in deepest humiliation and mortification, she ceased to fight. Alswitha was with her again, stroking back her hair from her forehead. Rhiannon lay still in shock, withdrawing deeply into her own mind. She tried not to feel the cold hands upon her. Tears came to her eyes as she was parted and probed. She dimly heard the doctor tell Alswitha at last that she was a virgin still and that her maidenhead was fully intact.

Never before in her life had she felt so mortified. She lay in so deep a pall of misery and shame that she could not even rouse herself to pray that at least this cross of hers might weigh heavily for Rowan's life.

She vowed that she would never forget the Viking scourge that had come unbidden on the wind to shatter her very existence. God could forgive her or no, she cared not. She would pray daily that Eric of Dubhlain might be erased from the face of the earth. And she would pray that when he died, he would do so in anguish and agony, cursing the day he was born.

Eric rode along the ranks of fighting men, calling a word here, applauding an action there, and warning a young Englishman that he left his right flank open to attack when he held his shield so carelessly. He rode to the end of the ranks and stared back at the action. The king, too, watched the war play from horseback. They would ride for Rochester in the morning. The heavily besieged town could not hold out much longer against the Danes encamped before it.

Eric watched as men worked with a field of spears, the mainstay of war. They practiced with swords and with maces, while in a distant field the archers practiced their aim. Before him, Svein of Trondheim swung his mighty double-headed ax. It was a particularly "Viking" weapon, since much of Europe had come to consider the deadly piece as uncivilized.

Eric had learned, though, even as a child, that his crafty old Irish grandfather had taken from the Vikings what he saw as expedient and powerful. He had been a match for both the Norwegian and Danish menace to his isle because he had been ever ready to learn from the foe. Most Irishmen had fought in leather armor before his grandfather's day, if they fought in armor at all. Aed Finnlaith had seen the chain mail upon the enemy and discovered that it saved lives, and so he had ordered his men to use mail.

Eric had noted that the double-headed ax was a deadly and formidable weapon, and he had encouraged his men, Irish and Norse alike, in learning the use of it. Tomorrow they would ride to do battle with the Danes, and the Danes could be fearsome adversaries. It would not be a civilized fight but a barbaric one. Eric was not afraid of death. He had been raised a Christian, but his mother had never denied them the study of the Norse religion. He was willing to believe in the gentle Christ and in a supreme God the Father. But he adhered to the Viking belief that no man could cheat death in the end, and it was always better to step forward; if he were to fall, he would honestly face the great gods of Valhalla, or even the Christian Lord of the universe.

He gazed across the field at the king he had chosen to support. Alfred sat a saddle well. He was not a large man, but a definite air of command emanated from him, the command necessary to be a ruler. Last night Eric had sat long with Alfred before his central fire, and though he knew that the Saxon king was usually sparing with his drink, they had both downed many a horn of the French wine Eric had brought in his ships. Dubhlain was rich in many ways, for ships constantly came and went from her ports. Since the Muslims had driven forward and claimed much of the Mediterranean, the wily Syrian and Jewish merchants had lost much of their trading power from the East. But in Dubhlain, spices and oils and fine silks and a multitude of wines could be had, for the Vikings who roamed the seas were willing to risk much in their pursuit of treasure.

The Saxon king had fascinated Eric as they had spoken. He was certain that Alfred had been fascinated in return and that he had envied much that Eric had taken for granted. By the age of ten, Eric had been able to read Latin and Greek, as well as his native Irish tongue and his father's Norse. He had read of the exploits of Alexander and learned the ways of the caliphs who ruled the Arab world from their seat in Baghdad. He had studied the efforts of Charlemagne and been taught mathematics, science, and music. He had also studied the Brehon laws of Ireland, so important to any man who would rule there, and he had attended the councils at Tara beneath his grandfather. He had heard the legends of the great men of Eire from St. Patrick to Cuchulain to the mighty tribe, the Tuath De Danaan. He had ridden to battle against the raids that had harried the Irish shores, but he had lived in a fine house of his father's making, a fortress with high walls and many rooms.

Alfred had often run in the night, and his home had many times been with the cattle and the pigs. His father, Ethelwulf, had won many victories, as had his brothers before him. But he had been just a lad himself when the last of his three older brothers, Ethelred I, had become king. And since then he had done little but practice warfare. Ethelred died when Alfred was twenty-one, and the fight had become his. In May of A.D. 878, Alfred rode out from the marshes to Egbert's Stone, and there England rallied around him. He met the Dane, Guthrum, in a massive battle, and Alfred was the victor. Guthrum went so far as to consent to baptism. Alfred stood as his godfather before the eyes of the Church. And Guthrum had kept his Christian peace—for a while.

Now Guthrum stormed Rochester. Alfred wanted him gone.

The King of Wessex was a curious man. He was not awesome in appearance, but he had the power to inspire men to greatness. He was passionate in the support of his church and a man of deep convictions. His word he held sacred.

He had been deeply troubled by the events that occurred upon the coast, that warfare had come between them before Eric had even reached land.

"Have you no knowledge yet of what went amiss?" Eric had asked him.

And the king had shook his head gravely. "I sent a lad, a trusted young fellow, with the message that you were to be received as my honored guests. I have not seen the boy again. Someone determined that my message was not to be given to the lady Rhiannon. I believe that dead men kept my word from her." He gazed at Eric quickly. "She would not defy my word, not against such odds! At least she would not have done so then. She denies any knowledge of it, and I believe her."

Eric was silent.

"You may still free yourself from your vows," the king assured him gravely. "If you believe her guilty—"

"I have no intention of freeing myself from my vows," Eric said. He would not cast aside this alliance and his dreams of his own land because of a wayward girl. He had seen her with Rowan by the brook. Perhaps they been interrupted before their affair had been fully consummated, but Eric did not believe that he could ever consider her innocent. She was a temptress; she was aware of her beauty and her power, and he pitied the poor man who had fallen in love with her.

His fury had abated somewhat. He was possessive, and he knew it. When they wed, she would learn that he was the law of her life and she'd never dare stray. He didn't like to think of the day when he had watched her, for the memory infuriated him anew. And more. He did not love her, certainly, and he was very wary of her. Yet she had cast some spell upon him. She was beautiful in the extreme and passionate and full of life. And she could be as seductive as a dream of glory. He had learned that he wanted her fiercely. She had created a fire in his loins that he could not squelch, and yet he was determined to hold away from her. He trusted Alfred; the king would not lie to him, neither would the king's physician, not about something so delicate as his bride's virginity. It was his pride, he thought, that had made him glad that Alfred had insisted on verifying Rhiannon's innocence. And she had to know that Eric could be blunt, stern, and demanding, as necessary. He had no intention of letting her pursue her visions of lost love for Rowan throughout their married life.

There were times when he had pitied her. He could not forget the chilling, tear-glazed dignity of her eyes when she had appealed to him in the king's house that day. Yet she had brought it upon herself.

Still, he remembered how it had felt to love, and in that she had his sympathy. He might well have risked everything for Emenia. He could not, however, think of her without a rise of heated ire, for he could not tolerate what she had done. The situation had been too precarious. And she had been promised to *him*.

He wondered, however, if her very fire and beauty were not the reasons he had chosen to see through his alliance with the king. Perhaps he could not love again, but he did want the lady Rhiannon. Now he rode to Alfred's side.

"I am still pleased with our alliance," he assured the king in greeting. "And I am pleased that the morning passed without the spilling of blood."

"Aye," the king murmured, looking straight ahead and barely seeing him.

As Eric followed the king's gaze across the field, he saw that Rollo was riding toward him, and he sensed that his captain's grave countenance had to do with the girl.

"What is it?" he demanded when Rollo reached his side upon a lathered mount.

The horse snorted. "Trouble among the men," Rollo said.

Eric arched a brow expectantly.

"They demand blood, they demand justice."

"Against . . . ?" he inquired coolly.

"Against the Welshman, Rowan."

"Why?" None had seen what he had, so none knew the seriousness of what had occurred.

"Rumors fly. You know the men. They will demand that you fight for your honor."

Eric sighed impatiently. "They want me to kill the lad?"

"Aye," Rollo said unhappily. He knew that they needed no discord among their own troops. "The boy will have to come before you. He will have to challenge you. And unless you choose to give the girl to him, you will have to kill him."

Even as Rollo finished speaking, a sudden silence came to the practice field. All the men watched and waited.

Another horseman approached Eric. It was Rowan. Men broke aside to let him pass.

The man was still ashen, Eric saw, but he sat his horse with his dignity intact. He stopped before Eric, but before he could speak, Alfred of Wessex had come between them.

"Rowan, how dare you come here thus? I have granted you the mercy of your life and you disavow me yet again!"

Rowan lowered his head. "Before God, I beg your forgiveness, Sire." He raised his eyes, facing Eric. "But I love her, you see. Eric of Dubhlain, I offer you no disrespect, for you are invited of my liege lord. But still, I challenge you, sir, to a test of arms, as is my right under ancient law."

"You would meet with me—and Vengeance?" Eric inquired softly, raising his sword.

The man's face grew even paler, but he nodded gravely.

Eric paused a moment. "The maid is not worth it, lad. No maid is worth it."

"Aye, this one is," he said softly.

Eric thought him a besotted fool, but he was a man and deserved his test of arms.

"At dawn, then," he said. "Upon this very field."

Rowan raised a hand in salute. "Here, then, Prince Eric, upon this field."

"And may God have mercy on your soul!" the king muttered gravely.

Rowan nodded in misery again. Eric decided that he liked the younger man; he had the courage to meet with sure death. Rowan turned his mount and raced back toward the annex buildings of the manor. A cry began among Eric's men, a battle cry. It rose with the wind and was like an echo of death.

Eric lifted his hand high in angry denial. He dropped it, and the cry ceased. The white stallion pranced, sensing his anger. He whirled the mount around, facing his men. "Do you then seek the death of our allies so easily? Nay—we fight the Danes, and if we must rejoice in death, let it be theirs!"

His temper rising, he, too, turned to ride from the throngs of warriors. He raced toward the wall, not bothering to seek out the gate. The white stallion soared over the barrier, and he rode out onto the meadows and fields and forest beyond the manor fortress. He rode and he rode, and he felt it again, a love of the land that utterly overpowered him.

He paused at last upon a high cliff that overlooked the valley where the king made his home. Despite the amassing of men and weapons, he could narrow his eyes and imagine a peaceful scene. He could see the sheep grazing, and the fat ducks as they waddled along. A mare raced with a foal, and the air carried the very taste of birth, of spring.

She loved the land, too, he thought suddenly. She had fought so fiercely for it. But he would prevail, he determined. He *would* prevail.

That night Eric was startled to see that Rhiannon had chosen to appear at supper.

Rowan was absent. Eric wondered if Rhiannon had heard about the challenge, and then he decided that no one had told her, for when her eyes, glittering silver, fell upon his, they were filled with such loathing that he knew she felt no fear whatsoever, that she knew nothing of the one-on-one combat that honor had demanded be fought over her.

She did not sit near him, nor did she appear before the king. Indeed she ignored both men.

She appeared, beautiful and in a curious splendor, for she walked with a pride and scorn that denied any wrongdoing on her part. Eric had assumed that she would avoid him and the king. She had chosen not to do so. She was the most stunning woman in the hall— likely in all of England, Eric thought. She was dressed in soft powder blue, a color that matched her eyes, except for the flinty look of hatred and anger that came to them when they fell upon him. Her hair was swept into a coil, and the clean lines of her throat and face were artfully highlighted. She walked in beauty, a sylph, slim and agile. When it was time to sit down to the banquet, she did not come near him or the king, or even Alswitha, but chose a place at the end of the table.

For his part, he bowed to her coolly and watched her with a certain amusement and curiosity. Tomorrow she was to be bound over to the women of a religious sect to assure her continued virginity until her wedding. Many women in her position would have shunned this assembly tonight, but not this one. She was here, aloof, condemned by many, and yet majestic before all.

He forgot her presence as he discussed with the king the grave matter of the plan of attack. Rollo spoke forcefully, as did a number of the king's men. Endless platters of food were served—quail, stuffed and still feathered; herring; boar; roast deer upon a spit. Ale and mead flowed freely. When the food seemed no longer appealing, Alswitha stood and nodded to the servants, and the platters were taken away.

"To the honor of our guests," she cried, "Padraic, seneschal to the great Lord of Thunder, Eric of Dubhlain."

Eric was somewhat surprised when his Irish storyteller rose and went to the rear of the hall, where he could be seen by all. The fire behind him added atmosphere to his tale. With great and dramatic clarity he described the family of Eric's grandfather. He spoke of the Irish kings and of the battles that had raged between them. He spoke in beautiful, beguiling poetry, and he honored the family Finnlaith, coming at last to Aed, who had united the kings of Ireland; who had given his daughter, Erin, to the Norseman Olaf the Wolf, so that Ireland could find peace and be strong. Then he told of Eric himself, of his travels abroad, of his defense of his father's realm, of the mighty battles he had waged and won.

When he fell silent at last, men raised their voice in loud, raucous approval. Alswitha flushed with pleasure, for Alfred was pleased and Eric surprised, and the company was highly entertained by the talented storyteller.

Then the noise died down and there was a stillness. Eric looked up curiously, to see that Rhiannon had come to where Padraic had stood before the fire. She had freed her hair, and the firelight played upon it and her gown, and she seemed a vision of flowing silk and sensual beauty.

"We have heard the tales of our great Norse host, and we have been greatly entertained. We thank our illustrious ally and pray that we may, in return, entertain him with our Saxon tale of pain and battle and . . . triumph."

The haunting sound of a lute filled the air then. Rhiannon began to sway, and it seemed that the music entered her limbs and moved them with exquisite grace. She spun and swirled. She cast back her head and lifted her arms, and all men were silent, watching her. There was not a sound in the whole of the hall except that of the lute, the soft crackle of the fire, and the fall of her delicate feet upon the floor. She wove a spell; she held them all enthralled. It seemed that the fire dimmed and the room darkened, and that all else paled except for the seductive and beautiful maid.

And then she began to speak as she swayed. She sang more than spoke, and her melody was a haunting one. She, too, told a story. A story of England.

Her eyes fell upon Eric with a bold, taunting challenge.

"The story I tell is of Lindesfarne. Lindesfarne," she repeated softly. Her eyes were full upon Eric, mutely challenging him. He knew why she had come tonight. She had come for revenge. She had come to do battle again—with him.

"I tell a tale of a beautiful place, stripped of God's grace, of beauty, of peace. Lindesfarne . . . And I tell a tale of the savages who raided there, fierce barbarians."

She smiled and began to move again—sweepingly, gracefully, seductively.

And not a man in the hall seemed capable of speech or movement as she began her damning tale.

Eric wasn't certain he was capable of movement himself.

He would listen to her tale.

And if she wanted battle, then battle he would enjoin.

Lindesfarne . . .

If he wasn't mistaken, there was danger in the tale. Alfred was watching Rhiannon warily, his fingers taut upon his chair.

Yet he did not move. None of them moved.

Indeed the tale was dangerous. She was dangerous. She had the power to enchant.

7

Surely some magic did lie over the hall, some deep enchantment. She cast some powder into the central fire, and it seemed to glow with special colors. The music continued to play, ethereal and hypnotic. She was bathed in the curious glow of that firelight, and her hair was a silken flame around her, her form lithe and fluid and haunting as she swayed and moved like Salome dancing to gain the Baptist's head.

"Lindesfarne!" She cried the name, and then she began to describe the monks who lived in that ancient and revered monastery. She spoke of their days, and her dance flowed to image forth the peace of the place. Then her voice rose, and the sound of the music became discordant, and there was a thundering sound against the floor, like the sound of a storm.

"Lightning came to warn them. Rain and wicked winds. The people were afraid and they wondered how they had offended God, for this church and this monastery, defenseless on an island off the coast of Northumbria, was the most sacred place of pilgrimage in all of England. St. Cuthbert had lived and worked there as an abbot a century before. . . .

"It was the year of Our Lord 793, and the thundering came again."

Rhiannon spun again and again, an exotic beauty in the fiery swirl of her hair; in the silver gems of her eyes; in the sensual, weightless sway of her elegant young form. Then she paused and fell to the floor, and the thunder crescendoed and then ceased. . . .

And then her voice came again. She told them how the horde had fallen upon Lindesfarne. How murder had fallen with the blade of the ax, how the fields had been trampled with blood, how the pages of learning had been cast into the eternal hellfire of the heathen who had come. She paused for effect. "Vikings, milords. Not Danes. *Norwegians.*"

Her arms stretched out, white and lovely. Slowly she unwound herself and rose, and still there was no sound within the hall. Eric himself did not move, though he knew that she fought with this last trick to discredit him before his English host. Her eyes reached across the mist of the darkness to his, and he knew that she would never forgive him for entering her life and radically transforming her destiny.

He longed to rise and strike her in fury. He didn't believe that she wanted bloodshed; she wanted him to suffer for being what he was, a Viking. She never seemed to grant him a drop of his Irish blood, yet it didn't matter. He *was* a Viking, and she had offended him deeply. She must imagine that there was nothing he could do. If he rose in anger, there would be bloodshed, for his men would rise behind him. She had spun such an aching tale, every Englishman must remember the raid that came long before their time and rally together in vengeance and hatred.

She had dared much, for the king, Eric could see, was furious.

For the moment, though, she had little to fear. The room remained silent; all eyes remained upon her. Her hair was a cascading shower of red-gold fire about her, and as she paused before them all, using the drama of the silence, she was achingly beautiful and magnificent, a woman for whom a man might readily die.

Well, she intended him to die, Eric thought dryly. He simply did not intend to oblige her.

She began to move again and to speak softly, and Eric, watching her narrow-eyed and pensive from his place beside the king, wondered how she dared defy Alfred again, when she had already suffered so for offending him. But she so smoothly changed her tale! No matter what his anger, Alfred would wait. He would not incite the men in the hall. She was clever. Dangerously clever, for while the men still sat, mesmerized by the startling beauty of the girl and the curious innocence that touched her tale, she carried her story onward. She spoke of Alfred's grandfather, and of his fathers and brothers. In wondrous, flowing words she described the greatest challenge of his career, when he had met the Dane, Guthrum. The year was 878. The Danes held Northumbria, had murdered Edmund of East Anglia, and they pressed hard against Alfred of Wessex. Despite all odds, the Saxon king refused to accept defeat, and the fighting forces held out in the island fastnesses of the fenlands. The Welsh of Cornwall were in league with the Danes, and the situation was desperate. But Alfred's cry went out, and the Saxon thanes of Devon came, ready to trust their fate to the great leadership of Alfred of Wessex, the one man who determined to hold an independent piece of England. The Battle of Ethandune was fought, and it was not the Saxons who were forced to seek terms but the Danish invaders. Guthrum vowed to leave Wessex for the land of Danelaw in the north. He was baptized to the Christian faith, but alas, Viking word was easily broken, and now Guthrum threatened the Saxons again.

Rhiannon fell silent. She raised her arms slowly and reached toward the sky, rising like a young deer upon her toes until she posed in a graceful line.

Then she dropped dramatically to the earth again, and her head fell as she paused once more. Then she raised her chin and her eyes to them all and her cry came out.

"Hail Alfred, King of Wessex!"

The fire brightened, and the hall was visible once again. There was silence, and then thunderous applause, and then a score of men were raising their leather tankards to the king.

And then silence fell again.

Her performance had been so provocative, so seductive, that they had all forgotten the birth of it, as well as the insult she had heaped upon the Norse. All of Eric's men, the Irish and the Norse and the men of mixed nationalities like himself, all of them applauded her like sheep, enchanted.

But then memory slowly returned to the men, their applause faded, and Eric, leaning back in his chair at the king's side, knew that they looked to him.

By all honor he was bound to challenge her, to punish her in some way, to meet her anger. But if he were to strike the girl who had just so eloquently praised the great King of Wessex, men who had condemned her this very day for her refusal to obey her guardian, the king would now rise wildly to her defense. She had cast him into a very dangerous and precarious situation, and he swore in silence that she would someday pay for her cunning.

She remained upon the ground, elegantly draped in her clothing, still beautiful in her pose. But her eyes were on his, and he saw the silver glint to them, the feline gleam. She knew exactly the import of what she had done, and she was sweetly savoring her triumph over him.

He sat still in the silence, and then he rose very slowly. He towered over the assembly in size and majesty in his crimson mantle with the banner of the wolf boldly emblazoned upon it.

He pushed away from the table and walked toward her. There was not a whisper of sound to be heard in the room. As she saw him come, wariness replaced the triumph in her eyes. She rose with swift and agile ease, but Eric saw then that she was not so calm as she pretended to be, for against the fine white line of her throat her pulse beat with the speed of hummingbird wings, and her breasts rose and fell rapidly with each breath she sought.

He paused before her, smiled slowly, and then bowed very low.

It was not what she had expected. She had been certain that he would lose his temper, demand some redress, and the king could not seek it for him now because she had said nothing that was not true. The first raid of note had been at Lindesfarne, and it had been Norwegians who'd savaged the sacred home of St. Cuthbert. None could deny it, and those who were reminded of it now had to see this new treaty as an unholy alliance.

His smile deepened, though she saw the clenched muscles in his jaw and the curl of his lips. His eyes captured hers, and where she had set out to hypnotize, she was caught in return, for she could do nothing but return his blue gaze. No chemist's powder touched the fire, but the room seemed to dim, and it was if they—and they alone—were caught in a curious, bold, glowing blaze; heat and light flowed between them. The air itself seemed to crackle, as with the portent of a storm, as if lightning flashed above and beyond them. Seconds passed—it might well have been eons, for she could not tear her eyes from the deadly aqua power of his. Her head fell back and she longed to defy him, and she swore that she would not cringe before him. A charged silence remained between them; the fire snapped and rose and danced upon the walls and within her very being. It was not the fire, she realized, but the power he emitted. His arms were bare beneath the flow of his mantle, and they glistened bronze, rippling with a play of muscle with each nuance of movement, with each breath he drew. She felt the warrior's majesty of him, the burning determination of sinew and brawn and savage confidence. And she felt, too, a different power—that of his mind—and in those fleeting seconds she knew that she had set out to battle not a fool but a man who would ever think and judge and carefully weigh his options. If he determined that he would have revenge, then it would be so. Once his mind was set, it would not be changed, and he would be forever ready to parry her every thrust.

His eyes remained fixed upon hers, and she did not falter or fail. He stared upon her, then spoke to the king.

"Truly, Alfred, you have offered me the fairest gem of Saxony. She puts the seneschals of my mother's country to shame, and likewise does she make fools of the skalds of Norway, for no man can tell a tale with so musical a voice and so lithe and beautiful a show of dance and movement."

He reached for her hand. Too late she thought that it might have been wise to withdraw, and she felt her slender fingers enveloped within the massive size and strength of his hold. Yet though he held her firmly, he turned her hand over and rubbed the callused tip of his thumb slowly over the center of her palm. She could not draw her eyes from his.

Rhiannon was vaguely aware that the king had risen. Tension continued to crackle on the air, taut and tangible, like a swirling mist, like the fiery heat that eclipsed them together, away from all the others.

"Indeed she is wondrous," Eric continued. "I would have jumped to my feet, longing to battle my own forebears, were they not ghosts now to ride the wind. I tell you, Alfred of Wessex, I was seduced. The fair lady here, this breath of beauty with which you welcome me to your shore, is indeed so exquisite that I am bewitched."

Suddenly, so fiercely that she nearly cried out, his fingers tightened upon hers. His eyes blazed with a true ice-fire, with all the savage windswept cold of the north, then he turned fleetly from her to the king, still holding tight to her hand.

"Good Alfred, I am so enamored that I would not

wait another moment to claim my bride. Let the seeds of discord of the past be cast onto the rocks, where they cannot fester and grow. Let us forget anything that has come before, and seal this alliance between us here and now. I would not dishonor your house, yet I would not live another night without this precious morsel of peace and goodwill away from my side!"

Her blood seemed swiftly to freeze, and she could not find breath even to protest. She had had her triumph, aye! She had savored her moments of victory, but he had taken them and twisted them heinously from her.

Alfred was frowning. A roar went up around the table; Viking laughter sounded, and with it the thunder sound of English approval.

"No!" she whispered.

It couldn't be done; it would not be decent or proper. Surely there could be no Mass celebrated now. The hour grew late and the moon was full; there was even a portent of thunder on the air. In the morning the men would ride away. She would have her reprieve.

Alfred was still frowning. Alswitha was whispering in his ear, and Rhiannon was certain that the queen warned him he would be sanctioning a heathen practice, no Christian nuptials.

"No!" she whispered again, and she worked diligently to free her hand from his grasp. It was not to be done. He had her with a touch of iron, implacable and unyielding. Despite herself, she shivered with fear. When he touched her, it would be with no tenderness. She had crossed him again and again, and she knew full well that any man might have despised her for the scene that he had come upon. Yet he seemed a Viking in truth, a man who would not heed propriety or care but would fight his way to what he craved, and claim it brutally . . . then discard it.

The king hesitated.

"It cannot be done!" Father Paul rose from the side of the table. "It cannot be done here and now—"

"We shall move to the church, where God always abides, is that not true, Father?" Eric demanded. "The banns have been cried to the people, and the betrothal is valid. It was my choice that we delay, but now I demand my rights." He slammed his fist hard against his breast and fell dramatically upon his knee, still holding tight to Rhiannon. He bowed his head, but she saw his eyes and knew that there was no humility to the gesture, just pure, driven fury.

"Before God I ride for the great and noble Saxon king, Alfred of Wessex. I face death eagerly for his pleasure, but since this night I have seen the beauty of my betrothed, I would make her my wife before I ride!"

The Norwegian host began to slam their tankards against the table. Many of them were drunk, and their Irish comrades were also.

Many a good Saxon was drunk, too, Rhiannon thought sourly.

And it was her doom. The clamor rose and she saw the king's features and knew that he weighed his choices of action. Tomorrow they rode to expel Gunthrum. He could not afford to risk the camaraderie and goodwill of all his forces. The wedding had been delayed at the Irish prince's request, but the king discerned that Eric had now chosen the only possible means of true peace among the warriors. Rhiannon had shamed them all; the prince of Dubhlain had magnanimously agreed to accept the bride, anyway, and when she had sought to subtly injure him, he had spoken of his desire.

None but those closest to him could have seen the fleet workings of his mind. Nor could any but those closest to him realize the extent of his wrath, for his control was so great, his rage so calculated and cold. None but those closest to him . . .

And Rhiannon.

The noise in the hall grew until it became a cacophony, crashing all around her. At last the king spoke. "So be it! The wedding shall take place immediately."

A roar went up, and Rollo stood, lifting his ale high. "A wedding. We eat and we drink and we feast while the bride is prepared!"

Light played upon the king's face. He was not pleased about the hasty ceremony, but he was compelled to follow through with it.

Rhiannon suddenly felt that her fingers were about to shatter and break. She saw that the Viking was staring at her again, and that he watched her with a wintry warning. While the shouts went on, he whispered, and she heard his every word clearly.

"No more trouble, lady. No further dissent. Do you truly care so little for men that you long for their deaths in mass carnage?"

"Nay!"

He lifted an arm to encompass the hall. "They are bred to war. The Irish here, the English, the Norse. All too easily hearts and minds can change, and in this society each insult must be avenged. I have done what was necessary. You will now play out the end of this drama you have spun."

She tugged again on her fingers, but she could not free herself. She saw that a number of women were coming, and that she seemed destined to be gowned for her wedding despite the events that had greeted Eric of Dubhlain's arrival at Wareham.

She thought of the warning pressure of his fingers upon hers, and a weakness pervaded her. He oft seemed created of bronze and steel; she did not think that any man could best him in a test of arms, surely no woman. His hatred for her was great, and his anger was staggering.

"You do not want to do this!" she charged him swiftly. "I know that you cannot want to marry me! Stop this from happening—you can do so!" His jaw remained locked, his eyes stayed cold and hard upon her, and she desperately goaded him. "What of— what of your fears that I bear another man's child? Physicians *can* be mistaken. Perhaps I did betray you. Stop this thing now and I will go to the holy sisters and—"

"And pray for my death in battle, no doubt. Lady, it matters not. I have forgotten nothing. I have no fears regarding you."

"But you saw me in the woods."

"And you are a fool to remind me," he told her with words so soft and chilling that they seemed to bring a cold finger to draw along the length of her spine. "I always said, my lady, that I would handle things within my own house. I can easily discern what a physician must seek. And if you have deceived the house of Wessex and carry a child, then you must carry that child to term." His eyes brightened and his voice deepened dramatically, and she did not know if he taunted her or spoke seriously. "You have displayed to me this evening your great and abiding knowledge of the Norwegian people. Ah, or is it the Viking you truly understand? No matter, I will tell you of the people who stay behind. You do not care to recognize my Irish blood. Nay, lady, nor do you deem me Christian. So I must think as a pagan, as a Viking. And often, when an unwanted child is born in the north, it is a matter easily settled. The child is merely cast into the snow and the ice, and the gods of Hel come to claim their own."

"You'd kill an innocent babe!"

"I merely told you what is done in the north. Perhaps in your next dramatic storytelling session the information will do you well."

"But . . ." She floundered, staring at him. The fire still rose behind them, her knees grew weak, and she felt again a terrible sense of heat surrounding just the two of them. She longed to beat against him, to hurt him. She feared to touch him lest the fire take hold of her, and she did not understand the feeling. She could hate no man with greater vigor, and yet she had never felt so deeply influenced by any other man, as if storms raged between them when the air was clear. Her heart beat raggedly, and she could not breathe. She feared his temper and hated him deeply. More than anything, she dreaded the night to come.

"I will hate you into eternity," she swore to him.

He smiled and bowed stiffly. "Unto the very halls of Valhalla, lady, you are welcome to do so. But you will not stop the wedding . . . or avoid the marriage bed tonight."

He started to move away. "Wait!" she cried out to him, and he turned quickly back to her. She stumbled for words. "W-would you cast out your own son to die in the snow? You'll never know!" she cried. "If you—if you—"

"If I bed you this night?" he inquired. "Lady, you seem to have far more difficulty with intimate words than with intimate actions. Is that what you mean?"

"Aye!" she stormed. "If you bed me, you'll never know whose child I carry!"

"But I am part Viking," he said smoothly. "Rape and ravishment and murder are my heritage. I shall fare well, lady, have no fear. I am set, I am determined."

"But if—"

"There are no ifs, milady. Whatever the truth happens to be, I will know it."

"No. Wait, listen, I am not a fitting bride. Not just Rowan but an endless assortment of lovers have been mine." Her panic was so great, she hardly knew what nonsense she babbled.

Rhiannon cried out softly, startled and in pain as he pulled her to him suddenly. She was forced to cast her head far back, and she felt the thunder of her heart echo against the hardness of his chest.

"Cease, milady, and cease now. Our marriage will be consummated this night. Don't think to make fools of all in the church, for my patience is already strained, and if you would truly know something of Viking vengeance, test it just one grain further!"

She could not breathe. She felt him with the entirety of her body, the bold strength of his legs, the vibrance of his arms, the staggering power of his eyes. She felt his touch keenly upon the naked flesh of her arms and shivered, aware that he would soon have every right to her, to take her and use her as he pleased. A quaking began deep in her heart, and she felt as if a wind had come, great and tempestuous and sweeping, and she could not fight the current of it. She was afraid and could not draw her eyes then from his hands, where they lay against her. Hands of great strength, with very long, handsome fingers. She wondered if they had ever dealt gently with a woman, and then she began quaking again, for she knew that he would never deal gently with her. Suddenly she was aware that her fate, her life, was being given into his hands, that she was to belong to this ruthless golden giant for the eternity of her days.

"Please!" she murmured desperately. "Think on this! It must not be! The years stretch out before us—"

"Lady, the years indeed stretch out. And they begin this night."

He released her abruptly. He turned and walked away, and the Saxon serving women who had waited a discreet distance from them came forward to escort her to the women's solar.

There were moments when she was bathed and dressed so carefully and tenderly for her wedding that she felt like falling to her knees, beating her breast, and tearing out her hair like a madwoman. She imagined just such a scene, and yet she imagined, too, that the Irish Viking would go through with the ceremony, anyway. He wanted something—and she was part of his quest, so that was that.

Alswitha brushed her hair while the other women set her train about Rhiannon's feet. The queen had brought her wine to sip to calm her, and Rhiannon quickly realized that the tankard she had been given held more than wine. She was glad of it, for she ceased to tremble, and though her dreams of redemption ran on, she stood still through it all, outwardly serene. Serene from sedation, perhaps, but serene.

She could walk down the aisle of the church and refuse to say the words. She could wait until she stood before the altar—and then reject him.

And still, she imagined dryly, he would go through with it, and all present would ignore her words if they were not the proper ones. Marriages were arranged, and hers should be no different from others. She knew that she could find little true sympathy even from Alswitha, for the queen had been of the Mercian royal house and her marriage to Alfred had been expedient. That they had come to love each other through the years was fortunate. There had been rough periods for them, too, Rhiannon knew, for the queen had at times found her husband self-righteous rather than good or pious, and she had once condemned him heartily for his unforgiving nature.

The longer she stood, the less anything seemed to matter. When an hour had passed, she was quiet and still and elegantly beautiful in the tunic that had been so carefully crafted for the occasion. Her hair was burnished to molten copper, and she carried the scent of rose water upon her skin. She did not protest being led from the manor longhouse and across the yard to the church. If anything, she appeared grave, understanding the solemnity of the occasion.

Whatever potion the queen had given her was a godsend, for she could walk with her head high and with her dignity intact. She knew that she hated the king, but she did not protest when he took her arm. And she knew that she despised the Viking—nay, he could not cloak himself as an Irishman!—who awaited her before the altar, appearing as grave as she did herself, though at the sight of her his lip curled slightly, and a touch of curiosity lightened his eyes.

He was quite splendid, she could admit, for she was able to feel distant from it all. He was taller than any man in the assembly, and his head gleamed high and golden above the others. His eyes were searing; no man could hide the truth from him. His head was fine and proud, and he was a striking bridegroom.

He was golden because he was a Viking, she reminded herself. And he was strong and powerful in build because he excelled in conquest, in dealing out death.

Father Paul was speaking. Rhiannon felt the king's hand upon hers, and it felt like dust. He handed her over to the Viking and she started, for his very flesh was searing. She looked around and saw the torches burning, and the faces of her countrymen and his swarming before her. Alswitha's face, the king's face, Allen, William . . . and Vikings and Irishmen in curious jerkins. One face caught her attention and she almost smiled, for it belonged to a man so old that his skin was wrinkled and browned like leather, and his beard fell nearly to the very ground. He watched her with a curious kindness, and her heart skipped a beat when she returned his very intense gaze. She found herself smiling at him. He nodded in some strange acknowledgment.

Father Paul cleared his throat endlessly. He spoke firmly of the Christian faith and of the importance of the sacrament of matrimony. He must have spoken too long, for at some point the Viking interrupted the ceremony.

"Get on with it, man!"

Then she was being charged to honor him as her husband and to obey him.

"Honor? Obey? A Viking? Oh, surely I think not!" she said very sweetly.

There was a silence, long and deadly. Then she felt herself whirled around and pulled hard against the crimson mantle of the man, the crimson mantle with its emblem of a snarling wolf. He touched her chin, and it was not a gentle touch or a kind one, but neither did it hurt. She felt, rather, the cobalt power of his eyes.

"Lady, you will honor, and I promise you, you will obey me." He stared at Father Paul. "Go on."

There were other things said. No longer did anyone wait for her replies. She was swiftly declared Eric of Dubhlain's wife.

Though it had been a Christian ceremony, it ended with a chorus of pagan shrieking and goading, and she was taken into her husband's arms. For one moment she felt his gaze again . . . and then she felt his lips, hard upon hers.

She thought to struggle. She pressed her palms against his chest, but they were like dust in the wind, and she longed to jerk her head away but she could not, for his fingers wound into her hair. He held her mercilessly still, as he slowly took his leisure. This was no brief peck, no swift brush of lips. His mouth molded surely to hers, and he overpowered her with the mastery of his kiss. His tongue teased her lips, then forced them to part. She felt that he consumed her. His tongue plunged with purpose into the dark recesses of her mouth and ravished her with wild abandon. He pressed her lips ever further apart and filled her ever fuller with the hot demand of his mouth and tongue. When she was able to breathe, she inhaled the scent of him—clean but male, threateningly male. She tried again to free herself. His arms were too strong, his kiss too powerful, a slow, sure, complete seduction of her mouth, tasting and delving and demanding with such startling insinuation that a ragged heat came into her, like an arrow cast into her very womb. She was struggling for breath, nearly losing consciousness and caught in the shocking force and intimacy of it all, when he suddenly released her.

She very nearly fell, but he caught her arm. She gazed into the curious blue fire of his eyes, and she brought her trembling fingers to her swollen lips. People were still shouting, in pagan chants that rose high in an endless series of crescendos. Men began to clap Eric heartily upon the back, then Alswitha and many wives of the English aldermen came to kiss Rhiannon's cheek. The sweet, dazed feeling remained with her, and also the awful, restless heat.

When he touched her, she despised him. She remembered all the infamy he had brought upon her, and she remembered what he was by birth—and choice, it seemed. But in the midst of the night she had realized, too, that when he touched her, she burned. She felt like a caged beast, desperate, seeking some freedom from the bars and barriers she could not see.

He disappeared from her view, and she was pushed along with many women. Warriors caught and held her and kissed her cheek and then released her, all of them boisterous and brimming with an intoxication brought on by the free-flowing wine and ale and the excitement of the night.

Then she was leaving the church and coming into the cool spring air. There was laughter then, and the sound of the lute, and a slow, seductive beat of a drum. And suddenly, beneath the moon, there was dancing, and she was swept into it. Wine flowed again, from Viking drinking horns now, and when one was pressed to her, she drank deeply.

She did not know where she was going until she was brought there, to one of the small outbuildings, distant from the longhouse of the manor. When she was borne within it, she discovered that the wood-and-daub structure was a single room, and within there was a large bed with fresh linen coverings, huge down pillows, and sheer gauze draperies. At the sight of it she paled and stood still, but the women were still with her. They laughed and spoke of their own wedding nights, and someone wondered if the sleek Viking warrior would be as gifted below the waist as he was in the shoulders while the others convulsed in laughter.

Her wedding finery was taken from her. She stood naked for several seconds, and then they cast a sheer gown over her head. She closed her eyes, feeling more naked and vulnerable than ever. The gown covered nothing but enhanced the shadows of the curves and mounds of her body. The sweet numbness that had sustained her through the wedding was ebbing away. The queen was not with the women now, and Rhiannon longed to see her, to plead for more of the potion so that she might endure the horror of the night to come.

Then suddenly there was silence. The women had paused, and Rhiannon spun in the sheer gown and saw that he stood in the doorway.

He ducked to enter the room. Men were behind him and they shouted raucous words of encouragement to the new bridegroom. Rhiannon suddenly felt, as she had before the fire that night, as if the known world had been eclipsed and she had entered into some distant plain, some place of magicians or Druids or gods. All sound paled; indeed, the world paled. All that she could see was the man, and she feared him, for her heart pounded, yet she felt alive, seared by blue fire and swept into the flame of it herself. She might loathe him, but he stood before her like a god, ever regal, indomitable. Since she had first seen him she had not been able to erase him from her mind. And now she was his wife. Certainly not to be loved. But to be possessed.

He stared at her, and she felt that his eyes roamed her like a lapping flame, that they invaded her very being. From head to toe he observed her, and the men fell silent behind him.

He did not turn. "Good night, friends," he said. No one moved, and he looked pointedly at her women.

And still no one moved, for they all seemed to stand in awe of him.

"Go!" he commanded. He took a step into the room, and someone squealed, then the women departed, following in the footsteps of Eric's men.

The door closed behind them. For several seconds Rhiannon could still hear the chatter and laughter of wedding guests, and then the sounds all ebbed into silence. The world faded away.

There was only the Viking.

His hands upon his hips, he began to smile. It wasn't a warm smile. It was as glacial as the color of his eyes.

She swore in silence that she would show no fear. She vowed to herself that she would despise him with pride and dignity, no matter what came.

But that smile of his was completely unnerving.

Watching her all the while, he cast aside his royal mantle with both grace and purpose. She started to tremble, despite her determination. She wished desperately that she had more of Alswitha's drugged wine.

"Lady . . . wife!" he muttered. He unbuckled his belt with its sword scabbard, and let it fall heedlessly to the floor.

Courage seeped from her, melting like ice with the coming of spring. She felt his gaze and the deep mockery of it. She gazed upon the naked gold power of his sinewy arms.

And then he took that first step toward her, and she saw that his smile was very grim and that his teeth were clenched hard against the cold, rigid line of his jaw.

A gasp escaped her. There was no sweet dullness

left now in her blood, and fear entered into her, electrifying her being. Belatedly she realized that she had pushed him far. She had fought him, injured him, betrayed him, and done her best to discredit him. Aye, she had pushed him far. Too far, perhaps.

Courage be damned, she thought. And pride and honor and even Wessex. She longed only to run and cared not where.

He took another step toward her, and she cried out and bolted, determined to slip past him and seek refuge in the darkness of the night. But she could not escape. His fingers locked into the fall of her hair, and he jerked her back to him, like a doll upon a string. She felt the impact of his body like a shaft of living steel, and she felt the furious wind of his breath against the softness of her cheek.

"Ah, lady! You think to elude me this evening? Nay, I think not. Sweet, sweet reckoning is mine at long last!" His hand snaked around her waist and he lifted her effortlessly, high against him. His eyes tore into hers with their icy blades.

Then he tossed her down hard upon the clean white expanse of their marital bed.

8

Stunned, Rhiannon gasped for breath, and for several
seconds she lay without moving, barely able to think.
He smiled at her, his eyes narrowed, and in those
swift, fleeting moments she realized that he clearly
remembered every injury she had ever done him,
from the deadly rain of her arrows to the insult of her
tryst with Rowan. She watched in shivering dismay as
he continued to disrobe, his eyes, cold and blue and
ageless, never leaving her face. Hose, tunic, and his
fine linen chemise all left him and fell carelessly
where they would lie, and still she hadn't found the
ability to move; nay, she had barely found the ability
to breathe.

Flames cast their glow upon the rippling muscles of
his shoulders and torso. Coarse golden hair covered
his chest, and beneath it, too, the sleek power of
sinew rippled gold and bronze in the play of the firelight. She tried to fix her eyes firmly upon his, but
they slipped, and she began to shiver. The beguiling
golden mat upon his chest slimmed and narrowed at
his waist and flared well beneath it, creating a masculine mat for the powerful shaft of his sex. She stared at
his turgid manhood and her throat went dry, her
blood racing in a sudden flurry. She longed to scream,

to deny, to disappear into the very air. With swift-rising horror she brought her gaze back to his eyes and was startled by the hard mockery and unrelenting pride within them. There was a strange and savage beauty about the man; it was in the carriage of his fine head, and even in the blazing mockery of his eyes. It was in the lithe, animallike grace of his sudden movement as he came toward her.

"A night to remember, my dear . . . wife."

"No!" she whispered. She sprang to her knees, dismayed and terrified, for she was certain that he meant to avenge himself in the most horrible way. She could not lie still and await what torture and brutality he would wreak against her.

She tried to leap from the bed. Before she could do so, he had caught her shoulders. He cast her back grimly and wasted no mercy or effort but crawled atop her, knelt astride her, capturing her wrists and stilling them beneath his weight. She struggled in maddened silence, but she could not begin to wage war against him, for his strength was so superior. Trickles of flame danced down the length of her spine as she felt his touch, bold and hard, upon her . . . as she felt his eyes, daggers that ripped into her, and pinned her soul as his body pinned her form.

"What shall I do first?" he inquired. "Beat you or rape you?"

"Let me go—"

She freed her hands, and he caught them again, pressing them to the sides of her face and leaning low against her. His breath warmed her lips and entered into her. She was filled with his scent, curiously clean and strikingly masculine and as alarming as his touch.

He whispered so close that his beard teased her flesh, as if the barrier of her gown did not lie between them at all.

"Ah, lady! There was a time when I had thought to use restraint! To prove to you, madam, beyond measure, that I was a product of a law more ancient than any English rule. I meant to be the epitome of a gentleman, madam, to display all the finer side of my sex."

She didn't know where his taunts were leading, but the deep tone of his voice was anything but tender. His body burned her. Even as he spoke, she was shatteringly aware of his splendid male build, of the very force of his hard body against her, of the searing, virile rod that nested against the gauze of her gown, and taunted her in greater measure than any words. She would have gladly died to escape him then, to escape that intimate surge of his body and the dreaded scorn of his voice, which made a mockery of his words. She did not want to feel the soft brush of his beard upon her, and she could not bear the vibrancy of his chest as his muscles rippled and constricted against her.

"Please—" she gasped out. There was a gray mist about her. She prayed that she might lose consciousness, that she might enter some netherworld where she was not at his mercy, where she need not know that he would rip into her at any moment, monstrous and cruel.

She would die, she thought. He would kill her.

"Ah, but there was a time when I longed to be civil! You had sent your arrows flying against me, you had fought me like a wildcat. But I was willing to believe in your innocence. Even when I caught you, a woman betrothed to me, with her lover in the woods, I tried to understand. But then you danced, madam. And you sang with such . . . eloquence. You tormented my heart and soul. And I thought of those distant ancestors of mine, sailing upon Lindesfarne and raiding it so brutally. I thought of the battle cries, and the blood lust, and the dark and rapacious need for ravishment that is surely born within us. Rhiannon . . ."

Her name was a bare whisper. It might have been spoken in tenderness. It might have been just a ripple of the ocean or the hungry flicker of a flame against the wind.

Then he leapt up, but he didn't release her. His fingers wound tight around her wrists; he dragged her along with him and stood her before the fire. "You've called me barbarian, and alas! The raw and primitive side of my nature has sprung forward. I have seen you in all your naked glory. I saw you shed your clothing like the most practiced harlot for your lover, and then I saw your movement as you danced. I saw the sinuous sway of your hips and the sensuous jut of your breasts, and the blood lust pounded within me until I could bear it no more. I knew that I must behave just as my ancestors did—brutal, merciless . . . hungry." The last word was a deep, startling, passionate whisper. It brought her keenly to life.

"No!" Desperate, she wrenched away. But she had won no victory, she quickly realized. He had released her on purpose, freeing his own hands so that he could catch hold of her again, drawing her back to him by the bodice of her nightgown. His fingers brushed the swell of her breasts as he forcefully tore at the fabric. The gauzy material shredded at his touch, as if melting away. Rhiannon grasped madly for the pieces of it, but he would not allow her to cover herself. With little care and certainly no mercy, he tore the remaining material from her shoulders. She swore against him and tried to strike him, but she was too quickly swept up once again and cast back upon the bed, naked this time. She tried to rise. Frantic, she sought to soothe him.

"You are no barbarian! You're an Irishman, a Christian. I was mistaken about you from the first! I find you are ever gentle—"

"You find me gentle? Oh, lady, you do lie!" he thundered, and fell upon her again. She was very aware of every nuance of his warrior's body, for he was careful to see that she was. He touched her lips with his own, and she twisted, growing frantic. She no longer sought to soothe him.

"Beast! Wretched wolf, wretched dog—"

"Ah, your words are fuel to the flame, my incredible beauty! We are ruled by passion and lust, and nothing more."

Wildly she tried to strike out, and her hands were imprisoned once again and pinned beneath her. She continued to curse him, for it was all that she could do to fight her fear.

"A wolf, a dog, a savage beast, and a barbarian!" he reiterated. "What did you intend to evoke in a man when you danced tonight, milady?"

She went still, afraid to answer him. His eyes held hers with a strange force that was as powerful as the knotted muscles of his limbs. His lip curled into a dry smile once again, and he touched her breasts, curving his hands around the fullness of them. She tossed her head and clamped her mouth shut and tried not to cry out as he moved his palms over the soft mounds, stroking and kneading her nipples until they hardened and swelled to taut peaks. Then, in shock, she lay still, barely daring to breathe. She felt horror and humiliation that her body should react thus to his touch. She despised this man, loathed him more deeply than she had imagined it could be possible to loathe anyone. But the fire continued to skitter through her, and though she longed to scream, she could not; she could merely lie there and pray that her face did not betray her, that it showed scorn, not confusion. He watched her like a hawk, stared into her eyes, and awaited her reaction with some keen emotion.

She swore then, savagely. She strained in wild and rampant fury and dismay and accomplished nothing but to feel him more firmly wedged against her, more insinuating, more intimate. She felt his sex between her thighs, felt the ungodly heat and the savage pulse, and again she thought that she would fall into some swirling vortex. . . .

"Rhiannon . . ." Her name again, that soft and searing lap of flame on the air, whispered, barely spoken. He moved his thumbs over her nipples and caressed the full swell of her breasts once more. He moved a finger down the valley between them, and she felt that mere touch as if it were a knife against her flesh.

"Alas, I am a Viking, a beast. 'Tis what you desired, your creation. But it is more. It is your beauty, lady, your most incredible beauty. I meant to be gentle and tender—truly I did. I meant to suffer your arrows in silence. I meant to forget that you had so willfully sought out the arms—and more—of another man when you were betrothed to me. I meant to leave you until battle had been waged. But your sheer, seductive beauty overwhelmed me. I wage a battle even now. Those eyes! They are the silver of the stars at night, and then they are the cornflower that grows upon a field in spring. They are all things, flashing with passion, gentle with laughter, evocative and cunning, and then seeking to portray sweet innocence again. And your hair. Red as fire, gold as the sun. And these breasts I touch, tipped with rose, and full and firm and beautiful. I am a Viking, so you tell me. I am savage and I am brutal. And I am on fire with lust, lady! Dying to plunge within you, to have you in blind and total possession. . . ."

His tone was mesmerizing despite his words; his body was like steel, his eyes like blue fire. His voice penetrated deep, deep inside of her, and she quaked and trembled in a way that he could not miss. His face was so close. His handsome countenance was dark and grave and his lips curled in contempt.

She should not be such a coward. She had gone to battle with less fear, with less sense of raw, quaking expectation. Where his hands lay against her she was shocked at the sensation, stunned by the warmth and the searing spirals of flame that were born within her from that touch. She could not bear the hot, thundering pulse of his protruding sex, could not bear the heat of his naked flesh or the power of it against her. Not for another second.

"Have done with it!" she cried. "Beat me, rape me, do what you will! But have done with it!"

He was dead still. Then he gently stroked her breast again, moving his palm upon it in such a fashion that she nearly screamed out again—with a shocking, newfound pleasure that mortified her more than the worst pain could do.

"No," he said simply, and then he sat back upon his haunches. He gazed at her still, and she could fathom nothing from his eyes.

"What?" she whispered.

"Ah, Rhiannon! I've no intention of beating you or raping you or any such thing. You, madam, are a seductress, and I guarantee you put savage thoughts into the mind of many a man tonight—Saxons as well as Vikings and Dubhlainers—but in cold truth, milady, barbarian though I am, I am trying very hard not to commit violence against you."

Aye, he was trying. Swearing, he pushed himself up and, descending from atop her, slowly paced the small confines of the room. He had meant to taunt her in repayment for so many things, then turn from her coldly and leave her be.

It was not so easy. She was his wife, and she had created all of the fires of hell within him. He had every right to her, and she probably did deserve to be ravished by the most brutal berserker ever to invade land.

He did not want her ever to expect mercy from him; she was too reckless a fighter, too dangerous a woman, and must never doubt his fury or the ironlike determination of his will.

But she haunted him, even when he was with her,

even when he gazed into the startling silver beauty of her eyes. He could not forget that he had seen her cast aside her clothing for a lover. Perhaps they had been interrupted before their affair had been consummated, but still he had seen her, her eyes sparkling like starlight, tenderness touching her face.

He did not love her! he reminded himself. He needed none of her tenderness. Neither did he want to be saddled with a wife who cringed at his approach.

She did not cringe. She never ceased to fight, he reminded himself half admiringly, half wearily. Even now. From the corner of his eye he saw that she was coiling to spring again.

Just as she leapt from the bed he was beside her. His fingers knotted cruelly into her hair, and he snarled sharply at her, "Don't! Don't ever think to escape me again. Were you to fly to the ends of the earth, madam, I would find you and drag you back. You are mine now, just like the sword I carry and the white stallion I seized."

"So I am the same as a horse!" she spat out.

"Nay, lady, for the white stallion is a fine mount and you've yet to prove to be so."

Outraged, Rhiannon went as still as stone. Then she cracked her hand across his face with a swift, startling force. The sound of her slap seemed incredibly loud against the sudden silence of the room. She could see the harsh red imprint of her fingers on his face.

His reaction frightened her more than if he had returned blow for blow. He did not move, his expression did not alter; indeed, if she weren't close enough to see the pulse that ticked furiously against his throat, she would have thought that he had not even felt her hand upon him. But she was close. And she was coming to know something about him, to read the ice that could form over his eyes, to see in the slight, swift tautening of his features the anger he betrayed in no other way. She thought that surely he would strike her in return and she tried to cringe from him, but his fingers were entangled in her hair, holding her close. Half choking, half sobbing, she tried to free her hair from his grasp.

Her bare breasts brushed over Eric's chest. He felt the rake of her nipples, pebbled and evocative against his flesh, and despite his anger—or perhaps because of it—he felt a new rise of desire within himself. Harsh, swift, and compelling, the longing to take her overwhelmed the control he had fought so hard to maintain. Her lips were but a breath away from his. "Lady," he said softly, "you are my wife. And thought I've no real wish to cause you harm, by God, through violence or tenderness, you will *be* my wife tonight."

Her eyes were on his. Her lips were parted and dry. "No!" she whispered.

"Yes."

His hold upon her hair eased. His hand cradled the back of her head, and he swept her into his arms, easing her back down to the bed. She trembled beneath him, but her dark lashes barely flickered and her eyes remained riveted to his, or perhaps he had been swept anew into the enchantment of her dance, of her seduction.

He lay down beside her before she could move, one leg cast over her limbs, his eyes never leaving hers.

Nor did her silver gaze fall from his. "You'd said that you'd not beat me or rape me. You promised—"

"I didn't exactly promise, but neither have I beaten you or raped you."

"But you intend—"

"It will not be rape. Cease to fight me. The battle is lost. It was lost before we came to this room tonight."

"No . . ." she whispered, shaking her head. There was a touch of desperation in her wide-set eyes. She knew that her protest was futile. He smiled, and placing his hand beneath the swell of her breast, over her heart, he felt the rampant beating. He curved his fingers over the fullness of her breast, and though she jolted with the new sensation, she caught her breath and did not speak or protest.

She could not protest, she was afraid to protest; indeed, she was afraid to move. She despised him, she reminded herself, truly she did; he was her enemy to the gates of hell, she was certain, and yet there was something mesmerizing about his very arrogance and confidence. He would do as he chose always, and damn the consequences. And there was something haunting in his voice. . . .

And in his touch.

She trembled, for she could not escape him, not his sinewed thigh or the strength of his arms, or the magnetic power of his eyes. Her lashes fell, and she could see his large bronze hand moving upon the ivory of her flesh. She did hate him, and she should hate his hands upon her, but what she felt was an ever-mounting fascination. An unbidden excitement swept through her. It seemed as if a slow-building fire had been ignited within her so deeply that she could not distinguish the source. Then she realized it was ignited from where his callused palm skimmed over her nipple, and it swept down into her, deep into her, into the very center of her being, into the apex of her thighs and her most womanly recesses.

"Please . . ." she whispered.

"I do not please."

"What if—"

"You are a liar, Rhiannon," he told her, and he did not cease to touch her. She was maddening, she was perfection, she was a dream of heaven and wicked delight.

"But—"

He smiled slowly, tauntingly. "Have done with your protests. I am no monk, and will not live as one. Nor are you such a sweet and tender bride. Still, we will soon know the absolute truth about your meeting with Rowan in the woods. There is nothing for you to fear. Barbarian that you call me, I could not harm an innocent babe. Should you carry the spawn of another man, that child will be promised simply and surely to the church. I would not kill the child of any woman, not even you, lady."

"I—I don't believe you." She moistened her lips. Her protests were futile. He would soon discover for himself that her tryst with Rowan had not been consummated.

Nor had proximity to Rowan ever made her feel as she felt at this moment. She loved Rowan, yet his kiss and his touch never had ignited such strange, startling fires as these, created by a man she hated.

He smiled, and it was a strange, crooked smile now, boyish, wistful, and nostalgic. "I've nine living siblings, lady. Six brothers, three sisters. My mother lost but one child, and yet for that child she grieved deeply and long. Barbarian though I may be, I have been taught that all life is sacred, and most especially that of a child.

"In truth, lady, I had meant to let you be this night. Aye, I meant to torment you, but then to leave you untouched until the battle was over, until I knew that the land Alfred gave me had been won. But I don't believe that you were ever really with your lover, and since you brought this on yourself, in all kindness, I must make you accept what you have done."

"What I have done!" she gasped. Candles flickered around them. The light danced upon his features and he was both forbidding in the ethereal glow and enchanting. Accept . . . this? She could never accept this stranger, draped so intimately upon her, this Viking with his blond hair and beard and piercing Nordic eyes and hard-sinewed body. He spoke softly, he seemed to take his leisure, and still she could feel the fires in him, the hard shaft of his sex, the lapping flames and the tension that sizzled between them. Fear surged through her once again as she realized that she was lying still when he touched her freely. She drew her hand up against his arm, but she quickly realized that the gesture was pointless. The corded muscles of his arm were like steel.

He caught her wrists and held them taut above her head, his gaze brooding upon her. "Men would have died for your reckless taunt this eve, lady. Alliances are precarious. I have come here to fight for Alfred because I believe in his cause, and I believe that he is a great king, a man to rival Aed Finnlaith, my grandfather, the Ard-ri. He is wise and he is pious, and he is a warrior-king with limitless courage. I have come here to find my own place, to seek out my fortress and my land, and I will not let you—or anyone—destroy what I have determined by my will."

He was done talking, she realized. He lowered his head, and though she thrashed aside, his mouth covered and claimed hers. His tongue parted her lips and thrust hotly and deeply into her mouth. He ravished with his tongue, caressed . . . and ravished again. It seemed he entered more and more deeply inside of her with the melding of their lips. In the flickering candlelight he seemed to steal away her very heart and soul, give them back, then take them once again. She fought the fires but they were there. She wanted to twist away but could not, and the kiss was so very forceful and demanding that she had no choice but to return it. His lips parted from hers and touched down upon them again and again, until her lips were swollen and her breath came raggedly.

When his lips left hers, they traveled a slow, demanding trail across her cheek to her earlobe, and she felt the hot moisture of his breath there, and then upon her throat. His eyes found hers. She wet her lips and tried to protest, but she had no breath for words. He freed her wrists but caught her hands, his fingers entwining with hers. He moved his body against the length of hers. She felt the rough hair of his thighs rubbing against her, and the power of his body as he wedged apart her knees, and settled his length between her thighs. His throbbing manhood lay intimately against her, and a desperate sound escaped her. His mouth covered hers, sweeping away her words and her protests. Then his lips moved again. He drew them slowly over her throat, pausing at the heartbeat that pulsed against a soft blue vein. His tongue flickered over her flesh, his kiss moving lower. His mouth closed slowly over her nipple, and the sensation of it caused her to gasp. Still he took his leisure, his tongue circling the rosy bud, his teeth grazing it, his lips moving once again. She whispered fervently and frantically, her head thrashing against the pillow. She surged against him, but their fingers were still entwined; his body was a prison of heat and muscle and sinew about her.

He trailed his kiss across the valley between her breasts to give attention to the second sweet mound, sucking the crest deeply into his mouth and causing new rays of fire to leap within her. He tasted the fullness of her, sweeping his tongue over the areola, then circling the very fullness of her breast. And his touch moved lower and lower.

She felt his hair, his beard, rough and evocative, moving over her belly. He swept his lips from one side to the other. He nipped lightly at her flesh, bathed it with the searing fire of his tongue. His hand moved over her, cupping her heat, stroking her thigh, covering the soft, downy mound between her thighs. She realized suddenly that her hands were free, that her fingers were now entangled in his hair. She tugged it, fighting the intimacy, whispering a frantic protest. He caught her hands again, recapturing her fingers. His eyes met hers with bold, blue determination and he smiled. Then he lowered his head once again.

Her thighs were spread wide, for he lay between

them. She gasped and choked and cried out at the intimacy he took then, surging hard against him. She tugged hard to free her hands, but he would not release his hold upon them. Slamming back against the pillow, she had no choice but to ride the startling, savage sensation that invaded her as surely as the shocking sweep of his tongue. Intimate, gentle, light, his lips just tasted her, barely caressed her. He teased, and then ravished and invaded. Still she twisted, still she fought, but even as she did so, the warmth seeped into her . . . deeper, deeper still. The little fires that had lapped into her body began to burn with a fright ening ferocity. She was moving against him in a rhythm, she realized dimly. Somewhere, somewhere in the very heart of the assault, she had ceased to battle. She did not seek to escape him but to know where the fires were leading. Slow, throbbing tremors built within her until they were unbearable. A honeyed liquid coursed through her veins and coiled and simmered in her heart and loins. Then it seemed that the world exploded, that stars burst forth to extinguish the candlelight, that everything within her melted into a feeling of ecstasy so sweet, she had never imagined such a sensation could be so. She was still and breathless, surrounded by darkness after the fire of the light, and then she felt that she was drifting back.

He was on top of her then. His whisper fell against her ear. "Did your lover ever know you so?" he demanded. "Did he taste your own sweet nectars with his kiss?"

Her eyes opened. The startling, shocking magic faded, and rage and embarrassment swept through

her. She cried out, seeking to strike him, but her fists
fell flat against his shoulders, and his lips claimed hers
with passion and fire. She felt the brush of his hand
against her thigh, and then she felt the searing heat
and strength of his sex as he moved into her at last.

She screamed with the sudden, blinding pain, but
her scream was caught by his kiss. He held very still,
letting her body become accustomed to the invasion
of his. Sobs rose in her throat and she twisted from
him, her fingernails curving into his shoulders.

He whispered to her, and she wasn't sure of the
words. And then he began to move. She did not think
that she could survive his thrusts, for she would be
split in two. But to her amazement the pain slowly
ebbed. And as it ebbed, the depth, the heat, the velvet thrust within her, the slow, sure rhythm . . . all
created little fires again. Flames that touched and
lapped at her, that danced throughout and heated
her blood. It was coming again, she realized, the startling ecstasy that was both terrifying and exalting. It
was building within her with each stroke of his body.
Drumbeats sounded within her head and her fingers
moved frantically over his shoulders. Muscles rippled
and corded beneath her touch, smooth and sleek and
shockingly powerful. A damp sheen of perspiration
covered them both. The earth pitched and rocked
and whirled madly, and still she felt the smooth slide
of his body claiming hers again and again.

He threw back his head, letting out a harsh cry.
Cords strained in his neck, his shoulders bunched and
tautened. And then Rhiannon felt him climax inside
her, and the magic within her was again released.
Sunlight burst upon her and then faded to near dark-

ness, and she thought that she was passing out or that perhaps in truth she had died. . . .

He rolled from her body and drew her close. It was then that she felt the pain again, a soreness between her thighs. She swung around within his arms and pummeled him fiercely. To her further fury he laughed, capturing her wrists and pulling her close.

"Bastard!" she hissed.

"A pleased one," he told her, his blue eyes mocking. "Your lovers' tryst was interrupted, so it seems."

"Then let me go now. Your honor has been satisfied. You've had your way—what more could you want?" she cried.

"What more? Oh, I want much, much more. I want everything, every little thing, that you were willing to give him."

"I'll never give you anything."

He smiled. "Oh, I think that you will. Indeed, my love, I think that you will."

9

"Never, I swear!" Rhiannon promised him vehemently. "All that you shall receive from me will be my ardent prayers for your swift demise!"

He laughed. "Because you hate me so deeply, madam? Or because you enjoy me?"

She swore softly and would have twisted away, but he caught her shoulders and pinned her with icy eyes. "Pray, then, for my demise. You had best do so. Yet if I do survive the coming battle, you had best then pray for your own soul. I will demand it as my due. I will demand everything, and I will have it—barbarically, if need be. I will always have what is mine."

She freed herself at last from him, shrouded herself in the bedcovers, and turned her back on him.

"I see that you have already begun to pray that I fall in battle."

She did not answer him. His hand fell upon her shoulder, and she shuddered, spinning around to meet him. He couldn't mean to—to start it all over again. But he could. It was his wedding night.

Her body quickened and burned at the thought. Did she despise him merely for being what he was . . . or perhaps she did hate him even more deeply for what he had drawn from her. For what he knew he had drawn from her.

She would give him no more, ever. Yet her eyes widened with alarm as he watched her because she had quickly learned a lesson this evening—he had the greater strength, and he did have the power to bend her will with his touch.

But he did not touch her again. "Go to sleep," he told her quietly. A glow fell over his features, over the mysterious blue power of his eyes, over the proud and handsome lines of his face, over his neatly clipped mustache and beard, over his shoulders, reminding her of their breadth and of his strength. She shivered. He stared at her a moment longer, then suddenly he swept his own covering aside. Naked and at ease, he sought out his sword.

In rising panic Rhiannon watched him. She saw him pick up the blade and stare at it almost lovingly, then run his fingers along the sharpness of the blade. He turned back toward the bed and began to stride toward her.

Something bubbled within her, a horror of death, some sweet instinct for life. He had lied; he meant to slay her, after all.

She paled. And as he came closer a cry escaped her. "Nay, you cannot!"

He paused, arching a brow. Then he began to laugh, and the sound of it was deep and rich and amused.

"Lady, with your temper, 'tis possible that I shall beat you at some time. But slit your throat . . . nay. Not yet, anyway."

He climbed back into the bed, laying the sword on

the floor by his side. "One never knows in foreign lands," he murmured. Then he turned his back on her, pulling the covers over his shoulders.

Beside him, she lay in shock, so vastly relieved that she was perplexed. She wanted to jump from the bed and blow out the oil lamps, for she craved darkness to shield her body and her thoughts. She could not bring herself to leave the bed, and so she lay still and listened for his easy breathing. His back was to her, and she saw the bronze expanse of his shoulders and began to shiver.

She had been wed to this curious demon, this beast who mocked her very fear of him and now had turned from her. She wanted no part of him; she truly wanted him to fall. She was in love with Rowan.

No, she could never be in love with Rowan again. Not since this man had touched her. She might despise him, but still she shivered because of him, shivered and burned. . . .

She swallowed, for she could not bear to see that broad expanse of back and those bronzed shoulders. She eased up at last and moved toward the trunk at the foot of the bed, where the two lamps burned. She leaned down to blow out the flame, and then she paused, for her eyes had fallen upon his sword.

She could pick up the blade and pierce his heart. Then he could no longer hurt or humiliate her, could never again claim her as his wife.

Nay . . . She smiled ruefully, scornfully, at herself, for she could not do such a thing. She could not take a blade against a sleeping man, no matter how she despised him.

"Vixen!"

The sharp, snarled word came from him in a startling rush of fury. She had not heard him move, she had not heard him breathe! But suddenly he was out of bed and was before her, holding her to him. He was hot and potent and in a seething fury, and she gasped with new fear as he held her, her head wrenched back and her soft form crushed against his hard one again.

"You would think to slay me! Your arrows did not find their true mark, so you would slice open a man you have wed!"

"Against my will!" she cried in her own defense. It would do her no good to claim that she had found herself unable to perform the treacherous deed. She quaked, and yet she forced herself to hold her chin high.

He swept her cleanly off her feet, into his arms. She felt his nakedness keenly. He cast her back upon the bed, but this time his back was not to her. His arm remained around her, and he pulled her taut to his body. Taut so that his chest and hips and loins were flush with her back and buttocks and he could feel each subtle shift of her movement.

And she could feel his body against her tender flesh. Pulsing, vibrant, alive . . .

"Go to sleep!" he snapped. "Move again and I shall promise to flay you with twenty strokes this very night, and then prove to you upon a later occasion that I can force myself to be very barbaric—and excruciatingly savage."

Tears stung her eyes but she did not move. She lay barely breathing, hating the intimate feel of him against her.

She did not sleep. She spent the next hours wide awake. She did not turn, twist, or shift—indeed, she barely blinked. When at last her eyes closed and sleep claimed her, she was entirely unaware that she eased against him for his great warmth.

Or that he, too, had lain awake, in truth far longer than she.

He had not mocked just her but himself.

For she was beautiful. Her naked flesh was truly exquisite. Her breasts rose voluptuously, firm and full, and they were crowned by tempting, rosy peaks that hardened evocatively to his touch. Her back was grace incarnate, her hips flared both delicately and lushly, and her waist could be spanned by his fingers. A rage against her burned within him. Despite his anger, he had taken care with her. He had nurtured the fires in her eyes and in her spirit, and he had known that she had obtained a sweet pleasure in the act, but nevertheless she behaved as if he had beaten her. She still fought him, still defied him.

She was still dreaming of another man.

Life was made of hard facts, he thought. She must accept that. She was his wife.

Another rage burned deep inside him too. He spoke in jest to shame her; yet he spoke the truth. They were enemies, keen and bitter, and she would fight and despise him at every turn. It was a brutal and ironic thing, for when he made love to her, he remembered love, the tenderness, the sweet laughter, the need.

This passion was no such emotion but a desire so strong that he did fight some savage beast within him, a wolf that yearned to howl and claim this woman. He did not want tenderness; he wanted to take her and cast her from him and keep that memory of love clean within him.

He gritted his teeth. She did not seem to recognize his Irish blood. She saw only the savage. Then be damned, he determined. He would quench the fever within him and be all that she saw.

He closed his eyes. He felt the rich fullness of her breast, and a fire pulsed inside of him again. He tightened his jaw. He had told her to sleep, but he could not allow her to do so.

His lips touched hers. His hands moved over her breast and he knew that he would take the vision of her beauty into battle with him and through the empty nights to come. He pressed his lips against her flesh and tasted the sweet salt of their first union. She moved, not really awakening. Her body writhed and arched instinctively to his caress.

Then he claimed her lips again, wedging his body between her thighs. Her eyes flew open with startled alarm just as he thrust into her with the hardness of his sex. It was too late for protests. A strangled sound escaped her, and she slammed her hands against his chest, but then her fingers curled over his shoulders, her nails raking his muscled flesh.

His lips left hers and he stared down at her. Her eyes were closed and her breath came raggedly through her barely parted lips. She might deny him. She might deny herself. But she was blessed with beauty and sensuality, and if she was not allowed to waylay him, she would learn the truth of it.

"You are mine," he whispered to her softly. "My wife. Remember it. Never forget it."

Then he moved within her.

His passion unleashed, he swept her into his great tide. Perhaps there was something of savagery in his demand, for he rode her at a fever pitch, and when he reached his climax, it seemed that the anger and tension spewed from him with the seed of his body. She was his, and she would know it now.

He felt her shudder, felt her release. He lay against her in the night until she cried out with outrage, trying to shove his weight from her.

He set her free, and she curled away from him. After a long time he saw the heaving of her shoulders cease. She slept again.

In sleep she was all innocence. Dark lashes swept over her cheeks, and her hair was an elegant tangle of flame covering her body like some finely spun cloth. She was very young. Seeing her so, he braced himself. He tried to remember how she had cast her clothing aside for her lover, intending to cuckold him. He remembered only the flow of her back and the beautiful flare of her hips, and he thought again how curiously she appeared as pure as winter's first snow, and as vulnerable and sweet.

He lay back and closed his eyes, and he reminded himself that he had to meet that very lover at dawn, and that he had gravely determined that he did not want to slay the lad. He would need his wits about him. Then the company would leave and they would ride to face Gunthrum at Rochester. He needed to be awake and ever aware, and his sword arm needed to be rested.

And still sleep eluded him.

* * *

The cock's first crow came at last, and the sky was lit with crimson.

It was time for him to meet with Rowan.

Eric rose and dressed quickly, belting on his scabbard and sliding Vengeance within it.

He paused, staring at Rhiannon. With morning's light she looked ever more innocent, ever more beautiful. Deadly beautiful, he thought, feeling his anger with her inflame him again. She might well have cost the poor fool lad his life, for they had to fight, and swordplay could always be deadly.

Rollo waited at the door of the wedding bower. He led the giant white stallion and carried Eric's faceplate and armor. They did not speak; there were no ribald jokes exchanged. Eric donned his mail and set the helmet and visor upon his head, adjusting it. He mounted Alexander.

"Is the king ready?"

"The king and the lad, Rowan, along with a number of the Englishmen, await us on the field."

Eric nodded.

"What will you do?"

"Slay him if I must."

Rollo smiled. "You never imagine that you will fall yourself?"

"Nay, never, for to imagine death is to invite it. And here I feel that I have the advantage, for the lad has not fought the long years that I have."

"This is bad between the Saxons and us," Rollo muttered.

"Aye, it is," Eric agreed. "But there is no help for it."

They came upon the field where they had practiced their deadly warfare just the day before, the place where the challenge had been issued and accepted. The king rode out to him, Rowan at his side. Alfred was grim and visibly displeased. And, Eric thought, he was also pale and pained.

The fight must take place; there was no alternative. But the king mourned the young man's death already. He had no doubt that Eric would take the victory.

They paused. The king raised his hand. "Swords only. The rush is upon horseback, and only when a man is unseated shall the fight come to the ground."

Eric nodded. Rowan, pale but determined, nodded too. Eric closed the visor over his helmet, and only his eyes, fire and ice, appeared behind the silver mask. The white stallion pranced and reared, the others backed away, and he raced toward his starting point. There was the sound of a horn; the men were aligned to fight.

The horn sounded again, and Eric slammed his heels against Alexander's flanks. Thunder rang against the earth and mud flew. The great power of the beast entered into him, and he rode as the lightning rode against the sky. Rowan, too, rode a great charger. The horses tore toward one another, breathing smoke, as if they were majestic dragons of legend, into the cold morning air. Thunder followed upon thunder.

And then they met.

Steel clashed against steel. Eric swung Vengeance with his battle cry upon his lips, and it was a chilling sound. Swords reverberated and shook. Their impact was mighty.

Eric compressed his lips grimly. He saw that the Englishman was well trained, but he must have felt that even his God was against him, for he fought weakly. Eric raised his sword again and cast it hard against Rowan's, and the younger man was unhorsed.

Eric instantly leapt from his mount, pressing his advantage for the moment. Rowan raised his shield but fell back, and then, in a pit of mud, slid to his knees. Eric smote him again, and Rowan's sword went flying, and then his shield, and he lay panting, his jugular pulsing, his eyes upon Eric's where they gleamed ruthlessly from the slits of his visor.

Eric held Vengeance to his side. Then, with purpose, he slid the blade against the other man's throat. He held it there, then raised it. He nicked Rowan's cheek. The lad reached instinctively for the wound and stared blankly at the Viking.

Eric turned to the king. "My honor is satisfied. This man is courageous, and if he is to fall beneath steel, I would have him fall in his quest against the Dane."

He awaited no reply. He turned and strode toward the waiting stallion.

There was movement behind him. Swiftly he spun, amazed, but wary lest the man intend him harm still. These English! he thought disdainfully. Ever ready with a sword at a man's back!

But the man did not hold his sword, and when Eric turned, young Rowan fell upon a single knee and cast his fist against his heart. "I thank you for my life, Prince of Dubhlain. I am ever your liege man." He stared up at Eric for a moment, then he lowered his head. "And as you know," he whispered, "in truth I never did lie with your . . . wife."

Eric reflected upon the words. "Get up. We'll all face death soon enough."

He turned and mounted Alexander. He saluted the king, then rode back toward his bridal bower. It was time to prepare to ride away to Rochester.

Rhiannon awoke slowly. She had never slept so deeply, she thought vaguely. Beneath her fingers she felt the cool smoothness of the sheets, and her head was cosseted by soft down. It was easy to remain adrift in a misted dream world.

But then she was wide awake. Her eyes flew open, and she tossed over in a panic.

He was gone. She was alone.

Nevertheless, she shivered again, remembering. Remembering the way that they had lain together, remembering his mockery and his touch and his promises . . . nay, his threats!

But even just thinking of him, her breath came short. And she felt the curious burning deep inside of her again. Her breasts ached, her nipples hardened, and the heat seemed to rise to her face. "Nay, nay!" she muttered vaguely, and pressed her face into the pillow.

Then she remembered her nakedness and she determined to rise and dress before he could return. It still seemed like early morning, too early for the army to have departed.

"Lady!"

There was a tap upon the door, and Magdalene, one of the queen's women, entered. She brought water to wash, and she wore a shy smile. "Your lord has gone, so I have come to help you dress."

Rhiannon nodded and tried to smile. Magdalene was a gentlewoman. Never married, she was tall, slim, gray-haired, and kindly. Alswitha had certainly sent her on purpose, knowing that she would not offend Rhiannon with laughter or jibes after the consummation of her marriage.

"Thank you," she murmured, and bit into her lower lip. "I am eager to dress."

Magdalene came in and set her water on the trunk. "I suppose that you are anxious to reach the field, for the men must meet with their swords soon."

"What?" Rhiannon demanded. She sat up, pulling a cover about her shoulders. She frowned and added more quietly, "What sword battle is this?"

"Why, Rowan did challenge your new husband. My lady, to be so beautiful that men would die for you! Ah!" Clasping her arms to her breast, Magdalene sighed wistfully.

"Die for me . . ." Rhiannon repeated. Then panic seized her and held her in a deathly grip. Rowan had determined to fight for her. She cared for him still, even if the night had changed her forever.

And he was no match for Eric of Dubhlain. He was not so well trained or so experienced. Nor was he created of steel, with an overmastering will and cold confidence.

"No—oh, no!" she said with a moan. She jumped from the bed, forgetting that she was clad only in the linen sheet, desperate to stop the fight before it could begin.

"Lady!" Magdalene called after her.

She ignored the summons. She burst out to the door, and the cool rush of the morning air filled her heart with dread. She ran into the dirt path that led toward the manor, and then she stopped, her heart seeming to miss a beat.

Eric was already mounted. His sword was in its scabbard. Her hand flew to her throat. They had not met yet. No blood dripped from the blade.

"My lord!" she cried.

His face was hidden behind the steel of his visor; she saw only his eyes—blue ice, blue fire. He dismounted, and his stride brought him quickly to her. She swallowed and lowered her head. Even before he reached her, she fell upon a knee in the dirt, keeping her head downcast.

"Please!" Her voice was husky and deep with heartfelt emotion. "Please, do not engage in this battle. Do not—do not slay Rowan. He is not guilty of anything, I swear it. You . . ." She paused as a flush covered her cheeks. How hard it was to beg anything from this man! "You know that we were never lovers in truth!"

He reached down. He took her elbows and forced her to rise. She gazed into his face, and still it was only the unfathomable blue fire of his eyes that she could see.

"Lady, what is this habit with you of walking about unclad?" he demanded hoarsely.

Miserably she pulled the linen more tightly about her.

"I speak of a man's life!" she cried.

"Your lover's life?"

"He was never—"

"No, madam, he never consummated the act of love. What he did receive from you—that tender scene in the forest!—was surely more than most husbands would endure."

"Please . . ." She opened her mouth to protest, but he had turned her around, and with a gauntleted hand heavy upon her waist, he pushed her back toward their wedding chamber. She looked behind her, then stumbled forward. He followed her. Magdalene remained inside. Eric cast her one swift gaze as he lifted off his visor, and she bobbed and hurried away.

Eric closed the door, and his back remained to Rhiannon for a long moment. Then he turned around.

"This man's life is very precious to you."

Rhiannon swallowed.

"Life is precious to me."

He cast his gauntlets upon the bed. "Except for mine?"

"Please, I beg you. Don't kill him."

"It's so intriguing to see you beg."

"You enjoy this!" she accused him.

"Indeed, madam, I do. Pray continue."

He was silent then and still, towering in the room, his hands upon his hips. She swallowed again, clamping her lips down hard. Then she walked toward him, hesitantly. And once again she knelt before him. The sheet and her glowing curtain of hair shielded her like a royal mantle, and she looked up to him at last with glorious, tear-shimmering eyes.

"Do not leave me now to go and slay him, and I swear to you that upon your return I—I will give you everything that you ask of me."

Eric leaned against the door and crossed his arms over his mail-coated chest with amused interest.

"You are my wife," he told her. "I can take what I want."

She flushed. "Aye, but you said that you wanted more than my body. What I'm saying is that I will not protest—"

"Protest or no, lady, when I return, this thing between us will go on."

Even as she pleaded, her temper was rising, yet she bit her lip lowered her eyes and began again. "Nay, sir, there are things that you cannot demand, and things that you cannot take, even as a husband." Her gaze rose with defiance and pride and reckless courage. "Spare him, I beg you, for mercy's sake. And spare him, I beg you . . . for me. I will repay you."

He lowered himself to her. She felt the radiating strength of him and inhaled his subtle masculine scent. She was trembling again despite herself, alive with the thing that tore into her breasts and spread like fire to her loins.

He reached out and lifted her chin, and his eyes burned into her. "What, Rhiannon? What will you do, how will you pay?"

"If he lives, I swear to you, I will come to you like the best of harlots. I will answer to your every whim. I will adore you like the most doting lover."

"If he lives? If I do not slay him?" Eric said.

"Aye!"

"You will pay so, you swear it?"

"I swear it."

He released her chin and moved suddenly, as if he had been scalded. She held her head down, then she gazed up at him. His eyes were fathomless once again, and her stomach did a somersault in panic. He was going to refuse her.

"Done," he said softly. Relief swept through Rhiannon, yet she frowned, for she was certain that the hint of a wicked smile played upon his lips. "Done, lady. I will return to you most eager for this payment. And so help me, madam and wife, you will make good the payment!"

"Aye!" she promised.

He stepped past her and she rose slowly. There was a tap on the door. Rhiannon pulled the sheet around her. Eric bid the caller enter.

It was Rollo, stating that the king needed to see him.

It was time to leave.

Eric took up his gauntlets, opened his trunk for his saddle roll and leather satchels, then swung them over his shoulder. He swept by Rhiannon, dismissing her. She watched him go, amazed that he could make such a bargain—one that her cost her all her pride and her dignity and her very soul—and then dismiss her as a matter of little importance.

"Lady?"

Magdalene stepped back into the room. She cheerfully went to Rhiannon's trunk, seeking out clothing. She chatted away, but at first Rhiannon barely heard her.

"They are all in awe, for it was such a noble fight! Lady, you are blessed!"

Rhiannon stared at Magdalene, then raced to her. "What fight?"

"Why, when your Irish prince battled Rowan. The

young man lost his sword almost immediately, but they tell me that Eric of Dubhlain only cut his cheek, then bid him rise and live to fight the Dane."

A horrible churning began in Rhiannon's stomach. "When—when did this happen?"

"Why, with the dawn. The entire place is a-buzz with it now, lady!"

Once again Rhiannon turned and ran to the door. She cast it open and ran back into the dirt road, clad only in her linen sheet.

They were mounting. They were ready to ride out. She saw Eric and she ran to him. Once again he wore only his visor, but his eyes condemned her with fury.

"Damn you, wife! Go dress yourself decently."

"Bastard!" she hissed.

He dismounted with no patience. He swept her up into his arms and carried her back to the structure. Furiously she pounded against him, bruising her hands upon his mail. "You bastard! You tricked me, you used me, you hated son of a rodent and a whore!"

He kicked open the door, ignoring Magdalene, who stood there, mouth agape.

He carried Rhiannon back to the bed and dropped her upon it. "Attack me, lady, all you will. But I warn you, never cast aspersions upon either my dam or my sire. And clothe yourself, lady, else my wrath will be great."

She tossed back her hair defiantly, yet inwardly she was frightened by the depths of his fury, frightened by the burning menace in the eyes that glinted from the mask of steel.

She would never let him see her fear! She vowed in silence.

"Is that all?" she managed to say with some semblance of courage and scorn.

He paused. She was certain that he smiled, slowly and with sure mockery.

"Nay, lady, it is not. Your young Rowan lives—I kept my bargain, though I did anticipate you. I will return, lady—and I will return demanding what is mine. Payment."

He bowed to her. He turned and strode from the room, and the door shuddered in his wake.

Then Rhiannon heard the sound of horns and a great clattering of hooves. She jumped up, ignoring her husband's command. She opened the door and stood there, huddled in linen.

And she saw him, Eric of Dubhlain, mounted upon Alexander. He wore full battle regalia, his visor concealing all his features but the blaze of his eyes, his mantle with its emblem of the wolf flowing behind him.

He did not look her way. The troops were moving. Already the banners were flying and the ranks forming. He called out a command to his Irish and Norse troops. There was thunder against the earth, and he rode out at the king's side.

Eric of Dubhlain, the Viking lord.

Her husband.

10

"The men of Rochester have held out against the Danes all through the winter," Alfred told Eric as they rode at the front of the king's great host of men. Astride the white stallion, Eric listened to the king while he shifted on his mount to watch the columns behind them.

His men were mainly upon horseback. He knew that it was a Viking habit that led them all to ride the horses of the land where they had made a conquest as they continued to do battle in that very land. The Saxons did not ride, or very few did so, and those who did were the captains of the forces and the king's closest advisers. The priest Asser was with them, not riding far behind, a quiet, often grave man who seemed to carry about him an air of wisdom. Rowan rode down the ranks, as did William and Allen and several other men. The ranks of Saxons walked in formation, clad in their leather armor. The house carls, or professional soldiers, were well armed, while the simple men, the small householders and landowners, carried whatever weaponry they had been able to gather together. Some walked with pitchforks, and some with scythes, and some with clubs they had fashioned from the heavy boughs of oaks.

His own men seemed remarkably well prepared for war in comparison. Irishman and Norseman alike, the men of Dubhlain had learned their lessons well. The truce that had been formed between Eric's Irish grandfather and Norwegian father had been beneficial to all Ireland. The Irish had learned shipbuilding, and a great deal about the fighting techniques of the Danes, for the Norse and the Danes were alike in many ways.

To a large part of the Christian world they were one and the same, Eric reflected—assailants, plunderers, rapists, robbers, and murderers all.

To his wife they were all the same. Vikings.

Annoyed with the rush of warmth that suffused him at the thought of Rhiannon, he determined to give his attention, and his advice, to the king. "If the Danes have been at the siege this long, they'll have built up their own fortifications." He paused, shifting in his saddle again to look back on the long file of men. Then he smiled to Alfred. "I'd dare make a wager, though. If word of the size of your army has reached the Danish jarls, they might well have quit their assault upon Rochester."

"You think them cowards?"

Eric shook his head gravely. "No Viking is a coward, Alfred. You know that. A Viking sets out to win glory and conquest. Death is not the Viking's fear, rather an inglorious death that might bring down shame upon him. To rest in the halls of Valhalla is a reward that goes only to the brave. And no man lives forever. 'Tis better to die a hero on a battlefield than to die in a battle against time, old and weathered and wrinkled."

"I have been fighting Danes all of my life," Alfred said. "I know about as much about the Viking as you do yourself, Eric Olafson," he said.

Eric smiled. "Not quite, for I am the son of a Norse Viking," he said, a smile of amusement curling his lip. "I don't deny any of my heritage. Even if my sire has come to be something of a hero upon the shores of Eire, he did come in conquest. And I have ridden dragon prows on journeys of conquest and adventure. I'll admit that once my father had settled down, he suggested that my uncle take me on journeys that threatened no Christian kingdoms. I rode to the conquest of pagans, and therefore such exploits were palatable to the Irish as well as to the Norse."

"You sound cynical," the king said, watching him.

Eric shrugged. "I have come to fight an invader with you. I am the son of an invader—and a proper Christian princess of Eire, I'll grant—but it is all an interesting dilemma. Very interesting. There are those who say that my father conquered much of Ireland. Those who know say that Ireland conquered my father, and that he is more a part of Eire than many a native son." He looked at Alfred and smiled again. "No matter how many times you beat the Danes, Sire, they will have made their conquest. Saxon lasses will bear Danish babes, and the names given to streams and rivers and hills and ridges by the Danes will often remain. The Viking, whoever he may be, has a habit of leaving his mark."

Alfred watched him long and carefully in return. "Well, I have already accepted one, haven't I? And close enough to my own kin."

"Sire?"

THE VIKING'S WOMAN - 215

"A Viking. A man who sailed across the sea in a dragon prow. I'm curious, Eric Olafson. Will you conquer your little patch of England? Or will England conquer you?"

Eric laughed, unoffended. "That is simple. England has already conquered me. Lulled, seduced, and conquered me. I have seen the land that beckoned to me, and you have made it mine. Therefore I am fighting not as any mercenary, not as any invited prince, but as a West Saxon, as yourself. That makes me more dangerous than my Danish cousins."

"But you say that they will be gone."

"I think it likely. They are no cowards, but neither are they men who will fight if they are grossly outnumbered. Not unless they are cornered."

"We shall see, Eric, we shall see," Alfred replied. He watched the younger man broodingly for a moment. "You've mentioned land. You've yet to mention your other Saxon acquisition."

"And that is?"

"Your wife," Alfred said with a certain irritation.

"Ah," Eric murmured.

"The lady is my kin, and my ward," the king reminded him.

"Your kin, Sire, no longer your ward," Eric replied mildly.

"My concern," the king amended.

Eric was silent for several moments. "I trust that you left her well," Alfred said.

"How did you think that I would leave her?" Eric inquired.

A slight coloration touched the king's cheeks, and

he stared straight ahead. "You'd certain reasons for anger—"

"And I am, Irish prince or no, a Viking," Eric finished for him. "I assure you that I did not cut her into little pieces and feast upon her for breakfast. Nor did I beat or abuse her, Alfred."

The king still did not seem satisfied. He inhaled and exhaled, looking ahead. "Did you find that your marriage was one . . . made in the good faith that we promised you?"

"Did I find my bride as innocent as your physician assured me that she was?" Eric asked with amusement. "Yes, I did."

"So you are well pleased with the marriage and Rhiannon is happy?"

"Oh, I don't imagine that she's terribly happy," Eric said. "But I would say that she is reconciled to me. And if she is not—well, then, she shall be very shortly."

Alfred wasn't particularly pleased with this answer, but there was no more that he could say, and there was no more that he had a right to ask a groom about a marriage that he, himself, had arranged.

He smiled, suddenly very sure that Rhiannon had suffered no truly grievous harm during the night.

"What is it?" Eric asked him.

"You dealt well with Rowan," Alfred told him.

Eric arched a brow.

"Well, he lives, and is no longer your enemy. I have heard that he is, in fact, your ever-devoted servant now."

"Tell me, Alfred, are you well pleased with your devil's bargain, then?"

"My devil's bargain?"

"Yes, that which you made with me."

The king smiled. "We'll know that once we've faced the Danes, I believe."

"*If* we face them," Eric commented.

"Oh, we will face them," Alfred guaranteed him. "If we do not do so now, most assuredly we will do so soon."

"You will have your pact of blood," Eric said.

"You have already received much of West Saxony," Alfred reminded him. "Yes, I will have my pact of blood."

"How strange," Eric commented easily as they rode. "It seems to me that you are speaking more about a woman than you are about land."

"Perhaps I am."

"Then let me assure you," Eric said, slowly, carefully, trying to hide the irritation in his voice. "Rhiannon is fine and will continue to do well enough. She is my wife—as was your will, not mine. But I take care of what is mine. In honesty, King Alfred, I do not trust her. Not for one moment. I am certain that she would dearly love for you to return with my head upon a platter for her. However, I find this amusing to a certain extent. I will live, Alfred, through all and any odds—to spite her wish, if for no other reason. Unless she crosses or betrays me, she will have nothing to fear from me."

"Perhaps she fears you, yourself," Alfred commented softly.

Eric shook his head. "No. She might despise me, but she does not fear me. Perhaps," he suggested to Alfred, "it would be better if she did. We still don't know what happened at the coast when I arrived. If she did not defy your wishes, who did? And yet you are her kin, a man she well loves."

"Loved," Alfred said in a weary breath. He still speculated about the night that had passed. Rhiannon had doubtlessly fought. And Eric had just as doubtlessly demanded his right to his wife. Rhiannon would surely be more than bitter against her king now.

Most women went to their marital beds with no choice, Alfred reminded himself. Yet he could not help but feel how deeply he had betrayed his godchild. Eric had allowed Rowan to live. He was a civilized man and showed a Christian spirit, but still . . .

The things that went on between a man and a woman were different from all others.

"Rhiannon did not betray me," Alfred said flatly. Then he wearied of the conversation, which was annoying Eric in any case. "It is growing dark. We will camp ahead, and in the morning we will reach Rochester." He called out to his men. The great body behind them came to a halt.

The king knew his country. They were not far from a stream where a secluded valley would give them cover for the night.

The ranks split. Eric and his men formed their camps, as did the Saxons. There were no fires lit, for they did not want to give the Danes warning of their approach.

There was a quiet as the men settled down to horns and skins of ale and cool water and dried, smoked beef and fowl and hard cheeses and bread. The only sounds to be heard as darkness fell were rustling noises and the occasional clink of steel as men cleaned and honed their swords and pikes and battle-axes.

Eric wandered from the camp, as was often his custom the night before a battle. By a heavy oak laden with the lush leaves of spring, he paused and stared up at the stars. The night was clear and cool and beautiful. He could hear the faint bubbling of the stream, the quiet movements of the men. Looking north and east, he could see the fires of Rochester. The Danes would have built woodwork and earthwork fortresses. They would have dug in deeply. Outside the walls of Rochester they would have plundered the countryside, taken the sheep and cattle, survived well off the rich offerings of the season. They were natural aggressors. He knew, Eric realized, because he had a certain affinity with them.

He still resented his wife's assumption that he was nothing more than an invader. His wife . . .

He sank down by the tree, his fingers knotting tensely together. She was a wayward child who must be dealt with. No . . . she was more too.

He would never forget the fire that burned in her eyes when she looked at him. Never forget her hatred, her arrows, her strength . . .

But there was more now that he would never forget. He would never forget what it felt like to be entangled with her in the silken cape of her hair. He would never forget the curve of her hip, or the fullness of her breast, or the sway and undulation of her body beneath him. He imagined now in the night air that he could inhale the intoxicating sweetness of her scent, that he could taste the nectar of her flesh, feel the frantic pulse of her heart.

If he closed his eyes, he could see hers. See their vibrant color, their shimmering passion, their fury, their surrender. . . .

Indeed, last night had been his.

Or had it?

He had expected a fight. He had expected her hatred and her fury, and he had expected tears. He had known that they would enter into battle, and he had known that for their future it would be imperative that he win.

He had even been aware that there was truth in Alfred's assertion that Rhiannon was perhaps the most beautiful woman in all his kingdom. Her hair carried the fire of her spirit, her eyes flashed with the silver sparkle of the tempest within her soul. There was beauty in her very motion—he had not known just how much until last night.

His hands clenched and he stretched his fingers out before him, trying to ease the strain within him. She had been glorious that morning, coming before him clothed in her linen sheet, going down upon her knees.

To plead for the life of her lover.

Glorious, as perfect in her beseeching as she was in all the other roles she had chosen to take on. Seeing her, he had wanted her, wanted her with a desire that had stormed his senses, seared his loins, and swept violently through him, pervading his every nerve ending.

It was not such a bad thing to want one's wife.

But she was no ordinary wife. It was dangerous to want her with such a desperate abandon. She was a dangerous woman and determined to see that a sword blade slit his throat if a Danish ax did not cleave his head.

And yet she had promised him. . . .

She had promised him what she had already given another, he reminded himself. He had awakened her passions, he had found a root of sensuality deep within her that she could not deny, yet she did not love him for it. Rather, he reflected, she despised him all the more. Yet he could not forget how she had appeared in the forest with Rowan. How magical it had seemed when she would offer herself and everything that she could give to a man she loved. . . .

He knit his brow. He did not love her. Love was an emotion he had experienced with the recklessness of his past, and he was not fool enough to love Rhiannon.

But she haunted him. He had taken her, and yet she had invaded him. And he had been pleased this morning that she still thought she had a bargaining power with him. To save Rowan's life she would do anything.

She was hoping fervently that her husband would be slain, Eric mused.

But he wouldn't be killed. Come what may, he would live. He had not lied to the king. He would live to return to his wife, no matter what.

Determined, he rose and returned to camp. Rollo, ever faithful, awaited him with a horn of ale. He took it and drank deeply.

"We've a victory tomorrow," Rollo said. "I feel it. I feel it on the wind."

"Careful," Eric warned him. "you're starting to sound like Mergwin."

Rollo laughed. " 'Twas Mergwin who assured me of

victory. I tell you, Eric, I miss him when he is not about, plaguing us all."

"I admit I miss him too."

"Why didn't he come? He hates to see you off to war alone."

"He was needed."

"Needed?"

"To watch my wife," Eric said. He finished the ale and handed the horn back to Rollo. "Sleep well, my friend. It never pays to be too assured of victory. Death comes quickly to the unwary."

"Death comes eventually to us all," Rollo reminded him.

Eric grinned and withdrew his sword from his scabbard. Starlight glinted down upon the steel blade of Vengeance. "Eventually," Eric agreed with Rollo. "But eventually is not going to be tomorrow. Not if it would mean that I would spend my eternity with every hero in Valhalla."

He turned, ready to seek sleep for the night. "Eric," Rollo called to him.

Eric paused.

"You're supposed to be a Christian prince."

Eric grinned. "For all the promises of heaven, Rollo, I will not die tomorrow!" he said. "Nay, I vow it. I will not die."

Her first day as a bride was a truly wretched experience for Rhiannon.

It seemed that she remained furious for hours. Her cheeks flamed, her heart thundered, and when she would try to calm herself, she would remember the amused blue ice in her bridegroom's hard arctic eyes and she would feel herself flame anew. And it seemed that there was no forgetting him. His scent remained about her—it touched the pillow where he had slept, it lingered on the sheets, it haunted and tormented her until she longed to scream aloud. To her horror she could relive the night, she could remember his words, his touch, and more. She could remember with a shameful clarity just how he had demanded things from her, just how he had subdued her . . . and how he had seduced her.

And then she realized that it wasn't so terrible that he had forced her to be his wife, but it was agonizing to recall the way he had made her feel, and the passion she had all too easily displayed.

She moaned softly and buried her face in the pillow, yet there was no forgetfulness there. Last night hadn't been enough for him. He had wanted more. That was what he had told her that morning, when she had pleaded for Rowan's life. And she had promised him exactly what he wanted. Anything that he wanted. She had sworn that she would come to him as she had come to Rowan.

Rowan! Panic seized her. She could not remember his face. She could only recall the strong, hard features of the Viking, his startling blue eyes, eyes that pierced through her, that raked over her, that saw everything and invaded her intimately. No one had ever known her so thoroughly, no one had ever touched her so deeply.

She sat up in a fury. He would have no more of her, he would take no more from her. It was all one vast amusement to him. He didn't want a wife, but he would take one to gain other things that he wanted.

He was interested in battle, and in acquisition. Her life lay in his hands like a toy, and he thought that he would dictate his will to her.

How very amused he must have been, watching her plead for the life of a man who had already been granted that life.

Well, she had been tricked, and she would never fulfill any bargain that she had made with him. He could not expect her to do so. God could not expect her to do so!

He would not best her, ever. She did not know how or when, but she would win in the end. So help her, she would not surrender to the hell in which he planned to imprison her.

His haunting male scent rose up to meet her. She jumped up, casting the pillow from her. He had marched to battle. With God's good grace he might have the decency to die.

But he wouldn't. Shivers trailed along her spine. She feared for the others. She feared for the king. But she knew, she just knew, deep in her heart, that Eric would come back.

Swearing aloud, she hurried to the door and threw it open. Magdalene was not far from her door, her eyes half closed against the waning sunlight as she leaned against a tree and watched a child tend to a flock of geese. Rhiannon called out to her softly, and she quickly leapt to her feet.

"How may I serve you, milady?"

"My hair, Magdalene, brush it out for me, please. And help me dress. Quickly."

"Aye, milady!"

Magdalene had magic in her fingers as she worked

on Rhiannon's hair. The woman began to chatter, talking about the fine display that morning when all of the men had started off to do battle. "The king is always so magnificent, and one never knows quite why. He is not taller, nor larger, nor more imposing, than other men. Still, he is Alfred. The Great. That is what men say. From other kingdoms, they call him Alfred the Great. So he is glorious in himself. But, milady, your lord is ever so imposing! He sits that great beast with such grace and confidence and beauty. And where his eyes fall, a maiden might well swoon. Oh, I tell you—"

"Please, Magdalene, do not tell me!" Rhiannon implored her. She smiled to take away the bite of her words. "They've all gone to war," she said hastily. "We must pray for them."

"Oh, your husband will survive, milady! He rode from here just like a god! He is magnificent, so tall, so golden, with such bronze muscles. Oh! I tell you—"

"Magdalene!"

"I am dreaming!" Magdalene continued despite Rhiannon's warning. She dropped the hairbrush and fell back on the bed, running her hands over the sheets in a way that annoyed Rhiannon to an extreme. "I tell you, I shall marry one of them! I shall have a beautiful Viking husband such as yours."

"He's Irish," Rhiannon found herself arguing perversely.

"He's all Viking," Magdalene said.

"Magdalene! The king and our good men have gone off to risk their lives against the Vikings. You mustn't speak so."

"Oh, of course!" Magdalene came quickly to her

feet and began to wring her hands nervously. "I meant no treason, lady—"

"I know that you did not," Rhiannon said wearily. "Help me with a shift and tunic, and I think that I will have you braid my hair. Then you may go."

"The queen wishes to see you!" Magdalene remembered suddenly.

Rhiannon sighed. She did not want Alswitha's sympathy. It was too late for that. But she had to see her and the other women, and she might as well get it over with.

She dressed quickly with Magdalene's help, then made her way slowly to the manor house. The children greeted her in the doorway and she found herself picking up the little ones and hugging them close to avoid Alswitha's eyes. But in time the queen insisted that she sit and have something to eat, and then it was all much worse than she had imagined. Alswitha tried to assure her that every woman's wedding night was a misery, even if she married a gentle lord, even if she married a man she happened to love. As the queen assured her that it would get better, that the pain would go away, she found herself staring down at the table. She couldn't speak, she could barely breathe.

"Did he hurt you so badly, then?" the queen demanded, distressed.

"No!" Rhiannon gasped out.

"Oh, dear—"

Rhiannon rose, clenching her fingers into fists at her sides as she fought for control. "He—he did not hurt me!" she said, vehemently. "Oh, please, for the love of God, Alswitha, must we talk about this?"

"No, no, of course, not." The queen was suddenly silent, looking behind her. Rhiannon realized that someone had come into the hall, that someone was standing silently behind her. She spun about.

It was the old man with the endlessly long beard and wrinkled and weathered face. He wore long robes and a curious hat, and he watched her with grave, fathomless eyes.

"Rhiannon," Alswitha said. "This is Mergwin, Eric's . . ." She had been about to say "servant," Rhiannon was certain. But looking at this man, she knew that no man or woman would ever dare call him a servant.

"I am Mergwin," he said to Rhiannon. "Some call me Druid, and some call me madman, but I am loyal to the Ard-ri of Ireland, and to his house. I have come to take you home."

"Home?" For a moment, Rhiannon's breath caught, and her heart seemed to beat too quickly. Home. *His* home? Did he mean to take her across the sea? She would not go, they could not force her to do so.

"Back to the coast. We will await Eric there."

"Oh." Her breath escaped her. She wanted to deny him, because she wanted to deny anything that Eric might have a hand in.

But there was nothing for her here. She loved Alswitha and the children, but she felt a certain distance from them now too. Alfred was gone to war, as was Rowan. And Eric too.

"Perhaps you should stay—" Alswitha began.

"No! No thank you, but I think that I would like to go home." She smiled at the ancient man with the long, tumbling beard. "Mergwin." She watched his eyes. Dark eyes, ancient eyes. She remembered how he had smiled at her during the wedding. He had been her only assurance, a man she had never seen before.

He looked as if he could be a testy old fellow, she thought fleetingly.

But she liked him. She sensed something in him, something warm and trustworthy. "Yes, I'd like to go home."

Alswitha said that arrangements would be made for horses and an escort, but Rhiannon was barely listening. She kept watching the old man.

Then she kissed Alswitha and the children goodbye and started out with Mergwin. In the yard before the manor, preparations were already being made. The majority of the men were with the king, but Rhiannon was to have an escort. Two lads, younger than she, were ready to ride, and old Kate from the kitchens was busy packing their bags so that they might have a fine meal when they paused for the evening.

Again Alswitha expressed her concerns, but Rhiannon kissed her quickly on the cheek, then mounted the bay mare Alswitha had supplied her.

For his age, Mergwin managed to mount his horse with a surprising agility and ease. He caught Rhiannon watching him and scowled. "When I'm too old to be useful, young woman, then I shall pass on to my just rewards!" He sniffed, and Rhiannon wondered what he would consider his just rewards to be. She lowered her head, hiding a smile. With the children and the king's household waving, they started on their way.

They hadn't ridden far from the complex at Wareham before Rhiannon rode up by the Druid's side.

"He will return, won't he?" she said. "You know that he will. Eric of Dubhlain will return from this battle."

He eyed her curiously. "Yes. He will come home."

"And the king?"

"The king is destined for very great things."

"Then he, too, will come home."

"For now."

"For now?"

The Druid's eyes were on her intently. "This is but the beginning, milady. The hornet's nest is being disturbed, and all hell will break loose. But it is all to come, and what happens as destiny unfolds is not clear to my understanding."

"How do you know this?" Rhiannon demanded.

He arched a snow-white brow. "How do I know this? Listen," he told her. "Listen to the trees, to the thunder in the ground, to the tempest in the sea. Listen and you will know."

Rhiannon tossed back her hair. "You knew that Eric would marry me. Before he and Alfred agreed upon it."

The Druid nodded.

"And you're going to tell me that it was destiny."

"Written upon the wind."

"I tell you," she cried suddenly, passionately, "nothing—*nothing*—is written on the wind! Or in the tempest of the sea, or in the breeze in the forest! We build our own destiny, and I shall have mine, despite your Irish prince!"

He was silent for a moment, ignoring her outburst. Then he smiled at her, amusement lacing his dark eyes. "He is *your* Irish prince now, wouldn't you say, milady?" Then he nudged his horse and trotted forward, and Rhiannon was left to stare after him, wondering if indeed she had encountered a new enemy or found a new, intriguing friend.

She nudged her own mount to a faster gait. She was going home. If nothing else, there would be solace in that.

The foot soldiers followed behind while the men with mounts thundered down the field toward the fortifications at Rochester. The Danes had built their own siege fortifications, but even as the first English troops bore down upon the ramparts, it became obvious that the Danes had chosen retreat.

Eric skirted the wooden ramparts of the walled town and chased around its circumference, certain that the attackers had taken a slow leave from their posts and sought the forests before them. They dared not let those Danes escape, for the Danish force would still be full and vital and ready for another attack.

On the great white stallion, Eric charged his enemies. His battle cry could be heard on his lips, just as his deadly standard of the wolf flew nearby as his men followed his line of attack. At the edge of the forest they engaged in battle.

Eric's first contestant was a fierce graybeard swinging a double-headed ax. From his position atop the stallion, Eric swooped low to avoid the deadly swing of the weapon and brought his sword down smoothly upon the man's neck. He fell in silence, already dreaming of Valhalla.

It would be a quick and merciful battle, Eric thought.

He bested others, for it seemed that the strength of the gods, Christian and Norse, were with him that day. Opponents streamed toward him, yet he was not so much as nicked. Rollo fought near him, and he, too, seemed to lead a charmed life. No matter how many men charged toward them, they neither faltered nor failed, and as time passed, they realized they stood alone in their field of fallen enemies. There was a certain commotion to their left, down one of the deep gullies by the forest. They exchanged glances, then swerved their mounts and hurried along the ridge to come riding down hard upon the scene of action.

Saxons were engaged with a score of Danes—berserkers, from the looks of many. The Danes were outnumbering the Saxons two to one. Eric grinned to Rollo. "Shall we?"

"Who wants to live forever?" Rollo queried him.

"Aye, who wants to live forever?" Eric echoed.

Riding hard together, they came into the fray. The ground was too rugged to maneuver the stallion, and Eric dismounted. He was quickly attacked by a young redhead who assured him that he had best kiss the sweet taste of life good-bye. "Child of a she-goat!" The Dane snarled.

Eric parried his sword thrust, leapt back, and caught the man in the throat with the point of his blade. He stepped over his fallen enemy. "Lad, I assure you, you never saw any woman quite so magnificent as my mother."

He looked across the gully. He was startled to see that several Danes, heavily weaponed and wearing chain mail and faceplates, were circling one lone Saxon defender.

The man was Rowan.

Certain death faced him, but the lad met it bravely and well, taunting his attackers. "Come, then, you sorry devils, come one, come all. Of course I shall die, but I shall take at least one of you with me. Who shall it be? Come, come on! You face me like a pack of women, you putrid and pathetic stench from hell. Come!"

Rowan was afraid, Eric sensed, but the man's show of courage was more than admirable. He waved his sword in the air, and the weapon caught a ray of sunlight that streaked through the trees.

The Danes would be upon him in a minute.

Eric wasted no more time but leapt atop the stallion and raced quickly toward the scene, his sword slicing and hacking. Men screamed and fell away, stunned by the sudden attack. He leapt from the stallion and fought on savagely.

Rowan cried out and entered into the battle himself, stepping forward aggressively and engaging the men who had taunted him and come upon him as a deadly horde. Within minutes Eric realized that Rollo had joined him, too, and they were then three against the horde, their backs their walls of defense as they came close to fight any new threat.

But the battle was over. Men lay dead upon the

ground in grotesque and haphazard abandon. Those Danes who had survived had fled.

Alfred came riding into the gully. He looked about at his own fallen men, at the number of the enemy. The king was silent for long moments. "We did not stop many," he said.

"They seemed many enough," Rollo commented dryly.

"Aye, good Rowan here was engaged with plenty," Eric said.

Rowan glanced his way, flushing. He looked at the king. "I'd be dead now, Sire, were it not for the Prince of Eire."

Eric shrugged and walked among the fallen, then stared up at the king. The priest, Asser, had come up behind Alfred. "We need to find and bury all of our dead. If the Danes decide to come back for the bodies—"

"We will take care of our own," the king quickly assured him. Their eyes met. They had both survived many a battle. They had seen what the Vikings, as victors, could do. Prisoners might well be disemboweled, burned alive, or find their organs used for cooking skins. The injured were best off dead, and the dead were best off in hell.

Eric mounted the white stallion again and followed the king from the gully and toward the walls of Rochester. The gates were opening, and the starving populace was rushing forward to meet their deliverers.

That night in Rochester they learned that the Danes had truly run in haste. They had left behind their prisoners and many of their horses.

Alfred was glad to claim both.

That night they feasted within the hall of a manor in Rochester. The fire lay in the center of the room, with a flue to the night above. Deer and sheep taken from the surrounding countryside were set on spits above the flame to roast for the hungry defenders of Rochester, for the king and his retinue. Eric sat by the king as the great haunches of meat were sliced from the roasting animals and served to the fighting men by lads and wenches.

The mood within the manor was triumphant and wild. English storytellers rose to speak of the exploits of their king, and one of Eric's Irish bards created a splendid recitation on his prince's prowess during the day. Eric listened with a certain amusement, but he was startled when young Rowan rose and lifted his cup to him. "To the prince who has twice saved my life! My undying loyalty, so I do swear it!"

Cheers went up. Eric rose, startled that he could feel so awkward among men. Rowan was advancing toward him. He knelt before him. "Your servant, my lord, always," Rowan swore humbly.

Eric reached down and forced the man to rise, taking him by the shoulders. "No, Rowan," he said smoothly. "Be not my servant. Be my friend."

The cheers went up louder and louder. Rowan's youthful, winning smile touched something deep inside of Eric. The young man was no coward, and no fool. There was strength about him, and humility and honor.

Rowan had loved Rhiannon, and Rhiannon had loved him. It had been easy to dismiss their youthful infatuation before. Well, perhaps not easy, for a certain rage and jealousy had admittedly plagued him.

But now he liked the lad, and he was sorry for the two of them. They had loved.

As he had loved Emenia.

As they stared at each other, a curious music was heard.

It came from a long flute, and once the music had begun, a hush settled over the room. The music was not the only entertainment beginning.

A dark-skinned girl with dark, almond-shaped eyes had moved before the fire. Her hair was ebony and fell well below her waist. She stood very still, and then her body began to sway subtly to the music before her limbs began to move.

She was incredibly graceful and beautiful. She was exotic beyond belief with her slanted eyes and warm, honey-toned skin, and when she moved, the sheer gauze drapery she wore floated about her and defined the full, sweet perfection of her figure. The music was slow, haunting; it swept into the flesh and the blood, and it was spellbinding.

Other than the music and the rustle of her movements, the room was silent. All eyes were upon the girl.

Eric watched her undulations, smiling for a moment. Then something about the dance reminded him of another such performance he had too recently witnessed. Rhiannon. When she had moved with sinuous grace, when she had told her tales with her soft, sultry siren's voice . . .

The room had been silent then too. Her hair had cascaded about her in sunset and golden waves as she taunted the men the way this vixen did now. She had held them all captive with her sway.

Even now, watching this almond-eyed temptress, he was reminded of his wife. He clenched his teeth and swore silently. He did not want to be reminded of her in his every waking moment. Nor did he want to dream of her.

Rollo sat down beside him. The smoke from the fire was rising. The girl seemed more and more a creature of myth and mystery, magical, elusive.

"She is one of the Dane's prisoners, left behind in their hurry to escape, so the steward here has told me. She was taken in a raid along the Mediterranean Sea, and it is whispered that she seeks a new master. It seems to me that her eyes are frequently falling upon you."

Were they? Eric didn't know. He had stared at the girl but had been lost in thought.

She swirled before him, to a faster, more exotic rhythm. The gauze about her was slowly disappearing as she cast various veils off and away from her body. Honeyed arms and shoulders and the mounds of her breasts were revealed. Slim pants hugged her hips, and a narrow band of the gauze barely concealed the tips of her breasts. She moved faster and faster, spinning before him in her bare feet. The music rose then suddenly ceased. She tossed her head back and forth and came to her knees before Eric.

Again the room was very still. There was not even the sound of music now. Eric could clearly hear the rise and fall of the girl's breath. She raised her head slowly, and her almond eyes touched his.

He felt the gaze of everyone in the room. He smiled slowly, then applauded.

The king spoke. "The girl is a slave. She is giving herself to you."

There was nothing in Alfred's voice to betray his thoughts. Eric was certain, however, that the king had a definite opinion on the proper way to handle the situation.

He turned to Alfred.

"I fought for your banner here today, Alfred. All that is taken today falls into your coffers, to be divided by you among the men."

The king, irritated, waved a hand, dismissing the woman. Unhappily she rose. Slowly, with several backward glances, she left the central hall of the manor.

The hounds began to nuzzle about the outskirts of the fire, seeking bones and leftovers. Men began to move again, rustling the rushes beneath their feet.

Eric stared at the king. "Neither of us watched this girl tonight, Alfred. Both of us were thinking of another such performance."

"One that brought you a wife."

"And you an alliance. The marriage was a contract between us."

The king's eyes narrowed. "So you intend to take the heathen harlot?"

Eric grinned and slowly shook his head. "Nay, Sire. I intend to give her to another."

The king's brows rose.

"Rowan," Eric said. "The lad has lost much. I think perhaps he deserves recompense."

Eric rose, suddenly very weary. He was losing his mind. He should not have given the girl away. He should have kept her to remind them all that he was his own man, that he would not be ruled by a woman, be that woman his wife and kin to the king.

He stared down at Alfred. The king looked up at him and said, "I am well pleased with our alliance. I would offer you anything taken here today."

"Even the girl?"

Alfred winced. "Even the girl."

Eric hesitated. "I don't want her," he said. "Good night, Alfred, King of England. She has reminded me that I am eager to return to what will be my home. There is much damaged, and I would see it righted."

He turned and walked from the hall. There were rooms surrounding the central hall in the manor with its warm central fire, and he had taken one for his own.

A rich down mattress lay atop a large rope bed, and there he stretched out. He closed his eyes; his sword, Vengeance, at his side, his hand upon it. He never slept out of reach of it.

The events of the day played before his weary mind, and then he began to drift toward sleep. He saw the almond-eyed girl dancing before him, half naked. Then the girl changed and she was his wife. Rhiannon.

Her hair flowed about her like the softest curtain of flame. It cascaded over her naked limbs and tumbled around her. Then she lay on her back, and the sounds around them were the sounds of a babbling brook. She beckoned to him, she smiled, she urged him to come to her. He lowered himself between the softness of her thighs and pressed her back into the lush green foliage of a sweet-smelling and verdant earth.

He stroked her hair and moved his fingers upon her, and he felt something sticky; it was blood.

He awoke with a sudden start.

All was still darkness around him. His door to the hall lay ajar, and men still lay about the fire sleeping or passed out cold, as if dead.

She was in no danger, he thought. Why did thoughts of her death haunt him so?

It was rather she who longed for his throat, he reminded himself.

He needed to sleep. The only physical wound he had received had been from her, but still, the day had been long and hard, if victorious. And tomorrow he wanted to ride like the wind. He had paid his part of his agreement, and he would continue to pay it. The Danes would certainly rise again to avenge the battle here today.

But for now . . .

He wanted to wake in the morning and ride like the wind. He wanted to claim what was his.

He lay back down and closed his eyes.

He dreamed again and slept restlessly. He kept dreaming that she was in danger, and he woke again and again.

She was in no danger. She was in Mergwin's care, and he would protect her from all things that a warrior might, and then some.

The dawn had barely broken when he gave up and rose. Irritated, he strode from the room and found Rollo by the fire, his great head cradled in his arms. Eric gave him a shove with a booted foot.

"Rouse the others," Eric commanded. "It's time to ride."

Rollo blinked, then quickly rose. There was movement as men began to awaken.

Eric walked out to meet the cool spring morning. Dew lay on the grass, and a soft misty fog closed around him. Rochester was an impressive town. The Danes had wanted it badly.

They would come back.

He called to a young lad and asked that his horse be brought from the stables and that word be sounded that he intended to ride with his men. Minutes later his men were ready with the Danish riches they had plundered from the fortifications. Eric was startled to see Rowan mounted to ride with him, the dancing girl seated behind him.

"The king does not come now," Eric said, riding to his side.

"I know. He has agreed that I should serve you," Rowan said.

He stared at the boy hard, his gaze cold and level. Rowan had proven to be many things—could he prove to be a traitor too?

He was master of his own will, and of his own house, Eric reminded himself. Rowan was welcome to ride with him. He would keep a keen eye upon the lad and on Rhiannon.

"Then we ride!" Eric told him.

He called out to his men and started forward.

For home, he thought.

And for his . . . wife.

And, he thought, a slow smile touching his features, for all of the promises she had made to him.

He would see that she kept them. Every single one.

11

It had been good to come home.

So many people near and dear to her were gone now, lost in the senseless battle with Eric's men. And still it was good simply to come home, to come to her own manor.

Nothing within her house had been touched, and in the time since she had fled the coast, much that had been damaged had been rebuilt.

And coming home, she had found Adela at last.

Her mother's cousin, Adela was nearing sixty. She was a sprightly lady with a keen eye and a quick wit, and she had been with Rhiannon for years. She had been hiding out in the household of one of the tenant farmers until Rhiannon had come home, but once Adela had seen Rhiannon's return and the careful, quiet respect given her by the Vikings left in charge, she had dared to venture to the manor. There, Rhiannon had laughed and cried and hugged her, and she was now reinstalled in her own room.

"Peter and his family were quite good, and they took a grave risk in shielding me!" Adela told her sagely, glad to dress again in her own clothing after she had bathed and stretched out on her large rope bed with the fine down mattress. "But, oh, what a place! Wee little ones everywhere, and a pile of straw and a dusty blanket upon the floor. Oh, my dear, I do tell you, my aching arse! Ah, but I do go on! What of you, my love?"

The question had been asked so tenderly that Rhiannon had taken great care with her reply.

"I'm fine. I—I fled from here to Alfred, and then, and then Alfred came here—"

"I thought that the king had come!" Adela said. "But I didn't dare come out in case he hadn't. That blond giant made a quick stop to any of his men abusing the people, but I didn't know what he might think about kin to the lady of the manor! So now, tell me more, how have you managed to come back?"

"I married the blond giant," Rhiannon told her quietly.

"Oh!" Adela said, stunned. "Oh, of course. But what of Rowan?"

"Well," Rhiannon said, trying to smile, trying very desperately to find a bit of humor to offer Adela, "I believe this means that my marriage to Rowan is off."

"Oh, my dear child!" Adela clucked, her soft blue eyes very tender upon the girl. Then she, too, managed to smile brightly. "Ah, well, the Viking is quite a magnificent man! You should have heard his voice ringing with command—"

"I've heard it ring with command, thank you."

"A fierce fighter, yes, but a man of mercy."

"Mercy!" Rhiannon exclaimed.

Adela nodded gravely. "Once the battle was done, he would allow none to be harmed. Oh, my dear Rhiannon! Are you suffering so very much, then?"

"Of course not," Rhiannon lied. "The king requested that I marry, and I have done so. This is my land and these are my people, no matter what the Viking may think. I will not relinquish what is mine. Most marriages are made for convenience. I shall be quite all right. Now tell me more. So Peter and his family are alive and well. I am so very pleased." She hugged her cousin again. "And I am so very grateful to see you, what with poor Egmund dead and so many others!"

Egmund had been given a decent Christian burial, Adela was able to assure her, and so had the others. "Beneath the great oak by the eastern gate, we shall go and pray for their souls, if that will please you, my dear."

Rhiannon had prayed for Egmund and the others. She had visited the tenants and the serfs, she had expressed her grief at their losses, and she had promised to help them with the rebuilding of what had been destroyed. Then she had proclaimed a day that was to belong to the people only—they would do no work in her fields or for the manor but use all their time for their own devices. She had deer roasted that night, and ale from the manor given to all the people. Not one of the Vikings in residence had lifted a hand to stop her in any of her charities. Not even the tall redhead with the massive shoulders who seemed to be in charge, the one called Sigurd. If he protested her giving away the contents of his master's larder, he made no comment. He barely spoke at all, not when he supped with her and Mergwin and Adela in the morning or at night.

She always knew, though, that he was there. That he watched her.

Standing upon the parapets with the dawn, looking out over her small walled town, Rhiannon could see that life was going on very much as before for the serfs and tenants and artisans. Men were at work in the fields. It was spring, and the most salient fact to the average man was that it was planting season. They all must eat to live.

Rhiannon knew that her relationship with her people was a good and an important one. The serfs were hers, not slaves but very much like slaves. They were born to her manor, and they would live out their lives there. They would work to serve her all of their days, or if someone chose to move on, then that person would need Rhiannon's blessing. She was a kind mistress, careful to fulfill the laws that had been set down for all men, and fair in disputes.

But a serf's service to his master or mistress was an ancient payment in return for protection. She had failed sadly to protect her people. Even if it had not been her fault, even if her fighting forces had been with the king, even if she had been betrayed, she had nevertheless let down her people, and it grieved her.

She sighed softly, watching the oxen and men move out on the multicolored fields. The Vikings had come. Eric had men in the house who, though painstakingly polite to her, watched her constantly. They made no move to interfere with her now that she had returned, but when she came down to sup in the morning or in the evening, they were there. Where poor Egmund should have sat was a Viking.

They might claim to be Irishmen, but they were Vikings.

She shivered. Would they say such a thing of her

children in twenty to thirty years? Nay, they are not
English, they are Vikings!

She paled at the thought. She could not possibly
have children with the blond giant who so recklessly
and heedlessly claimed his own way. He was a
stranger.

He was no stranger, she thought. Not after their
wedding night. A flush touched her cheeks, and she
remembered the long ride home with Mergwin and
her escort. She had been fascinated with the old
Druid who had entertained her with various tales on
the way home. He had told her about the coming of
St. Patrick to Eire, and how he had chased all of the
snakes away, and about the meaning of Irish hospitality and how no man could be turned away if he
needed a bed or a meal; about Aed Finnlaith, the
great Ard-ri, who had gathered the many kings together to meet the Viking threat.

"And still," she remarked, "the Vikings took Dubhlain!"

Mergwin smiled and shrugged. "And formed a pact
with the Ard-ri. And since then, other than sporadic
Danish raids, there has been peace. The Ard-ri
spends much time in Dubhlain, and his many grandchildren tame the land and subdue restless nobles.
Olaf the White, the Wolf of Norway, speaks the Irish
language far more frequently than his own. He
dresses in Irish royal splendor and creates strong Irish
fortifications. He is far more the defender of the land
than an invader."

"Now," Rhiannon insisted. "But he came as an invader."

"His children are part of Eire. Just as the child you carry now will be part of Alfred's united England."

She gasped, staring at him sharply. "I carry no child—"

"But you do."

"You can't know that! You can't possibly know that!"

He shrugged. "As you would have it. But it is a boy, and you will call it Garth."

Again she had gasped, because if she had ever had a son and a choice, she would indeed have named him for the father she had loved so dearly and so briefly. If a Viking would allow such a thing. How could this man know such things?

"You have been talking to Alfred," she murmured.

He didn't answer her, and she knew that was not the case. And now, staring out across the fields blindly, Rhiannon remembered his words so clearly. He could not know! No one could know so very soon.

She sucked in her cheeks. She could not bear the Viking's child. A legal heir was something he might truly want, and she couldn't bear the thought of giving him anything that he desired.

She closed her eyes and remembered the night of their wedding, wondering if it could be true. "Dear God, by all the saints, preserve me!" she whispered aloud, then shuddered. "I shall not listen to the heathen gibberish of a Druid!" she swore.

Then she started, staring hard over the parapet.

Riders were coming. At first she could only see the great mass of a large group of riders on the horizon. They were racing hard. Dirt flew and spewed about them. Then, as they came closer and closer, she could make out the individual riders. She could see the standards flying.

And in the front she could see the great white stallion and the chain mail that Eric of Dubhlain wore to battle glinting in the sun. He rode with his visor up, his silver helmet atop his head, and he rode with the confidence of a god. Behind him, a man rode with his standard carried high, the sign of the wolf.

They'd come back! And so very quickly too. She had prayed for the king's victory, but she had not expected it to come so soon.

She had not expected to see Eric of Dubhlain so soon.

The horns began to sound, heralding the warriors' return. Rhiannon stared down from the parapet for what seemed like forever, feeling the pounding of her heart. Then she determined that she would come down, greet him, doing so with tremendous dignity.

She didn't owe him anything—he had tricked her —but she would greet him.

She hurried down the steps and into the manor and to her own room. She looked around, feeling a strange quivering seize hold of her again. Her room, yes, but he had claimed it when he had come. His trunks were there—trunks filled with clothing and furs and with weapons, and maps and books painstakingly created by Irish monks in monasteries. She had tentatively, then boldly, searched through his belongings, and she had thought most seriously about choosing another place to sleep. But despite her unwillingness to admit it, she was afraid of him. Or perhaps what she felt was not so much fear. Perhaps it was merely that she was coming to know him very well. If he chose it, then perhaps his wife might be allowed to sleep elsewhere. If he did not choose, then he would hunt her down and drag her back, and he would consider it his right.

And all the laws of England would uphold him.

She found her brush upon her dressing table and drew it through the length of her hair, then smoothed down her tunic and quickly assessed her choice of clothing for the day. She wore a white linen tunic with finely stitched embroidery about the bodice and sleeves. It was not a gown for a royal occasion, but it was an attractive one that enhanced the color of her hair.

What did she care what she wore? she wondered. Perhaps she must take care to wage a more civil battle against him now, but they were still enemies. To the death.

She came down the stairs to the main hall and strode across the room. Adela had been busy by one of the windows with her needlework, but she was smiling with mischief in her eyes and was quick to rise when Rhiannon came. "So the giant returns."

Rhiannon cast Adela a quick gaze and swallowed down a nervous retort. "Yes, Adela, come. You must meet him. Don't be afraid of him."

"Oh, I'm not afraid at all!" her cousin assured her.

Adela followed her out the heavy double doors to the yard before the house. Far to her left, the gates were being opened. Sigurd and Mergwin were already there, awaiting their lord.

Her heart beating wildly, Rhiannon clenched her hands to her sides as she stood in the early-morning sunlight. He must have ridden through the night, she thought, to arrive so early.

The horses began to thunder through the gates. Eric still rode in the lead. His silver helmet lay in his hand now; his great wolf standard still flew high behind him. Arriving in the yard, he quickly dismounted. Stable lads were quickly there to take the white stallion from him. Huge in his mail armor, Eric smiled at Mergwin and Sigurd, and then his eyes roamed quickly to the steps where Rhiannon stood, her hands still clenched tightly at her sides. She thought there was grave amusement in his eyes as they flickered over her. Perhaps there was a challenge.

He stood tall in the sunlight, watching her with those startling blue eyes. She wondered if perhaps he was thinking that she should come to him, but that she would not do. Then it was no matter, for Sigurd had stepped forward and was demanding the news of the battle, and Eric had clapped him on the shoulder and assured him that it had been a total rout. He greeted Mergwin and asked after his health, and then he was coming toward Rhiannon. She was having difficulty breathing.

She suddenly could not forget how he had first come to this hall; she could not forget the raw physicality of that first battle and meeting.

He stood before her, his visored helmet still beneath his arm, his armor adding bulk to his already huge size. She was certain then that his eyes held a challenge, along with the amusement. "My lady, my wife, how pleased I am that you have come here so anxious to greet me."

She was certainly not pleased to greet him, and he must know it very well. Nevertheless she smiled, feeling as if her face had cracked. "I would inquire after the king, Eric of Dubhlain."

"The king fares quite well. Would you not inquire after *my* health?"

"I am not blind, my lord. I can see very well that your health is excellent, is it not?"

"Most excellent. I've a nagging scar upon a thigh from a previous arrow wound, but I come from this foray unscathed. I am sure that must please you greatly to hear."

Her smile was frozen in place. "Greatly."

He leaned low, taking her hand, whispering for her ear alone, "What a liar you are, milady. You were desperately wishing that I would arrive with my entrails hanging from my tattered flesh."

"Nay, my lord, I was desperately wishing that you would not return at all," she said sweetly. She raised her voice. "You must be very weary from your long ride."

"I'm not really weary at all," he told her. "I have ridden quite furiously for the promise of . . . home."

She turned about, ready to enter the house and have done with the charade they must play before the others. But it wouldn't end, of course. Rollo would enter with him, and perhaps others of his captains, and they had to be served ale and whatever meal could be quickly assembled. She would see to that for him. And then she would see to it that she managed to be somewhere else for the day.

She nearly tripped over Adela. Eric saw the woman

then for the first time, for he frowned, pulling Rhiannon back. "And who might this be?"

"Adela, milord! Your wife's woman."

"My cousin," Rhiannon corrected, giving Adela a stern look.

Adela bobbed prettily and gracefully, her light eyes dancing. "I'm quite pleased to see you back, safe and well."

Eric smiled slowly, and then he started to laugh. "Adela, eh? Come, then, and drink with us. I'm sure that my wife is most eager to drink to Alfred's latest victory."

Rhiannon said nothing. His every word seemed to be double-edged. He did enjoy taunting her so very much. But she would never be his hapless victim, she vowed; she would never surrender. Let him have his little joke now; the last laugh would be hers.

Rollo came up behind her husband then, greeting her with a kiss upon the hand. Others began to fill the hall.

Rhiannon's heart seemed to flutter fiercely and then seemed to cease beating as she noted a very familiar face among the crowd of warriors.

Rowan's face. Her onetime betrothed had followed her husband to the very hall that should have been his own.

She felt the blood seep from her face, and more. She felt her husband's eyes hard upon her, even as he responded to something that Adela had to say to him.

Rowan.

He was laughing at some man's jest when his gaze met hers. The laughter faded quickly from his eyes.

Gravely he bowed his head to her in acknowledgment, then turned away.

A heavy, gauntleted hand fell upon her arm, pulling her around. She raised her face, pale and translucent, to meet her husband's searing blue stare.

"Aye, wife," he said to her softly, "young Rowan is with me. Alive and quite well, as you will notice."

She determinedly pulled her arm from his grasp. He let her go. "Why is he here?" she demanded. "What new cruelty is this?"

"No cruelty, madam. He chose to serve me."

"I don't believe you!"

"Do you see the man in chains? No, my dear wife, he walks about freely. I happened upon a chance to wrest his life from certain Danes, and I believe that he is grateful."

"You saved his life?" His smugness and arrogance irritated her beyond all reason. "You are a fool, great Irish wolf," she said very sweetly, spitting out the last words. "Perhaps I am still mindlessly in love with him. Perhaps he is still mindlessly in love with me. And perhaps we will both betray you in this very place."

He was silent for so very long, not a muscle twitching in his fierce, striking face. Despite herself, she felt a churning in her stomach and wished that she had not spoken so.

But then one golden brow arched high as he stared at her, and she wondered desperately what he was truly thinking. He shrugged, and she nearly screamed when he took her hand between both of his, bending low once again to brush her flesh with his lips. "I think not, my lady. Truly I think not. Rowan will not betray me for his honor. And you will not betray me, for if you do, I shall flay your naked back and buttocks until your lesson is well learned."

This time when she tried to wrench away from him, he chose not to let her go.

"Leave me be!" she whispered desperately. "You've a hall filled with companions! Would you not be a welcoming host?"

"Nay, I would be the lord, madam. I intend to bathe and change before supper."

"Don't expect me to entertain your men!" she protested.

"I do not," he assured her. "I expect you to entertain me."

Her eyes widened, and she wrenched her hand away in earnest. "Eric, you cannot mean—"

"But I do, my love. Your endearing words regarding Rowan have brought sharply to mind a vision and a memory. I see again my wife, cloaked in little more than the splendid beauty of her hair, promising me anything if young Rowan should live. Promising to serve me in any way. Any way at all."

"But he lived already!"

"I could not have promised not to slay him had he already lain dead, my love."

"Oh! You know what I mean. You tricked me. You had already made up your mind. You sat there atop that stallion of yours—of mine—and you let me make a fool of myself—"

"You promised to give me all that was owed to me."

"I owe you nothing."

"On the contrary," he told her, his eyes blue fire as

they bored into hers, his grip upon her nearly merciless. "You owe me much and I have come to collect."

"Not here, not now—"

"Adela!" he called sharply, interrupting Rhiannon.
Adela turned about quickly. Eric gave her a handsome smile that seemed to charm her at once.

It chilled Rhiannon to the bone.

"Lady, would you be so kind as to order servants to
see that the tub is brought to my lady's and my bedchamber? And see that much steaming water is
brought, and perhaps some wine. And then, Cousin
Adela, perhaps I could also count on you to see to the
welfare of my men within this hall. I imagine you
were accustomed to such a role within this place before the confusion of our coming. Since we were not
expected, I imagine that it will take some time for
meat to be roasted and a supper prepared. If you will
see to things until then . . . ?"

"Certainly, milord," Adela said, and quickly turned
toward the kitchen entrance to carry out the task she
had been given.

Watching her go, Rhiannon spoke up quickly.
"Eric, surely such behavior on our part would be
most rude—"

"Walk by my side, lady, or over my shoulder. I care
not which way you accompany me, but accompany
me you shall."

"You are doing this to me because Rowan is in the
hall!" she accused him stubbornly.

"Nay, my lady and wife. I'm doing this because it
will give pleasure to me—and perhaps not to me
alone."

An ice shield seemed to fall over his eyes as he

gazed down upon her. Deep inside she felt the chill, and then the cold was gone, and she felt a searing heat instead. Her mouth felt dry and she was trembling. She wanted to hate him—she did hate him—and despised what he was doing to her. But despite herself, she was remembering their wedding night.

And the feel of his hands upon her, moving over her. The feel of his lips brushing her mouth, searing her flesh.

She shook her head desperately. Rowan was in the hall. She had loved Rowan.

And he had never, never made her feel like this.

"Eric, I will not come with you now!"

"Give battle, lady, and I will best you every time!" he warned her.

"You will *not* win every time—"

"Aye, for I have been taught to win, or else there is nothing but death, and so I take all my battles to heart."

She opened her mouth to protest, but he was determined and did not make idle threats. He bent low and swept her up over his shoulder. The laughter and conversation within the hall suddenly ceased, and even as Rhiannon strained against him, he spoke with a light touch to those assembled in the hall. "Men, drink deeply and enjoy the rest that battle has awarded to us! My lady and I will rejoin you shortly."

There was laughter, and a promise of understanding from the crowd. Eric turned about. Rhiannon was swept against his mail-clad body as he headed swiftly for the stairway. Within seconds he had traversed the steps despite her whispered threats and flailing fists. Then they were within the bedchamber, and he tossed her down carelessly upon the bed with such force that she thought the rope supports would be torn to shreds. She quickly came up on an elbow, longing to scream and rail at him, but she only seethed inwardly as she realized that the wooden tub he had requested had arrived, that the kitchen lads were bringing pail after pail of steaming hot water into the room. Old Joseph from the kitchen set a leather gourd of wine with two silver cups upon a table. He never looked her way. None of them did. Eric was easy with the servants, thanking them when they departed and firmly bolting the door when they had gone.

He leaned against it then, watching her.

"Well?" he demanded at last.

"Well?"

"Come serve me, my love."

"You've lost your mind. One battle-ax too many has come across your skull, *my love.*"

"What a delightful cadence those words have upon your lips! I have not lost my mind. On the contrary, my memory is excellent. And I remember, love, that you—"

"You tricked me!" she reminded him.

He started to stride across the room to her, formidable indeed in his mail and the heavily padded garments beneath it.

She leapt from the bed before he could reach her.

"Eric—"

"Rhiannon! Come give me assistance with this mail now, or I vow you will come to regret it!"

"Don't threaten me."

"It is a grave and sincere promise."

"I can't—"

"You can. I'm quite certain that you've assisted often enough with armor. Come, assist me. Serve me. Perhaps that is all that I will require of you."

She stood still, her heart beating fiercely, and then she tossed back her hair and strode over to him impatiently. His helmet he had already cast aside. He reached low for the hem of the long, tuniclike piece that composed the bulk of the protective garment. He dipped low on one knee, and she helped slide it over his head. It was heavy; she lost her grasp and the metal thudded to the floor. "It is no matter," he told her impatiently. "My man will come for it. Get the straps."

He stood again, and Rhiannon silently walked around to his back, uncinching the leather ties that held his tunic in place so that he could bear the weight of the mail. He tossed the garment aside impatiently. Beneath it he wore only a linen shirt and hose and boots. He could manage those quite well himself, Rhiannon thought, and moved away from him.

But he sat in a chair and lifted a foot and stared at her. "Oh, come! You can remove your own boots."

"Yes, I can. But I prefer that you assist me." He smiled pleasantly. "I promise that I shall assist *you* in removing your clothing any time that you should desire."

"Thank you, but I shall not desire," she retorted pertly. He was still staring at her, still waiting and smiling. And even as he watched her it seemed that the heat crept slowly within her, swirling low within her belly and rising at long last to color her cheeks. "Oh, for the love of God!" she muttered. She strode over and pulled off his boot. He rested his hose-covered foot upon her backside as she set about removing his second boot. She jerked the boot from him as quickly as she could, and swirled about. Those Nordic blue eyes were still so hard upon her, yet his smile was in place. Lazily his lashes fell to half cover his eyes. "Thank you," he said mildly, rising. With his back to her, he stripped off his shirt and hose.

Rhiannon swallowed tautly as she saw his naked back and buttocks, the taut muscles that rippled with his every movement. She turned, staring at the wall as she heard him step into the tub."

Endless minutes seemed to pass. "May I go?" she inquired, fighting to keep her voice level and low.

"May you *what*?"

"Go! Leave this chamber! Attend to our guests."

"Attend to our guests? You mean that you are anxious to hostess that horde of Vikings out there?"

It was impossible to maintain her grasp upon her temper. She wasn't going to grovel and beg. She wasn't even going to ask his leave any longer. With an impatient oath she swung about and started for the door.

His voice cracked out at her like a whip.

"Don't do it," he warned.

To her great annoyance she felt her breath catching in her throat, her heart beating too quickly.

She did not open the door; she remained paused before it.

She was not a coward, she assured herself. But if she tried to leave, he would step naked from the tub and stop her. And after that . . . she did not know what he would do.

She swung around, crossing her arms over her chest, and stared at him. "You said that if I assisted you—"

"But I need more assistance," he said pleasantly.

"What do you want?"

"Come scrub my back. The rigors of battle are exhausting. I crave some comfort and peace."

Comfort and peace, my arse! Rhiannon thought, but she did not say the words aloud. Instead she waged war with the seething tremors inside of her and strode to the tub, trying very hard not to look upon his nakedness. She wrenched the cloth and soap from him and went around to his back. She scrubbed him with a desperate wish to remove his skin. She swallowed tightly as she covered the bronzed breadth of his shoulders and felt the vitality and sinewed heat beneath her hands. His golden hair lay dampened upon his flesh, curling over her fingers.

"There! I am done!" she told him impatiently, dropping the linen cloth and the cube of soap.

But he caught her wrist and dragged her around until she was beside him. The pressure he bore upon her brought her down to her knees, where his heavily lashed gaze met hers.

"But you are not done. You have only just begun."

"I—"

"Your touch upon my back was so very gentle and tender. I do know that I am well bathed. My chest now desires such a gentle caress."

Rhiannon lowered her eyes because she could not take the feel of his upon them anymore. Tensing her jaw, she caught hold of the cloth again and began to scrub his chest, averting her gaze from the parts of his anatomy that lay beneath the water. Huge expanses of muscle rippled beneath her fingertips, and her hands shook so that she could scarcely continue her task. "I did pray for you to die!" she whispered fiercely to him. She still could not meet his gaze, but she knew that his eyes were hard upon her.

"Ah, you must have been praying to the Christian god. You should have been praying to the gods of my father and the Danes. Perhaps Thor would have taken me in battle then, and carried me away to the halls of Valhalla—instead of delivering me unto your bedchamber."

"Perhaps," Rhiannon said. "I shall remember that next time." She started to stand, but he caught her wrist again. "My love, you're not finished."

"But I am."

He made a tsking sound. She knew that she reddened as he watched her, but there was no escape; his fingers were like iron handcuffs wound about her wrists. "To think of the long, lonely nights when I lay awake thinking about you and your sweet promise."

"You lie, milord. I'm sure that you rode to battle and did not give me a second thought. Perhaps you thought about your newly acquired lands, but—"

"Aye," he interrupted gravely, "I did think about the land." Their eyes touched and he smiled slowly. "I love the land. I love its ruggedness and its beauty and its bounty. I love the laughter of children at play in the meadows. I ache to see the people at peace so that the richness of the earth might increase. You love it too," he told her.

He did love the land; she had always sensed that about him. And she had to admit he seemed to have a high regard for human life—for a man who spent so many of his days at battle.

But Alfred battled too. Alfred, who cherished learning, his family, his home, his hearth, his god. Alfred was a warrior-king. He was still a compassionate man.

It was not easy to realize that this man, her enemy and yet her lord and husband, could also be a compassionate man. One who knew her perhaps better than she would care to have him know her.

Her eyes fell. "I love my people, milord."

"Aye, but the people are intricately interwoven with the land, are they not? And obviously you deal with this inheritance of yours well. The place has thrived in my absence."

Her eyes met his once again, locked in challenge. "But it is no longer my inheritance, is it?"

He smiled, leaning back comfortably, a smile curling his lips as he closed his eyes. "You are mine and the land is mine. I cherish you both."

"As you cherish Alexander."

"He is a remarkably fine stallion."

She lifted the bath cloth, heedless of repercussions, ready to douse his face with the soapy water. But his relaxed appearance was deceptive. Before she could move, he had opened his eyes and wound his fingers around her wrist. He held her tight, speaking in a deep, husky voice that held her to him with an even greater strength than that of his powerful arms.

"My wife, I did think of you. Night after night. I thought of the words of your sweet promise. You asked me not to slay your lover and he lives. Let me see if I can recall your exact words. Alas, I cannot, yet

I do remember you telling me that you would grant me anything, anything at all."

"You tricked me."

He shrugged. "I'll have what I want," he told her. "And I don't think that you mind your wifely duties so much as you protest you do. I do remember our wedding night with the greatest pleasure. Those soft, sweet—and not so soft and sweet—sounds that escaped you haunted my dreams when I lay alone in the darkness."

Again waves of crimson seemed over rush to her face. "Viking menace—" she began with all the dignity she could muster. But then she emitted a startled gasp as his arm suddenly snaked about her, dragging her, fully clothed, into the tub with him. Water sloshed out upon the wooden floor and she pressed hard against his chest, but he laughed, ignoring her. His fingers threaded into her hair, and he held her still as his mouth descended hungrily upon hers and his tongue began a foray over her lips and mouth that was both savage and seductive. Her heart hammered, and the steam of the water and the hard heat of his body surrounded her. And then his lips broke from hers as his fingers found the laces of her tunic. "You promised to come to me, to seduce and enchant as you did that day in the woods with your lover."

She caught his powerful fingers where they lay atop her breast. "You want what you cannot have, what you never earned, what I shall never give you! I was in love with Rowan—"

"In love!" He snorted derisively. "You toyed with a lad. You need a man."

"Ah, so you, sir, are so very old! Alas! Give me the

youth! What maid would require such a decrepit lover?"

"Not so decrepit yet, I think!" He laughed, then caught her hand and slid it slowly down the length of his body, adjusting her weight upon him. She gasped as he brought her fingers low beneath the water, over the steel planes of his belly, to close around his masculine shaft. Life and pulsing heat surged beneath her fingertips, seeming to swell ever larger with an awesome strength and desire. She wanted to wrench her hand away, but his remained over it. She wanted to turn from him, to cry, to protest. Her eyes remained locked with his and she did not cease to touch him.

He smiled slowly. Impatiently he shoved free the laces of her tunic, baring her breast. He pulled her close, and his lips closed over the fullness of her soft, feminine mound. His tongue bathed the growing hardness of her nipple and he suckled fiercely there, bringing a startling wave of intense pleasure to her. She cried out, and her fingers delved of their own volition into the length of his hair as he availed himself passionately of the sweet fruit of her body. His hand was beneath the sodden length of her garments, sliding along her bare flesh, stroking her upper thigh. His touch teased the very heart of her heat, then swept within her, deep within her, stroking, rotating, bringing her to the edge of abyss where she shuddered fiercely, alive with fire, longing to fight, knowing that she was lost. Stroking, stroking, touching so softly, so deeply . . . words caught within her throat and she choked and gasped, and then his lips were upon hers, sweeping away her protests and her cries.

He rose from the tub, cradling her within his arms.

Great sheets of water spilled from his naked body, as well as her sodden-clothed one. His eyes remained upon hers for long moments as the water drained from them, and then he set her down before the tub, caught her garment at the bodice, and rent the wet fabric with such strength that the many layers of her shift and once beautiful white gown fell in a heavy heap to the floor. She silently railed against herself for the color that came again to her cheeks and flooded her body, but she did not turn from him; she met his gaze with all the boldness and challenge that she could. And she was even somewhat glad of the slow, admiring smile and the light that touched his eyes as he gazed upon her. Aye, they were enemies, but despite herself, she was gratified that he admired her and was elated by the sight of him, by the sheer masculine beauty of his size and strength, by the raw and exciting power that lay within him. Aye, she was even glad of his arrogance, for perhaps it was that very confidence within him that lit the fires within her.

"You have utterly destroyed my gown," she told him dryly.

"You have others."

"Ah, sir, but I am your wife, your property, your chattel! What is mine is yours, and therefore, destroyed, is a loss to you. You will not always best the enemy. There will not always be new riches to conquer!"

"Alas, no, for my dear wife will now pray to the proper gods to see that I am destroyed!"

"You will not always win!" she persisted.

He reached for her, lifting her from the remnants of her clothing, sweeping her high into his arms once again. His eyes caught hers with their endless crystal-blue power, and his smile curved the fullness of his lip. "But, my love, I beg to protest. I do always win, and I promise you I will always do so."

She longed to deny him, but he was already moving, striding on long, muscular legs to the bed. This time when he deposited her upon it, he lowered his body along with hers. And she would have spoken, but he again claimed her lips. When his mouth moved from hers at last, it was to travel with tempest and heat to her earlobe, where he whispered that she was damp and delicious. His hand caressed her as his eyes met hers again, and he told her huskily where he would kiss and caress the lingering dewdrops of the bath from her body. His palm touched lightly upon her breast, and then his lips were there, and he laved the tightening sweet bud with his tongue, swept it into his mouth, grazed it with his tongue, and bathed it anew, leaving her gasping, surging against him, and tearing her fingers into his shoulders and hair. Any thoughts of denying that she wanted anything other than all that he offered her slipped away like the last, lingering rays of the setting sun.

He licked a final drop of water from her navel and traversed down the length of her belly, planting his weight between her thighs. And then he dared her to protest as his strong hands slid beneath her thighs, parting the sinewy length of her legs still further, and then began a soft, full caress of the pink petals of her deepest longing. His touch was light, sweeping, exploring, so taunting and seductive that rather than protest, she felt herself surge against him. And he obliged the sweet demand of her body, thrusting, sweeping, seducing with the touch of both his fingers and his tongue.

Deep, dark fantasies she'd never imagined began to burst forth within her. Soft cries tore from her throat once again, and she undulated without inhibition as he brought her higher. Great, shocking waves of ecstasy began to sweep through her. She shuddered violently as the peak began to rise within her like myriad starbursts on a velvet sky. And just when she thought that the pleasure was beginning to fade away, he caressed her deeply, all the way into her womb, and then he rose above her, filling her with the throbbing fullness of himself, and as he drove fiercely into her the waves of rapture began anew.

She bit into his shoulder, her fingers raking over his back. Shamelessly she clung to him, winding her legs around his waist, moving with him as he commanded her, finding the drive of his rhythm.

She did not want this, she thought very briefly. She did not want to give to him; she had promised to do so, but he had tricked her and betrayed her. . . .

Yet he was what she wanted more than anything in the world. Her kisses fell against his chest; she met the ardor of his mouth with an all-consuming passion. She marveled at the strength of the muscle beneath her fingertips, and she reveled in the strength of him that thrust with such great thirst and power between her thighs. The great, staggering waves of pleasure began to grow and build within her to renewed heights. Then it seemed that a sweetness so good that it was nearly unbearable filled her. The world blazed with light, and she was aware that he entered her even deeper . . . and deeper. . . .

The ecstasy peaked, sweeping through her. The shattering light turned to darkness even as she heard the harsh, guttural cry of her Viking husband, and he found the violence of his own release within the sheath of her body.

The light returned slowly. She still gasped for breath, and her body was being racked by tiny after-shudders.

He lay by her side upon an elbow, watching her. A wild tangle of her hair, still partially damp, created binding skeins of fire and gold between them.

He touched her cheek gently. She knew that he studied her, but she closed her eyes and did not move. She still trembled inwardly, wanting nothing more than to lay her head against him in exhaustion and find peace.

"I did dream about you, my love."

She wondered at first if the whisper was real, but then she knew that it was, for he pulled her gently against him until her head rested upon the great expanse of his chest. He stroked back her hair, smoothing out the tangled mass.

"I dreamed about this place, about the hues of the rocks and the cliffs. Mauves and purples and the green of spring."

"Ireland is green, so I hear," she murmured against his flesh. She couldn't see his face, but she could sense his smile.

"Aye, it is green. Beautiful, bountiful green. Yet Eire, too, has her colors. Her rocks and her cliffs. Her beauty and her peace."

" 'Tis not so peaceful here at all," Rhiannon said

softly. "Most often the gale winds blow. And the sea is treacherous. Storms are frequent."

"Aye, that is so," he agreed.

" 'Tis part of what you love, definitely your style."

He laughed softly. "And yours, too, I believe, milady. Aye, perhaps we are well suited."

There was still a tenderness to his voice, but suddenly it was frightening to her, as was the comfort she found at his side. It could not last. He did not love her, he toyed with her. He cared for her as he did the land —and Alexander! She must never allow herself to come too close to him. She must never depend on him.

Need him.

His hand moved along her back now. Idly. His fingers gentle and still arousing in their subtle touch. He caressed her shoulder and her arm. His touch teased the flesh on the underside of her breast. And it seemed all too natural that they should do so.

She bit her lip and raised her head as she tried to tug her hair free from him. His laughter, low and husky, taunted her. He raised himself over her again, his weight balanced upon the hard-muscled length of his arms.

"Alas, sweet wife, perhaps you might discover that you are in love with me—decrepit old man that I am!"

The sweetness of the passion and soft-spoken words between them was fading. All that remained was a sudden picture of his strong, handsome, and gloating Viking face, and the memory of the wanton desire he could draw from her so very easily.

"I shall never love you!" she promised hoarsely.

"This is just my conjugal duty. You give me no choice about that!"

His eyes did not seem so light; indeed, it was as if a glacial shield covered them, yet still they remained upon her. His smile did not alter. "Aye, lady, you've no choice. Bear that in mind always. You need not love me—you need only serve me. Perhaps we shall do very well. Love is such a painful emotion."

"You do not love me!" she reminded him.

"Good lord, no," he replied curtly. Still he did not move. His knuckles brushed over her cheek, and he added almost softly, "Heaven help the man who loves you! Heaven, Valhalla, and all of the gods, Christian and pagan."

Then abruptly he pushed up and leapt away from the bed with the grace of an acrobat despite his size. She started to turn away, reaching for a sheet to cover herself. She was yielding to the drowsiness that crept over her when his steely voice splashed across her like cold water. "Get up, my love, you've guests to entertain in the hall."

"I've guests to entertain?" she said coolly.

He reached for her, drawing her up before him. And God help her—just the touch of her body against his hardness warmed her anew, even as she met his gaze, hating him.

"As I've said," he whispered softly, "you need not love me. But you are my wife and you will serve me."

"I am not your slave!"

"Nay, Rhiannon, you are lady here. And so you will reign within the hall where you were born. And you will lie with me within this room, when I, as lord, demand it."

"We shall see."

"Indeed," he said, laughing, "we shall."

He pulled her into his arms once again and kissed her. The kiss ran passionate and deep, and she could not fight it. And then, mingled with the passion, there seemed to be the slightest touch of tenderness, and when his lips broke from hers at last, his eyes were nearly a cobalt blue, so hypnotizing that she could not begin to tear hers away. "Indeed," he murmured, "God help the fool who dares to love you, Rhiannon!"

Then he turned away again and reached into one of his trunks, dismissing her. "Dress quickly, we have lingered long enough."

"*We* have lingered? I did not—"

His eyes met hers again, silencing her. "But you did," he told her, his voice teasing, playful. "And you will do so again. And again. Now come."

Seething at his insinuation and at the sharp command in his voice, Rhiannon spun about to find some new clothing for herself. She kept her back to him as she donned a shift, and then she turned just slightly.

He was clad again in hose and slipping on a shirt, and she bit down hard upon her lip as she felt a trembling begin anew deep within her. His waist was so trim, his shoulders so broad. His arms were like steel, with their bands of muscle, and his thighs were as hard as tree trunks. Even now she longed to stroke the taut bronze of his skin and marvel at the feel beneath her fingertips.

He did not love her. . . .

He was her husband, and fate had cast them together.

She would not serve him! She would not!

And yet . . .

He cared for this place. For the land. For the people. For the children.

He started to turn, some sixth sense telling him that she watched him. Hurriedly she turned and drew out a new undergown and tunic, slipping into the more elegant powder-blue ensemble. Then she knew that he watched her. When she turned again, he was clad as an Irish prince in his shirt and ermine-lined short tunic, royal-blue hose and crimson mantle and brooch. He adjusted the dagger he was never without into the sheath at his waist and extended his hand to her.

"Shall we go, milady?"

"You dragged me here. Now you rush me."

"Alas, if you would rather stay, I would be very glad to ignore all rules of hospitality and linger with you awhile! You learn so swiftly, lady and wife, and yet there is so much more that I might show you. Surely my haste was unseemly, and I had nothing but dreams so long after the truly astonishing raptures of our wedding night. . . ." His voice trailed away, and the deep, husky sound of his laughter filled the room.

Rhiannon, herself, had determined to hurry. By the time he finished speaking, she had brushed her hair, donned her shoes, and quickly swallowed down a measure of the wine that had been left them. She stood at the door, jutting her chin proudly against his laughter.

"I see that you are ready, after all," he said. He took her hand and led her from the room.

In the hall he paused, kissing her hand, his eyes very blue as they probed hers in the shadows.

"You are, my love, incredibly beautiful." A wicked grin twisted his sensual mouth. "The afternoon has waned in splendor, and already I am anxious for the night."

She returned his gaze steadily, praying that he could not hear the fierce flutter of her heart or realize that just his words warmed her with small, sizzling fires of excitement.

"We've guests waiting," she said.

"Indeed."

He took her hand, leading her toward the stairs and the hall below.

And as they walked, she suddenly shivered fiercely.

God and heaven help the woman who was fool enough to love him! she thought.

Indeed, God help her.

12

On his fifth morning home Rhiannon discovered that the Viking was again gone from her bed.

She awoke to find the linen sheets rumpled where he had lain, but the blond giant who had returned all too swiftly to plague her life was gone.

She leapt up, as if she needed to escape even the haunting memory of him beside her, and stared at the bed as if it, too, were a living, breathing taunt of all that marriage meant. She clenched her fists at her side, wishing desperately that just once she could give him a sound thrashing. Not that he had really raised a hand against her. It was just that his word was law, and he knew how she loathed his dominance and therefore seemed determined to rule the bride who had brought the land as well as the land itself.

She shivered, realized that she was naked, and dived into a trunk for a shift and hose and tunic. Half clad, she turned to the ewer and bowl on the stand by the mantle and scrubbed her face and throat and hands. Then she finished dressing, brushed and braided her hair, swept a fur-trimmed mantle about her shoulders, and left the room quickly.

High upon the stairs she paused. She did not hear her husband's voice within the hall, but there were others there. Rollo told some tale of battle, and others listened and interrupted with a question here and there. Rhiannon hurried on down the stairs quietly, unnoticed. She inhaled sharply as she saw Rowan and the other young men who had been in King Alfred's service now within her hall.

Her husband's hall, she thought bitterly.

Well, they had been there since his return. They had greeted her politely that first night, and with all due respect and even tenderness when she had descended the stairs on Eric's arm. Even Rowan. He had touched her hand, bowed deep over it, and had kissed her cheek with Eric right there, greeting her like a sister. Such conduct had made her feel abandoned, for the fact that he had dared touch her so before Eric was somehow a deep and disturbing disavowal of all that had been between them.

Love was over, she thought. Once it had bubbled soft and light and beautiful, like a spring, but it seemed now all a childish game of pretend. Or maybe it was just that Eric was here, so very real when dreams had all become fantasy. Maybe it was the way that he had touched her, putting some brand or claim upon her that she could not, even in the deepest recesses of her heart, deny. She had known Rowan for years, yet Eric now knew her better. She had believed for years that she would cherish Rowan until the day she died. Yet already the thought of Rowan's gentle kiss was hazy and innocuous, while the very memory of the passion of Eric's lips brought forth a new, dizzying heat to her blood and a flood of color to her cheeks. . . .

And a longing stirring deeply inside her.

She would be foolish to love him; she did not love him and she never would. Even if they did share a love of the land and of spirited animals and vulnerable children. Even if they did share certain values—an abiding respect for their elders and the traditions of their respective heritages; a taste for the exotic; and a reverence for learning. No, whatever rapports might exist between them, she would never love him. Nor would she ever, ever honor or obey him.

She slipped hurriedly and unseen from the hall. One of Eric's men, an Irishman, stood guard by the door. He bowed to her as she passed. She knew not where she was going, just away, far away from the hall to which Eric might too quickly return.

She walked quickly, passing smiths and artisans within the walls, then left the gates—and more of Eric's guard—behind her. Her destination was away from the sea. She hurried along a path that led to the grass-carpeted cliffs to the north. Fifteen minutes brought her to a huge oak with heavy branches that waved over a cool, quickly moving stream.

Egmund had been buried here. Egmund and Thomas. Adela had brought her to the graves, and she had spent much time in prayer for their souls. She had thought to have them reinterred under the chapel floor, but then she had realized that she loved coming to the oak, that it was beautiful and peaceful, and there was no sign of the sea, or of the dragon-prowed ships that lined what had once been her coast, her domain.

She sank to her knees in the grass and bowed her head, praying again for the friends she had lost, yet her mind was not on her prayers. She sat back on the grass, idly chewed a stem, and stared at the swift-moving water. She was numb, she thought. She had not been prepared and he was back. There had been a certain peace in returning home in his absence. She'd had the illusion that life was almost what it had been before. She had sat in the hall and listened to the complaints of her serfs and tenants and freemen, and she had carefully judged them by Alfred's laws. She was just in her ordering of compensations. There had been very few complaints among the people, though. They had been too busy rebuilding their homes after the futile battle they had fought to bring strife against one another. But men were men. Disputes would arise and Alfred's domain was known for the fairness of its laws.

But now . . .

A Viking was lord of these people. Eric had entered the hall and demanded that all within it be at his beck and call. He had dared carry her up a stairway before all assembled, and just as arrogantly he had led her back down to dine within it. Yet all through the meal she had been conscious that it had been postponed until the master had first enjoyed the fulfillment of another basic hunger. And each time she had reached for the chalice of mead that they had shared, she had brushed his fingers, had met his eyes, and had known that he laughed at her embarrassment.

Yet others seemed to find him civilized, and not merely for brief moments, as she herself did. Adela thought him striking—and charming. Charming! The servants found no difficulty in answering his every command. Alfred's men joked easily with him. Even

Rowan—damn Rowan!—seemed to honor him deeply and like him.

Men, she thought with avid disgust. So he went to battle and slayed others with ease; so he was a hero. He had been reared to dole out death, and that was all.

To dole out death—and the power of his will.

She had escaped him after dinner the first night to see to sleeping arrangements for all the men who had accompanied him home. Some would be within the hall; some would need quarters within the cottages before the walls; some would take over property outside of the walls; and so forth. Then, too, there was extra grain and hay to be acquired for all the horses, and so much else to be done. And so she had escaped him until very late, and when he had found her at last, she had been in the kitchen, ordering the meals for the day to come. She could still see him in the doorway, his hands upon his hips, his eyes crystal blue and very hard upon her. He lifted a hand and bid her simply, "Come!"

She had swirled about with all the noble defiance she could muster. "My lord, I am busy," she had said, her tone one to dismiss the staunchest warrior.

But not this lord of the wolves. She had barely turned her back upon him before his hand was upon her shoulder. He didn't argue or even speak again but once more swept her into his arms and kept her there in a viselike grip. Their eyes met, and neither of them had a word to say. He carried her past drunken, drowsing men in the hall, up the stairs, and to their room, and his eyes never left hers once. And when he placed her upon the bed, she told him that she hated him, yet even as she watched him shed his clothing in the candlelight, she wondered if she spoke the truth. She repeated the words as he crawled over her, his magnificent chest bronze and richly matted with platinum hair, and knew she whispered lies. "You are my wife," he reminded her. "And I will have my way." His throaty laughter filled the air, taunting her, but then his touch became a sweet caress, and her furious protests died within the sweet, demanding hunger of his lips. Her words were swept away as cleanly as her will. The candles burned low, and in time it was her soft cries of desire and fulfillment that he took from her with the fervor of his kiss.

Seated upon the bank, Rhiannon exhaled sharply and came suddenly to her feet. The next day he had gone riding until the wee hours, and she had pretended sleep when he returned. He hadn't touched her, and so she had played the game again the third night. But he had been the victor, laughing, rolling her about to tell her she was a sorry little deceiver and that she could welcome her lord home.

She had done so but now regretted it.

But last night . . . last night she had wrested a victory. No matter how exciting his touch, she had resisted. She had not given him battle; she had simply lain as cold as stone, tears filling her eyes in the darkness as she fought not him but herself.

And then she lay awake in the darkness as long as he.

And now this morning . . .

She could still feel him upon her, breathe in the scent of him, remember the rich tenor of his laughter, the fierce ardor of the man as his body impaled her own. She could feel the rock-hardness of his muscle, the shudder within him, within her, the sensation as he filled her with himself, with his seed. She could never be free of him. Never, never forget the memory. And she hated herself more vehemently than she hated him, because she couldn't deny that he did appear something of a god, that his naked chest—and hips and thighs . . . and manhood—were indeed awesome. That his eyes were commanding—and not just his eyes but his whole personality. That he was, in truth, the new lord here.

No, never.

The leaves of the tree rustled and whispered above her. She was all alone here and at peace. She cast aside her mantle and quickly took off her shoes and stripped away her hose and hurried to the water. It was icy cold but delicious and cleansing. She glanced about again, then shed her tunic and shift and walked into the thigh-high water and shuddered furiously as the cold struck her. Then she sank down so that the rushing water covered her to her shoulders, soaking her hair. She dived within it quickly and felt the full force of the cold, rose, and shivered delightedly. She felt free. Free of his touch, of his command.

"Rhiannon!"

She gasped, swinging about then sinking low, as she heard her name called with a sharp, worried tension. She gritted her teeth, praying that Eric had not discovered her even here, then relaxing at nearly the same moment as she recognized Rowan's voice.

"Rhiannon!"

"I'm—I'm here!" she called out.

She saw him then, mounted, coming around the

bend of the oak. How young he looked! she thought briefly. She felt as if she were his senior by many years. Rowan was still a lad, she reflected, and she no longer a girl but a woman. He dismounted quickly and came rushing toward her. He paused as he realized that her clothing lay strewn upon the bank. He choked out an expletive, then swept up her mantle and walked to the water's edge with the garment uplifted for her.

She rose and walked toward him, remembering the ill-fated morning when she had come to him so. Dreams had been alive then. But now . . . now she hurried for the shelter of the garment, and he averted his eyes.

"What is it?" she asked softly, sweeping the cloak about her.

"You were gone," he said harshly. "You were gone and the guards had seen you leave, but no one knew where you were, and I—I feared for your safety."

"My safety?" Puzzled, she stared up at him. Then she smiled slowly and ruefully, squaring her shoulders. "I see. You thought that I might contemplate casting myself over the cliff to the sea?"

Rowan's color darkened. "I—I don't know." She was startled when he suddenly fell to his knees before her. "I beg your pardon, Rhiannon, for last night I realized that my presence added to your wretchedness. Please understand. I—"

She pulled her hand free from his touch. "You have determined to serve a Viking, Rowan. I have not. That is all."

"You should see him in battle—"

"I have seen him in battle, I saw him attack my

home, and I am not in awe of a man for his ability to kill other men."

"You don't know him—"

"It is I who beg your pardon, Rowan. I am coming to know him very well."

He stood very close to her. "Rhiannon, for the love of God, please try to understand. He saved my life, not once but twice. By all that is holy, I am honor-bound to serve him."

He seemed so desperate, so very wretched himself, that her heart was torn. She slipped her arms around him, knowing that she would always love him, though not in the way she had once. She loved him as she might love a brother. There was nothing in her gesture except for that love.

Yet even as her arms entwined about his neck and she whispered his name with tenderness and sorrow, she felt a chill slowly seize her. She stared past his head, and the chill became icy shafts that raced along her spine.

Eric was watching her.

Seated upon his white stallion, he stared at them from the shadows beneath the tree. She could not see his eyes, nor read his features, but she could see the golden glitter of his hair and the easy, powerful way he sat his horse.

Then he nudged the great white stallion and came toward them, dressed that day as an Irish prince, his scarlet mantle held over his shoulder with a large emerald brooch, inscribed with the sign of the wolf.

"Oh, God!" she breathed.

Rowan quickly moved away, spinning around to see the danger. He released her and stepped forward, ready to meet this wolf, no matter what his fear, ready to come between her and the danger.

"My Lord," Rowan began. "I swear to you—"

"No!" Rhiannon cried, rushing around him. Rowan reached for her arm, trying to stop her.

"Rhiannon!"

She pulled free. Her mantle flew in the breeze. Even as she swept it about herself it became evident that she wore nothing beneath it. Silently she swore. But she was determined not to let Rowan suffer for his concern for her life. "There was nothing wrong here!" she declared hotly. "Do you understand me? There was nothing wrong here at all."

Cold blue eyes, as chilling as an icy winter wind, swept over her. Not a muscle moved in the hard planes of his face.

"My Lord—" Rowan said.

"Rowan, go on. I'll speak with you later," Eric interrupted him curtly.

"But, my lord—"

"Damn you, man, go!"

Rhiannon froze. Her eyes locked with Eric's, and they listened as Rowan hurried to his mount.

And then rode away.

Eric's eyes remained hard upon hers. Despite the cold of the water that still dripped from her and the glacial quality of his stare, she felt a prickling of sweat break out upon her forehead. She would not let him do this to her. She would not! she swore.

She stamped a foot furiously upon the ground. "This was innocent, I tell you. And you've no right, no right at all, to look at me so."

"How am I looking at you?" he inquired.

From a great height, she nearly said, and so it seemed. Upon the stallion he was ruthlessly tall, and yet she preferred him there, upon the mount, rather than on the ground and near to her.

She did not answer him. Instead she said, "I tell you that we are both entirely innocent. And if you were at all civilized—"

"Ah, but we've agreed! I'm not one bit civilized. I am entirely pagan. Viking. I slay my enemies. Death is the very creed by which I live!"

He began to dismount. Her breath was lost to her as her heart hammered wildly. She took a step back, but he had paused to gaze at the scattered array of her clothing upon the ground.

He took another step toward her. She swallowed her fear—and her pride. She must clear Rowan's honor, which she had compromised. She fell gracefully to one knee, her head bowed. "I beg of you, listen to me—"

"Get off the ground. False humility does not become you."

Her eyes flashing furiously, she rose. She pulled the mantle more tightly about her and saw his grim smile as he met the fury in her gaze. "That's more like it, my love."

"I am not your love. And I never shall be, so you claim."

"So you're not," he said smoothly. He started to walk around her, stroking his chin. "Not my love—but indeed my wife. My wife! Bound within the sanctity of holy matrimony to honor and obey. And yet I shall be damned, madam, if I am not always finding you in various stages of undress."

"One would think it your favorite way of discovering a woman, my lord," she snapped back, "since when I am fully clad, you seem to make great haste to strip away what I wear."

"It's not your nudity that disturbs me," he said, and again she felt a horrible chill, for he was at her back and paused there. She could not see his face; she could only hear the tremor in his voice that betrayed his anger, despite the lightness of his tone. "It is your repeated nudity before other men. Before Rowan."

She swung around, unable to bear him behind her anymore. She was trembling and had to moisten her lips to speak. She suddenly regretted her victory of the night before. Perhaps he would not be so furious if she had not been so cold. He could not know what it had cost her. "My Lord, I do swear to you that Rowan is innocent—"

"There are so many ways to die, are there not? One can hang a man by the neck with rope until he is dead. It is not a pretty way to die. If the rope is too short, he slowly strangles. If it is too long, the head could be wrenched entirely from the body. But then, a man might simply be beheaded with the swing of a battle-ax or the slice of a sword."

"Eric—"

"But then, of course, a woman's neck slices far more easily than a man's. Your neck, dear wife, is so very slender. . . ."

She backed away, facing him. "Then have done with it!" she started to cry, but her words broke off because he touched her at last, his fingers threading into her hair at the nape of her neck as he wrenched her to his chest. His fingers tugged hard upon her dampened hair, forcing her eyes to meet his. "I would never slay you so, my dear. I would never deny myself the pleasure of wrapping my fingers about your throat and squeezing the very life from you!" Even as he spoke, his free hand found the opening of her mantle, and his fingers spread over the beating of her heart beneath her breast. "To stop this treacherous pulse!" he hissed.

And then suddenly he released her, thrusting her from him. He walked toward his horse, his back to her. "Gather your things and come. Now."

Rhiannon desperately inhaled and exhaled, staring after him. He hadn't hurt her yet, but she still didn't know his intent. Was he dragging her back to have done with both her and Rowan in her very own hall?

"Wait!" she cried.

He went utterly still and turned around slowly. Again she lost her breath. She fought for several seconds to regain it. "Wait, you haven't listened to me. If you dare to hurt Rowan—"

They were the wrong words. His long stride brought him before her in a matter of seconds, and she was soon back in his powerful grip. His eyes commanded hers as he stared down upon her. "I dare anything, madam—that you should well know by now! But as far as young Rowan goes, I intend him no harm. I trust *him* implicitly."

"Wha-what?" Rhiannon stuttered.

"I'd not punish the lad because *your* behavior is that of the careless whore."

"What!" This time she did not stutter; the word lashed out with all her fury. It wasn't enough. She struggled against his hold, managing to claw at his chin and kick him in the shin. He swore savagely, catching her arm and wrenching her around. She fell in a tangle of her mantle, and he came down quickly, straddled over her hips.

Her temper rose to salvage her from complete humiliation. "Truly, if there is a God in heaven, you will rot beneath the stroke of some battle-ax, you will slowly molder and decay, you will—"

"Do go on," he encouraged.

"Get off me!"

"What? Now? Why, I am enchanted to discover how you feel beneath me. It's interesting to discover what it would be like to be the man for whom you so eagerly shed your clothing."

"I did not shed my clothing for Rowan!"

"You would tell me that Rowan performed the deed?"

"No! Of course not. I—"

"Ah! I've got it at last. You came here and shed your clothing and cast yourself into the water to play the seductress, just in case I, your legal lord, should wander by. How intriguing a thought. Especially after last night."

"I did not—"

"Careful, careful, lady!" He leaned nearer, and she did not know if the gleam in his eyes was from amusement or fury, or some other emotion altogether. "I rather like the sound of that. And I don't like the sound of my other suggestions half as well."

She opened her mouth, then allowed it to fall shut. The leaves of the great oak above her cast shadows over them both. He picked up a lock of her damp hair, winding it around his finger. "An early-morning tryst with my wife beneath the shade of an ancient oak, in the coolness of a bubbling brook . . . it does hold a certain appeal, don't you think? Rather tickles the fantasy?"

"No!"

"No! My heart is broken. Alas! Within my bed lies a lifeless log, when I know that I married a woman of vibrance and passion. Does she exist only for others now? Perhaps I am wrong. Perhaps I shall have to speak with young Rowan to discover—"

"Stop!" she whispered.

He arched a golden brow. She lifted her chin. "A tryst with my dear lord and dearly beloved husband sounds like a—a fantasy indeed!" she choked out.

A gleam of deviltry touched the blue of his eyes, and she wanted to strike out as just the corner of his lip twitched with humor. But before she could raise a hand against him, he was on his feet, casting his mantle aside, unbuckling his scabbard. The sword fell to the ground beside her with a heavy thud. He tugged off his boots, stripped away his hose, then his tunic and shirt, and she twisted to her side and glanced longingly at the sword.

His bare foot landed on her hair, and her eyes shot to his. "I promise if you even think about bringing a weapon against me again, I shall carve my initials and the emblem of the Royal House of Vestfald upon your backside!"

She choked out in fury, leaping to her feet, flying against him. He caught her and fell with her, his laughter filling the air as they rolled to the water's edge. Her mantle had fallen free, and she lay between the chill of the water and the sizzling heat of his body. She writhed beneath him, trying to free herself from his weight but bringing herself into deeper, further contact with him instead. She swore vehemently, which caused him to cast his head back in laughter.

"What would you have of a Viking? You have labeled me, and I give you what you desire! Let nothing stand in my way. I will take what I want and have it by the grace of my sword, lady. And I shall have no more cold creature beneath me again, but all the rage and fire and sweet passion that is due me in turn!"

"I owe you nothing! Bastard—"

His eyes met hers, alive with blue flame, with passion. And his whisper touched her cheek. "Take care, milady! Take care! Convince me that you longed for me and no other."

She inhaled sharply, longing to tell him to go to hell. Her anger was as fierce as his.

Nevertheless, she wanted him too. Her traitorous body wanted him in the stream, in the coolness of the water, in the breath of the day, in the shadow of the oak. She trembled, feeling again the strength in his arms, in his touch, in the power of his chest. Aye, she wanted him. She wanted the passion and more. She wanted the comfort of his arms. She wanted the tenderness of his whisper. She wanted the man she was coming to know.

The leaves rustled, and the brook bubbled softly by them. She felt the cool peace of the day keenly and, against it, the seething currents that had erupted between them.

She stared at him, then slowly she cupped his cheeks with her hands, meeting the fire of his eyes with silvery sparks of her own. But then she drew his head down to hers, and she touched his lips with a sweeping, savage kiss to defy any demand of his. She flicked her tongue tauntingly, seductively, against his lips, then she delved past the barrier of his teeth and played a hostile, sensual duel with his tongue. Her fingers entwined into his hair, and she pressed her breasts high and excitingly against the roughness of his chest.

A guttural groan escaped him, shattering the quiet of the day. And then she felt the peace no more, not the coolness of the water, nor the shadow of the oak. His lips seared her throat and her breast, and she was pressing against him, and then kneeling with him, their lips entwined. She stood and felt the roughness of his face against her belly, against her thighs. She cried out softly and moved sensuously down upon him, using all of her body to stroke him, then kissing, nipping his shoulders, rubbing her hair and head slowly down the taut, rippling planes of his belly. She hesitated just briefly, but then the fantasy seized her, and she gripped the fullness of his thrusting shaft between her palms and nearly jumped at the heat and size of him beneath her touch. His whispers encouraged her to further boldness, wantonness—wickedness, perhaps—but it didn't matter. She didn't remember her hatred or the bloodshed or anything that stood between them. She knew only this man, this lover, and the sweet, savage things he had evoked inside her, and the startling, swift beauty that could come from it, sweeping away thought, indeed stealing consciousness, even moments of life. She moved upon him with her kiss, with the lap and stroke of her tongue, the caress of her mouth.

Fierce, hoarse sounds escaped him. He gripped her shoulders, shuddering fiercely, then he pulled her up and against him, and his mouth covered hers voraciously as he bore her down. He parted her thighs ruthlessly, and parted her still further with the questing stroke of his fingers, then both consumed and filled her with the hot, wet thrust and lave of his tongue until she was nearly delirious, sobbing for him, barely aware of what her words demanded. He obliged, dragging her fully beneath him. She cried out, startled as he entered her with the driving force of a huge, majestic machine, blazing his way in, filling her, becoming a part of her. His lips covered her cry, his warmth swept her into the vortex of his desire. Lightning seemed to fill her as thunder shook the earth, and the very ground pulsed around her and within her. She was swept to Valhalla and beyond. The ecstasy rose within her until pleasure was nearly pain, and still he brought her higher. Then the sun seemed to blaze and burst within her, and she was filled with a stream of the man, even as the dazzling beauty exploded around her, and night reigned supreme.

Seconds later the daylight returned. Her eyes fluttered open, and she discovered Eric at her side, leaning upon an elbow, carefully studying the paleness of her face.

Suddenly the coolness of the water and the air seemed to strike freshly upon her. She shivered and tried to move, but her damp hair was caught beneath him and she could not.

He touched her face, drawing a line down her cheek, and she tried to twist from him. He would not allow her to do so. "Why did you come here?" he demanded.

"To please you, obviously!" she snapped, and then she was instantly sorry, for the Nordic winds seemed to touch his eyes again. A swift tick appeared at the base of his throat, and she said quickly, "I—you'll not, you'll not—"

"I'll not what?"

Her eyes fell. They lay naked still, bathed in the brook and in the sheen of their mating, and yet the distance between them was suddenly and incredibly vast. "You'll not hurt Rowan?"

He pushed away from her, rose, and walked into the brook. The water came only to his knees, but he sank into the coldness of it, his back to her. Then he rose, ignoring her, and walked, naked and confident and careless, to the shore. He swept up his shirt and slipped into it.

"Eric?" she whispered, rising up slightly on an elbow, a sudden fear seizing her again.

He pulled on his tunic and laced the leather strands, then glanced her way. His eyes flicked over the length of her naked body, half in the water, half out of it. "Rowan was never in any danger of my wrath," he told her flatly. "As I told you earlier, I trust his sense of honor, even if yours is nonexistent."

She started as if he had slapped her. Tears stung her eyes, but she spun away from him, walking blindly into the water herself. Still his harsh words followed her. "I told you once, a woman will never influence my actions, not even by so sweet a display as that you have just offered."

She did not want to see him. She wanted to sink beneath the water in her misery.

And so she stayed there. Stayed, her back to him, letting the water rinse her hair and chill and cleanse her body. She closed her eyes and waited, praying that she had waited so long that he had gone.

But he had not. When she rose at last, dripping and shivering, he was there, on the bank, completely clad and leaning against the tree, watching her curiously. She strode by him with her chin high. She spoke softly, pausing before him in all her naked majesty. "You wanted to know why I came here. I came to bathe away the memory of the night."

She awaited his fury but none came. The wind rustled around them. "And you gained nothing but the new memory of the day," he said at last.

She turned away. He caught hold of her arm. Tears were still burning within her eyes, tears she could not understand. He pulled her back to him. "That is why you came?"

She wondered at the tension in his words. Moistening her lips, she gestured toward the tree. "Egmund is buried here. And Thomas."

He frowned, and she explained, "My captains. My father's men. Men who watched out for me all of their lives, slain in our battle."

He stiffened. "Traitors, madam," he said.

She shook her head passionately. "Nay, never traitors!"

"Then, lady, you defied your king, for you did attack me!"

Again she shook her head. "I did not betray King Alfred! I do have a sense of honor, my lord, even if you cannot see it!"

"I have seen you attempt to betray a marriage betrothal."

"A betrothal I did not freely enter into! Can't you understand?" she cried suddenly, passionately. "You have undoubtedly had countless women, willing and no! I was being sold, bartered—betrayed!—into marriage. I wanted—oh, never mind!" She tried to wrench free of his hold but he held her tight.

"Willing," he said.

"What?"

He smiled. "They were all willing, all my women."

"Oh!" she swore. "Well, I was not!"

But his mood was no longer playful. He had grown serious, and his words were filled with tension. "Someone betrayed Alfred," he said very softly. "And me."

"I tire of proclaiming my innocence!"

He held her still, very tightly. Then he released her, his eyes locked with hers. He walked by her, collecting her clothing where it lay strewn upon the ground, then brought the garments to her, thrusting them into her hand. "I tire, my lady, of finding you running about naked in places other than our own private domain."

At least the lethal tension seemed to have ebbed away from him. She snatched her clothing from him. "You'll not find me naked again, you needn't fear."

"Ah, but I like you naked. In fact, I prefer you naked. Your temper seems ever so much better when you are so."

"You'll not find me naked again," she repeated. "Ever."

"I shall, I think," he said tauntingly, "for I shall make you so. At my will and leisure, of course."

She choked down an epithet and swung around. His laughter followed her. Her back to him, she dressed as quickly as she could. Then she turned back to him as she fastened her mantle with the brooch, not liking to have him at her back.

He was watching her very curiously again. To her vast surprise he seized her hand and kissed it. Then he backed her against the tree, and his enormous hand cupped her chin, his curiously sensitive fingers stroked her cheek, and his lips descended softly, almost tenderly, upon hers. And when they lifted, he murmured, "Thank you."

"For—for what?" she breathed cautiously.

"For this morning. The fantasy was more than fulfilled. Tell me, did you really barter again, so fiercely, so thrillingly, for another man's life? Or was there perhaps just the slightest desire to please me, your husband? Mayhap despite the involuntary nature of this marriage and the horror of a Viking in your bed, you are falling just the least little bit in love?"

"No!" she protested furiously.

"And yet you are so magnificent!" he whispered.

"I shall never, never fall in love with you!" she promised. "Just because you haven't a horrible stench and I—and I—"

He was laughing again—she was spared from going any further. His lips touched hers once more, softly, briefly. "And you needn't fear, vixen, I shall never, never fall in love with you." He was not looking at her, and he seemed suddenly far away. "Contrary to your belief, milady, I do remember love," he said softly.

The breeze picked up and whispered by them. Then his eyes focused hard upon hers again. "You have, I assume, fallen out of love with Rowan?"

"I—I—" she stuttered, "of course not!" But she had, and she was blushing furiously, and she didn't know if she had answered foolishly and foolhardily again, or if she had only managed to amuse him further. "I mean—"

He shook his head. "The boy is safe, lady. Come now. There are petitioners here among the people, and I would learn Alfred's laws from you."

He strode swiftly to the white stallion, then paused, waiting for her. Slowly she followed him. He swept her up, setting her upon the horse, then mounted behind her.

He paused before the tree. "I do already know something of the king's laws," he said. "Treason against the king is the highest crime within the land."

"They did not betray him!" she insisted softly.

She felt his whisper against her ear. "Treason against one's lord is the second-highest crime within this land."

He was silent, waiting. She said nothing in reply, and he spoke again at last.

"Rhiannon, you will do well to remember that whatever your heart, or your mind, I am your lord."

She didn't answer him, and he touched her chin, turning her head slightly so that he could read her eyes. She freed herself quickly from his touch and lowered her gaze to the pommel of his saddle, where his left hand lay easily, grasping the reins. They were such large, powerful hands, his fingers exceptionally long and somewhat tapering, as graceful as they were strong.

"Rhiannon—"

"I do not forget that you are my lord," she said, and tossed her head to meet his eyes again, defiance rising to her own once again. "It seems that I am not able to do so!"

He smiled, and then his jovial laughter filled the air and the harsh planes of his face were eased, and in the sun he was every inch the prince, all-powerful, striking, golden in the light, indeed the Viking lord of the wolves.

"You are, milady, quite remarkable."

"Am I?"

"You do well enough in my absence. Indeed you do marvelously well. And you grind your teeth with my return, yet I've really not come to do battle. We both seek the same goals."

"Nay, milord, we do not!" she insisted sweetly.

But he smiled again. "Aye, lady, we do." He stretched out an arm to encompass the land around them. "We both seek the best for this place. Prosperity, laughter, peace. Careful judgment, greater learning—our own golden age, perhaps."

Her eyes widened with mock innocence. "Milord! What power have I? You've just taken the gravest care to remind me that I am little more than a servant beneath your overlordship!"

He shook his head, amused once more, completely aware that any humility she offered him was false. "Rhiannon, you test your power with every step you take, or so it seems! Lady, you are my wife, and any man makes demands of his mate. The reins that pull upon you are easy ones, my love, just as long as you remember that they are there."

"As I have told you," she said softly, "you need have no fear. You do not allow me not to recall at all times that you are the lord here!"

"I care not how, as long as you do recall it!" he told her, and then he nudged the stallion hard with his knees and the great beast leapt to life. She felt the great, thundering motion of the animal's gallop beneath her thighs and the warmth and strength and curious security of her husband's broad chest against her back, even as his arms encircled her.

Perhaps there could be something almost like peace between them. . . .

Yet even as the sun rose shimmeringly high on the new day and they approached the walls of their home, all thoughts of peace vanished. From the cliffs they could see that the gates were open and that horses and men bearing Alfred's colors were back upon them already.

"What is it?" Rhiannon murmured.

Eric reined in Alexander and stared down at the scene of milling horses and men.

"More Danes," he said wearily. Then he added wryly, "Alas, my love, you may yet find reprieve. I think that I must ride back to war already, and that a Danish battle-ax shall ever be waiting!"

He nudged the white back to a full gallop.

She never had a chance to tell him that she did not really wish for a battle-ax to catch him.

Indeed she would pray for his safe return.

13

There was a great assembly gathered in the hall as
Rhiannon followed Eric quickly through the doorway. Among them were many of Alfred's top men:
serious, grim Allen of Kent; Edward of Sussex; Jon of
Winchester; and William of Northumbria. William
had been engaged in some heavy discussion with
Rollo by the north wall; he leaned there, twirling his
fine dark mustache. As soon as Rhiannon entered the
room, she felt his eyes upon her, brooding and dark,
shielded behind the droop of his eyelids and his thick
lashes. This is a dangerous man, she thought uneasily.
Then she tried to dispel the idea because he was so
trusted by the king. All the same, he made her un-
comfortable, she realized. He had never liked the
power that she held. But he was important to Alfred,
and Rhiannon knew that she must grit her teeth and
accept him into her home.

She had no choice. Eric would do so.

Still, it was obvious that Alfred's men had not come
to stay—they had come to collect warriors again for
some new battle.

"Eric!" It was Jon, headstrong, passionate, always
first into the fray, who approached Eric even as he
entered the hall. "Gunthrum has heard of the rout at

Rochester and plots retaliation! Even now there are plans for an attack from the sea! We need ships to be sent to the king's command. And we have been warned by a captive that a host of the bloody invaders will arrive just north of here. The king requests that you take your men and stop this group from joining with Gunthrum's host!"

"My fleet is at the king's command," Eric assured Jon.

"And we'll bloody best any Dane who dares step foot ashore upon this coast!" Rollo boasted.

A wild cheer went up, and drinking horns were raised. Rhiannon determined that Englishmen could behave as barbarically as any pagans when it came to war.

"We need the ships immediately," Allen warned, stepping forward.

Eric nodded, hardly needing to glance Rollo's way as he spoke to his second in command. "Rollo, see to it that the captains are ready to sail."

The huge Viking nodded and walked swiftly from the room.

William of Northumbria left his place by the wall at last. He came forward, offering his hand in a strong clasp to Eric. "Viking ships against a Viking invader! It will surely bring us victory." He laughed, clapping Eric hard upon the shoulder. Eric did not reply, and for a fleeting moment Rhiannon wondered if her husband shared her uneasiness about the man. But then Rowan stepped into the breech.

"There are none so fleet, so fine, at the craft of shipbuilding as the Vikings. We must thank God that the great Ard-ri of Ireland accepted the prince from

Norway as a son-in-law, and that the Ard-ri's grand-son has now brought us the great craft of his ships."

"And the great craft of his sword arm!" William added.

"Well, I do thank you for the welcome," Eric replied wryly. "Let's see if our Viking ships bring assistance to this new conquest."

"How long until they can sail to meet the king?" Jon asked anxiously.

Eric's lip curled in a subtle, sardonic smile. "A Viking ship, my friends, can sail at a moment's notice." He turned to William. "And a Viking host can ride at a moment's notice. We'll leave within the hour." He swirled around and found Rhiannon behind him. "See to the comforts of your Englishmen, will you, my love?" he said. His voice carried a soft taunt, yet she wondered suddenly if he were angry at her, or at something said within the room. He shouted to Rowan to join him, and for a moment her heart seemed to grow cold as she remembered the events of the morning. He had seemed willing to exculpate Rowan readily enough—indeed, he appeared genuinely fond of the lad, but might he not yet reflect that he'd breathe easier without such a rival in proximity to his wife? Eric would be giving Rowan his orders in battle. . . . But no, her husband would never do anything so underhanded, Rhiannon realized. Whatever faults her Viking had, even she must concede that deviousness was not among them. Eric was an honorable man. But he was angry with her, if not with Rowan. He blamed her for the morning's encounter; he mistrusted and even disliked her. And she had told him, albeit falsely, that she still loved Rowan. Might he not try to hurt her through the lad, though he bore Rowan himself no grudge?

She hadn't the time to say a word, nor would she have begun to do so with men like William and Allen in the room. She swept by her husband even as he hurried to the yard to call forth his grooms. She greeted Jon and Edward.

William stepped before her as she neared the kitchen. "My dear Rhiannon! We have all worried so for you. How do you fare?"

She didn't like the question from him at all. There was a light about his eyes that glistened like grease. He had been the one entirely eager to throw her to the wolf.

"I fare very well, very well indeed, William. Thank you and excuse me, I'll see what we have to feed this host."

He reached out a hand to stop her, but she evaded him and hurried into the kitchen. Adela was already there, and it seemed she and the steward had things well in hand. "Ah, there you are, dear! Well, we've ordered out numerous kegs of ale and mead, and we've just brought in scores of fresh fish and the boars they killed out hunting the other day. We haven't the time to roast huge haunches, so we've sliced and skewered much of the meat, and the table is to be set right now. Have I missed anything?"

"Not a thing. It's quite the best anyone can do on such notice. Adela, you are a godsend."

Adela smiled, plump and complacent. She patted Rhiannon's hair. "Did you have a nice swim, then, this morning?"

"What? Oh, yes, lovely, thank you," Rhiannon muttered. She noticed that Mergwin was by the cook fire, stirring something that simmered in a pot over the flames. He turned to her, and his ancient eyes studied her, then he gazed again at the pot. Rhiannon smiled briefly to Adela and found herself hurrying over to the magician.

"What is it?" she hissed at him.

He looked up with some surprise. With his free hand he stroked his beard, taking his time to reply. He looked back to the pot. "Did you tell him?" he inquired.

"Tell him what?" she whispered tensely.

He studied her again. "About the child."

Instinctively she touched her stomach. He couldn't have known! This fascinating, frightening man couldn't have known the truth she was just beginning to suspect herself. As the days passed, so did the time when she should have had her monthly flow. And there were other, oh so subtle changes too. Mergwin was right, and she knew it. But she could not tell Eric. She argued that she was not sure—despite Mergwin's words. The truth was that her pride would not allow her, not when her husband treated her as a possession —to be taken and discarded at his will, according to his own word!

"There is nothing to tell him!" she insisted. Then she felt a chill, for the way his eyes touched her, she knew instantly that he was aware of her lies, that he saw all the way into the depth of her soul. Defensive, she softly and accusingly cross-queried him. "Did you tell him?"

"It is not my place but yours, my lady," he told her, bowing with a humility that was certainly mocking.

She started to turn away, but he caught her arm. "I don't like this."

She pulled free, not understanding him. "What do you mean? I did not ask for this, any of this—"

"I'm talking about this new summons. I do not like it. Something is wrong."

She tossed back her drying hair. "Something is always wrong with battle," she said softly. "Men die."

She liked the way that he looked at her then, with thought and a certain new respect. He made a move as if he would touch her, but just then long, heavy strides brought Eric thundering into the room. "My God, I've raised an army already—can't we feed a few men in the same amount of time?"

"The meal comes, my lord, at this very moment!" the steward hastily assured him. The kitchen came to life with lads and lasses hurrying about with plates and knives and tapered spoons for the stew and great skewers for the meat. Mergwin slipped quietly out the back entrance, Rhiannon saw. She was about to follow him when she felt Eric's hand upon her arm, stopping her.

"Come, my lady, take your place at my side."

She had little choice, for his fingers were like steel, and his will seemed akin to God's. She nodded but pulled back, trying to caution herself to take care but desperate to say something with so little time remaining to them. Rowan would ride with him again. She had to know that the two men, at least, were at peace.

"My lord, have you spoken with Ro—"

"Aye, lady, I have." His fingers tightened so that she nearly cried out, but she swallowed back the sound. From the doorway that the servants hurried through she could hear the laughter and the booming voices of the men. And still Eric nearly whispered as he continued, "By God, madam, how many times must I assure you that I do not blame the lad?"

"You blame me!" she choked out.

"Aye, that I do. Now, milady—"

"It's just that you leave for battle again—"

"And though you would gladly have a Danish ax cleave my skull, you fear that I would, through malice, cast away the boy's life?"

She paled, sensing the rise of his anger. "It's just that—"

"I assure you," he hissed, very close to her, "that your honor or lack thereof is not worth the life of one warrior, be he Irish, Norse, or English. Now, lady, I do suggest you follow me quickly, before I forget that I am supposed to be among civilized English company and take you yonder to redden that flesh you do seem so determined still to expose to others."

She jerked free and swore, heading for the hall with her head high. She was brought back swiftly, swallowing down a cry, as his fingers knotted into her hair. He released her quickly enough, caught her arm, and proceeded out with her once again.

Eric led her to the head of his table, while the others grouped around them, according to their rank. That left William at Rhiannon's side; Jon by him; Allen and Edward to Eric's left; and Rollo, courteously giving up his own seat, down the plank with Rowan and others of Eric's own host. Because of the seating, Rhiannon should have shared a chalice with William that day, yet despite the anger still emanating from her husband, he came to her rescue when William offered the chalice to her first.

Eric caught her hand when protocol would have demanded that she accept the proffered cup, and he apologized to William with a pleasant ease. "William, you will excuse us, I beg, and indulge us. My wife and I have had so little time to explore the wonders of matrimony—it seems that war must always intrude. My lady will share this cup with me, as it is still a fascination just to have my lips wander where hers have touched before them."

He spoke loudly enough for all to hear. Edward laughed and applauded, and Jon stood up with his chalice raised high. "My lords—English and other!— we have gained not just an able warrior but truly a man of wisdom and wit, a prince and a poet. My dear lady Rhiannon, I admit—if you'll excuse me, Prince of Eire"—he bowed quickly to Eric, then looked to Rhiannon again—"we who watched you grow with courage and beauty were honor-bound to see to this match, yet in our hearts we bled. And now we discover that you are wed to a man who has gained more than our deepest respect and admiration, and who, by his very words, cherishes you deeply as well. Lady, to you, and to your Lord of Wolves!"

There was thunderous applause. Rhiannon found her husband's eyes upon her with their mocking light. He lifted his chalice to her and drank from it deeply. She stood swiftly. "Aye, my lords, I thank you one and all for your care. What can I say? This marriage is indeed fantastic! I wonder what new fantasy each day shall bring. And I am astounded. Cherish! Why, trust me, my friends. His every word and his every motion contain tenderness and care. He is most certainly a prince among princes"—she paused just briefly, staring into his eyes as she continued with dripping sarcasm—"unique among all men."

She sat as more cheers arose. Eric lifted the chalice to her once again, and she nearly snatched it from him to swallow down a great quantity of the mead. But then the laughter and the cheers died down, and the talk turned swiftly to war. Rhiannon glanced to the side and realized that William was gone.

She turned and found Eric watching her once again. "Why did you start that?" she hissed to him. "What lies, what mockery, what—"

"That man covets you," he said curtly, interrupting her. She fell silent, and he inclined his head, indicating William's empty seat. "And I think that you even prefer me to him, so I suggest that you take grave care in his presence."

The color drained from her face. There was so much about her that he read with appalling ease. She did despise William. No matter what she had ever thought of Eric, his touch had never dismayed her, it was true. While the very feel of William's eyes upon her . . .

Long, powerful fingers closed over hers. Eric's gaze held hers once again, startling, deep. "He'll never touch you, I swear it."

She shuddered despite herself. Then Eric's words both warmed and chilled her, for he added, "Rest easy, for I swear I should kill him if he ever stepped too close."

He released her hand then, rising quickly, and asked Allen casually where William had gone.

"I sent a messenger ahead to find the king and assure him that you had sent the ships and would lead your men against the menace just north of here. William has just gone to make sure that the lad has got off all right."

"It is time that we were all gone," Eric said, and it was a signal. About the table, men rose. They shifted outward until Rhiannon realized that she sat alone at the table.

She jumped up and hurried out. The grooms and stable lads had brought the horses, and the warriors were being assisted into their mail and helmets.

Eric was already clad in his mail and shimmering helmet and seated atop the white stallion. He turned, sensing that she had come from the house. Across the sea of men, his eyes, blue as the fjords of Norway, fell upon hers. She shivered anew and watched him from the step. He nudged the stallion, and the animal broke its way through the others and then Eric loomed high above her on his steed.

"Lady, you may yet have your wish. If I am slain, you must immediately make your way to the king, do you understand?"

She tried to swallow. "No Danish ax would dare to slay you. You would simply command it not to do so."

"Take heed of what I say. You will go to the king."

He was angry. She answered again, her words barely finding voice. "I will go to the king."

"There is scarcely an army of defense left to you here. If there were to be an attack, you'd have to run into the forest. No heroics, lady. None of your flying arrows. The house and the walls I can rebuild. The land will remain mine no matter who seeks to wrest it from me. But you, lady, you are to seek shelter in the forest, do you understand? Leave the men to try to hold the walls and to protect those serfs and tenants who remain to us. Do you understand me?"

"I—"

"Do you, lady?"

She nodded again.

Suddenly he was off the horse. He cast back the face shield of his visor and swept her into his arms. His kiss was so savage and bruising that her lips tingled with the pressure, and yet she realized dimly that she was clinging to him.

And that she was afraid.

He released her and mounted the white stallion once again. He cried out to the men. She stood upon the step until the dust from the horses and the foot soldiers had died away, and then she wearily reentered the house.

She bent down before the fire upon the balls of her feet and studied the flame. Why did it feel so very empty to have him leave? She could still feel her lips tingling from his kiss.

And she could still remember the passion deep within her soul.

"Come, dear, come upstairs." Adela said, touching her shoulders. "Perhaps you should sleep awhile. It's been quite an eventful day."

How recently she had loathed his presence. Eric was gone and the house was empty. What did the hours change? He had certainly grown no more tender!

But then, that was not his way, despite his flowery words at the table. Yet he had known that she de-

spised William—aye, even feared him—and he had
offered his protection—no, he had sworn it.

Ah, but she was his, like the white stallion. He let no
man ride the stallion, and surely, ironically, he would
let no man ride her.

Only a fool would love him. She did not love him,
would not love him. . . .

She was losing her mind! And, aye, but she was
weary!

She stood quickly. "Adela," she said, hugging the
woman fiercely, "I do love you. And I *will* rest."

"Yes, dear, I know," Adela said cheerfully.

Lying down felt wonderful. But she did not sleep.
She remembered Mergwin's words in the kitchen,
and she felt the subtle changes in her body. Mergwin
had been right all along; she could not deny it. And
perhaps she should have told Eric. Perhaps he would
meet with death and never know.

And perhaps, despite their wedding night, he
would disclaim the child. Maybe he would allow himself to wonder if the child was his. Other men might
wonder as well. . . .

Restless, she rose and sat before the fire. Even as
she brooded there, she heard a tap upon her door.
She absently bade, "Enter," expecting Adela, and
started when Mergwin entered her room.

"Two messengers were sent!" he said, pacing the
room.

"Mergwin, I do beg your pardon, but—"

"Two messengers left. One was sent to Alfred. I
know not who sent the other, but I learned from the
grooms that two lads set out."

"Perhaps they were anxious that someone make it to the king in case of accident—"

"Or perhaps someone was sent to the Danes."

She leapt to her feet, staring at him. A trap? To warn the Danes of Eric's approach, to see that he was ambushed?

And he still suspected her of the last treachery. Of betraying Alfred, of attacking him by choice upon his arrival. He would instantly assume that she was the traitor once again.

"No, it can't be—"

"You must send someone. I am too old, I cannot travel quickly enough to catch him anymore." She had never heard the Druid swear, or lament his age before. Now he did, his leathery hands trembling. "My God, to see and not to see clearly, it is a curse! You must send the guard immediately!"

"No one can catch them! They'll be riding hard, into the valley. And Alfred's men will have already turned to reach him at Wareham. I don't—" She broke off and ran to the window, studying the landscape. "I can go!"

"What?" Mergwin demanded, amazed.

She swung around. "See, Mergwin—see the cliff just north, above the valley? I shall take my quiver and shoot a warning down the valley. I can stop them!"

"You could shoot them," Mergwin muttered.

"Ask your lord, Eric!" she told him. "I never miss. Well, I can be sure not to kill anyone, and I can send many messages, and surely they will notice the arrows, take cover, and discover the messages."

"No. You cannot go. If you were hurt—"

"I won't go alone. I'll take the Irishman Patrick of Armagh with me."

Mergwin hesitated, then shook his head. "Send Patrick. You must not go. You must not go. Do you understand?"

What was the meaning of this? She had ruled this land in her own right, and now these invaders were all telling her what she could and could not do. She started to argue, then smiled instead.

"As you wish, Mergwin, as you wish."

"I shall go find Patrick."

"I will change and see that the warnings are written," Rhiannon said serenely.

As soon as he was gone, she hastily found heavy hose, a short leather tunic, and a dull brown mantle with a hood. She brushed and braided her hair and sat down with a quill and ink and wrote out the warning of treachery ten times, then decided on five more. She raced downstairs and found that Patrick was mounted with an English quiver of arrows at his back and an English longbow rested over his saddle. Mergwin was at his side, giving him instructions. The old Druid brooded so that he didn't seem to notice Rhiannon's apparel. She was grateful for that small mercy.

She smiled and offered up the warnings, and thongs with which to secure them, to Patrick, then she bid him Godspeed. As Patrick rode away, Mergwin sighed and reentered the house.

As soon as he was gone, Rhiannon raced to the stables.

No one other than Mergwin was left behind to defy her will. Rollo was with Eric, as were all the others high up in his command. When she ordered a horse, the stable boy, who had always done so in the past, thought not a thing of obeying her now. When she rode beyond the gates, she left word behind that she was merely catching up with Patrick and would return with him.

No one thought to waylay her. None could have stopped her except for the Druid, and she had deceived him, so she was free. If she hurt him, she was sorry, for he had already become very dear to her. This was something she had to do. She could not let Eric think that she had betrayed him again.

Patrick had not left so long before her, yet it seemed to take her hours to catch up with him. By the time that she did, it had long been dark, and she knew that there would be no way to warn Eric and his men that night.

When she came upon Patrick in a clearing, he had drawn his sword and stood wary, ready to face down an opponent. "Patrick, it is me, Rhiannon!" she called out quickly. By the light of the fire he had set, she could see the puzzlement that touched his features, as well as the dismay.

"My lady! What are doing here? It is not safe. If the Danes are moving in so close—"

She interrupted him with the ironic laughter that suddenly seized her. She saw the dismay cloud his features, and a certain irritation, and she tried to sober quickly to reassure him. "I'm sorry, Patrick, I really am. It's just that I so recently fled this very way, and you and your . . ." She paused because Patrick was every inch an Irishman, a descendant of ancient kings, and she had no desire to insult him. She had no need to. He supplied the end of her statement softly to her on the night air.

"Vikings?" he suggested.

She shrugged, dismounting from the mare she had chosen and joining him by the fire. They stared at each other a long moment, then she apologized. "Yes, Vikings, Patrick. I'm sorry, but they are Viking ships—"

"And Eric is the son of a Viking king," Patrick supplied. He smiled, his freckled face showing deep dimples as he did so, then he swept off the mantle he wore over a simple shirt of protective mail and laid it out upon the ground. "My lady, would you sit? What roasts is a plump hare, and I believe it will be quite tasty."

She smiled and sat and he joined her. His warm brown eyes were steady upon her. "You mustn't judge all Vikings by those you have come to know."

She lowered her head slightly, trying to hide the curious war of emotions within her. "I know no Viking as well as Eric, Patrick."

"I refer to those who have ravaged this land. You would like Eric's father very much. He never allowed slaughter—"

"But he seized land that was not his!" she protested.

"He has returned to Ireland tenfold anything that he ever took," Patrick said, proudly defending Olaf. "He and his sons have fought time and again for the old Ard-ri, his father-in-law. Dubhlain rises as a great town—the greatest, perhaps, in all Eire. There are schools for the children and great monasteries that he supports. Musicians and scholars come and . . ." He paused, grinning. "That is the Irish way. Do you know what one of the greatest crimes in all Ireland is?"

"What?"

"To refuse hospitality to those in need. You might travel anywhere beneath the jurisdiction of the Ard-ri, or of the great Irish kings, and be welcomed with warmth and kindness. It is our way. And in Eire a woman may readily own property, and she may be heard if she desires to plead her own case in any dispute. Why, the Ard-ri himself, my lady, is the most responsible man in the land, for it is the Irish belief that the higher a man's status in life, the greater must be his forfeit for crime against a lesser man. Moreover, Ireland is beautiful, lady. You should see the land. Achingly green and beautiful, for mile upon endless mile. Yet the seasons bring change, and colors in mauve and purples and glorious oranges and—"

"Patrick! You should be at home, setting all these wondrous thought to paper, not facing war upon foreign soil!" Rhiannon exclaimed.

Patrick flushed deeply in the firelight. "Lady, I have told you these things because you must understand. Eric of Dubhlain is not a pagan or a barbarian. He is a cross between the lusty seafaring talents of the Viking and of the fine and ancient royal lineage of a land where civilization—in a golden glory!—has long flourished. He speaks many languages, has studied Greek and Roman verse, knows much of astronomy and astrology, and plays many instruments. It was never, ever meant that any here should suffer from our appearance from across the sea. Only the enemy we mutually fight, the Danes. I—I wish that you could see the difference between Eric and Gunthrum."

"Patrick," she said softly in the face of his sincerity, "I have come tonight because I wish to help."

"You should not be here!" he exclaimed, suddenly remembering why he had been sent himself. "It is not safe!"

"I am the best archer I know," she said flatly. "I must be here."

He smiled slowly at her after a moment. "What if I requested that you turn around and go home?"

"Ah, but it would not be safe to send me in the night. Further, you could request that I leave, but you could not order me to do so, and I am commanding you to serve me now. As I am your lord's lady, you are beholden to me."

He was silent for a moment. "Tomorrow, with the dawn, we will cross that ridge. When the dew lifts and the fog clears, we should be able to see their progress along the coast."

She nodded. Patrick decided that his hare was well roasted, and he pulled the meat from the fire and they shared it. She drank warm ale from his horn and settled down upon his mantle.

He slept little through the night, she knew. He kept a careful vigil over her until the dawn broke and morning came upon them.

Less than an hour's time brought them to the ridge. As they had both anticipated, the cliffs and valley of the coast were clearly visible to them for miles and miles. Patrick was the first to catch sight of Eric's party, winding through a trail far, far below them and many miles to the southwest. The distance was greater than Rhiannon had expected, and her heart thundered against her chest as she weighed her chances of striking the trees before the men as they rode. Then she nodded to Patrick, and he stepped aside. She used all of her strength to set her arrow carefully within the crossbow. A brief second later she let it fly. They watched the arrow as it arched and flew. Moments later she cried out with delight as she saw it fall into the trees on their path. "Another!" she called quickly to Patrick. Over the next ten minutes she sent arrow after arrow.

Then she could shoot no more. The crossbow was heavy; it took tremendous strength to use. Her arm was in agony, and she doubted that she could shoot another arrow to save her own life.

She sank to the ground, dropping the heavy crossbow. " 'Tis all right, lady! They've come across one at least!" Patrick assured her, stooping down beside her. "Look, they've paused! See there! They are forewarned and cannot be ambushed."

She leapt back to her feet, finding new strength. Staring far down, she could indeed see that the riders had stopped and gathered together. She sighed with pleasure, then frowned as some other movement caught her eye. "Oh, dear God!" she whispered. "Look, Patrick, look! Behind them! The Danes are already behind them!"

The enemy had allowed Eric and his men to pass, and were now quietly following behind them. From her vantage point Rhiannon could see that the trail would lead them to a rise of cliffs that had to be carefully ridden. Eric would be trapped against the rise of rock. "We must warn them again! Patrick, have we any of the parchment left, any of the cords?

Quickly, help me." Patrick moved with haste, finding the remaining warnings and the leather cords.

"Oh, but what shall I use for ink?" she wailed.

"Don't despair, lady, give me a moment."

She thought that he had gone daft, for he knelt down, gathering twigs and dried grass and branches. He drew flint and a striker from his saddle and started to build a fire.

"Patrick—"

"Ah, just one moment!" He smiled, then drew a branch from the fire. "We need only a few words. Write with the burned end, milady."

In seconds she had crudely scrawled out the warning "Behind you." She nearly cried out with the pain as she sent another arrow flying, but then the deed was done, and she closed her eyes and prayed. Then she and Patrick knelt upon the cliff together and watched anxiously.

"It's been found!" Patrick said.

"How can you tell?" she demanded.

"Watch them; watch the battle formation they are taking. They are ready and waiting. They will slice down the Danes like dogs when they think to attack!"

The sun rose high. A trickle of sweat ran down Rhiannon's cheek. From high above, she and Patrick watched the battle. Watched as the Danes approached . . . watched as Eric's men countered their attack before it could begin.

Then Rhiannon let out a ragged sob, for she could not tell in the melee of death who was taking the field.

"The crest of the Wolf still flies, my lady. See? I

cannot so clearly make out the standard, but I know my lord's colors, and they are clear!"

She could make out nothing for the trees and foliage below them. Horses lay dead, men lay dead, and she had to believe that Patrick knew what he was saying. Then she realized that they had spent the entire day upon the cliff—her vision was impaired because night was already falling.

All that was left to do was pray.

She was alone, she realized suddenly. Then, when she turned about, rubbing her eyes, she saw that Patrick had renewed the fire. He stood behind her with a large partridge, grinning. "My lady, I do try to make each meal a different treat."

She smiled wanly. "Patrick, I could not possibly eat."

"You must," he told. "You cannot change the outcome of the battle by refusing to eat."

He was right. And suddenly she remembered that there was another reason she should keep up her strength.

"Let me help—"

"Nay, I can pluck this bird in no time," he assured her.

He cooked the bird and found a stream, and she discovered that she was starving and could wolf down quite a portion of the food and fresh water. They were both tense that night, more anxious than they had been the night before, and even through the long hours of the day. They were quiet, at ease with their silence with one another—they both knew they waited the dawn.

Very late, Rhiannon finally slept, curled up and covered by the width of Patrick's cloak. Surprisingly she slept dreamlessly, and deeply.

The harsh clang of swords was a rude awakening to her.

At the first clash of steel her eyes flew open. She leapt wearily to her feet, glad that at least she had carried a small dagger, sheathed at her ankle. But she had no sword, and the heavy crossbow was no weapon for hand-to-hand combat. She heard a curse, and again the clash of steel, and she swirled about. Patrick was nowhere in sight, yet she knew that he was near, for she could hear the fight. She raced for the edge of the cliff and saw him upon a shelf below. The stripping of the grass and the upturned soil quickly told her that the battle had begun much closer to her and that Patrick had waged his war as far from her as possible to give her time to escape.

"Why, bless you, Irishman!" she whispered aloud, then rushed back to the dying fire. Perhaps she could use the longbow, after all.

Sweeping up the bow and hoisting the quiver of arrows to her back, she hurried back to the cliff. There were two of them against Patrick—dressed in crude skin boots, no hose upon their calves, belted tunics clothing them to their knees. Both wore conical steel helmets and wielded heavy shields. They were adept fighters.

But so was Patrick. He held his own against the two burly giants, yet he could not last forever, Rhiannon thought.

She nearly screamed aloud with the pain in her arm as she drew back on the bow and set and aimed her arrow. She let it fly and watched as it caught one of the men in the shoulder. She didn't know if it was a mortal wound or not, but it caused him to bellow out in pain and drop his sword. Patrick, with barely a breath, dispatched his enemy with a neat, clean thrust, and then looked up to wave to her.

He smiled, but then his smile faded. A look of horror masked his features and he cried out a hoarse warning.

Too late, Rhiannon spun around.

There were three of them before her. Ragged, weary, filthy, and bloodied—Danes.

She screamed, then reached for her dagger, desperately vowing that she should not be taken. Yet there was no hope, and she knew it. She plowed at one in fury and with such speed that she managed to slice through his leather tunic and scratch his flesh. But that was all. She was seized from behind. The force set upon her wrist caused her to drop the dagger. She was dragged hard against the man who had seized her. She tried to bite his hand, and he laughed, lifting her from the ground.

She swore and called them swine and the dung of rodents in their own language, enunciating carefully, making sure they understood every word that she said.

"A she-cat with long, long claws!" Her captor laughed. She twisted to see him. He had dark blond hair, ruddy cheeks, murky dark eyes, and brows that met heavily across his skull. She kicked backward at him with all of her strength, and she must have caught some important piece of his anatomy, for his smile faded and he swore. "A she-cat I will tame here and now, by Odin!" He snarled.

The third man, a younger, slimmer blond with long, matted, and bloodied hair, stepped forward, wrenching her to him. His eyes were light gray, and she felt ill at the way they slid over her. "A she-cat with young, curved breasts and wicked long legs and a fine-shaped rump, my friends."

"A bitch!" growled the man she had wounded, stepping forward. He, in his turn, wrenched her from his younger companion. Rhiannon gasped and staggered back in pain as his hand slashed out, cuffing her brutally against the chin.

She fell, tasted the dirt. Tears stung her eyes, and she realized suddenly that there was indeed a difference between Vikings. These would grant her no mercy. They would tear her to shreds right here upon this cliff.

She didn't know what panic seized her, but she rose and leapt toward the cliff. She would attempt to roll, but if she caught rock and broke her neck or cracked her skull, then so be it. She would prefer the quick and merciful death.

But it wasn't to be hers. She had barely given flight before her hair was caught and she was pulled back into the arms of the dark-haired man. His mouth split into a broad smile as he held her. His teeth, those that remained in his skull, were blackened and horrible. He watched her for a moment with that ridiculous smile, then he hurtled her toward the earth.

"I took her—she's mine first!" he proclaimed. He lunged toward her, and she knew his intent. She leapt up again, but he screamed out to his comrades, "Take her arms, you fools!"

In a second they had her. She writhed and bit

blindly, then she was slapped hard in the face again, and her head began to ring. She heard a pounding and realized that it was not just in her head. Before the dark-haired menace could make another move, a voice rang out.

"Fools! Come, the Irishmen are returning!"

"We've caught a vixen, Yorg, a—" the dark-haired man began.

"And she is mine first, as are all the spoils of this war!" the rider called out sharply. "Give her to me! We ride."

The blond man wrenched her up. Dizzy, Rhiannon realized she had to fight and escape these men before they could take her. She bit the blond, and he yelped out in pain and fury.

"What is the problem?" the horseman, Yorg, demanded.

"She bites!" the blond proclaimed.

"Bind her!"

Her last hope disappeared as Yorg tossed down leather thongs. She still hadn't had a good look at him. Her arms were bound behind her back, and she was tossed up before him on the horse, stomach down. The horse reared as Yorg viciously turned it about.

And they rode.

She thought it was perhaps an hour that they rode, but she did not know in what direction, for she was miserable and dizzy and the movement in her position made her feel wretchedly sick. She was very glad when they stopped, and as she was lifted down, she realized that Yorg was perhaps Eric's own age, well muscled in the shoulders and arms, a warrior with scars, and one, it seemed, well trained to battle. Dark, shaggy hair fell down his shoulders, but his face was clean-shaven, displaying a long scar down his cheek that marred his appearance. Like the others, he was covered with blood, filthy, and ragged in appearance.

He set her upon her feet, studying her in turn. He lifted her cloak and felt the quality of the material. Then he ducked to a knee and felt her hose. She started to kick him, but he grabbed her ankle, causing her to fall. Laughter rang out around her.

"I think, my friends, we've captured a lady of some standing," he mused in his native tongue. "Perhaps we can trick her into giving us her identity, eh, Ragwald?" he said to the blond man.

"She speaks our language very well," Ragwald informed him, a slight edge to his voice that told her there was a great struggle for power among them.

"Does she? Hmm, a lady with learning. Perhaps she comes from Alfred's very house!" he mused. "Well," he said pointedly to her, "do you?"

She spat at him. He roared with fury and came to her, wrenching her arm hard. "So she bites and spits and swears and fights, eh?" he thundered, and he swerved around, dragging Rhiannon with him. Tripping, she followed along, and the others did, too, laughing and applauding their leader. Stumbling, still ill, and wretched, Rhiannon tried to remain on her feet and yet see the terrain. They had come to a farmer's cottage—she could see the corpse of the farmer in his field. There was a broad stream that led down a length of the cliff to the sea, she was certain. And it was to that stream that Yorg dragged her. In the water he pressed her to her knees, then pushed her facefirst into the water, holding her by the length of her hair. She could not breathe, she was going to drown, her chest was bursting. She would die, she thought, and when the pain was gone, perhaps it would be best.

Yorg pulled her from the water. She opened her mouth and gulped in air. He walked around her, and she staggered to her feet. "You'll be tamed, vixen," he promised. He turned to his men, his hands on his hips. "She is a beauty, a prize. I applaud your bringing her to me. Hair like the sun and fire, eyes like precious jewels, lush, ripe . . . indeed a prize. A royal prize. When I have done with her, she will draw a goodly ransom!" He chortled.

Her ties were binding her, but fury and dreadful, horrible fear sent her catapulting forward, striking Yorg with her body with such a startling impact that he pitched forward into the water himself. His men roared. She backed away quickly and desperately as he rose.

There were more of them, she realized with sick dismay. Suddenly they were all around her—the men who had seized her and more. All of them bloodied, some of them limping, they had come to this quiet glen, murdered the farmer, and taken the place to hide out and nurse their wounds. She could never escape.

And now Yorg was up on his feet, shrieking like a wounded bear, thrashing through the water to reach her side. She tried to run. He caught her and spun her around. She flinched instinctively as his fist raised to come against her cheek, but the blow never fell.

"By all Valhalla, she is mine, and you will give her to me or answer with your life!" A voice rang out.

Yorg's arm fell. Everyone turned with amazement to see what effrontery had brought a man to argue the rights over a woman with Yorg.

No one's amazement was greater than Rhiannon's, for a single rider had come among the men. He was mounted on a small brown pony and seemed immense upon it. He was as blond and golden as the sun, except that his hair was matted with blood. He wore no clothing she had ever seen before but was clad like these men in skins and fur-lined boots, tattered and ragged from battle. His face was dirty and grimy and barely recognizable, but there was no mistaking his eyes.

It was Eric. Eric, alone, calmly walking into this sea of the enemy and demanding that she be given to him.

She was too startled to cry out, and in a minute she was grateful that amazement had taken her tongue, for she realized that he was pretending to be among their number.

Yorg let go of her and strode through the water to the horseman. "Who are you? And who in the name of all the gods do you think you are to demand anything of me? Do you know who I am, you fool?"

"I demand her because she is my captive, taken by your men."

"Who—"

"I am sent by Gunthrum—whom you have failed, Yorg!" Eric dismounted and thrashed through the water, straight toward Yorg, to wrench Rhiannon away from the Dane and drag her along with him in a method every bit as crude as Yorg's. She cried out, falling. He dragged her back up to her feet, slipping a dagger from the sheath at his ankle and slicing the strips of skin that bound her.

"What do you think you're doing?" Yorg snarled.

"Taking back what is mine."

"She's mine now. And I had her tied."

"You had her tied because you are not even warrior enough to hang on to a woman," Eric said, sneering. "And she is mine because I seized her first, and I am ordered to take her to Gunthrum."

"What care I for Gunthrum?" Yorg demanded.

Ragwald stepped forward. "We found her upon a cliff. You were careless with your captive. The bitch was sending messages," he spat out. "She was the one raining down the arrows that warned the bastard Irish-Norseman of our attack. You were not warrior enough to hold a woman!"

Eric stepped back, drawing his sword. He smiled, and the smile was an eerie one. "Come. Test the warrior that I am."

Shouts went up. It seemed that Ragwald regretted his challenge, but he drew his own sword and stepped forward. "A man dies of old age and is forgotten!" he yelled. "A warrior sits in Valhalla, and you will sit in Valhalla this night!"

They were brave words, but Rhiannon had never, until that moment, quite realized the full value of her husband's prowess. Barely had Ragwald moved with a battle cry on his lips than Eric had countered that move, swinging his heavy sword as if it were a twig. Even as Ragwald bore down upon him, Eric swung his sword again and shifted his weight.

There was never even a clash of steel. Ragwald fell

before Rhiannon, and the pool of water before her began to spread out red.

She screamed as her arm was forcefully yanked, and she was pulled against her husband's side once again. "She's mine!" he roared. "Mine, by Gunthrum's order. Who else would dispute me?"

There was no sound. Then Yorg spoke, more carefully than he had before. "She is from a royal house, perhaps Alfred's own. She is worth a great deal and has been in our keeping. What will you pay for her?"

"The brown pony," Eric said, indicating the horse.

Yorg spat into the water. "The brown pony? You offer me a pony for a treasure?"

"A treasure!" Eric snorted. "She is not worth so much."

"Her hair is gold and flame!" Yorg argued.

"It is tarnished brass, no more," Eric said flatly. Rhiannon spun on him, startled. He held her tight, ignoring her. "Take the pony in trade."

"Worthless compared to this woman!" Yorg insisted. "She is young, with breasts as ripe and sweet as fruit and legs as long and as tempting as willows."

Eric laughed good-humoredly. "Breasts like sagging melons, my friend, and legs as knotted and knock-kneed as a willow, if you would."

"Take care! She understands your every word!" Yorg warned Eric.

She did indeed. Rhiannon could not resist. He was directly by her side, and she swung about to kick him, hard. After all, she was a captive—whether theirs or his. She had every right to fight.

Yorg laughed, and someone warned Eric that she bit worse than a rabid dog, and before she knew it he had his hand in her hair, pushing her down into the water again, and pinning her angrily before him. Sodden and both furious and terrified, she listened as the negotiations continued.

"Her temper is worse, indeed, than that of a rabid dog," Eric told Yorg.

"Then why would you have her?" Yorg craftily demanded.

"Because I took her first, and therefore she is mine, for all that she is a vixen."

"Give her to me this night—she will be yours tomorrow."

"She is mine now."

They were at a stalemate, Rhiannon realized. It was insane. Eric could not battle them all, not if they rushed him. Why had he come alone? she wondered.

She cried out, startled, as he ripped her mantle from her shoulders, along with the sapphire brooch that held it there. He tossed the sodden garment to Yorg. "It is all that I offer, and it is worth much." He shoved Rhiannon ahead of him with such force that she nearly fell. Staggering, she swirled in protest. He thrust her forward again with a thunderous expression and greater force. "Go!" he roared.

She moved. She walked past Yorg, and then she felt that they were all around her. Eric pushed her past the brown pony and the others, and across the open field where the farmer's body lay. He walked calmly and with purpose, with his long stride, his arrogance, his determination.

Finally they reached the forest, and there was a trail within the darkness of the trees. He shoved her once again, and she swung around on him, terrified and swearing. "You bastard! Why—"

He had no reply for her except another furious order. "Run!" he commanded, and he took her hand. Even as they started thrashing through the trees and foliage, she realized that Yorg and his duped comrades were coming after them at last.

14

Eric passed by her, catching her hand, dragging her along at a speed that soon stole her breath away. Her chest burned ferociously, and pain streaked down her legs, then shot back upward from her calves. Tree branches and brambles caught and tore at her hair and her clothing, but despite her gasps, Eric kept his steady runner's pace, amazingly fleet considering the steely bulk of his muscles.

At last she tripped over a root. Her hand was wrenched free from her husband's and she went sprawling into a pool of mud. He stopped, swirled around, swore vehemently, started to reach out a hand to her, and then paused.

The woods were silent. They had outrun Yorg and his men. Eric's continued silence assured Rhiannon that it was true.

"Well, milady"—he scowled, exasperated— "would you care to get up so that we may keep going? Or do you wish to rest so there?"

Her fear of Yorg died away with a renewed birth of fury. She closed her fingers around a handful of the mud and slung it Eric's way before leaping swiftly to her feet to circle him carefully.

The mud caught him right on the nose. She would

have laughed out loud except that the dark color of the earth framed his eyes as neatly as the silver tones of his battle helmet and his eyes had become a very lethal blue.

"I wish to rest here!" she exclaimed, fighting for breath to maintain her fury. "Oh! Of course I do not wish to rest in mud! I can barely move, milord. What on earth were you doing there!"

"What!" He had circled around her with purpose but now stood dead still, his hands upon his hips as he stared at her. "Madam, did you wish to remain in the Dane's embrace? You had only to say so!"

"Oh! And you would have let me remain? I seem to recall that there was once a place I longed to remain, and my longing had no effect upon your will!"

He moved quickly toward her, and before she could escape on the slippery earth, he had caught her. He tossed her heedlessly over his shoulder and started to move.

"What are you doing?" she cried.

"Returning you to the Dane!" he thundered. "You are a vixen and a shrew, and you bite, and, quite frankly, your hair is currently the color of a dung heap."

"Oh!" She slammed her fists against his back. "Put me down!"

He released her and she slid back into the mud. She started to reach for another handful of it, but suddenly he was on top of her, as caked with the brown earth as she. All that she could see of his face was the blue of his eyes. His fingers wound tightly around her wrists, and then she saw the white flash of his teeth as he smiled. "I was trying to rescue you, though heaven alone knows why!"

"You fool, you could have been killed!" she railed in return. "You've command of hundreds of men, yet you entered into Danish horde alone, in rags—"

"My God, woman!" he exclaimed heatedly. "Don't you know what they would have done to you had they realized that you might be seized by a Norse-Irish host? They'd have killed you before we could have entered into battle!"

His words chilled her to the bone. She had heard tales about the atrocities committed by the raiders. Tales of men nailed to trees, forced to watch as their entrails were sliced from their bodies. Beneath the dirt on her face she paled, then trembled. She felt his weight against her and knew that he had not realized the meaning of her silence, for he continued on in a fury. "I should strip the flesh from your back myself, madam, that you should have come to put us both in such a position!"

"I came to warn you!" she cried out.

"You were told to take care! Not to expose yourself across the countryside."

"My God, how dare you! I saved you and your men from the treachery of another!"

He pushed up and demanded furiously, "Was it another? I have felt the shaft of those well-aimed arrows of yours—remember, my love?"

"But—"

"Ah, you're a remarkable actress, too, Rhiannon. I seem to recall a night when your performance nearly incited hundreds of men to bloodshed. It was our wedding night, remember? Perhaps you sent the message, then came out to 'warn' us in a pretense of innocence."

Fury filled her until she was choking. Her emotion was such that she managed to thrust him from her. He slipped in the mud even as she rose and nimbly ran from the pool.

"Rhiannon!"

In a second he had caught up with her. She tried to struggle free from his grasp, but she stepped down hard on a root and cried out as her ankle twisted. He swept her up in his arms and continued walking, his gaze straight ahead, his face masked in the mud but for his eyes.

"My men should now be descending upon the Danes hiding in that camp," he told her at length. "We'll meet with them by the fork in the brook tomorrow."

She did not reply. She was filthy and her throat was parched and every muscle within her body ached and burned. She leaned her head back, exhausted, and closed her eyes.

Despite the jar of his movements as he walked, she must have dozed. When she opened her eyes again, the world was still and darkness had fallen. All that lit the forest around her was the glow of a bright full moon and a twinkling of stars. Then she realized that a fire also burned nearby, that some meat roasted upon it, and that she rested on the earth on a pillow created of Eric's shirt, heavily padded to support the weight of his mail. She could hear water running close by and knew that he had not rested until he had reached the point where he had said that he would meet up with his men.

She still felt dizzy and closed her eyes. They flew open once again as something cold touched her forehead. Eric was at her side, stripped down to his hose, cleaning the mud from her face with a length of material from his over-tunic. She quickly sat up, warily backing away from him.

"Rhiannon, I was merely trying to—"

"I can take care of myself, thank you!"

"Can you?" he demanded.

"You are putting more mud on me than you are taking off!"

"Well, that, madam, can be most easily solved."

She shrieked in protest, pounding his chest as he swept her from the ground and headed with her straight into the cold water of the brook. It was deep here, where the waters met to rush out to the sea. And when the wetness came to his hips, he dropped her into it. She came up sputtering and choking and swearing, increasingly infuriated by his laughter.

She swirled about, and he caught her by the material of her tunic. "You've soaked my clothing, and I shall now drown of its weight or freeze if I do not die of the sheer longing for your demise!" she told him.

He jerked her into the hold of his arms. "Well, love, we mustn't have drowned," he said. "If thine own eye offends thee, pluck it out—a good Christian platitude, is it not? Your clothing is hardly an eye, but if it offends you . . ." And with his words he caught the hem of the garmet and stripped it from her despite her writhing, her flailing fists, and her oaths. When he was done with that, he heedlessly tipped her back into the water to take off her hose. He tossed both to the shore as she dived deep to escape him. Far across the brook, she crossed her arms over her chest and stared at him in a quivering fury.

"Come back here," he commanded.

"You are insane!"

"Rhiannon, we could not stay so encrusted with mud. Come over here. I only wish to rinse out your hair before it is so matted with the stuff that we'll have to cut it out."

"Well, what would be the loss of such a tangled mass of tarnished brass?" she retorted.

He was silent, and then his laughter suddenly rang out. "Alas, what vanity is this?" he teased. The water rippled as he strode toward her within it. She dived in the moonlight, swimming far beneath the water, surfacing only when her lungs were bursting.

And still he was not far behind. "Rhiannon . . ."

She dived again. This time she chose her direction poorly, and he quickly captured her foot. He pulled her against him, his hands sliding along her naked thigh, hot against the chill of the water. She choked and struggled, but her breasts were taut against his chest, and she was suddenly staring into the very deep blue of his eyes in the moonlight. His knuckles brushed her teeth. The sizzling light of passion came to burn within his blue eyes.

Breathlessly she demanded, "What would you have with hair so tarnished?"

His fingers curved over the rise of her buttocks and swept seductively along her spine, then lowered again, pressing her close to him so that she could feel the rise of his sex hard against the apex of her thighs.

"What would you have had me tell him?" he asked her softly. "Aye, indeed, it is glorious hair. It shines with the light of dawn, and that of the sunset too. It blankets me with softness, with beauty; it caresses my naked flesh with a life and wonder all its own." His fingers stroked her soaking hair, smoothing it back, then wandered down her cheek and fell slowly over her throat and collarbone. His palm teased her chilled and hardened nipple even as his fingers closed warmly about her breasts. She caught her breath as his touch there started a bonfire within her that burned even between her legs, and she leaned back, resisting him. "My lord, I would not have you insulted by allowing you to dally with a breast that was ever so like a rotten, sagging melon!"

A smile flickered over his features, and they were shatteringly handsome in the dusky light. "Aye, but if I had told him yes, indeed, they were the lushest, sweetest fruit, hard and firm as apples, alabaster tipped with rosebuds, and glorious in their beauty, alas! He might have determined never to let you go."

His stroke was light and magic. His palms moved with a tender, scintillating rhythm over those rosy crests, and she feared that her knees would buckle, even as he held her. Then, without warning, his touch suddenly shifted with bold intimacy to sweep searing heat betwixt her thighs, and she shuddered and held tight, forgetting her protest. Yet he had not forgotten his words, for his denial of them still rang out softly as he whispered against her ear. "Knock-kneed, madam? I dared not tell him that the feel of your flesh was finer than any fabric raided from the masters of the east, that your legs were indeed long and shapely, and that they could wrap around a man to give him ecstasy so great, it was indeed paradise here on earth.

I could not tell him that the taste of you was sweeter than any wine, that it was possible to drown in the beauty of your eyes, that the wanting of you could knot a man inside and out, and that I should readily die to retrieve you, for I had tasted your sweetness and would defy any man, any god, to have you once again."

He taunted her; surely he taunted her. Yet as she raised her eyes to his there seemed to be no mockery in his gaze. He lifted her from the water to carry her to the shore, and there he set her down again. Again he spoke of the alabaster beauty of her flesh in the glow of the moonlight. And as he spoke of each of her perfections he planted there a tender yet sensual kiss, until it seemed that she was dried from the chill of the water by the heat of his lips and tongue, and then it was his body that warmed her, and the startling, seductive tenderness gave way at last to the searing rise of passion.

Later, so much later, when the moon at last begin to sink in the blackness of the heavens, when passion had been heavily spent and exhaustion had nearly claimed her, she felt his arms again, lifting her, carrying her beneath the tree and setting her there upon the warmth of his own mantle. She had nearly drifted off to sleep when he nudged her and offered her some of the meat, now well-charred, that he had set upon the fire. She did not think that she could eat, but the food was delicious, and she found that she had acquired a ravenous hunger.

When they had finished their meal, he came down beside her and held her close against his naked heat. Lost in the warmth and comfort of him, Rhiannon thought that this was almost like being cherished, almost like being loved.

Yet it had been an illusion of the night, she thought as the first bright rays of dawn awoke her. For when she opened her eyes, he was gone from her side. The mantle was cast down carelessly upon her, and as she wrapped it about herself, shivering as she sat up, she saw that Eric was dressed and stood some distance from her, one roughly booted foot balanced on a stone as he stared out pensively at the water.

He seemed to sense that she had awakened, for his sharp gaze quickly fell on her as well. "Get up, dress," he told her curtly. "The men will be here soon."

Stunned by his tone, she gritted her teeth and rose regally, his mantle cloaked about her. She walked to the water and knelt down and drank deeply, then cleansed her face. She felt his eyes upon her all the while. When she rose and swung about to face him, he was still watching her with a chilling gaze. Anger and irritation simmered deeply within her. Tenderness was a tactic with him—he waged battles with her according to strategy, as he did his enemies. When the need was gone, he cast tenderness aside as he might an empty dish.

"What are you staring at?" she demanded. "Just what is it that you want from me now? Aren't you accustomed to merely taking anything that you desire?"

"If I could take the truth from you, my love, know it —I surely would."

"What truth? What are you talking about now?"

He was slow to answer, and then he shrugged. "If

not you, Rhiannon, who? Who is the traitor within your own home?"

She stiffened, inhaling sharply. She had risked her life to warn him, and he still suspected that the treachery had come from her! "Bastard!" she hissed at him, and that was all. Swinging about, she collected the pieces of still damp clothing. She was about to stamp around the tree when he caught her arm, her eyes raising furiously to his.

"I did not accuse you—" he began.

She wrenched free. Tears were stinging her eyes, and so she swung at him blindly. Her arm was caught and she stood tightly against him. "I asked you who, Rhiannon, that is all! You must have an idea of who or what is behind this!"

"I don't!" she flung out. "I don't know! Let go of me!"

"Rhiannon!" His voice grew gentle, and he moved to smooth the hair from her forehead. She tossed her head back to elude his touch. "No! Don't give me your pretenses of gentleness, for the lies are useless by the morning's light, are they not? There is no sweet emotion lost between us, milord!" She wrenched free from his touch, backing away from him, afraid that the tears that stung her lids would fall and she would betray the fact that many emotions were rising terrifyingly within her. "Accuse me if you would, but do so honestly. I despise the lie of—of tenderness from you!"

She saw the tightening of his jaw and the lighting flash within his eyes, and still she was not prepared when he came toward her, drawing her close again with a grip that threatened to smash the fragile bones within her wrist. "Despise me, loathe me, spend your every waking hour ruing the day that I was born! But obey me, Rhiannon, in all things. And answer me with a civil tongue when I ask you a question!"

"Then ask me civil questions!" she tossed back, praying that he would release her. She would break, she would cry, if he did not to do so quickly. Only a fool would love him. Only a fool would succumb to his whispered words in the velvet of the night. Only a fool.

Dear God, she was slowly but surely becoming a fool, needing him, seeking his approval, yearning for those whispered words. . . .

Craving his silken touch in the darkness.

"Who is doing this?" he repeated.

"I don't know!" she answered once again. And then she smiled through clenched teeth and reminded him, "Surely not Egmund nor Thomas—my men, mi-lord!—unless you believe that their ghosts rose from beneath a tree to betray you and Alfred ever fur-ther!"

He was not able to reply, for at that moment there came a thrashing through the trees and a cheerful, if somewhat anxious, cry on the morning breeze.

"Eric! Are you here?"

Eric's eyes remained sharply upon her as he cried back. "Aye, Rollo, we are here!"

Rhiannon tugged frantically upon her wrist once again, her anger and hurt momentarily forgotten. "My lord, I am not dressed!" she reminded him. But it was too late, for horses were moving into the clearing —Patrick's and Rollo's first, Rowan's close behind.

The mantle was about her, but her clothing now lay strewn at her feet.

Patrick quickly dismounted and hurried before her, catching her free hand, falling to his knees. "Bless our Holy Father and all the saints, my lady! I was so frightened for you."

"Patrick, please!" she said softly, wondering what Eric thought of this display. "Please, get up."

But he did not. "You saved my life, lady, with that arrow, and risked your own. And though I found Eric quickly enough, we could not charge in upon them, for in danger the things that the Danes sometimes do to captives are best never spoken. But, lady, you are here, and safe, and we are so grateful—"

"And the Danes?" Eric interrupted dryly.

"They hadn't a chance," Rollo assured Eric from his mount.

"Not this group," Rowan added quietly. Rhiannon's eyes touched his. She felt a soft color rise to her cheeks as she remembered that her clothing lay at her feet.

"We must ride for Eric," Rollo said quietly.

Patrick, who had realized he knelt upon her tunic, rose awkwardly. "We shall ride on past the clearing and await you," he told Eric.

Rollo was not so delicate. He burst into laughter. "Alas, but we have spent the night in deep worry, and milord and milady have spent the night as if they played in some paradise. Indeed, excuse us, Eric—we shall wait beyond the trees."

Patrick remounted, and the riders were quickly gone. Rhiannon turned her back on Eric and tried to stumble into her clothing with the mantle still about her shoulders. He was silent for a moment, then his voice thundered out with irritation. "What is this, madam? Some new game?" He pulled the mantle from her, and she shivered in the coolness of the morning air, facing him furiously. His eyes raked over her and then met and clashed with her own. "I know every tender inch of your form, Rhiannon, and I would remind you that you are mine, that I am not a man of patience, and that I will not tolerate this foolishness."

She stared at him, longing for some power to hurt him. She tossed back her head and set her hands upon her hips, heedless of her own nudity. "Fine!" she tossed back, and reached down for her hose. Ignoring him, she donned them. He watched her in a cold silence all the time that she dressed, and when she had finished and started walking for the clearing, he caught her by the arm and pulled her back. "I warned you, milady—hate me but obey me."

"I shall try not to send messages again," she said sweetly.

"In all things," he said sharply.

"I will see that delightful meals are served at all the proper times."

He smiled, the corner of his lip just curving, his eyes wicked with a searing blue taunt. "In all things," he repeated softly. "I will have what I want at my whim."

She inhaled, her heart thundering. "And what of my whim, my lord?"

"I shall be delighted to serve your every desire."

"And what if my desire is not to be so served?"

He laughed and pulled her very close, and she did

not know if he was angry or amused. "I think perhaps you must learn to mesh your desires with mine, Rhiannon, and then we shall both be served." And then the laughter was gone, and his voice was very low and rang with a hint of steel. "I have warned you to obey me. I will have my way, so do not ever think that it shall not be so."

"You will have your way?" she queried, determined to challenge him. "Well, it seems that I have disobeyed you now, great Eric of Dubhlain. Either I betrayed you or I disobeyed in running about the countryside. I'm no better than Alexander, certainly no more valuable a property! What would you do with an errant stallion or with a disobedient serf? Why not hang me, milord, or slice my head from my shoulders and have done with it!"

"Ah, but that would be too final!" he said lightly. "Trust me, madam, I am seriously considering some wounding punishment to your flesh, but one that I alone shall administer, and in privacy. Now, my lady and wife, shall we go?"

She flashed him a glance of pure loathing and spun around with all haste. "Some Danish battle-ax shall get you yet, my lord!" she cast back sweetly.

"Not in time for you, beloved wife," he replied in every bit as pleasant a tone.

It seemed a battle lost. With her head held high, Rhiannon was determined on retreat. She didn't say another word but hurried out of the clearing where Rowan, Patrick, and Rollo awaited them at the head of a contingent of men. Patrick brought her a mare and helped her to mount. She watched as Rollo brought Eric the white stallion. Eric smiled, greeting the animal as a friend, stroking its nose and whispering a word of welcome before leaping gracefully upon its back.

He was far more pleased with the horse he had acquired than with his wife, she thought bitterly, amazed again at the sharp pain within her. How could she care? He had invaded her land, he had stripped her of everything. Even pride. Her taunts and show of rebellion were an illusion, she thought, her last effort at waging war against him. She could not surrender, ever, or she would be lost.

They started the ride home, Eric in the lead. Rhiannon held back, riding between Patrick and Rowan. *I will not love you!* she vowed silently to Eric's back. *And I will not fear you!*

Here, amid them all, none could accuse her of anything improper with Rowan, and so she discovered that she could easily converse with him and Patrick, of whom she was growing very fond. She smiled and talked, and she and Rowan listened while Patrick gave wonderful descriptions of his native land and assured them that St. Patrick, his namesake, had indeed driven all the snakes from Eire many, many years ago.

" 'Tis a pity he cannot come back and take care of the Danes!" Rollo said with a woeful smile, turning back to them. Rhiannon laughed delightedly, her eyes sparkling, her lips curving. But then her smile faded, for she saw that her husband, too, had turned back and studied her curiously. She bowed her head, then tossed it back once again, ignoring him. She asked Patrick to tell her another tale, and he did, assuring her this time that there were little people who lived in the rocks and the crevices and in the caves far beneath the ground.

The ride was pleasant, and Rhiannon was surprised at the ease with which they returned. Yet even as night approached again and they came upon the last leg of the journey home, she felt a change in the air.

Clouds had formed over them, bilious and black. She felt a chill wind coming in from the sea.

As they approached the walls of the town Eric held up a hand, and the entire party came to a stop. Between the men's shoulders Rhiannon could see that Mergwin stood in the road, awaiting them. He stood alone, and yet it seemed that he commanded all of the road, as well as the sky and even the sea beyond them. The wind caught his white hair and whipped the length of his beard. His eyes seemed as gray and as heavy as the clouds, shrouded in misery.

"What is it?" Eric demanded sharply, dismounting from his horse. He came to the old man and Mergwin clutched his hands, and Rhiannon suddenly saw the frailty in the old Druid and rune master. Even as she stared at him she saw past him to the sea.

The coast was filled with Viking ships again, great ships with intricately carved prows of beasts, dragons, and serpents.

Her heart began to hammer. What new invasion was this? How often could they battle the Vikings? King Alfred had been doing so forever and forever, so long that he had been forced to use Vikings to battle the Vikings.

But Eric did not seem alarmed by the ships. His attention was all for the old man who blocked their path.

"It is the Ard-ri," Mergwin said.

"Grandfather," Eric breathed. He looked steadily at Mergwin. "He is dying."

"Your father has sent for you. You mother needs you. If you sail with the morning tide, you will see Aed Finnlaith once again."

Eric shouted that Mergwin be brought a horse, then he mounted once again. Silence fell over the party as they rode onward through the gates.

Eric quickly dismounted before the manor house and entered the hall. Rhiannon started to dismount and discovered that Patrick was there to help her. His eyes were sorrowful. They even gleamed with a hint of tears.

"He will definitely sail for Ireland?" she asked. *Please, God*, she thought, *let him go. Keep him away from me so that he does not touch me, so that I can learn to hate him again! Don't let me care, please, don't let me care. . . .*

"Aye, indeed, he will go! The Ard-ri is beloved of all men, especially his children and his grandsons. He is a great man; he forged the peace and he kept it, and he gave justice and compassion to all men. You would have loved him too."

She nodded, because Patrick seemed to feel the pain of the Ard-ri's coming loss so keenly. She tried not to show her relief that her husband would be leaving her.

She hurried into the hall, thinking that she would escape quietly to Adela's room and stay there, away from the preparations for the journey, out of sight and out of mind. Yet even as she came through the hall she stopped, for Mergwin awaited her in the entry, his eyes gray and brooding and accusing. How had he known she would enter right then? With all else on his mind, how had he thought to find her?

"I begged you not to go!" he reminded her, and there was pain in his voice, and worry, and she was suddenly very sorry that she had hurt him so. She cared for him—she could not help but care for him. He was frightening in his way, but he was her friend too. She knew that he believed in her. He had even wanted her as Eric's wife.

She shook her head. "I'm sorry. Truly, Mergwin, I never meant to hurt you. And I am sorry, too, for your Ard-ri. He seems to be so admired and loved, he must be a very great man. I will pray for him with all my heart. All of us here will pray for him."

She had not noticed that Eric had quietly come behind Mergwin in the hallway until his voice, crisp and cold, snapped out to her a sharp command. "Madam, you needn't pray for him. You will accompany us with the morning tide."

Her gaze quickly flew from Mergwin's eyes to those of her husband. In the shadow of the hallway they were cobalt. She thought that he did not want her with him—he simply wasn't going to leave her because he knew how anxious she was for him to go.

She swallowed, fighting to be soft-spoken and reasonable. "Eric, I am afraid that I would be in your way. It will be a very difficult time for you—"

"And I would not increase that difficulty by wondering what you are up to here—if the Danes have come to seize you or if you have decided to go walking into a Danish camp," he said harshly. "You'd best look into packing your things, although Mergwin has already advised Adela to pack for you."

"But, my lord husband—" she began carefully.

"Rhiannon, cease your act and make haste. The dawn will come quickly."

She looked imploringly at Mergwin but knew that he wasn't about to help her—she had duped him once. And Eric . . .

"I shall not go!" she swore, furiously striding past him.

He stopped her, catching a tangled tress of her hair. When she cried out, he calmly studied the lock and then smiled icily at her. "Rhiannon, you will come. Willing or no, you will come." His blue eyes seemed to strike hers. "I suggest that you make it willingly." He released her hair and strode by her, returning to the hall. Rhiannon glanced wretchedly at Mergwin, then went tearing up the stairs.

Adela was in the room. A warm bath, clean towels, and rose-scented soap awaited her. Adela assured her with a certain awe that they had all been anxiously awaiting her return—and yet Mergwin had assured them time and time again that no harm would befall her, that she would eventually come home. "And when we saw the Viking ships again and realized that they were not our own returning, why, we were all in a panic! But Mergwin quickly assured us that they came from Olaf the White, King of Dubhlain. To watch them was fantastic! And then you returned, just as Mergwin said you would! And now you will go to Ireland! Oh, Rhiannon, I shall miss you dearly. You must take the greatest care!"

"I am not going to Ireland!" Rhiannon said desperately.

"But, my dear—"

"I am not going!"

Even as she spoke, there was a tap upon the door, and it opened before either of them could call out. Rhiannon shivered as she thought that it might be Eric, that he might have heard her defiant words.

But it was not Eric. It was the girl, Judith—the one who seemed to adore Eric so very much. She came in with a tray of food and set it upon one of the trunks, then bobbed a curtsy to Rhiannon. "My lady, Lord Eric has said that this should be brought to you and that you should eat and then rest, since it will still be dark when you must rise again."

Watching the pretty girl, Rhiannon knew that Judith would gladly serve Eric in any way. Had she done so already?

"Thank you, Judith," Rhiannon said. The girl stayed there, looking about the room.

She could not bear the thought of Judith in his arms, or in his bed, or in this very room. She fought hard to curb her temper. She would not make a fool of herself. "Judith, thank you, that is all."

With a sigh the girl left the room. "I'd watch that one!" Adela warned her.

"Mmm," Rhiannon murmured wearily. She wanted to be alone. She turned around and gripped her cousin's hands. "You've done so well for me already—my trunks packed and my bath complete. I'm fine now. I'm going to comb out my hair, eat quickly, and go to bed. You do the same. You must be exhausted."

Adela's eyes were troubled. "If you're sure—"

"I am. Please."

Adela kissed her, then left.

As soon as she was gone, Rhiannon began to pace the room. Then she sat at the end of her bed and idly began to comb her hair. It was raggedly tangled from her nights in the wilderness, but she set to it with a will, and in time it began to dry and untangle and fall softly into her hands and over her shoulders and down her back. She held still for a moment, then dived into her one of her trunks and searched through it for a bed gown. She found a sheer linen one with delicate embroidery about the throat and wrists and with material so fine that it covered almost nothing at all. She slipped into it swiftly, wondering how late it was, then if Eric would come to her at all that night. She glanced at the tray of food that she had not eaten, discovered the mead upon it, and gulped it down. Then she swept her comb through her hair once again.

There were footsteps outside her door. She set down the comb and plunged into the bed, draping her hair about her.

The door opened. She heard Eric's footsteps as he moved about the room. She listened as he closed the door, and she seemed to freeze as he paused, then walked over to the bed and stood staring down at her.

He was there several long moments, then she heard him move away, aware of the thud of his boots upon the floor and the fall of his clothing as he stripped in the candlelight. She heard him swear softly as he climbed into the now very cold water of her bath, and she heard him splash about for a moment, then rise and come from the tub.

He would come to the bed and accuse her of faking sleep. And she would rise and remind him that all life was by his whim, and she would try very hard to please him and convince him that she would anxiously await his return—if only he would leave her.

But when he lay down beside her, he did not touch her. He turned his back on her.

She opened her eyes. He had snuffed out the candles, but the moonlight came through and played upon the sleek muscles of his back. She bit her lip, hesitating, frustrated. She tried twisting about, brushing his naked back with her backside and tossing a long lock of her hair upon him. Still he made no move.

She lay back and stared at the ceiling.

"Eric," she said softly at last.

He rose up on an elbow. In the moonlight she could feel him watching her.

"I am sorry about your grandfather. Truly I am."

He said nothing. After a moment he started to lie back down, but then he swore a soft oath and set his arms about her stiff shoulders, pulling her back. She allowed soft tears to glaze her eyes, and as he held her to him, he paused, and she whispered, *"Please* don't make me go! I am so afraid!"

"Oh?" he said, braced above her, studying her features.

She was beautiful in the moonlight. Her eyes so soft, shimmering, liquid, her lips trembling, as red as the rose that had given the nectar to the scent that lingered sweetly over the length of her. Beneath the frail barrier of the gown her breasts rose and fell rapidly with the intake of her breath. The mounds seemed larger, fuller, more tempting than ever; her nipples were larger, darker, duskier, more fascinating, more seductive. Her hair lay about her as soft as down, curling over his nakedness, entangling him. But then she had done that already, entangled and enmeshed him with those skeins of gold and fire, with those eyes of shimmering silver, with the beauty of her lyrical voice and supple form. It was not love, he thought harshly, never love. But she was his, and he desired her beyond any desire he had ever known. He wanted to take her gently into his arms, to reassure her, to hold her.

But he knew her. Knew her well.

What new game was this? It did not matter, he thought wearily. She might as well play it.

"Eric . . ." She said his name softly, seductively, with a whisper, with a trembling innocence. "My lord, please, I would be a good wife, I would obey, I would . . . serve you in all things. But please, not this! I beg you, don't make me go to Ireland. When you return, I will be here. And I will strive to be everything that you want of a wife."

He stroked her hair, finding fascination in the length of it as his fingers moved over the shining softness. "Will you?" he asked her.

"I will."

Her lashes were low, her eyes soft and seductive. He eased himself down her body, nuzzling her breasts, then closing his mouth gently over one mound and stroking the hard-tipped crest with the length of his tongue over the texture of the sheer linen. She exhaled a sharp gasp, and her body surged against his, her soft woman's form contacting the rod of his masculinity and quickening the rise of heat and savage need within him.

"I will be whatever you want!" she promised, digging into his locks. She rose with him, draping her hair around him, wrapping her arms about him. Her quick kisses rained over his shoulders and his chest. She held the length of her hair and stroked his body with the soft, silky strands. The sweet-smelling tresses aroused him wherever they touched. Her lips fell upon his and lingered there, and then traveled over his body again. Softly, subtly, sweetly, she seduced him. Desire became a storm within him, shattering, fierce, a whirlwind. She knew how to touch him just where he needed to be touched. She knew when to tantalize, when to tease, when to give. She could blind a man, seduce him until nothing mattered but the fulfillment of his desire. . . .

He caught her savagely, dragged her atop him, then flipped her down over onto her back. He saw her eyes, and for a moment, before her lashes fell rich and thick over them, he saw a certain triumph there. Fury shook him suddenly, and he breathed in, bracing himself lest he give in to the very ferocity of it.

Hold! he commanded himself, for he would give her the game she played. He smiled, and he tenderly kissed her lips, tasting the sweetness of her mouth. And then he took his time and his leisure, making love erotically through the sheerness of the garment, searing her belly through it and below, touching her ever more intimately, to the pink core of her own desire, with the lapping wet heat of his tongue over the rougher texture of the gown. Whispers and cries met his thrusts, and soon she trembled uncontrollably beneath him, writing, twisting, undulating.

He ripped the gown to shreds, finding her naked flesh, voraciously taking all of it. And when she nearly lay limp from all the shattering climaxes he had mercilessly orchestrated in her, he pulled her beneath him, sheathed himself passionately within her, and demanded everything once again.

And everything was his. He had never known such a sweet and savage explosion of release as that which came to him that night, as wild as the sea in the rage of a storm. Fierce, racking shudders seized him and he filled her again and again with himself, then fell upon her, for a moment at the most extreme peace, sated as he had never imagined that he could be. He closed his eyes and felt the thunder of her heart beneath the fullness of her breast, and he knew that he could touch her, that he could draw from her many, many things that she did not want to give.

But he knew, too, that she had deceived him, that she loathed the very idea of being his wife.

A bitter smile tore at his lips, and a heaviness fell painfully over his chest. God! If he could cease to want her! If he could forget her very existence . . .

But he could not. When he was not with her, she taunted his dreams. When he thought of her in danger, he was pierced as with a knife. She was his wife.

And, by God, she would learn that she was so, and that her tricks and deceit could not change things, that she must obey him. . . .

He wondered still at the pain within him, and he

gritted his teeth hard against it. Then he pulled her to him and whispered softly in the night, "So you would love me when I return?"

Her breathing was still ragged. He cupped her breast as he held her, and still he could hear the pulse of her heart. "Aye, my lord," she whispered huskily.

"When I return . . . you would honor and obey me?"

"Aye!"

He kissed her forehead and pulled her against him. He stared at the ceiling and then closed his eyes. Damn her! Aed Finnlaith was dying! The thought tore into him, and he could not face it. His grandfather was in Ireland; he was the country's peace, he was its grace. He had brought Ireland her golden age, and he was wise and wonderful. Eric would never forget him—his wisdom, his teachings.

And she would cause him havoc even now . . .

His arms tightened for a minute. She made a slight sound of protest, and he eased his hold. He needed to sleep, if only for a few hours.

But he did not. He lay awake. And when the first hint of dawn rose, he tossed aside the linen sheet and came to his feet.

She must have known, even in sleep, that he had left the bed. A soft smile curled her lip and she stretched out comfortably, her hair a golden cloak about her. He clenched his jaw, turned away, and dressed quickly, pinning his finest mantle to his shoulder, donning his scabbard and sword. It was a sad occasion, and he had to arrive in proper attire.

He came back to the bed and stared down at his

wife. For a moment his fingers trembled, and he gripped them tightly as he stared down at her, for she was beautiful indeed. Perhaps she hadn't sent a message to the Danes. He didn't believe that she had. But she must know something, and if she was beautiful, she was every bit as treacherous.

He would bear a scar from her arrow wound all of his life to prove it!

Eric smiled coldly. "Get up," he said curtly. "It's time to go."

"But I'm not going!" she protested.

"You are, madam. I told you so last night."

"But—" She broke off, her face coloring. "But you said—"

"I never said a thing."

"Oh!" She realized her folly, and her color deepened ever further. "How could you let me—oh, you bastard!" And with that she was flying at him.

He caught her quickly, even as her arms flailed at him. His heart hammered and a rushing noise came to his brain. He could want her even now, even when he had known again and again the sweetness of her taste.

He held her wrists as he stared into the fiery storm of her eyes. "I will haul you upon a ship—naked or dressed, my lady. I would just as soon bring you clothed before my mother, but I will bring you one way or the other. I told you yesterday that you would accompany me. And I've warned you many times that my decisions will never be swayed by the games of a woman—no matter how charming those games." He pushed her from him, then inclined his head slightly, still carefully holding her wrists.

She would fly at him again, he knew it. Her finger-nails were clawed out like a cat's, and that wild look was still creating fire in her eyes. Words were choking out from her. *Bastard* among them. *Rodent.* Then she seemed to have slipped into the Welsh language of her father. He didn't know it well. It didn't matter, he understood the general meaning of her outburst.

"Ten minutes, my dear lady wife!" he thundered. He tossed her back upon the bed, and she gasped and stared up at him in silence at last, her eyes damp with tears, her hair beneath her, her form not just naked and beautiful but oddly vulnerable.

"Ten minutes," he repeated. And before she could rise or gather her breath to speak again, he threw open the door, exited the room, and slammed it behind him.

He paused there, startled, and he heard her sobbing softly. Then he reminded himself that the whole scene had happened because she was so eager to be free of him. After all, he could sink to the bottom of the Irish sea or meet with his demise some other way, and perhaps she would be free of him forever.

There could be war. With the Ard-ri dead, there could be war against Niall, his oldest son, as the Irish kings competed for power. The Danes could realize the weakness in Ireland. But no matter what, his father would hold Dubhlain, Eric knew that.

Still, his father would support Niall, his brother-in-law too. Indeed, there easily could be war, and Rhiannon might be granted her wish.

He strode away with grim determination and purpose.

In ten minutes she had best be ready to walk, he thought darkly. If not, he vowed, she would reach Ireland wrapped in a blanket and chucked over his shoulder.

15

The passage had been rough across the sea, and yet they had traversed the water with amazing skill and speed.

Rhiannon's decision to accompany her husband had been one made with little effort—she had never doubted that he would carry out any threat, and so she had walked to the ships well before he had come to join her and had awaited him while the preparations had been made, while the voyagers had loaded their dragon-prowed vessels, while the shouts had rung out and the riggings had been made secure. Alone upon the shore, wrapped in a crimson mantle, she had stared at the ships with their serpents' faces; at the prows rising so high out of the water; at the beautiful, chilling, and sleek designs; and she balled her hands into fists, fighting the temptation to run. She could not believe that she was about to embark upon a Viking ship.

She had tried to avoid her husband's ship, but no one had stepped aboard until Eric had appeared on the shore. Immediately his eyes had sought hers out, and she had been infuriated by the cold triumph in his gaze—he had known too easily that she would obey him.

And then, too quickly, he had been at her side, and when she would have fled to climb aboard the vessel taken by Patrick and Rowan, his hand was upon her arm. "My wife will accompany me," he informed her. She cast him a regal, chilling gaze and stepped aboard his ship. There she found a certain freedom, for Eric stood at the prow, and she found a seat far to the rear of the rowers. They left with the tide, but the wind was not to be theirs; nevertheless, that did not daunt her husband's purpose. Shouts went up as the red-striped sails were set to catch the best of the wind, and the talented seamen set to their oars with a gusto.

Morning came curiously to the sky. The reds and pinks of dawn did not become bright, but gray clouds crowded the heavens. Lightning bolted across the sky and thunder clapped with a deafening force.

The Vikings were supposed to be a superstitious lot, or so Rhiannon had heard, refusing to sail if the cast of the runes was not right, looking to their gods against this sort of weather. But even as the dragon-prowed ship pitched against the rising, swirling waves, the red-bearded fellow nearest Rhiannon smiled at her reassuringly. " 'Tis just Thor, perhaps, riding across the heavens, throwing down his thunderbolts."

"Aye," agreed another, "for even the great Norse Thor weeps and laments with all good Christian man that the Ard-ri should pass from this world to the next."

Rhiannon tried to smile, but her lips were white and her stomach was churning fiercely.

"Don't fear, lady!" the red-bearded oarsman urged her. "We are the finest seamen alive!" he boasted.

She did not fear sinking into the sea or being swallowed up by the blackness of it. Indeed, she might welcome such an event. That, at least, might move her husband, for Eric still stood at the prow, his arms crossed over his chest. No matter how fierce or wild the tempest of the sea, he boldly stood upon the deck of his ship, and his blue eyes were fixed upon the land that they approached, the land that seemed so very distant from her own.

She stumbled to her feet, gripping the rail at last, and was violently sick. She wondered how the ship was still moving, for it seemed that every man upon it had come to witness her humiliation. "Lady, are you well?" "Take care the pitch and sway of the waves!" "By Odin and God above, have we lost her?"

Mergwin, his eyes no longer filled with condemnation over the deceit she had played upon him, was then at her side. While men whispered that a violent sea could do such a thing, even to a seasoned sailor, Mergwin stared upon her with a knowing gaze. It was the growing babe that had caused her upset, and they both knew it.

With a cloth dampened by fresh water, he cleaned her face, then offered her a drink. She closed her eyes and leaned against him, accepting his ministrations and finding a curious comfort in his ancient arms. She wished that she could touch his weathered cheek and tell him thank you, beg his forgiveness, and confess that she was indeed coming to love him.

But when she opened her eyes, she saw that Eric was standing there, towering before her, his eyes as sharp as a whip, his hands upon his hips, his muscular legs still riding the rise and swell and tempest as easily as he rode a war-horse. A dark blush stained her cheeks and she folded her lips tightly together.

"She is all right!" he called to his men. He didn't need to say more; they all returned to their positions, and she was left there at the bow, in the shelter of Mergwin's arms, beneath his condemning stare.

"They thought that perhaps you had been about to pitch yourself overboard. I wondered that myself for a moment," he said.

She tried to rise from Mergwin's shoulder but could not. She swallowed tightly. "Alas, sir, you do distress me, but not enough that I would go against God's commandments!"

His jaw tightened, and she saw a pulse tick furiously at his throat. " 'Tis good to know I have not driven you to the sea, milady." He bowed mockingly. "My deepest regrets, lady. I had not realized you would be so poor a sailor."

He returned to his vigil at the prow. She nearly lashed out that she was a wonderful sailor, that it was his fault, that there was a babe inside making her so wretchedly ill. But she clamped down hard on her lips and did not speak. When she looked at Mergwin, his mysterious gray eyes were upon her, but he did not question or condemn her. "This is a rough time for him," Mergwin told her. "For all of us. You do not know the Ard-ri."

Mergwin loved the dying high king, too, she thought. But she said wearily, "All times seem to be rough these days, don't they?"

He smiled and shook his head. "There will be sorrow, but you will find happiness here, you will see."

"I shall not be here that long," Rhiannon said.

Mergwin started to speak, paused, then shook his head. She touched his knee. "Mergwin, I shall not be here that long. It isn't—it isn't my home, don't you understand? It is his, never mine. I mean no insult, but here, everyone will be different. . . ."

He leaned back and his eyes fell closed, and for a minute she was afraid, for he seemed so very old and fragile himself. Then he sighed wearily. "There will be war," he said softly, and then no more, and she wasn't at all sure of what he meant.

The threatened rain never fell. The sky and the sea continued to roil and churn with black clouds and fierce wind, but rain never fell. The darkness was still all around them when Rhiannon first saw the rugged coastline of Ireland. She stared at the land, alien and seemingly threatening in the wild grayness that prevailed. Then they entered into the river that would lead them to Dubhlain, and she watched everything around her for what she could see. There was beauty in Ireland—stark, green beauty as the land bowed to the heavens. Much of the land was barren, some of it fascinating, and all curiously familiar, much of it like home. Subtly different, though. For the meadows endlessly stretched out from the cliffs, in truly emerald hues. Fluffy white sheep grazed in the fields.

In time the walls of Dubhlain rose before them. Rhiannon was amazed at the work in stone, at the splendor, at the strength of the walls, rising white against the darkness. And even as the ships found their berths upon the river she saw the crowds awaiting them upon the shore. Mergwin helped her to rise. For now, it seemed, Eric had forgotten her. He had stepped ashore all ready.

Rhiannon paused, her heart pounding, as she saw a woman break away from the crowd. Her hair was as black as the night, sweeping free to her waist, and she was as lithe and slender as a young doe. She came racing forward, calling Eric's name.

Rhiannon froze, swallowing tightly, thinking she had never hated him with more vigor. Why had he brought her here? To witness his tender reunions with an Irish mistress? She wanted to be sick all over again. The woman greeted him with such care, such tenderness, and even in the shadows she was so very beautiful. And when she was not hugging him, she was speaking earnestly with him.

"Rhiannon, come," Mergwin urged her.

"I . . . can't!" she whispered. Then she froze, for Eric had turned back to her at last, and he came back aboard the vessel and to her side. Before she could protest, he had taken her arm and was dragging her forward, and then he swept her into his arms to set her firmly upon the Irish shore—and before the dark-haired woman. "Rhiannon, this is Erin of Dubhlain; Mother, Rhiannon, my wife."

The woman with the ebony hair smiled, and seeing her up close, Rhiannon realized that she was not a young woman, although she seemed ageless. Her eyes were a dazzling emerald green, her smile infectious. "Rhiannon, welcome. This is a sad time for us, but anything we can do for you we will. We Irish are famed for our hospitality, you know. This is my son's home and therefore yours, so all within it is utterly at your disposal." She squeezed Rhiannon's hands, then flashed her beautiful smile to her son. "Eric! She is lovely beyond measure, and I daresay, you don't deserve her one small whit. But come now, please. I am afraid to be away too long."

But they did not leave the ships so quickly. Erin of Dubhlain saw Mergwin waiting silently behind her. Not a word passed between them, but she went into the old man's arms, and there they hugged each other in silence as time slipped by. When they parted, Erin's eyes were damp with tears, but she took Rhiannon's hand and smiled again, and Rhiannon spoke softly and quickly, trying not to stumble over the Irish language she had so seldom used. "My lady, I am so very sorry to have come at such a time. Your father is clearly a well-beloved man and king, and my prayers are with him and with you."

"Thank you," Erin said. She continued to hold Rhiannon's hand, leading the way past the walls to a manor built also of stone, huge and impressive. There were paths against the walls of the town where people could step and avoid the mud and manure of the open ground. The wooden walks were amazing, like nothing Rhiannon had ever seen before in England or in Wales.

"It was here that he collapsed," Erin was explaining softly to her son. "I know many thought that I should have returned him to Tara to die, but I was desperate to gather my brother and sisters, and father's grandchildren. He sleeps and he wakes; he has good moments and bad. He knows that he is leaving, and he often speaks his will. I could not risk his death upon the road."

Eric replied that his mother had been right. Rhiannon felt like an intruder, but Erin's hand remained firm upon hers, and Rhiannon followed along. When they entered the manor, they came upon a huge, great hall, and it seemed that there were at least a hundred people gathered within it. They gave way as Erin entered. In the center of the room they came to a bed covered in embroidered linen. Within it lay a very old man with snow-white hair and a completely weathered face. His eyes were closed. Erin paused, and Eric stepped forward quickly, falling to his knees, taking the old man's long, thin hands into his own. Rhiannon noted dimly that there was a nun on the other side of the bed, her head bowed deeply in prayer. And then Rhiannon started, for at the head of the bed stood a man so like Eric that he could only be Olaf the White of the House of Vestfald of Norway, King of Dubhlain, and Eric's father.

Time had trod gently with this man, as with his wife. His golden hair had touches of white, but he stood as tall as his son, with endlessly broad shoulders and handsome, striking features. His eyes were the shocking, piercing blue Eric had inherited. They fell upon Rhiannon, and for a moment she could not breathe. Like his son's, they offered no apology but studied her keenly. Then his mouth twisted into a small smile and he nodded, and she knew that he had determined her identity and was welcoming her. Her heart fluttered suddenly, for it was that same smile upon Eric's face that had captured her senses and, upon occasion, her heart.

There were many others within the room. At the Ard-ri's feet was a tall man with dark hair and shadowed green eyes who resembled Erin, except that he seemed much older. Beside him was another dark-haired man, but his eyes were blue and his features akin to her own husband's. All across the room there were men and women, striking brunettes, Celtic blonds, and all shades in between, and it suddenly occurred to Rhiannon that everyone within the room was a relation, in one way or another, of the Ard-ri.

She began to hear Latin chants and realized that they had all come to pray. There was a priest far beyond the Ard-ri's bed, and his words droned on and on. Then there was silence, and then a shuffling, as many of the people left the room. There were a few soft sobs and the sniffling of children, and then it seemed that things were very quiet again.

Then the Ard-ri opened his eyes and a smile touched his features. He didn't try to sit up. He glanced down to the foot of the bed, and then he glanced up at the Viking King of Dubhlain. His voice was soft but very assured. "Olaf, you are here."

"Aye, Aed Finnlaith. Always."

"He has been as good a son as any, eh, Niall?" he asked the man at the foot of his bed.

"Aye, Father. As he has been my brother."

The old man then glanced at Eric. "A wolf like your sire, Grandson. Eric, you have come! You will not leave me now. You will not leave Ireland just yet." He winced suddenly with pain, and Erin bit down upon her hand as just the whisper of a sound escaped her. The Ard-ri closed his eyes and spoke again. "God help us, for the kings will go to war! The peace I have sought all of these years is such a fragile thing! 'Tis not the law that the High Kingship should go to Niall because he is my son but because no man is more qualified. All of these years, Olaf, I have been strong because you have been beside me. By God, I pray you stand by my son!"

"Aed, by the oath that bound us years ago," Olaf assured the Ard-ri, "rest now with peace. The walls of Dubhlain will ever be Niall's fortress. My sons, your grandsons, will ever be the great sword you claim we have been. Indeed, Aed, my father, I am your son."

The Ard-ri's eyes opened again, and they seemed to be glazed with tears. Then they fell shut. Moments later they opened again. They were heavy with pain now.

And they were on Rhiannon. The Ard-ri freed a hand from Eric and reached it out to her. Startled, Rhiannon moistened her lips and looked uncertainly at Erin.

"Please!" Erin whispered.

Rhiannon stepped forward. The Ard-ri's fingers closed upon hers with a startling strength. "Forgive me!" he whispered heatedly. "Forgive me, forgive me. I loved you then as always, so fiercely!" Clearly, he thought she was someone else, Rhiannon thought, but who?

A silence fell then. Frightened, Rhiannon held still, staring down at the man with the glazed eyes. "By God, I loved no one more! But there was always the land, you see. And the fight. I had to do what I did." He paused, bringing her hand together with Eric's. Rhiannon wanted to shriek and pull away, but she caught her husband's sharp blue gaze upon her with its raw command. She did not move, she could scarcely breathe, and then the Ard-ri continued, tearing into her heart, seeing things that no one should have seen. "I knew the man, you see, the things a maiden could not know. I knew his strength, and I prayed fiercely that you would forgive me. I prayed that you would love him, that time would tell, that days together would bring peace. It was for Ireland, you understand. Tell me, child, that you forgive me!"

Stunned speechless, Rhiannon felt tears stinging hot behind her lashes as she stared into the haunting and anxious gaze of the dying man. Eric's grip tightened upon her hand until she thought she would scream. Then Eric was whispering to her harshly, "Tell him! Damn you, woman, tell him what he wishes to hear!"

"I forgive you!" she cried out. She freed her hand and touched the old man's cheek, and suddenly her tears were falling down her cheeks and she was saying the things she was certain he wanted to hear. "Of course I forgive you. I love you. And everything you thought was true, and all is fine now—you cannot imagine how fine—and you must rest, and know that I love you and that everything is forgiven you, and there has never been such a king. . . ."

His eyes had fallen shut again. Erin, pale, was at her side. "Bless you, child!" she said softly, then pleaded to her son, "Eric, take your bride to her room, then come back. They do not believe that he will last the night."

"As you wish, Mother," Eric said. He brought her hands to his lips, then took Rhiannon's elbow and led her from the room with strides so long, she could barely follow. He hadn't a word to say to her as he led her through the magnificent stone residence, up a flight of stairs, and along a long corridor. They turned at a second hallway and moved left, then Eric thrust open a door and urged her inside. Rhiannon nearly flew past him, came to the center of the room, and then paused. It was every inch a man's room—Eric's room. The carved wood bed was enormous, like a massive sleigh. The trunks in the room were heavy, and the tapestries that protected the walls depicted scenes of war and triumph. Fine wood tables offered drinking horns and a heavy pitcher and bowl for washing. The fireplace was on the far side of the room, and before it lay a huge, heavy rug that had once been a tremendous white bear. Furs also lay strewn over the bed, and upon the walls were mounted various weapons, an intricately etched sword, a large bow, several pikes, and a shield with the insignia of the wolf.

She ceased looking about the room and gazed back at Eric, startled to find him staring at her intently.

"What—what was your grandfather saying to me?" she whispered. "Whom did he think I was?"

"I'm sorry, I haven't really time to talk now," Eric said curtly. "The manor is well staffed. Someone will come to you soon with food and drink and anything that you require." He still stared at her, and she shivered. He did not seem so cold now but distant, and she realized suddenly that he was suffering but that he would never betray it. She wanted to reach out to him.

He had dragged her here. He cared nothing for her, or for her feelings. He cared only that she obey, that he speak and she jump to his commands.

She turned away, tears again spilling from her eyes. She could not love him! She could not be so great a fool, nor could she cast aside pride so very easily. He used her constantly. He menaced her with his strength. She would not give him anything, not even sympathy. "I shall be fine," she told him stiffly.

Still he did not leave. Then, moments later, she heard the door open and close.

She sat down on the bed and sobbed, and she didn't know if she cried for herself, for Eric, for Erin, for the Ard-ri, or perhaps for all of Ireland.

In time her tears dried. A girl named Grendal came to the door with a rich stew and warm mead. The girl assured her that a bath would not be difficult, and many lads came with a fine carved tub and buckets of water, and just as efficiently they removed the tub when she was done and dressed in a new bed gown of finely embroidered Irish linen. Grendal quietly left her be then, and Rhiannon crawled into the massive bed with all the furs and slept.

Sometime later Rhiannon awoke but did not know why. Then she realized that she was not alone in the room. Eric sat before the fire, his legs outstretched before it, his golden head heavy between his two hands. The fire snapped and crackled, but no sound came from the man. Rhiannon sat up and paused, and she reminded herself that he had been cold and brutal in the extreme about her coming here, but then she rose, anyway, remembering the whispers of the lover he had been at the stream. She could despise him, but there was something binding them together. She rose and found the mead and brought him a horn of it. She knelt upon one knee at his side to offer the drink to him. Startled, he turned to her. He took the mead, watching her warily. "What is it that you want now, Rhiannon?"

She started, moving back from him. "That I want?" she repeated.

"Aye," he said wryly. "When you come to me so, it is always for some purpose."

She rose swiftly and gracefully, ready to spin about and leave him. He caught her hand and held her there. "You are not going home," he told her.

"I did not ask to go home," she said coldly.

He stared at her, then nodded and gazed absently at the fire again. "He is gone," he whispered softly. "Aed Finnlaith is gone, and so is the peace of many decades."

"I'm . . . sorry," she said softly. She could feel his pain, but she longed to ease it.

He released her hand. She stood there awkwardly. "Truly, Eric, I am sorry."

"Go to bed, Rhiannon."

Still she stayed, uncertain. "Is there anything—"

"Go to bed, Rhiannon. I wish to be alone."

So dismissed, she swung about. She wanted to run from the room, from him, but she did not dare, not when he was in his present mood. He might let her go . . . and then again, he might not.

Miserably she crawled back into his bed, and she wondered what he had been like as a little boy; she wondered about the man who had grown up with this castle as his home.

Hurt, she curled to the far side of the bed, leaving him plenty of room. Cold, she shivered, pulling the furs about her. In time she drifted off to sleep again.

Once more, before the dawn, she awoke. He lay beside her. He was upon his back, and she was curled upon his chest, in the shelter of his arm. She was no longer cold.

Nor could she pull away from him. He slept, exhausted. Her hair was caught beneath his naked back. She tugged upon it gently, then realized that her simple movement had awakened him, and his gaze was hard upon her. "Forgive me, madam, am I touching you?"

With a soft expletive he shifted, releasing her hair. Naked, he rose. She watched him, biting her lip, longing to say something but unable to, as he quickly dressed, then slammed out of the room.

She lay back down, but she did not sleep again. Much later Grendal came to her with fresh water and a meal, but she was not hungry and could not eat. She did not know what to do, and so she remained in Eric's room throughout the long morning.

Later in the afternoon she wandered into the hallway, took the curve, and came to the top of the stairway. From the great hall below she could hear tears and wailing, the deep sounds of mourning. Rather than intrude, she swung around and hurried away. She stopped short, for the hall was blocked by the height and breadth of a man. In the shadows she blinked fiercely, thinking that it was Eric, then realizing that it was not Eric but his father, the King of Dubhlain himself. A true Viking, she thought fleetingly, and a rosy flush colored her cheeks as she thought of all the times she had railed against and taunted Eric for his paternal parentage. Yet surely Eric would never have mentioned her hatred to this man.

"Why do you turn away?" he asked her.

"I . . ." She stared at him blankly, then realized that he meant she had turned away from the stairs. "I —I did not wish to intrude, my lord."

"Ah, Rhiannon! You are my son's wife and therefore our own daughter, and in this moment you do not intrude—you are deeply welcome. My father-in-law knew this, for as his life ebbed away, he reached for you, and you answered that which he needed to hear. Come, take my arm. Eric is downstairs."

He reached for her gently, and still she withdrew, shaking her head with sudden fear. "You do not understand, my lord."

"Ah! You cannot take the arm of a Viking, even one so very many years upon this shore?"

"No!" she cried out, stricken, then realized that a subtle smile played on his ageless features. The years would deal with Eric so, she thought. Until the end he would be so very straight, so formidable—so dominating!—and yet still have the ability to charm with the curve of a smile.

She lowered her lashes, flushing, for it seemed this man quite easily read her mind. She shook her head. "It is not that." She paused. How could she tell the king that his son did not want her with him? "I—I don't think that Eric—"

"My Lady Rhiannon . . . daughter!" he corrected himself. "Come, take my arm. No man forces a maid across the sea to a foreign land if he does not wish her presence there."

"But—"

"Come," he said, urging her gently. And yet this gentle urging was every inch a command, and she took his arm. As she walked down the stairs she won-

dered how these men were so able to bend her will,
the one she had married with his ruthless demands,
this one, his father, with a gentle force every bit as
strong.

When they came below, he led her to the Ard-ri's
bed, and the high king was adorned in all his glory, in
royal blue and crimson, the crests of Ireland and Tara
emblazoned on his mantle, a golden cross resting on
his chest. She bent low with the Viking king of Dubhlain and said a prayer, and when she rose, she was still
on her father-in-law's arm. Men, kings of Ireland,
came to speak with Olaf the White. To each he presented Rhiannon as his new daughter, and every man
there gave her welcome and the respect demanded
by the king. She was led across the hall, where a meal
awaited them, and there Erin, her beautiful face betraying the stains of her tears, came upon them. She
led Rhiannon to the high dais that fronted the long
tables, but before Rhiannon could be seated, she felt
her arm taken once again, and she turned swiftly.
There was Eric, clad much as his father, wearing a
crimson mantle trimmed with ermine and emblazoned with the insignias of the wolf, of the kings of
Tara, and of the house of Vestfald. "Mother, I thank
you. I will take my wife now, if I may."

His words to his mother were so gentle, so tender.
Thank God, Rhiannon thought, that he was not so
gentle with her, for the tenderness would play too
painfully upon her heart. She needn't fear, she
thought wryly as, seeming to growl, he demanded
that she come with him. He seated her at his side and
next to his father, and though she shared a chalice
with her husband, it was her father-in-law who

thought to speak with her, to engage her in conversation, to tell her about their customs. When the meal had ended, Eric led her back up the stairs, opened the door, and ushered her into the room. She turned about to see that he was already closing the door, leaving her again.

"Eric!" she called.

"What is it?"

She shook her head. "I just . . ." She paused and inhaled deeply. She remembered her father-in-law's assurance: No man brings a woman across a sea to a foreign land unless he desires her presence there.

Or unless he merely seeks to frustrate her own desires, Rhiannon thought bitterly. But she lowered her lashes softly and said, "I do not like to see you suffer so."

He was very still for a moment, and she thought she felt a coldness like an icy rush of air. Then he stepped back into the room, closed the door, and strode to tower before her. His touch was none too gentle as he raised her chin and forced her to meet his eyes. "You do not wish to see me suffer? Why, lady! I thought that it was your dearest wish to have me boiled in oil!"

She pulled away, alarmed by the tears that stung her eyelids. "Indeed, I had forgotten. So it is!"

He did not come for her, yet she thought that there was the slightest ghost of a smile upon his face, and watching him, she felt her heart seem to cartwheel. She dug her nails into her palms because she was tempted to run across the room to him, he was so striking there, so regal in his attire, so tall that he dominated the room, so golden that he seemed to radiate light. "I suffer the loss of my grandfather, yes," he told her very softly. His smile faded, but his gaze remained gentle upon her. "But you cannot understand the gravity of it all. Grandfather was the backbone of the island. He *was* Eire. He was . . . much as Alfred, you see. He was a very old man, over ninety years old, and he lived a great and majestic life. He will be welcomed in heaven, and the Norsemen he has known will save him a place at the table in Valhalla." He paused, then came toward her, the gentleness gone. His eyes were alive with a glacial radiance as his fingers threaded through her hair, forcefully tilting her face to his this time. "My father is strong, my brothers and I are strong, and now we must turn that strength to the aid and assistance of my uncle, Niall of Ulster. Do you understand this?"

"You are hurting me!" she told him.

His hold did not ease. His lips moved above hers, and his whisper warmed and taunted her. "There will be war. And you will remain here, within the safety of these walls, for the length of it." He did not release her but awaited some protest from her. Levelly she returned his gaze and allowed him no answer, no protest, no tears, and no fight. "My Lord, you are pulling on my hair!"

Then he did release her. He swung about and was gone.

She paced the room for what seemed like forever. Her trunks had been brought to the room; however, she did not change into her own bed clothing but chose the beautiful gown of Irish linen she had worn the night before.

The fire grew very low, and Rhiannon was cold

when she at last slipped beneath the sheets and furs of her husband's bed.

It was later still when he entered the room. Wearily he took a chair before the fire and stared into the flames.

She watched him in the firelight for what seemed like eons. There was such harsh tension in his features, such pain in the depths of his eyes. Her father-in-law was wrong. He certainly did not love her, and now, here, he did not even want her.

But she was falling in love with him despite her better judgment, despite all that had passed between them, despite the man himself. Nay, she *was* in love with him. . . .

She rose and walked before the fire. His eyes met hers, and he arched a brow in surprise and taunting question.

He would reject her. She should run and bury herself in the covers.

She did not. She pulled the tie upon the embroidered gown and allowed the linen to fall softly to her feet. More slowly still, she walked to him, meeting his gaze. Before him, she fell to her knees, took his hands, and lightly kissed his palms.

A sharp sound escaped him, and he was up, swinging her into his arms. He placed her upon the endlessly soft texture of the furs and began to make love to her. His kisses seared her flesh. His hands aroused her to a frightening ecstasy. She had longed to ease his soul, had meant to make love to him. Yet she had no chance, for it seemed that she had opened up the floodgates to his passion, more powerful and fierce than the storm that had threatened the sea and sky on the day of their arrival. Now that she had unleashed this tempest, she could neither guide nor control it; she could do nothing, indeed, but ride out the storm.

And it was sweet. He maneuvered her upon the fur, ravenously played his lips and teeth and tongue upon her, sweeping her back, her spine, and her buttocks with his soaring desire, then turning her and positioning her to his leisure once again. She felt the wind inside of her, and the gold of his sun, and she cried out, obliging his every whim, accommodating the dark and windswept passion that rose with a pulsing crescendo between them. The world seemed to rock when he was inside her, to pitch with the wicked, awesome force of the sea, to spin like a whirlpool, then explode in a frenzy of brilliance and light and sweet, sweet nectars.

At last he held her very close. He said nothing but stroked her sweat-dampened body. Words rose to her lips. *We're going to have a child.* She tried to open her lips, to utter them. She could not. In time she slept.

In the morning he was up and dressed before she could open her eyes. Exhausted, her hair a tangle within the furs, she realized he was standing above her. "You are not going home," he informed her harshly.

"What?" she whispered, amazed at the change in him. He might not love her, but she had thought, in the night, that there had been, at the least, a caring between them.

"You are not going home."

"I did not ask—"

"Whenever you seduce, madam, you are asking. You seek payment like the harlot, you—"

He broke off as she furiously tossed a down pillow into his face. He held the pillow as tightly as he held his temper. "Rhiannon, I do not pay. You should know that by now."

She pulled a fur over her quivering breasts with what dignity she could muster. "I asked you for nothing!" she spat out. "Nothing, my lord, at all! I sought to *give* something to you last night, but you needn't fear, I shall never think to give you anything again!"

He tossed down the pillow and reached for her face. She started to turn away, but his fingers moved so gently upon her flesh that instead she froze, stiff and miserable. "I stand corrected, my lady," he said softly, and his voice touched her, causing a warmth to shiver down the length of her spine. "And I thank you."

His lips brushed hers lightly. Then he was gone. She hugged a fur to her and stared after him, then sank back down into the bed. She would never know him. In a hundred years she would never know him.

Grendal saw to her needs once again in the morning, then she dressed and waited, wondering if she should go down or if Eric would come for her.

Eric, most probably, would not come for her.

In the afternoon there was a tap on her door. The nun she had seen by the Ard-ri's bed the first night of her arrival came in, smiling gently. "I am Bede, Erin's sister," she introduced herself, and took Rhiannon's hands and kissed her cheek warmly. "This is such a very hard time to have come upon us all! Truly we are warm and welcoming, and if you could have known him, you would have loved my father so dearly!"

"I am sure that I would have," Rhiannon said politely.

"You did so very well with Father."

"I did?"

"You did indeed" came a voice from the open doorway. Erin of Dubhlain was there, glancing at her sister, then smiling wryly at Rhiannon. "You must have been terribly confused when Father grabbed you so."

"I—" She broke off, determined to say nothing more. *Your father read my mind and my heart!* she wanted to cry, but she did not, and she was glad, for Erin quickly continued.

"You see, he thought that you were me."

"Your pardon, milady?"

Bede laughed softly, and even Erin cast her an affectionate smile. "Aye, she can laugh now! But this fine, saintly sister of mine once conspired with Father—"

"I did not conspire!" Bede protested.

"Hmmpf!" Erin said. "They tricked me into marriage, you see. I would have taken on a gnome or a dwarf or a large ugly boar rather than a Viking," Erin explained. "But you see, there had been war—awful, horrible war—and Father and Olaf formed a peace, and I was the assurance for that peace."

"Oh!" Rhiannon exclaimed. "But you seem now to be so . . . so . . ."

Erin smiled delightedly, catching Rhiannon's hands, bringing her to sit at the foot of the bed. "No woman has ever been so blessed with a marriage—or with a man. The years have been exceedingly kind to me, but they did not start off well."

" 'Twas hard, you see," Bede informed Rhiannon,

"for Erin and Olaf had known each other. Erin was running about the country in golden armor, you see, and she had battled her own husband."

"Bede!"

"There was much that Father never knew," Bede said affectionately.

"Rhiannon, I thank you again with all my heart for what you said to my father."

"Please, don't thank me. I—I'm just so sorry that he is gone."

Erin leapt up and paced nervously. "And now that he is gone, all those men who so honor him in this hall are plotting war against my brother!"

"I don't understand," Rhiannon said. "Why should they do so?"

Erin shook her head. "I don't know, I've never understood. When I was a child, there was always war among the kings. Then the Vikings came, and Father formed a peace so that they could be met. And now . . . now they will fight again. God help Niall!" She spun back around. "Have you everything that you need? Your trunks arrived from the ship all right?"

"Indeed, milady, they did. Thank you."

"Milady?" She smiled broadly, her emerald eyes bright, and again Rhiannon thought that she was an uncannily beautiful woman. "I am your mother-in-law. You musn't be so formal. Except that now you must excuse me, because there is so much to be seen to." She headed to the door, then paused, looking back. "Bede, see to it that Rhiannon meets the family, will you please? Yesterday was so difficult, but today . . . we must go on." She started to leave, then came back and smiled at Rhiannon. "I am so glad that Eric has found you. He has been quite a wanderer, going a-Viking to far-distant lands, and I am actually quite amazed that he has found a beautiful young Christian wife at King Alfred's court. Pray believe that I welcome you with all my heart!"

She left then, and Bede suggested that Rhiannon come down to the hall and meet the family.

Rhiannon followed Bede. Down the stairway she could see the hall where the Ard-ri now lay to receive the homage of his people. A multitude of men in elegant dress, mantles emblazoned with their mottoes and insignias, stood by him in silent prayer. Rhiannon did not see her husband.

As the day wore on, Bede guided Rhiannon about the manor of the King of Dubhlain. In a room across from the main hall she caught a glimpse of Eric at last. He sat with a large group of men, his brothers and uncles, she assumed, and they were engaged in a heated discussion. Bede led her onward. In the grianon, or the women's sun room, a beautiful girl with Erin's ebony hair leapt to her feet and raced forward when Rhiannon entered. "Aunt Bede, you've brought her at last! I was so intrigued to meet you last night. Do you remember me? *Can* you remember us all? I'm Daria, the youngest and last of this brood, Eric's sister. And these are my sisters, Megan and Elizabeth. You'll get to us all eventually. The boys are Leith—you might have seen him last night at Grandfather's bedside—and let's see, Bryan, Conan, Conar, and Bryce. And Eric, of course. Father's double, that's what we call him. Please, come in! There's been so much sorrow! Tell us about Alfred and England, and that awful Gunthrum. Oh, please, do come in, and don't be shy. We're never able to be so ourselves, you see." She laughed, and Rhiannon was instantly enchanted by her candor and ease.

"Well, I can tell you a bit—" she began.

"You're Alfred's kin, aren't you?" Daria interrupted.

"His cousin."

"Do tell us something, please. We've all been so wretched over Grandfather—we'd love to escape to some faraway land!"

Rhiannon found herself in the midst of the women —Eric's aunts, sisters, and sisters-in-law—with her natural storytelling ability coming to the fore. She repeated the story of Lindesfarne, refraining now from mentioning that it had been Norwegian Vikings that had wreaked havoc, and she told endless tales of Alfred's heroism and nobility. When she was done, Daria demanded to know how Eric had managed to sweep her away.

"Rather against my will," Rhiannon admitted calmly. "You see, he came a-Viking, stole my manor and lands, and Alfred decided that we should be wed."

There was a sudden silence. She had made the statement lightly, almost jokingly, and yet they were all staring at her. She had offended them, and she was sorry.

But then she realized that they were all staring at the doorway. She swung around, startled and dismayed to discover that Eric was there, staring at her. Comfortably leaning against the door frame, his arms crossed over his chest, he watched her with his crystal-blue, fathomless, but surely condemning gaze and waited.

"She's a wonderful weaver of tales, is she not?" he inquired politely of the group. "Alas, my love, I do believe that you neglected part of the story. My wife is quite the heroine herself, you see. We arrived, and before I know it, I'm wearing one of my dear lady and wife's arrows in my thigh. No Viking has ever held much sway over this fair lass, I do assure you."

"You—you shot Eric!" Daria exclaimed.

Rhiannon flushed. "I did not mean—"

"Oh, Eric!" Daria giggled, leapt to her feet, and hugged her brother. Rhiannon saw the easy affection that passed between them, the lightness, the smiles. He'd never have such a smile for her, she thought, half wistful, half bitter.

"I see that you came out of it well and good," Daria told him.

"Little sister"—he scowled playfully—"I wear a horrid scar upon my flesh."

"Oh, well, you wear other scars!" She winked at Erin. "You really hit my brother with an arrow?"

"She has excellent aim," Eric said, "if very little common sense and a dubious quantity of loyalty. But now, if you'll excuse me, I must retrieve her for the moment. Rhiannon?"

She rose, wishing she had a bow and arrow in her hands at that very moment. How could he say such a thing before his sisters and his aunts?

She strode to the doorway, then paused right before him. "Alas, my lord! What would you have of me? If my loyalty is so dubious, perhaps my aim is also. Take care, young lord of the wolves, for the future.

My aim could improve, along with my common sense. Were it just a little bit better, we need not have married at all, as there would have been little left for you to consummate such an arrangement!"

Daria, close enough to hear her words, burst into laughter. Eric studied Rhiannon and slowly grinned. Then he took a step forward, swept Rhiannon into his arms, and lightly tossed her over his shoulder. "Excuse me, ladies, I must deal with my wayward wife." Bowing, he took her from the grianon and down the hall, heedless of anyone about them. Stunned and short of breath, Rhiannon could make no protest.

Then she discovered that she was on her feet again. They had left the manor behind and stood in a courtyard before it. Men were everywhere, saddling and bridling horses and adorning them in their king's and prince's colors. Rhiannon started to protest Eric's manhandling of her but fell silent, gazing around at all the activity.

"What—"

His eyes were steady upon her. "There has already been an attack upon Ulster in Niall's absence," he told her.

"You—you're riding away now?" she asked in amazement. "Your grandfather's body has not even grown cold!"

"We will escort Grandfather's body to Tara and ride on to Ulster," he said. His hands were firmly crossed across his chest; his eyes were chilling as they rested upon her. "And you will stay here, in my mother's care, until I return."

She opened her mouth to reply, then shut it, for she saw Rowan across the courtyard, conversing with another of the men of Wessex who had accompanied them. She glanced at Eric, finding it difficult to breathe. "Rowan will ride with you?"

He seemed startled, then he stiffened. "Aye, by his own choice."

"He should not . . . he should not die on foreign soil!"

He pulled her suddenly and hard against him. "Do you seek his return and not mine, milady? Alas, I see that it is true, but then you never pretended to seek other than a Dane's battle-ax for my skull. But, lady, if this lasts days or years, you will remember that you are my wife; you will remember me!"

She tried to jerk free; he was hurting her. Her stubborn pride wouldn't let her tell him that she loved him, that her concern for Rowan was now a ruse to protect her heart. She could not tell him that she could not bear the world if he did not return; she could not even tell him about their child.

"Eric—"

He lifted her up into his arms. His lips descended upon hers with startling force. He kissed her passionately, ravished her lips and her mouth, and when he set her down, it did not seem that he had done enough.

"Eric!" She whispered. "You must watch out for—"

"For Rowan?" he demanded cuttingly. "By God, madam!" he swore fiercely. Then a cry escaped her as he lifted her violently into his arms. She held tight to him, for his strides were long and careless as he burst back into the manor, took the stairs two at a time, and brought her back to his room. There he tossed her heedlessly upon the bed, and before she could rise or protest, he had cast his own weight upon hers. "Stop this, you Viking . . . bastard!" she cried in alarm, but there was no stopping him, his anger, or his passion.

He shoved up the hem of her tunic and briefly adjusted his own clothing. She cried out once again, hysteria rising in her voice at the depth of the violence within him. "Eric!"

Something in her voice reached him at last. He went very still, then eased his weight down beside her. He murmured something that she couldn't understand. He started to pull away, and she should have been glad but she could not let him go. Tears were damp on her cheek, she realized.

She felt his kiss upon those tears, a gentle kiss. She held him more tightly against her, feeling a quickening within her body. His lips found hers and there was a fierce, seeking hunger in them but no longer the violence. His tongue entered deep into her mouth and seemed to reach secret recesses. The hard feel of his body against hers brought a sweet, moist warmth seeping through her. It seemed that his very hunger filled her. She wanted him. Desired him with a fiercely growing need that filled her heart and her limbs and her very being. He was leaving again.

"Lady, you will remember me!" he whispered softly against her ear. He repeated himself, and she felt a great trembling seize hold of him. Moaning softly, she reached for him, drawing his lips to hers, pressing herself against him with a welcoming undulation of her hips.

"Rhiannon . . ."

She heard the whisper of her name.

She didn't want to speak. She buried her face against his throat. "Please!" she murmured simply.

There was no more that she needed to say. He was within her, and she held tight to him with the first startling impact. He began to move, with every thrust he came deeper into her, and in seconds she was meeting his frenzy, matching it with her own. He made love as if he could forever leave his imprint upon her; she made love as if her longing for him could keep him from war. Thunder seemed to rock the air around them as their rhythm and tempest rose to nearly unbearable heights. Then she cried out, for the climax that then claimed her exploded with a searing fire that left her tasting ecstasy, then robbed her briefly of consciousness. When she saw light again, she felt Eric's great weight shuddering above her, and again she was filled, flooded with the searing warmth of his seed. She closed her eyes, savoring that warmth.

They were still for what seemed like forever. Then he enwrapped her in his arms and held her close. "Remember me," he whispered once again.

She opened her eyes and met the cobalt storm of his. She tried to smile but could not. And she tried to speak loudly, but her voice was a whisper. "Indeed, my lord, I daresay I cannot forget you. I—I am going to bear your child."

"What?" Still looming atop her, he lifted his weight above her and searched out her features.

She inhaled and exhaled. "We're going to have a child."

"You do not lie to me?"

She smiled at last. He seemed so very fierce. "Milord, I cannot believe that you have not guessed already. There are changes . . ."

It was his turn to inhale sharply. Then he drew his body abruptly from hers, adjusted her tunic, and touched her cheek tenderly. "You little fool!" he exclaimed. "Why did you let me—"

"Let you? My lord, when have I ever managed to stop you?" she challenged. Then she added hastily, "Eric, I wanted—I wanted you too. You did not hurt me or the babe!"

He touched her cheek, then he kissed her. "You will take care. You will take the utmost care."

She nodded. He did not mean to take care of herself; he meant that she must take care for the child.

He rose, reached a hand down, and drew her up and into his arms. For a moment he held her tenderly, achingly so. "Aye, my love, take care. . . ." Then he released her, touching her cheek. "I will watch young Rowan. I will guard him whenever I may. You needn't fear."

The sound of his voice was harsh and bitter once again. His lips touched hers and then he turned and strode away.

The door slammed.

Tears stung her eyes. "It is you I love!" she whispered. But it was too late.

He was gone.

16

As evening fell, a chill wind swept the northern coastline. Standing high upon the cliffs, the wind whipping
his mantle furiously about him, Eric stared out across
the darkened, fog-shrouded distance of the sea.
Somewhere far away lay the land of the Scots, so
named for the tribes that had left Eire to settle there.
It was a land far north, far, far above the English
kingdoms Alfred fought so hard to wrest from the
Danes.

Indeed, they had come very far in the past months.
And now, with the harshness of winter facing them,
they had come to the end of the fight. One by one the
lesser kings of Ireland had bowed to the supremacy of
Niall mac Aed, but now they battled along the coastline of his uncle's own Ulster, battled a man born
much as himself, Lars mac Connar, the son of an Irish
lass and grandson of a Danish jarl.

The decisive battle would come tomorrow. To the
north, far ahead of him, Eric could see the fires of the
Danish camp. Emissaries had run back and forth between the lines all day, and it had been decided.
Whoever took the day tomorrow would take the strip
of Ulster. With all of the country now sworn to support Niall, it seemed unnecessary to wrest this strip of

land from Lars. But few knew the Irish sentiment more thoroughly than Niall, Olaf, Eric, and his brothers and cousins. If Niall did not hold his own kingdom, he would hold nothing else. The warlike factions would split and splinter, and there would be dissent throughout the land.

Everything hinged on the morrow.

Then they could return to Dubhlain.

Eric felt the cold wind rush over his face as a fire ignited within him. How he longed to return!

They had not departed so swiftly as they had first planned—there had been his grandfather's funeral to deal with despite the imminent threats upon them. When he had left Rhiannon to return to the courtyard, he had discovered that there was a council under way, and that his immediate presence was required. He had sat with his uncles, father, brothers, and cousins, and they had decided that it was too risky to allow Eric and the women to see Aed to his final resting place at Tara with only a guard. They would not show fear and they would not show any weakness, but all of the family would proceed north with the Ard-ri's body and attend prayers at his graveside with the monks from Armagh.

Then they would swiftly turn to the business of securing the loyalty of the lesser kings.

And so he had had some time. . . .

Not so very much time, for the journey with such a number had been slow, and he had never been at leisure to ride with his wife during the day. Then there had been the constant messages coming and going to the various kingdoms. Niall had recognized the various kings of Ireland—and demanded their recognition in return. The days had been exhausting.

There had also been the messages from Wessex.

Gunthrum had cast himself into the fray after the fall of Rochester. Alfred had taken a great host of ships—Eric's among them—and attacked the Danes under Gunthrum.

He had made a clean sweep, capturing endless ships and riches. But then the Danes had attacked in return, and the prizes had been swept away again.

By spring, Alfred would attack and harry the Danes from London; or so he vowed. He implored Eric to return by the spring.

Eric looked out to the sea. Always there was warfare.

He sighed, closed his eyes wearily, and remembered that at least for a time the nights had been his. On the long, slow journey to Tara the nights had been his.

Even then he and Rhiannon had spoken little. Sometimes their party had slept in tents upon the road, sometimes they had found the rich hospitality of an Irish farm, and occasionally there had been the luxury of a lesser king's manor house. It had not mattered. He had been too exhausted for words; she had never demanded them. It had been a time of discovery for him, for indeed she had changed, and he cursed himself for a fool that he had not noticed. Her breasts were so very full as they spilled into his hands, and her abdomen had already begun to swell. It seemed that even her eyes were brighter, her cheeks more lustrous. . . .

But then she had always been beautiful. He had

never denied that. Never. From the very first time he had seen her high atop the wall, she had arrested his senses. Now she still plagued and haunted him in his dreams, for there were so many memories of her to be conjured up and recalled. In his dreams she came to him, as she had come to solace him after his grandfather had died. Came to him naked, lithe, the burning gold and fire of her hair a maiden's cloak about her, casting her in a spell of both innocence and intrigue. Soft and rippling like the rays of the sun, like the dance of the fire, skeins of hair in rich, thick beauty fell upon her naked flesh and covered but did not hide the fullness of her breasts, the rose-colored hues of her nipples, the curve of her hip, the curling thatch of fire and mystery between her thighs. He could smell the sweetness of her flesh within his dreams, and he could see her eyes, feel her flesh, as she came to him and poured herself upon him. So very much lay deep within her. So very much was contained behind the wondrous silver lights of her eyes. Pain too swiftly betrayed, too swiftly hidden away. Laughter, so very seldom for him; tenderness; and the anger of a storm, the tempest of the sea, the rage of a tigress. All these things lay deep within her, and her mood, ever volatile, changed with the ripple of the wind.

Only a fool would love her. . . .

But he did.

He wondered briefly when it had come about, when his heart had so changed, when she had captivated more than his lust, when she had conquered his heart. Had it been in discovering that he could best her time and again, and yet she never surrendered?

Had it been in touching her, in drowning with the fire of her hair, the tempest in her eyes? Had it been in knowing her, in learning the beauty in her heart and mind? Had it been in wondering if she had indeed left the manor to send her arrows flying in his defense?

Perhaps on that day he had only admitted that she was his and that he would fight as ferociously and as blindly as any wild animal to keep what belonged to him. When had it changed so that he was forced to admit, if only to himself, that he loved her? Nay, what he felt for her was deeper than love. It was deeper than any emotion he had ever known before. It was a part of him, waking and sleeping.

He had loved before. . . .

And he had learned the pain of it, and he was keenly aware that love could be a two-edged sword, a weapon greater than any invented or perfected by man. By God, too many things still lay between them. Countless men had died needlessly because she had attacked him when he had arrived upon her shore.

And too many things had come to pass since then. Perhaps her men, long in their graves now, had been innocent, for in truth, no ghosts had later warned the Dane Ragwald of his approach.

But someone had done so. . . .

If not his wife, then someone frighteningly close to Alfred. Who? Rhiannon had to have some idea. She had been Alfred's ward; she knew them all and knew them well. Was she protecting someone? Or was she as innocent as she claimed?

Perhaps she still desired his death but had learned with cunning to be patient, to await it more calmly.

No, he could not believe such a thing. That she still cared deeply for Rowan he knew. She had implored him once again to care for her countrymen when they had parted ways at Tara; there were at least twenty men of Wessex with them, but he had known that though she cared for the others, it was Rowan to whom she referred.

They were going to have a child. If he fell in battle now, he might well leave a son behind him. His hands trembled suddenly, and he looked up to the sky and prayed, though he wasn't sure to which deity he offered up his prayers. He wanted to live. He wanted to live more than he had ever realized before. He wanted to see his child, be it a son or a daughter, and he wanted a chance to live the life he had carved out for himself. He could never betray his uncle, Niall, and he would always come to Leith's support if Dubhlain was threatened. He would always be an Irishman, just as he would always be his father's son, a Norseman. But his life now lay across the sea, and his soul now rested within Rhiannon's slender hands. Somehow he had sent roots for himself deep down into that earth in Wessex, and he wanted nothing more than peace, time with his wife, time with his child. Time to luxuriate forever amid tendrils of fire and gold, to nuzzle and hug Rhiannon before a blaze in winter, to create a world together. His wandering days were indeed over; his time to go a-Viking had ended when Alfred had placed her hand within his. He had thought it was the land that he craved so fiercely, but it was not. It was the heart of the woman who had given him his home.

There was the softest sound behind him, and he swirled around, unsheathing his sword.

High upon the cliff, Mergwin stood before him. Eric lowered his sword with a sigh and resheathed it, swearing softly. "By Odin, Mergwin, but you do come like a wraith from the darkness!" Mergwin should not have been with them, Eric thought. Aed Finnlaith had left this life in his nineties. Mergwin was even older than Aed; far too old to follow a battle trail. And yet he had insisted.

Now the wind whipped his hair and his beard, and his eyes caught the glow of the midnight moon; he appeared the magician, the wizard, in truth. "I have come to warn you that much will be amiss with tomorrow's dawn," Mergwin said.

Eric smiled. "Very much, Mergwin. We'll go to battle against a fierce and talented warrior, and the future of all the land and of the houses of Aed Finnlaith and the Norwegian Wolf will be at risk."

Mergwin shook his head. "That is battle, open and simple."

Open and simple? Eric thought. Battle was never simple. It was always a horror of blood and pain and death. But in his lifetime Mergwin had witnessed countless battles, and it seemed that he knew things could be even worse.

The old man cast him a wry glance and came to sit upon the cliff. He stared out at the night, at the ripping wind. "There is something gravely amiss. I followed you to England because I sensed it. I stayed with your bride because I feared it. And now, here, it has come close again." His fingers knotted into fists.

"By Odin and all the hosts in heaven! I can feel this thing, but I cannot touch it! I can only warn you to look beyond the obvious. Duck the battle-ax, parry the thrust of the sword. And beyond that, too, you must take care."

He rose again. He looked at Eric, and Eric studied him gravely. "Aye, Mergwin, I'll take the gravest care. And if I manage to stay alive, I will try to see what is hidden."

Mergwin nodded. He started to walk away and then paused, looking back. "By the way, my prince, it is a boy."

"What?" Eric said sharply.

"Your child. It is a son."

Mergwin disappeared into the darkness as he had come. Eric watched after him and smiled slowly, and then his smile faded.

What was it that Mergwin sensed but could not touch?

Could something treacherous have followed him from Wessex unto these cliffs?

It was impossible. The impending battle was making Mergwin uneasy. Since Aed had died, Mergwin had not been the same.

Eric needed to sleep.

But when he returned to his men and his tent, he did not find rest. He dozed and tossed with the night. Visions came before him. Visions of battle, men carrying swords and axes. Visions in which she walked to him . . .

Slowly, beautifully, naked in the moonlight, the glow illuminated her every curve and hollow.

But she never reached him. A sword fell between them, and he awoke with a start.

The dawn had come. It was time for battle.

He had left the white stallion behind in Wessex, and from his father's stables he had chosen a favorite, especially bred for war, a massive black with sleek lines, a startling speed, and a rugged stamina against the strains of battle. Eric led men into the first fray along with Niall and his father and his brother, Leith. No true king ever hid behind the flesh of his people, his father had taught them as children, and it had been a lesson he had learned well, one that had attracted him to Alfred, for like his father and grandfather, Alfred was a warrior-king.

The sons of the Wolf met the first clash of steel, and they bled the first blood.

Eric felt the first wound penetrate his lower thigh, but his mail protected much of his body, and those thrusts he could deflect in the first fray bruised him but did no great harm. After the first rush the battle was enjoined so that he was more at his leisure to meet his opponents. He had learned to fight well with his family. When his younger brother, Bryan, was caught between two axmen, Eric was able to sweep down and dispatch one. Later, over his shoulder, he realized that his father had severed the throat of a berserker about to leap upon his mount.

Horrible, frightful battle continued for several hours, until the ground beneath them grew slick with the blood that had been shed.

Then a retreat was sounded by Lars, and the battle began to ebb.

Eric remembered his promise to Rhiannon to guard Rowan, and he swore fiercely. He had not seen the lad in some time. "Some of your Englishmen were caught in the fighting behind the trees!" Leith called to him, and Eric nodded in response and hurried the black stallion toward the copse. He arrived there to find Rowan and several others still in the midst of battle. Rowan was taking on at least four of the men trying to escape.

Eric rode hard up behind him, swinging his sword, taking down one and then another. Rowan pierced the heart of a third enemy, and the last man made good his escape through the trees.

"Thank you, then, milord!" Rowan called to Eric. "I daresay I hate to admit that I was in need of assistance, but alas, so I was!"

"We're all in need of assistance now and then, my friend!" Eric assured him. "Knowing this can make a man a great warrior!"

Rowan tipped back his visor, smiled, and waved. Eric swirled his mount about and returned to the crest where his father, brothers, and kin were gathering.

Lars had offered terms. He, himself, would bow down before Niall of Ulster if his men would be granted pardon, his wounded returned to his women, and if Niall would grant him a small spit of land in his own right.

An emissary went back. Niall would do so if Lars would sign an oath of fealty before his man, claiming Niall his overlord.

Darkness fell. Leith ordered that their own wounded be tended to, that their dead be gathered for Christian burial. His father, his brothers, and his immediate family had survived the battle, and for that Eric was grateful. But as he watched the bodies of old friends and faithful followers being laid out before him, he braced himself against the onslaught of pain. Then he started as he saw Rollo carrying forth a certain body, and he swore and rushed forward, taking the corpse from his friend.

It was Rowan.

Rowan, pale in death, handsome, young, still, a thin trickle of blood trailing from his lip. Eric laid him down upon the ground. Moving his hand from beneath the lad, he saw the pool of blood that stained it. "By God!" he swore, "I left him at the battle's end! What happened? Who saw this? I swear that the reward shall be great if someone here can tell me!"

One of the Englishmen stepped forward, leaning heavily upon his sword from some leg wound. It was an older man, one who had often been at Rowan's side, a man called Harold of Mercia.

"My lord, I swear that I, too, saw him alive and well at the battle's end! But the Danes were slipping through the trees, and Rowan would pursue them. Sire, we do not know how he met his death."

Grief and guilt fell hard upon Eric. He sat there, fury seizing him, staring at the men gathered around him. "He would be a warrior," someone commented.

"Men fall in battle, 'tis the way of it," Rollo reminded him quietly.

Eric, again bearing his burden of the fallen lad, stumbled to his feet. He carried Rowan's corpse over to the others; monks had already gathered around the fallen. Bitterly he placed Rowan among them, and he paid a small, weathered monk a gold coin to have additional prayers said for the lad.

The English youth deserved to go home, to be buried within the soil of Wessex. But Eric could not bring Rowan's body home, he knew, not when the journey was so long and the weather still so changeable. Rowan would lie here, in the north of Eire.

Eric saw to his men, and he saw to his duties as Olaf's son and Niall's nephew, and then he retreated hastily to the cliff and stared out upon the water. Rollo found him there first and offered him a dagger. Eric stared at the bloodied earth, then looked to Rollo again. There were no Celtic designs upon the dagger, nor did it seem to be of Danish make. He had seen similar weapons in Saxon England.

"What is this?"

"I did not wish to speak to you before the others," Rollo told him. "But that is the weapon that killed young Rowan. I thought that you should have it."

Eric looked at Rollo, nodded slowly, and rolled the weapon in his hand. "Thank you."

Sensing that Eric needed to be alone, Rollo left him. Eric sat upon the shelf of the cliff as Mergwin had done the night before. The battle had been taken. It was time to go home.

But how dearly he dreaded that now. Mergwin had warned him. But what had the warning been? They had seen fierce battle. Rowan had fought bravely and well. And then Rowan had fallen.

It wasn't right. Eric simply sensed that something about Rowan's death was *not* what it appeared to be.

There was a step behind him, and Eric swirled about. He exhaled as he saw his father there in the moonlight. Olaf hunkered down beside him, and for long moments they both stared out at the sea. "A man fell in battle," Olaf said at last. "He chose to fight that battle. It is not your fault."

Eric grinned ruefully and turned to Olaf. "But I swore to protect him, Father. I, in my arrogance, assumed that I could keep him from death. And I failed."

"No man can keep another from death, Eric. It was the lad's time, and nothing can change that."

Eric nodded slowly. "It is *how* he died . . ."

"If you question his death, you must find the truth of it," Olaf told him.

Eric showed his father the dagger. " 'Tis English, is it not?"

Olaf studied the weapon slowly. "It is not Irish, nor of any Viking design that I have seen. Yet Vikings seize their weapons from many lands—and many fallen enemies—so you must be sure of what you suspect. And you must watch your own back."

"Aye, Father, I will do so," Eric assured him.

Olaf clapped him on the back and left him to find his own peace with the night wind. They were very much alike, and it seemed that Olaf knew his son needed the shelter of the darkness to ease his soul.

It was a cold day in late December, and Rhiannon sat in the grianon with Daria and Megan and Erin, anxiously listening to the last message from the King of Dubhlain about their final victory when the first contraction wrapped mercilessly about her back. She leapt to her feet and gasped with the startling onslaught of the pain. "It's the child!" Daria exclaimed.

The messenger went still, and Erin smiled, very calm as she bent over her needlework. "Pray, do go on with the message. Rhiannon, I'm afraid that we shall have a bit of time before the baby truly arrives. Let's hear the sweet music of this victory first, then we will retire to your room and await this new grandchild of mine."

Daria arched a severe brow to her mother, but Rhiannon could already feel the pain beginning to ebb. She sat again, and the messenger cleared his throat and continued. When he had finished, Erin just as calmly asked him, "My husband made no mention of my sons?"

"None other than the 'all is well' line, milady."

"Then all of them are well and will return," Erin said softly. Then she set her needlework down and turned to Rhiannon. "Eric will return, Rhiannon. And return ecstatic to find a new child."

Rhiannon lowered her lashes quickly. Would he truly be ecstatic? She had hoped that the child would take longer. She closed her eyes, wondering if it had even been a full nine months since their wedding night. He had seemed well assured then that he had taken her maidenhood, but would he believe so now? Would he doubt that the child was his?

She closed her eyes tightly, remembering the few sweet weeks that had been theirs. So sad an occasion —the funeral procession for the great Ard-ri! And yet for them it had been a first taste of peace, a time when they had met without anger, without suspicion. And if no words of love had been whispered, neither had words of hatred or of wrath. And he had touched her breasts with a new tenderness, had lain his head softly

against her while he caressed the growing roundness
of her belly.

Dear God, she thought, *don't let this be destroyed
now! Oh, please, let him know that this is his child,
let him love the babe, let him love me. . . .*

He would never love her; he had said so.

A second pain seized her, and with it she gasped
aloud and stared reproachfully at Erin. Erin laughed
and told her, "Dear Rhiannon, I have done this
eleven times, you must recall, and I assure you, we've
still a while to go!"

They did have quite a while to go. Erin brought
Rhiannon to her room, and Daria and Megan took
turns at her side. Grendal came with fresh linens to
change the bedding and Rhiannon's gown when her
waters broke and soaked everything about her. And
still the hours went on and on, and the pain became
ever more severe.

With nightfall she was frantic and severely in pain;
the contractions now seemed to seize her one a minute. She fought tears and swore instead. She bitterly
railed against Eric and swore that she despised all
Vikings and wished that every one of them would be
swallowed up by the sea. Then she saw Erin's emerald eyes bright above hers; gasping, she tried to apologize.

Erin laughed. "My dear, do not apologize to me!
Trust me once more. Eleven times I swore against all
Vikings myself, wishing that they would be swal-
lowed up by the sea." She smiled reassuringly, cooled
Rhiannon's forehead with a cloth, and held her when
a scream seized her.

Dawn came, and when Rhiannon thought that she

could truly take no more, that she would die of the misery and exhaustion and pain, Erin called out with delight, "The head is crowning! Oh, Rhiannon, this is it! Just a little more effort. Push now, push!"

She tried, but the effort was too great and a pain seized her again.

"I can't! I cannot!" she cried out. "Oh, I cannot!"

"Indeed you can!" Daria pressed her. "If you managed to pierce my brother with an arrow, you can surely bring forth his child!"

"Come now, push!" Erin urged her.

"Think of it as thrusting Eric into an icy fjord," Daria suggested.

"Daria!" Erin chastised.

"I'm just trying to help, Mother. Now come, Rhiannon, come. Oh, this is it! Press down hard!"

She did, and this time the babe came rushing from her, and the relief was tremendous and wonderful. She fell back, too exhausted to inquire about the child's sex. But she did not need to.

"A boy! Oh, that arrogant brother of mine will be so pleased!" Daria said affectionately. "Oh, Rhiannon, a son!"

A son. Mergwin had told her that it would be a boy. He had told her when she hadn't even believed that she could be carrying a child. A son. Eric would have a son. All men wanted sons.

Unless they thought that the child might not be theirs. . . .

"Here, Rhiannon! Oh, he's beautiful!"

Beautiful, squalling, swaddled in linen, still wet and slick and wrinkled. She laughed, holding him, then something swept over her, some emotion so deep that she shivered and trembled and fell instantly in awe and in love.

"Rhiannon, you must push again," Erin told her. "The afterbirth must come now. Daria, take the babe back. Rhiannon can have him soon enough."

She obeyed her mother-in-law without another thought of pain. She was so anxious to hold her son again that she obediently changed her gown, moved so that the bed could be changed again, and then blissfully reached for her infant. Erin said that she must let him suckle for just a few moments and so she did, and when the tiny lips tugged with such startling force upon her breast, she was forever lost.

She loved the babe so fiercely. So very fiercely.

Just as she had come to love his father, despite her denials. But the babe she could love without fear, while Eric . . .

He gave her his passion, his protection, the fires of his heat, deep in the night. But he held from her his thoughts, his secrets, and his heart.

Please, God, let him love this child! she thought, and then she drifted, exhausted, into sleep.

The journey home seemed endless, and yet at last the walls of Dubhlain rose high before them. Horns were sounded, their return was announced, and soon the endless parade of warriors rode through the courtyard. Their number had decreased, for Niall had remained in Tara with his sons and his men, and several of those called to arms had also returned to their homes.

Still there was tremendous commotion in the courtyard. His mother was upon the steps to greet his father. She seemed like a girl—beautiful, fresh, and young—as she awaited her lord, as she had done so many times. Yet even as Erin rushed forward and was lifted by her golden husband, Eric realized that she held a bundle carefully within her arms.

He left the black stallion with its reins dangling for a stable boy, and his strides lengthened with every second as he hurried toward his parents. A chill, and then a warmth, and then a wicked rush of blood seized hold of him, and at the end he was running. Then, before Erin, he slid to a halt and she spun around, her eyes wide, and then she smiled and greeted him. "Eric!" With her free arm she caught him and kissed his cheek, and he found he had voice. "Mother! Mother, is this—"

"Indeed, Eric, this is!" Laughing, Erin cradled her bundle in her arms and moved a patch of blanket from a tiny face. "He is ten days old, and we christened him Garth, since we did not know when you would return. Rhiannon was hesitant to name the child without your consent, but it was her father's name and I—"

"Garth! It is a boy."

"Eric, I said 'he'!" Erin laughed. "Take him."

He scooped the child into his arms, muttering, "Mergwin! That old Druid said it would be a boy!" His arms were trembling as he tried to study the child. He walked away, hurrying for the entrance to the manor. The news had gotten out among the returning men. A cheer went up, and Eric swung around, smiling, lifting an arm in thanks for the approval of the men. He gazed at his child, at the enormous blue eyes, at the near platinum hair, so light and yet in thick abundance. Ten days old. His son seemed to study him with equal curiosity. His son.

Eric paused, gazing back at Erin. "Mother, Rhiannon—"

"She is fine and well and sleeping. I heard the horns, but I did not waken her because she slept so soundly and still tires easily. It has just been ten days, you see, and the babe does not sleep through the night."

He smiled and nodded. Erin made her way to him and proudly touched the babe's cheek, then pulled Eric on inside. "Really, though, she is fine." Even as Erin spoke, the babe stared at Eric, waved his tiny fists in the air, and let out with a hearty scream. Erin laughed. "He not only looks like you, he even sounds a great deal like you! Take him to his mother, he is hungry."

"Is he?" Eric demanded. "Well, I'm glad that he hasn't merely decided that he does not like my face." He kissed his mother's cheek and strode hastily into the house and up the long stairway. He thrust open the door to his room just in time to see Rhiannon rising. She was dressed in white, her hair a flaming tangle about her, her eyes heavy-lidded and both sweetly sensual and arrestingly innocent as they fell upon him. They widened to silver saucers, and she whispered his name with surprise. "Eric!"

He strode across the room to her, laying the child at her side, capturing her hand and kissing it before drinking deeply of her lips. And then her eyes were on his again, wide and luminescent. A rueful, shy smile touched her lips, and she said anxiously, "Do you like him?"

"Like him? I adore him. And I thank you with all my heart."

She lowered her lashes quickly as tears rose to glisten her eyes. He caught her chin, raised it up, and studied her eyes demandingly. "What is this? What did you expect?"

She went very pale and tried to twist away, but he would not allow her to do so. "Rhiannon, I would know what is going on in that mind of yours."

"I—I was afraid!" she whispered.

"Of what? Of me?"

Her lashes fell despite his command. And then he smiled and counted days; it was probably an exact nine months since their wedding night, and there certainly had been tension regarding it.

He threaded his fingers through her hair, turned her face to his, and seized her lips with a startling passion that brought her eyes flying open to meet his. "My dear wife, I have always known that I bedded a maid that night. Whatever caused you to take me for a fool at this late date?"

She flushed and freed herself from his touch. Staring down at the babe, she felt her temper returning with a rise. "Well, you didn't notice the child when he was coming along quite nicely within me!"

He shrugged, a grin upon his lips that tore at her heart and caused it to thunder with a new excitement. "I'm afraid, my love, that I was fairly well versed at sex but quite unaccustomed to the matter of siring a child. Rhiannon, we have made a son. God, he is gorgeous!"

"Hmmph!" came a voice from the doorway. " 'We' made a son! You should have been here for the labor.

And according to Rhiannon at that time, you should have been swallowed up in the sea for your part in it all!"

Eric spun around to see his sister Daria standing there smiling. He stood and caught her when she rushed into his arms and kissed him fiercely. Tears stung her eyes. "Oh, Eric, I am so grateful to see you all home and alive and well!"

"I'm grateful to be here," Eric said, holding her close. Then he looked down at his wife. "I should have been swallowed up by the sea?"

She flushed furiously, and Daria laughed. "I'll be back for Garth, Rhiannon, when you two have finished doting, to give you a few minutes alone."

She left them, and there was silence for a moment. Then Garth started to scream again, and Rhiannon flushed and murmured that he was hungry. She adjusted her gown and led the babe's questing mouth to her breast. He latched on hungrily, letting out startling little noises. Eric laughed. Forgetting his travel-stained clothing and weapons, he stretched out beside his wife and felt a warmth and languor steal over him. So this is it, he thought briefly. This is peace and happiness, a taste of it at least, a taste to reach for. Feelings surged hotly within him, the desire to protect against all odds, to hold his son, to hold Rhiannon both with passion and with tenderness. There had never been anything so beautiful in life as the sight of his wife cradling his child.

He touched her cheek as she fed the child. "Did you really wish that I should pitch into the sea? You merely could have prayed for a battle-ax to take me."

She kept her eyes on her son. "You don't understand, Eric. I'm not at all sure what I really said at the time."

"It was so painful?" he asked her tensely.

"It was horrible!" she replied, but then she smiled, and her eyes turned to his at last. "But worth it! Oh, Eric, he is worth . . . everything! Everything."

He inhaled, watching her eyes. He touched his son's platinum hair. "You love the grandchild of a Viking from the house of Vestfald," he reminded her.

She watched his eyes, and then she smiled very slowly. The blood within him heated, and he warned himself that he musn't feel so, that it was far too soon after the birth of their child for him to be feeling desire at all.

"I like your father very much," she told him primly.

"Do you?"

"Indeed."

He smiled, then caught her hand and kissed it. They stared at each other for a long moment, and then Rhiannon let out a startled "Oh! Take him, Eric, he's sleeping already, and he really must burp."

He swept up the baby, casting him over his shoulder with ease. Rhiannon adjusted her gown and pushed up on the bed, shivering with the pleasure of her husband's return and his delight in their child. "You do that very well," she murmured, and indeed he did. The splendid warrior with his golden head, royal crimson mantle, and massive sword arm seemed completely at ease with the child upon his shoulders.

"I am an uncle many times over," he reminded her, grinning. Then the baby burped, and Rhiannon laughed, and Eric playfully charged his son with insurrection for spitting up on his father's formal attire.

"Oh, Eric! I was so afraid so many times!" Rhiannon admitted, watching him.

"Afraid?"

"That you would not come back," she said, and again her gaze fell and she plucked at the covers. She could not give too much to him. She did not dare. "But you see, you have returned, and your father is well, and your brothers, and your mother is so happy, and I am so very glad. . . ." Her voice trailed away. Eric suddenly had gone very still.

"Eric—?"

"Garth sleeps. I shall have Daria take him." He strode to the door. Daria was down the hallway, talking excitedly with Bryan. Bryan, seeing Eric's eyes, seemed to know that the time had come to tell Rhiannon that her countryman had been slain.

"Daria, go get our nephew," Bryan told her. Eric nodded briefly to his brother. Daria frowned but quickly swept the baby away. Eric reentered his room, closing the door. Rhiannon was sitting up now, staring at him with deep concern in her eyes, a frown knitting her brow.

"Eric, what is it?"

He couldn't hedge; he couldn't ease his guilt or her pain. "Rowan was killed," he told her simply. And then he watched her features as she comprehended his words, watched the anguish seep into her eyes, the tears rise within them. His voice became rough as he continued. "I swore to protect him, but I failed. I had him buried with special prayers. I could not bring him back; circumstances would not allow it. I—I'm sorry."

He wanted to touch her but knew she would not want him to do so. She had loved Rowan. Loved him with youth, with innocence, with passion, and with laughter. She would not want the man who had destroyed that love to soothe her now.

"I'm sorry," he repeated. Then, awkwardly, he added, "I'll leave you. If you need me, send for me."

He left the room, closing the door behind him. He heard the soft sobs that escaped her, then winced and hurried down the stairs.

She did not need him, or so it seemed. The hours in the long day passed, and she did not send for him. He ate with his family as dusk fell, then he found solace before the fire with a horn of ale as the night darkened and the hour grew late.

No one intruded upon him until quite late, when his father came and sat beside him, staring into the fire. "You should go to her," he told Eric.

"She does not want me," he said simply.

Olaf leaned forward, watching the flames. "Once I came back from a battle and I had to tell your mother that both a very old friend—the Irish king she might have married—and her brother had fallen in the same day. And when I did, I stayed away from her. I left her to cry alone."

"So what would you have of me?" Eric asked him.

Olaf smiled slowly. "I made a mistake. I would not have you make the same mistake. Go to your wife. Hold her. Ease what pain you can."

"What if she does not want me?" Eric asked bitterly.

"She wants you!" a soft voice answered him as Erin came out of the shadows to stand behind her husband and smile down at her son. "I know she wants you. She needs you. Just as I needed your father. Go to her, Eric."

He rose, looking at them both. Then he left behind the light of the fire, strode up the stairs, and walked down the hall to his room. There he paused, then he pushed open the door. He found her in their bed, tears still glazing her eyes. He lifted her into his arms and carried her before the fire, and he held her there, close. Her arms wound around his neck and she sobbed softly, but she laid her head against his chest.

He lifted her chin and gently kissed her tearstained face. He smoothed back her hair, and then he murmured, "Let me hold you, my love. Just let me hold you."

Her arms tightened about him and she trembled. He asked her what was wrong.

Her silvery eyes looked into his. "I am just afraid that you will let me go!" she whispered.

He stared at her for long moments and then replied, "Never. Never, my love."

She leaned back against him, sighing softly. And then her eyes began to close.

She slept there in his arms, slept until the very wee hours of morning came, and they were both awakened by Daria's appearance with their very precious —and very loud—son within her arms.

Another day would soon begin. They had weathered the night, Eric thought.

Indeed, perhaps they had begun anew.

17

Christmas Day came upon them and was celebrated with Christian fervor. Eric presented Rhiannon with an elegantly jeweled and golden filigreed mantle brooch with a Celtic design, and her gift to him was a very fine dagger she had purchased from one of the peddlers who brought in Viking treasures from the Baltic lands and a fine tunic sewn with gold thread that she had fashioned herself in the long months when they had been gone.

It was a happy occasion for her. She had come to love Dubhlain and Eric's family very much, and it was difficult to remember that she had loathed and despised the very idea of coming here.

Two things disturbed her, though. One, that Rowan had died, and had met his death in a foreign land, one where he had come—albeit indirectly—because of her. The second thing that disturbed her was that she had long, empty hours to dwell on Rowan's death, because after the night in which he had offered her comfort, Eric had chosen to move across the hall, stating that he was afraid to disturb her or the babe.

Her son was still her absolute delight, and it seemed that when she would she let her mind wander to the pain of losing Rowan, Garth would cease his suckling and stare into her eyes with wisdom and wonder, and she would smile again and be eased.

There was Daria, too, so close to her own age, such a very good friend. And Olaf the White, King of Dubhlain, who sometimes spoke with thunder, more often with gentle tones, and who was definitely the master of his house. Erin, with her quick smile, was as beautiful as any young girl, a whirl of energy and sweet wisdom. In truth, Rhiannon enjoyed all of the household, all of Eric's many brothers and sisters and nephews and nieces. It was a home filled with laughter, and sorrow, too, as on the night when Aed Finnlaith had departed to his heavenly rest. Yet they were all fiercely together in their sorrows and their joys, and perhaps that was the enchantment of the place.

But even as the January winds whipped and tore at the great stone walls of the town, Eric rode out daily. His ships were repaired and provisioned for the journey eastward, toward her home. It seemed that he was far more eager to leave than she.

A date was set for the end of the month. Rhiannon found her husband in the simply furnished room he had taken as his own and protested their departure. "You would bring your son across a frigid, wind-tossed sea! Eric, we must wait—"

"I cannot wait," he told her impatiently. Seated before the fire, he carefully honed his sword blade with a stone. He called the sword Vengeance, she knew. Even the death he wielded had a name. He looked up as she remained there, his eyes as frosty a blue as she could ever remember, distant, chilling.

Nothing had really changed. He was master of his own destiny, and she was still his property to command, even if he did love his son. "I cannot wait! I vowed my sword to Alfred of Wessex. I left him to do battle for my kin, which Alfred understands, but he plans his assault on Gunthrum in the spring, and I must be with him."

"Eric—"

"My lady, it is a matter of my honor."

Tears stung her eyes. "Is death so very honorable, then?"

His eyes fell upon her once again. "Indeed, milady, 'tis the only entrance for a man into the halls of Valhalla."

She swung about and left him. They seldom spoke as the days passed, and Rhiannon watched the gray and forbidding skies. Then came the date that he had set, and she was relieved to see that the wind had calmed somewhat, even if the sea did still seem to be alive with froth.

Rhiannon found her father-in-law and pleaded with him to attempt to stop Eric, but Olaf smiled gently at her and offered no help. "He must return. He has sworn to support Alfred. He has taken the land, he has taken you as his wife, he has his fine new son. He must return."

"But—"

"Rhiannon, there is no stopping him. Come, it will be well. Mergwin has predicted a fine sailing, and he is never wrong about such things. Indeed, I shall miss him most sorely."

"He is coming with us?"

Olaf nodded and wrapped his arms about her

gently and kissed the top of her head. "It is time. There is no other course that a man can take. If you ever wish to return, if you ever need us, do not hesitate. The sea is truly not such a vast distance between us."

There would be no help for it at all. They were leaving. But Mergwin had said that they would be safe; yet he was coming with them. If he was so certain that they would be safe, why was he coming when his heart lay in Ireland?

The household came to see them depart down the river. Rhiannon found herself clinging fiercely to Erin, who assured her that there would be better times ahead and that they would meet again. Rhiannon thanked Eric's mother for her hospitality and expressed her condolences again for the loss of Erin's father. The queen smiled and assured her, "I feel that Father merely bided his time since we lost my mother a few years ago. I believe that they are together again and that they guard us all. Take care of my son and grandson, I beg you."

She could not take care of Eric, no one could, but she did not tell Erin that. She kissed her mother-in-law's cheek again, and Erin bundled the fur of her mantle high about her throat as Megan kissed her and handed over the well-bundled Garth. Then Rhiannon discovered that Daria had decided to accompany them, and she was very glad.

Rhiannon had already stepped aboard her husband's vessel when she saw Mergwin saying good-bye to Erin. He held her like a daughter, hugged her close, whispered something in her ear, and embraced her very tenderly again. Then he, too, came aboard.

Moments later he had come past the rows of sailors and sat with her at the bow of the ship. Daria, Rhiannon saw, was sailing on Patrick's vessel.

Cries and commands rang out, and on that very gray morning she watched the magnificent walled town of Dubhlain slowly fade from her view. Warm fingers curled over hers. She turned to see Mergwin's eyes upon her. "It will be well," he assured her.

She nodded and held his hand tightly. She thought of his great age and wondered again why he had chosen to make the journey.

The sea was choppy indeed, and it seemed that they were constantly tossed about. The wind whipped at Rhiannon's face and hair, chilling her greatly.

Hours out, Eric at last left his stance at the dragon prow and walked back to her. "Are you faring better this time?" he asked. It was a polite question. It seemed distant, though, and nothing other than a courtesy.

"I am faring very well, milord. I am an excellent sailor, as long as I am not with child."

"Ah, well, if you had thought to mention to me that you were with child, milady, I might have been better prepared to make your voyage more comfortable."

He did not wait for a reply. Swinging about, he headed for the prow once again and took up his vigil. She glanced at Mergwin and saw that he was smiling slightly. But then she noticed, too, that the smile did not quite reach his eyes, and she was worried. "Are you ill?" she asked him anxiously.

He shook his head. "Somewhat sad, that is all."

"Why?"

"I will never see Ireland again," he told her softly.

A chill settled over her. "You mustn't say that!" she told him. "Please, you mustn't—"

"Speak the truth? I am a very old man, Rhiannon. Very old."

"But I need you!" she insisted.

"And I will be here as long as you need me," he assured her. Then he swiftly changed the subject. "His temper simmers slowly at times, you know."

"Eric's?"

Mergwin nodded. "What makes him so tense, I wonder, like a great caged wolf prowling about his ship?"

"The mere fact that he is an arrogant Viking male," Rhiannon retorted quickly.

"A wolf alone, prowling about. They mate for life, wolves do, you know, milady. And if a wolf loses his mate, he prowls the woods and howls out his pain and fury."

"Ah, but does the wolf love his mate?"

Mergwin's smile deepened, and his ancient eyes seemed to glisten with silver. "I've seen this wolf in love once before—a long time ago on a distant shore. She was killed, and I watched him suffer and prowl until there came . . . you. Yet even then, you see, it was different. It was a different time, a different life. I do not think that he knew the full meaning until this time. You hold the wolf within your hands, Rhiannon. You have only to see that."

"He is going to war again," she said softly. "He will always be going to war."

"A tempest precedes a calm. This will be Alfred's

last great battle, and he will prevail and go down in history as the only king the English will call 'Great.' "

"But will we survive the tempest?" Rhiannon asked.

He was slow in answering. The wind came hard upon them, and his hair and beard were lifted. Garth, who had been whimpering, quieted, and it seemed that even the sounds of the shouts of the men and the whipping of the sails grew silent and subdued.

"You must survive it!" was all that he would say.

Then Mergwin, too, rose and strode to the prow. Alone, Rhiannon held Garth very close to her heart and tried to cease the shivering that had begun inside her.

They did make the winter's crossing, and made it very well. By nightfall she was home, stepping upon the soil of Wessex. Adela was there to greet her, and there was a hot bath prepared in her room, and warmed mead with cinnamon awaited her on the fire. That night, as soon as she had bathed and Garth had been fed and put to bed in the tiny nursery that adjoined her master's room, she fell into her own bed and slept, too exhausted to feel hurt when Eric did not join her, too exhausted to do more than hope that Daria had been well cared for.

The days passed. Rhiannon anxiously wondered about her sister-in-law's impressions of her home after the grandeur of Dubhlain. But Daria was enchanted with the place, and Rhiannon was relieved and grateful.

The preparations for war went on. In the cleared courtyard men practiced with their arms. The blacksmiths were busy forging weapons of steel. At night men honed their weapons. The messages had come in. When the spring broke, Eric must meet with Alfred, and they would attack the Danes, led by Gunthrum.

A cold war was already taking place within the house, Rhiannon thought. She could not understand why Eric stayed away from her for so long. Garth flourished, and Eric enjoyed the babe and was comfortable with him, and yet he continued to sleep elsewhere. Hurt, she felt her own temper rise, and the awkwardness of her situation added fuel to the flames. Had Eric wanted her, he simply would have swept her into his arms and taken her. She hadn't the strength to carry him off anywhere. And she had too much pride to ask for his presence. He had held her and promised that he would never let her go.

And he hadn't touched her since.

February turned to March. The day came nearer and nearer when he would ride away, and she did not think that she could bear it. Mergwin was edgy and said nothing, and so she was very afraid. Determined to say something to Eric before he could leave, Rhiannon made her way to his room. She tapped upon his door, and as it had stood ajar, it opened of its own accord. She saw that Eric was deeply ensconced in a steaming bath. And there was no young serving lad at his side to assist him but the doelike maiden Judith.

He had not heard the tap, and he did not see her there, as a hot cloth covered his face while his head rested on the rear of the tub. Rhiannon lifted her head proudly and moved into the room. Judith's eyes widened at the sight of her. Rhiannon smiled very sweetly and indicated that Judith should leave, closing the door behind her.

"Ah, Judith, give my back a scrub, eh?" he said.

Rhiannon emitted some strangled sound of agreement and came around behind him, stripping the cloth from his face. He edged forward, baring his back to her. She dexterously scrubbed his back, biting her lips to keep from lashing out at him. At his next words she started violently. "Now you've done my back, lass, how about my front?" The husky edge to his voice gave very little question to his meaning.

"Oh, my lord! I should just love to take care of your front—permanently!" she snapped out. And before he could respond, she had splashed up the water, soaking his face and beard. And then she was done with him. Spinning about, she tore from the room, tears stinging her eyes, fury raging in her heart.

"Rhiannon!" he bellowed after her in sharp command. She ignored him and kept running.

Down the stairs she ran, past Patrick and Rollo and the men in the hallway, past Adela and Daria, both of whom sat at a tapestry.

"Rhiannon!" he thundered again. She caught up her heavy mantle at the door and went racing to the stables. Brushing past the lads, she bridled a mare and leapt upon her bare back, then galloped past the sentries at the gates.

She didn't know where she was going. She rode for what seemed an endless time, and then realized she must give the poor mare a rest. When she had slowed her pace at last, she became aware that it was snowing and that the night was bitterly cold. Darkness lay all about her, and she, who knew this land like the back of her hand, was very nearly lost.

It didn't seem to matter. "Damn him!" she cried to the night wind. And then tears trickled down her face. She paid no heed to her movements and was taken entirely by surprise when the mare suddenly whinnied and reared. Rhiannon grasped with her thighs too late and went sliding off the animal onto her backside. Stunned, she lay upon the ground.

Then the traitorous little mare went tearing off alone—toward home, toward warmth, toward a stable of hay.

Rising and dusting off her bruised derrière, Rhiannon felt her heart tug even as she started to shiver. Garth! He slept through the night now, but he would awake in the morning, hungry and crying and alone. They would see to him, surely. Adela and Daria were there; they would never let him suffer. There was goat's milk for him to drink. . . .

She could die out here. No, she would not die; she knew her way, she just had to start walking. . . .

The thunder of a horse's hooves came to her, and in seconds she saw Eric appear out of the darkness, on the great white stallion. She quickly wiped the tears from her eyes and tried to right her snow-dampened hair and mussed clothing. He stopped before her, staring down at her, and she was certain that there was amusement in his eyes. How dare he!

She started walking in the direction from which he had come.

"Rhiannon!"

She kept walking. He did not stop her but slowly

walked the stallion behind her. "I thought you might need some assistance."

"Whatever gave you that idea?"

"The mare that rushed by me, for one thing."

"Oh. Well, I had thought that I wanted to ride. Once out here, I realized that I far preferred to walk, and so I sent her on home. You are quite welcome to leave me."

"Am I?"

"Indeed."

She had not heard him dismount, she had not heard his footsteps in the snow, but suddenly he was behind her and sweeping her up into his arms. She struggled against him, but he ignored her flailing fists. "You're soaked! You'll be ill!" he scolded her. In seconds he had lifted her up with him onto the stallion. Still she fought his hold.

"What difference should that make to you!" she raged. "You find your entertainment where you choose."

"Garth would be quite heartbroken!"

"Let me go . . . Viking!" she charged him.

The sky suddenly seemed to break. From the darkness came millions upon millions of snowflakes. Eric swore, then urged the stallion forward. Even as they moved, Rhiannon regretted her impetuous run from the house. The weather was worsening. They would never make it back. The thick, wet snow was beating upon them mercilessly now.

But Eric was not heading for the house. She realized a moment later that he was headed for one of the small hunting cottages that nestled in the woods before the cliffs. He led the stallion beneath the eaves, then dismounted from the horse and dragged Rhiannon down into his arms. He battled the wind to bring her inside, then nearly cast her from him to close the door once again. When that was done, he turned and leaned against it, and his blue gaze fell upon her with a sharp and dangerous gleam.

"Ah, my love! Here we are! On a night when we could be safe and warm before our own fire!"

She ignored him, turning her back on him and trying to wring some of the dampness from her skirts. He strode past her, and for a moment she froze, but he did not touch her. He came to the central fireplace and swore anew as he built up the tinder, then brought out flint and striker and managed to start a blaze. The warmth was hypnotic. She did not want to come near it, yet she shivered mindlessly.

Eric rose and looked about. Straw pallets lay in the corners of the small room, covered with fur blankets. There was a large, simply carved table to the left of the fire, several drinking horns upon it. He strode to the table and tested the first horn. Then his eyes fell upon Rhiannon again, and he moved toward her. She backed away and he paused, a devil's gleam in his eye as he passed the horn to her. "Mead. Drink it. I am planning on bringing you back alive."

"I don't—"

"I said to drink it!"

She took a long swallow of the mead. It was warm and delicious and raced down her throat and to her stomach. She took another swallow, then handed the horn back to him. "Your every command obeyed, milord," she drawled sarcastically. "Is there anything else?"

"Indeed. Take off your clothes."

"I will not!" she spat out furiously. But he had already left her, dropping the horn onto one of the pallets and pulling a fur blanket from another.

"Let's see, how shall I phrase this? Milady, you may remove your clothing of your own accord or I shall do it for you. Actually, it's been quite a while. I should dearly relish the task."

"Oh!" she cried out, rage sweeping through her. "Bloody invader, Viking bastard!" she lashed out. Smiling, he caught her arm, dragging her toward him. She fought to free herself, and her mantle came away in his hand. She raced to the corner of the room, but he came after her, pinning her there. She pummeled his chest, but he caught hold of her wrists and held them high above her head, bracing her there in the corner. With his free hand he rent the blue wool of her tunic and the linen of her shift beneath. She tried to kick him and in her fury cried out anew. "It seemed to me that it was Judith who was to 'do' your front, Viking!"

His laughter was husky, his breath on her cheek was warm and sweet with the mead, and his body was very close to hers. "Rhiannon—" He broke off, as she managed to slam up a knee and inform him, "Milord, that is all that I shall do for your front!"

A second later she was lying flat upon the pallet, winded, desperate. She flailed about to maintain her meager hold on the remnants of her clothing, but he snatched them from her with an awesome force. Shivering fiercely, she clasped her arms about herself, but then a fur landed atop her, covering her and warming her. Startled, she scrambled up to discover that Eric was peeling away his own soaked clothing and reaching for a fur for himself.

Then he turned back to her. She tried to shoot up, but he pushed her back and straddled her. Tears lightly stung her eyes again. The fur just covered his shoulders. His naked chest was rippled with muscle, smooth and sleek and fascinating, and it had been so long since she had seen him so. His sex rested upon her belly, and that, too, filled her with warmth and desire, and seemed to cause a scalding liquid to dance deep within her. But now that she had come to need him so desperately, to desire him during her every waking moment, to long to touch him with tenderness and yearning; now that she loved him, he betrayed her. He wanted the harlot Judith.

"Don't you touch me!" she whispered, afraid that her tears would soon fall, that her pride would be broken.

Again he caught her wrists, then leaned low against her body. Her breasts touched his chest and she longed to have him cup them, caress them. His lips paused just above hers, and he whispered huskily, "However can you do my front if I don't touch you?"

"Damn you—"

He silenced her with a kiss. Deep, passionate, then sweet and tender. Coercion became seduction. He stole her will and her breath with his honeyed kisses, and he gave warmth against the storm. When he broke from her, he touched her lips still again and again with his own. And then the tears were about to spill from her eyes and she twisted her head aside and begged him, "Eric, don't!"

"Rhiannon, I knew that it was you."

Her eyes met his, wide and disbelieving. "How could you—"

"Because you have a sweet scent all of your own. Like roses. It is the soap you use, and the fragrance always lingers about you. I know it as clearly as I know the color of your hair, the hue of your eyes. I know it because it has haunted me since the day we met. It drifts into my dreams and calls to me when I am away. It covers me like the softness of your hair when we are together. No other woman will ever wear it."

"But . . . Eric, she was in your room while you were bathing!"

"She brought up towels. My love, she is a servant in our house."

"And you have . . ." She paused, then inhaled deeply. "You have stayed so very far away from me!"

"I did not wish to hurt you or the babe."

"But it's past the time!"

"Rhiannon, you told me that the birth was very hard. I thought it best to keep myself away for a time. And then . . . well, you made no suggestion that I should return."

She moistened her lips, staring at his eyes. "Because I thought you did not wish to come back!"

"Do you want me back?"

She inhaled again, torn, afraid, wanting to believe the tenderness in his eyes. "Oh, my God!" she breathed. "I do not believe that I am saying this to a Viking! Yes, yes . . . I want you back. I want you . . . I . . ." She paused again, shivered, and then she felt the startling warmth of him and all the beauty that she had missed for so long—the hardness of his thighs, the thunder of his heart, the searing heat of his body fitting against hers. And his features, striking and strong, hewn from two cultures brought together at their very best. His eyes . . . so endlessly blue, so gentle now upon hers. She dared to whisper, "I want you, Eric. So badly. I love you."

Eric started violently at the whispered words, staring down at her then with wonder and amazement and a love that matched hers for him. Her eyes were slightly damp, and they glistened in the fire's glow, silvery blue and beautifully fringed by the thickness of her dark lashes. Her hair, always her crowning glory, swirled around their nakedness and the furs, entwining them in the flame-colored tresses. Her lips were the color of mead, her face slightly flushed, and her body was even lovelier than the memory of it that had taunted his dreams during the long nights. Her breasts were still enlarged and very full, her nipples a deep rose and turgid with desire, and her limbs creamy and smooth beneath him.

And she was whispering that she loved him. . . .

"By God, I was so afraid!" he told her. "Afraid, too, that I had lost forever what little of you I held when Rowan died. I could best the man, you see, but never his ghost. I thought that he would lie between us, and so I waited, but I . . ." He paused, and her eyes searched his out, confused and questing. "I was so afraid to love you, Rhiannon. Love leaves a man vulnerable. It is such a wicked weapon to be wielded. I fought against it, yet I know not when I lost that battle, only that I did. Perhaps it was lost from the start, from that day I first saw you high upon the wall. Perhaps it was when I held you beneath me. Or when I watched you move and sway when you taunted men to violence. Perhaps, then, it was only the desperation to have you, to possess you, and then again, once I had done so, I was indeed lost forever. I do not know when it came about. But, my wife, I, too, love you—with all of my heart, all of my life, all of my soul."

"Eric!" she whispered, and then the tears were spilling down her cheeks and she was speaking so quickly, he could scarcely understand her. "I loved you long before Rowan died. He was still dear to me and I grieved for his death, but I'd have rather had you back a thousand times in his place. I could not understand how I could love you when you ordered me about constantly, arrogant and demanding—"

"Arrogant?"

"Indeed." She laughed, and then her words died away and she whispered, "Oh, Eric, can this really be?"

"I know that you are now my life and that I love you beyond understanding or reason!" he whispered. And then he groaned, and his knuckles moved over her cheeks as he told her, "I watched time and again as my son lay at your breast, and I longed to be there myself!" His lips touched hers once again, then moved to her breast, tasting her as he caressed her. She cried out with the deliciousness of it, cradling his golden hair against her. Then he rose above her and whispered that he loved her eyes and the sweet entanglement of her hair and the beautiful swell of her breasts. He fell against her, touching her, exciting her, and rising to whisper again with crude, blunt, evocative words just what else he loved of hers, and with his every whisper he touched and tantalized and stroked and caressed and aroused with kisses and the great, hungry sweep of his tongue her limbs, her flesh, her most intimate and secret places. In turn she rose from the nest of the furs and wrapped her arms around him, and her whispers caressed him, as did the soft, fragrant tendrils of her hair. Boldly she stroked and touched and explored him, assuring him sweetly that she was delighted to serve and obey in any way, that she was eager and surely competent to do his front; then she proceeded to prove that it was so. He laughed until the breath caught within him, and he swept her to him and beneath him. Before the glow of the fire, they consummated the words and vows they had exchanged that night, this new thing admitted between them, the wonder of their love.

Late into the night they held each other and listened to the snow fall and the fire snap and crackle. They touched again and made love again, and when Rhiannon at last expressed concern about their son, Eric was certain that he would be all right until the morning and that no one would worry, for they were all aware that Eric had come after her.

"And they know that we will be all right because you are invincible?" she asked teasingly.

He laughed. "Aye, perhaps."

"You are very arrogant."

"And always will be, I'm afraid. Do you mind so very much?"

She sighed with mock resignation. "I shall try to live with it."

"Will you? Bear in mind that you, my love, are willful and proud and impetuous, and that I will forever wear a scar from your arrow!"

"You are demanding and autocratic as well as arrogant," she reminded him sweetly, stroking the area of his scar and assuring him smilingly that she would spend many nights trying to atone for the deed. Then he held her again, loved her again, and they drifted into a lazy half sleep.

Dawn came, and she turned in his arms and told him worriedly, "Eric, I never did betray you—or Alfred. I swear it. He is my king and was my guardian, and I love him and never would have defied him. I did not betray you."

He caught her hand and kissed it. "Hush, love, I know that." He said no more, but his mind raced back, and again he saw Rowan alive and well in his saddle as they fought the Danes, and then he saw Rowan again, dead upon the ground, and he saw the dagger.

He pulled her close and kissed her forehead. "I know, my love, I know."

Minutes later they rose, and he dressed her in his mantle and wrapped her in furs. Then they came outside, where the snow had stopped but where the world lay, a beautiful, pristine white cocoon. They mounted the white stallion and the great animal carried them home.

A time of peace ensued, so very sweet that Rhiannon could scarce bear knowing that Eric would ride out any day. She clung to him through the nights, wishing that time could be magically arrested, the future kept at bay.

But it could not. One bright spring morning the men prepared to leave. Rhiannon waited within the courtyard, Adela and Daria at her side, Garth within her arms, and she watched as Eric led the white stallion toward her. His mail covered his chest, his mantle emblazoned with his arms was draped about his shoulders. His helmet sat atop his head, and through the open visor she could see the startling blue of his eyes. She trembled, thinking how deeply and dearly she loved him and just how magnificent he was, even as he prepared to go to war.

He pulled aside his helmet as he approached her. He tenderly kissed his son, and then handed the babe to his sister. He took Rhiannon into his arms, then, and kissed her long and tenderly, until she thought that her heart would break.

A shadow of fear swept over her as he broke away. He was in so much danger. Mergwin would not have come with them to this shore if he were not afraid of danger to Eric. She could not let him go.

"Eric . . ."

"It will be over and I will be home before you know it, my love."

"No . . ." she whispered miserably.

"I will come back. I have said that it shall be so, and so it will," he assured her with a tender smile.

"If only . . ."

"What?" he demanded.

She shook her head and lifted her chin. She would not send him into battle oppressed with her fears. "God be with you, my love. God, and all the deities of the house of Vestfald!"

He held her tightly once again. "You'll be safe and well. Patrick is staying to guard you, Daria is here, as well as Adela. Watch over our son, madam."

"I will."

"And Mergwin will be here."

"Mergwin!" Startled, she pulled from him. "Mergwin is staying here? He is not riding with you?"

"He wishes to stay with you. He is a very old man. I am not pleased when he insists on riding to battle."

She nodded and felt a chill wind sweep over her. Then she managed to smile.

Mergwin did not think that there would be danger for Eric. He thought that the danger would come for her.

She kissed Eric again, warmly, passionately. Then he whispered that he must go, and they tore from each other. And she watched as, resplendent in his war apparel, he mounted the stallion, and she managed to smile and to wave until he was gone from sight.

Then a sob ripped from her throat. She spun about, entered the house, and raced to her room, to *their* room, and there cried until she had no more tears to shed.

Lying there, she prayed then in silence. *God help him, God help him, God be with him.*

And pray you, dearest Lord, be also with me!

18

The fighting was swift and merciless.

Within weeks they had forced the Danes to London, and in the days that followed they battled fiercely within the old Roman town. Alfred was like a man possessed, determined, driven. But then the events that had taken place in Eric's absence had brought him to this bitter point.

Gunthrum had signed a treaty in which he had agreed to settle East Anglia, but hearing of the assault on Rochester had apparently been too much for him, and he had rejoined the battle. Alfred had sent all of his available ships, including Eric's, against Gunthrum on the Thames, and Alfred had prevailed, capturing Gunthrum's fleet and all the treasures within it. But as Alfred had ordered his men toward home, the Danes had assaulted his heavily laden ships and won away all that had been lost and more.

They had come this far, trailing carnage in their wake. Alfred had ordered countless villages and towns burned, and there had been tremendous bloodshed. The king was demanding absolute loyalty from the people and would accept nothing less.

Now Eric sat atop Alexander and stared down upon the ruins of London. It was a charred and desolate

place, unfit for human habitation. Men with carts carried away bodies and limbs; women and children
were just beginning to appear among the debris,
scrounging amid the ruins for food and sustenance.

If nothing else, Eric thought wearily, it was over.

And he had survived it all once again, he and Rollo
and the vast majority of his men. Alfred had forgiven
him his absence when he had crossed the sea to Ireland, and so, in all honor, Eric had felt himself obliged
to ride forward in every fray, to bring his battle cry to
his lips and race first into the battle line of the enemy.
He was adept at warfare; life had given him that. But
today, looking down at the ruins of the pathetic town,
he was sick to death of the slaughter and pain and the
desolation, and he was heartily glad that he would
start for home within the next few days. Home . . .

There was to be a new peace treaty. Scribes were
already working on it. Gunthrum the wily Dane had
also managed to survive the battle very well.

England was to be divided into two parts. The
boundary would run along the River Thames, then
along the River Lea at its source, then directly to
Bedford, then along the Ouse to Watling Street. The
Danes would hold Essex, East Anglia, the Eastern
Midlands, and the land north of the Humber. In the
south Alfred would reign as king, and none would
dispute his sovereignty again.

There would be peace. If only the peace could
last. . . .

He turned the stallion away from the desolate
scene and led the horse toward the multitude of tents
on the outskirts of the city.

He quickened his pace suddenly as he heard a high,

drawn-out cry, followed by the clang of steel, and then again the sounds of fierce swordplay. He nudged the stallion to a gallop, and by a copse of trees he found a group of men, mainly his own and some of those belonging to the king's closest retainers, vehemently engaged in battle with what seemed to be a Danish raiding party. Quickly he drew his sword and entered into it, finding Rollo already in the fray. Eric leapt from the stallion and hacked his way to his friend's back, and there they formed a fierce and deadly fighting machine together. "By the halls of Valhalla!" Rollo roared out. "What is this? On the very day that a treaty is to be signed?"

"I know not!" Eric claimed. Nor could he care at the moment. The enemy was coming at him two at a time, and it took all his great strength to move his sword with sufficient speed to save his skin. He nearly tripped over one fallen attacker, but that proved to be his salvation, for a sword, ripping through the air, missed his skull. He straightened and skewered his assailant, then inhaled sharply as he noticed that high atop a knoll a single horseman was staring down at him. He squinted against the morning air, trying to make out the emblems on the man's mantle.

He swore, lifting his shield as the man raised his hand, then sent a small silver blade hurtling through the air toward him.

The dagger caught on his shield with shattering force, and fell to the ground.

The horseman quickly raced away.

Eric knelt down and picked up the dagger. It was the same type that had killed Rowan. They might have been identical.

The surviving Danes in the glade had melted away, disappearing into the trees. Eric shouted to Rollo that he had to catch the horseman, then went racing out to find the white stallion. He galloped from the glade, but the horseman was gone, and he had little clue as to his direction or destination. Swearing beneath his breath in every language he knew, Eric rode wearily back to the glade where Rollo and the others were gathering up their wounded.

Young Jon of Wincester, a favorite of the king, was bending down by one Danish body. He rose with disgust as Eric came riding to his side. "What bloody treaty can we ever trust when men come forward such as this?"

Edward of Sussex, Jon's good friend and once a loyal companion to Rowan, came to Eric's side as well. "I'll be damned if I can understand it! It was as if they cared not for battle or gain but were intent upon murder and nothing more!"

"Not so strange for Danes," Jon said bitterly.

"I don't know," Eric said, shaking his head. "Even for Danes. Men battle for gain or for defense. Why else?"

None of them had an answer. They gathered the wounded and headed back to the camp. Eric washed the blood from his face and hands and changed his tunic, then made his way to Alfred's tent. The king was there, listening as a scribe sent from Gunthrum rambled on and on about the particulars of the treaty.

"There's not a word of truth in the bloody thing!" Eric interrupted.

Alfred looked his way. "We've already sent word to Gunthrum, accusing him of infamy and treachery.

He has denied the attack and has sent me a daughter of his as hostage to verify his word."

"Then," Eric said coolly, "there is some traitor among us. Some traitor who has wished me harm—rather, death—since I came to this shore. It began when your message failed to reach Rhiannon and my ships were so vehemently attacked. Then, when I went on your behalf, Alfred, to battle the Danes in the far south, they were warned of my approach. Moreover, I have very good cause to believe, Alfred, that young Rowan did not fall in simple battle in Ireland but that he fell to a murderer, to create greater turmoil within my house."

There was a shocked gasp from the opening of the tent. Jon of Wincester came striding in, decked in mail, his features tense. "By all that's holy, my lord of Dubhlain! You say that Rowan was murdered?"

Eric tossed the dagger that had been aimed at his throat upon the king's table. Alfred and Jon both strode for it, Jon giving way for the king.

Then Alfred studied the dagger and its design. Pain etched into his weary features and he fell back into his chair. "What is it?" Jon demanded.

Alfred waved a hand that Jon might pick up the dagger. He did so. He inhaled sharply. "It's William's. William of Northumbria's. 'Tis his dagger. There must be some . . . mistake."

William of Northumbria. Indeed William and Allen and Jon and Edward had all come into his house, into Rhiannon's house, when Alfred had sent him orders to see to the Danes in the south. William had not accompanied them to Ireland, but there had been many men of Wessex with him, as well as many sent directly under Rowan's command.

"There is no mistake," Eric said. "I've two daggers. One taken from Rowan's back in Ireland, one just hurtled at me in the glade."

"In Ireland—"

"Find a man called Harold of Mercia. If he has survived this latest warfare, he might shed some light upon these events," Eric suggested.

Alfred strode to the opening of the tent. He ordered his guard to find Harold, and then he paced back and forth upon the cold earth floor, his hands locked behind his back. In seconds the older man who had stepped forward at Rowan's death in Ireland came hurrying into the tent. He knelt before the king. "My lord, you have summoned me."

"Get up!" Alfred commanded. Harold did so. Then his eyes fell upon Eric and Jon, and he paled visibly. He looked to the table and saw the dagger there and suddenly turned about in a raw panic. He started to run from the tent.

Jon stepped before the opening. Eric seized Harold by the shoulder and dragged him back before the king.

"Were you in the service of William of Northumbria when you went to Ireland?"

"In William's service? Why, no, no, my King. I served young Rowan, I did."

"Did you serve him?" Eric asked coldly. "Or did you slay him, for gold provided by William?"

The man's pallor sealed his doom. A harsh, anguished cry escaped Jon, and he stepped forward, his knife bared, and swiftly slit the man's throat.

Alfred turned his back on the scene, his pain and weariness evident in the slope of his shoulders. "By God, Jon, I have fought for this land to give it laws! You have done murder here and now!"

"And I will gladly pay his survivors, and perhaps they will be as pleased to make gain upon death as this man was! By God, Alfred, he murdered Rowan!"

"At William's command," Eric interrupted. "I'm going for William."

He hurried from the tent and made way quickly for the section where William and his followers were encamped. He strode past William's men and threw open the flaps to his tent.

There was no one there. Outside he caught by his shirt the first man he could find, and demanded to know where his master might be.

No one knew, and no amount of threatening could change their story. William had ridden out that morning in the company of Allen of Kent, and he had not been seen since.

As Eric stood there among William's men, Jon, with Edward close behind him, came riding up hard upon him. "William has not been seen in hours. Neither has Allen. William must have known that you had the dagger—and proof against him. He has ridden south."

"We must follow," Eric said.

Jon glanced at Edward, then began speaking rapidly. "Aye, we must ride, and very quickly. We've already told your man, Rollo, and he is gathering your weapons and bringing your mount. We have to head for the coast, for your manor, with all haste."

Eric felt the cold enter him, felt the fear that had plagued Mergwin since they had come to this land.

"To my manor? Why?" he demanded huskily.

"Because we believe . . ." Jon began. He inhaled quickly, but Edward was continuing for him.

"We believe that William of Northumbria has long coveted your wife. There were comments that he made to Rowan, things that we saw, others that we suspected. We used to joke about it. But he always thought that if Rowan was gone, or if Rhiannon lost the king's favor, he would be the one to have her. And now he will have lost everything, and so we believe . . . we believe that he will make all haste to vent his hatred and anger upon her now."

Eric's fingers tightened into fists at his side. He cast back his head and let out a battle cry tinged with anguish and with fury, a sound that shattered the very sunlight and the day. The battle cry of the house of Vestfald, the tearing, horrible cry of the wolf at bay.

Rollo appeared upon a spotted mount, leading the white. Eric leapt on the stallion and started out at a hard gallop, and the others were hard pressed to follow behind him.

For Rhiannon the days passed slowly.

It was spring, and the earth was coming alive. The fields seemed fertile with planting and there was an abundance of animals, squirrels and rabbits and countless deer. In the stables the horses were restless. Daria was anxious and restless, too, and despite her happiness and delight in her son, so was Rhiannon. Only Mergwin and Adela seemed calm, and Rhiannon wondered if age brought peace, or an ability to realize that time would pass at its own pace and that there was nothing to be done.

There was news from the battlefront. Eric sent a man back every week, so she knew where battle had been engaged and that he was well, and the king also; and that the fighting was going in their favor. She knew that they had come to London; that it seemed that there would be a new peace treaty. But the treaty had yet to be signed, and until it was, she would worry about Eric. She knew that despite his apparent calm, Mergwin waited, too, and that he seemed to watch not only her but also the sky and the wind and the sea. Often he walked away alone; she knew not where, nor did she know what he did during his long absences. Until Eric came home, she would worry.

She blessed Daria for being with her. Daria told her Norse tales about the gods Odin and Thor, and Irish tales about St. Patrick and about the little people who lived in the glades, and the banshees who came and cried when death was imminent. The two women laughed and joked about men, and Daria described her dream lover, and they spent long spring afternoons by the fire with the baby between them, whiling away the hours, and the endless days.

But when William of Northumbria arrived at the gates one afternoon, Rhiannon was alone. Mergwin was out in the forest somewhere, and Daria had accompanied Adela to the shore, where a small ship had just arrived from Olaf and Erin, laden with gifts.

The guards, recognizing William's colors, had instantly opened the gates, and the servants summoned Rhiannon. She hurried to the door, certain that the news must be grave indeed if William, himself, had come to her home rather than a servant or a carl.

She ran out to the courtyard to meet him, her heart pounding fiercely. He seemed to have ridden in great haste, and that, too, alarmed her. He was alone except for his constant companion, Allen. Rhiannon quickly greeted them both, offering food and ale. But William dismounted from his horse and caught her shoulders between his hands. "Rhiannon, there is no time. Have a servant bring us ale to carry—and some bread and cheese, perhaps. We must make haste."

"Why? What is it? What has happened?" she cried in alarm.

"Eric has been wounded. He cannot be moved. He asks for you. I have promised to bring you with all haste."

"Oh!" she cried with horror. And suddenly she could not move, could not think. "I must—I must get Adela and my things—"

"No, you must come right now. Send a man for food and drink, then come with me. Now. There's no time."

"I must get Garth—"

"What?" William demanded, stopping her.

"My son. I cannot leave my son."

William's fingers moved pensively over his mustache, twirling the dark length of it. Then he smiled. "Yes, of course, my dear. You must bring your son. But hurry."

She did. Trembling, she moved in terror, her knees quaking as she tried to walk. This was it, the horror that had been descending upon her for so very long. Eric had taunted death one too many times. He was a great warrior, perhaps one of the greatest, and he could wield a sword like no other man. Yet every man was mortal, and now he lay, hurt and perhaps dying, when he had finally become everything in life for her. He could not die! No matter what the omens, he could not die! She would not let him do so!

Garth had been sleeping. She ignored his protests as she swept him up into her arms and bundled him in a huge linen blanket. She caught up a mantle and came hurrying back down the stairs. By then the servants had brought food satchels and drinking horns, and a mare awaited her in the courtyard.

Patrick had arrived. Tensely he listened to William's tale of the battles fought.

"I should ride with you," Patrick said.

"No!" William replied sharply. "Eric especially requested that you remain behind with his sister and Adela at the manor. He needs you . . . here."

"Oh, Patrick!" Rhiannon said, shaking. He held her tight, then helped her upon the mare, securing Garth within her arms.

"He will be well, milady, he will be well! Eric is created of steel, I know it. You must keep faith."

She nodded, afraid to speak for the tears that choked her.

"Milady, come!" William urged.

"Yes, let's make all haste, let's ride!" she whispered. "Oh, please, bring me to him as quickly as you can!" she pleaded. "Patrick, God be with you."

"And Godspeed to you, milady!"

William led his mount about. At a swift canter he led Rhiannon and Allen through the gates and toward the cliffs. Tears stung Rhiannon's eyes. She scarcely noticed in which direction they rode.

But Mergwin, emerging from the forest, did notice. He clenched his fists and closed his eyes tightly, then raced for the stables. Ignoring the painful thundering in his heart, he leapt atop a bare-backed mount. Ignoring the concerned shouts of Patrick and the stable hands, he went racing after the riders.

They were already far from the manor, already entering the copse of trees. Mergwin pounded hard after them, catching up with them as they entered upon a shadowed trail.

"Rhiannon!" he called to her.

She reined in her mount. "Why does the old fool delay us?" William demanded, exasperated.

"I must wait for him!" Rhiannon insisted. She turned back. "Mergwin! Eric has been injured!" she called. "I must hurry to reach him."

Mergwin rode slowly before them. He stared at her and at William. Then he looked at Rhiannon again and said softly, "He has not been hurt. Eric of Dubhlain has not been hurt."

"How do you know, you old fake?" Allen demanded curtly. "We have been with him. We have come from the battle. He has sent us for his wife."

Mergwin shook his head slowly. He edged his mount between Rhiannon's horse and William's. "I would know if Eric of Dubhlain were near death. Do not go with them, Rhiannon. Take your babe and race homeward—now!"

He cracked his hand down hard upon the mare's rump. Rhiannon cried out as the mare leapt forward, nearly dislodging her. She clutched Garth close to her breast, and fear rode through her as she started to obey Mergwin's order, her heart racing. Yet even as she led the mare down the narrow path, William shouted, and Allen was quick to cut her off. She could not manage to evade him, not while holding Garth and desperately trying to see that he did not fall or come to injury. She heard a sharp, dry cry and a thud, and she spun her mare around in time to see that William had struck Mergwin and that the old man fell from his horse to hit the ground with cruel force.

She dismounted quickly from her own horse and hurried to his side, clutching Garth tightly. She gazed up at William with loathing and hissed in fury, " 'Tis the truth he tells! What game is it that you play?"

With Garth carefully laid at her side, she brought Mergwin's head to her lap. His eyes opened, gray as the twilight, mystical, pained.

"Leave him!" William commanded her.

"You've hurt him!"

"I meant to kill him."

"Bastard! Alfred will hang you!"

"Alfred, madam, will never see me again."

"Mergwin," she whispered, ignoring William. The ancient eyes remained upon her, then he winced, and she cried out, "I have to get him home! He will die here!"

"Lady, he will die, and you are not going home."

"Mergwin, hold on, I beg of you! Hold on to life, cherish it dearly. Adela or Patrick or Daria will come, I know it—"

"Rhiannon," he whispered. She alone could hear, and only then by bending very low to his lips. "Fear not for me, for my years have been many. I have warned you, and mayhap not too late, for with every moment Eric comes closer. Take what time you can, make the journey difficult, and if I have thwarted this traitor, then my purpose here is done and it is time that I join those I love in a better life."

"No!" she cried out, feeling the dampness of tears fall upon her cheek. "No, Mergwin, no!"

She leapt to her feet, facing William. "You will help him or I will not make a move."

William smiled and leaned down from his saddle. "You will move—and quickly, milady—or I will have Allen wrest your brat from you and ride hard with his knife set upon the babe's throat. Have I made myself clear?"

She choked in fury. "You would not!"

"Allen—"

"No!"

She scooped up Garth and held him close, and then she looked down at Mergwin. His eyes were closed. His face was white and shadowed, already a haunting mask of death. She could not leave him!

But neither she could not risk her son.

"Milady?" William said. She did not move. "Mount your mare or I shall come for you and give the child to Allen. Do not try to outrun me. I will hurt you, and I will hurt the babe."

Her only chance was to escape him on horseback and hurry back for Mergwin.

She had to escape him, had to . . .

But when she mounted the mare, William took her reins. He would lead her himself.

"We must make haste!" Allen warned him.

"To where?" Rhiannon demanded.

"To join the Danes," William told her briefly. "I've given Gunthrum much in the way of warnings and information. I've been promised a place in his household. You will share it with me."

"Alfred will demand my return."

"Perhaps. But by then, my love, you will be far too weary and ashamed to want to return to your husband. Nor would he want the wife that I should return, eh, Allen?"

Allen started to laugh. Rhiannon nudged her horse closer to William's. His hands were lax upon the reins. Clutching Garth tightly with both hands, she slammed her heels against the mare's sides. The poor creature burst into a gallop with such force and speed that the reins were wrenched from William's hands.

Desperately, still holding the babe to her breast, Rhiannon tried to retrieve the trailing reins as she thrashed wildly through the forest. Branches caught at her hair and scratched her face, yet she didn't dare slow her pace. She was blinded by the brush, and the reins eluded her as the mare chose an ever more erratic path, until suddenly she reared so abruptly that it was all Rhiannon could do to maintain her seat. And when the mare's hooves struck the earth once again, William was before her, lean-featured, tense, his eyes glittering anew with anger.

"One more antic like that and I promise that I shall set the child's skull beneath my horse's hooves. He is adept at crushing larger heads in battle—one little head will be as nothing to him."

She lowered her head, shivering. She had to believe that Garth would survive this horror, to which she had so foolishly fallen prey.

She lifted furious eyes to him. "Lead on, then, milord."

"If you doubt my threat—"

"Oh, I do not. I believe you completely capable of the murder of a helpless infant. 'Tis battle against men that must be beyond your capacity."

He rode his mount very close to her. The back of his hand lashed across her cheek, and she gritted her teeth against the pain, fighting for balance upon the mare. William watched her face and then smiled slowly.

"You'll learn courtesy and respect, milady. We have very long days and nights ahead for you to learn."

Days and nights . . . her heart sank. She realized that in truth the nightmare had just begun.

Where was Eric? Still with the king? Mergwin had come to warn her but was too late. Tears stung her eyes, and she wondered if he still lay dying upon the path, or if he had already gone on to the great Valhalla of such men as he, if he embraced the loved ones he had lost. *Oh, Mergwin, be with me still!* she thought. *Someone be with me, oh, God, please!*

He knew as soon as he reached the gates of his home that William had come already. Riding in, he gave no pause but called to the sentry on duty to find Patrick.

The alarm on Patrick's handsome features quickly proved that something was very wrong. Eric did not dismount from the white stallion but questioned Patrick from the saddle.

"Has he come? William of Northumbria. Has he come here?"

"Indeed, Eric. He said that you were wounded, and my lady Rhiannon took the babe and fled with him."

"How long ago?" Eric demanded harshly. They had not dared to sleep during the night, trying to close the gap of hours between their departures. For nearly three days they had done nothing but ride, and still William had beaten them.

"Perhaps an hour, maybe two. Thank God you are all right, milord! But then, why did William—"

"Eric!" Daria, who had heard their arrival, came running from the house. "Eric, you're all right! But we had heard—"

"Daria, I will explain all later. Right now I've got to stop William and find my wife."

"And child," Daria said.

"The babe? He has taken the babe too?"

"Aye, Eric. She left so quickly, neither Adela nor I were here. Father sent ships, you see. Oh, Eric!"

"Where's Mergwin?"

"With them, perhaps," Patrick said. "He went leaping onto a bare-backed mare when they left. The mare just returned alone. We were preparing to search for him before the daylight could fail us completely."

"I will find him," Eric said.

He turned the white stallion about, heading for the gates. Rollo, Jon, and Edward quickly followed. "Wait!" Daria pleaded. "Let me come with you! Maybe I can help."

Her brother barely paused. "Daria, go back inside!" Eric told her. "By God, Daria, I would not have you at risk too!"

But when he had turned again, Daria was already

heading for the stables. She was her father's daughter —and her mother's, he thought admiringly.

Eric was already hard set upon the trail. He had snatched Rhiannon away from Yorg the Dane easily enough, but this would be different. William was a very desperate man, a man guilty of much but mainly of treason against the king. There was no help against the king's wrath. He would care nothing for his own life, only that he bring Rhiannon and Eric down with him into the darkness of death.

And the child! If only she had left the child behind! But she would not have left the babe; he knew that well. And he knew, too, that she would do anything to protect Garth. Sweat broke out upon his brow, his hands trembled upon his reins, and he knew that if he found William, he would gladly rip him asunder with his bare hands.

He frowned, aware of a body in his path, against the trees. He leapt from the white stallion and came down beside the crumpled form. It was Mergwin, as gray as death, his eyes closed against the shadows of the coming night.

"God!" Eric choked on the word and dragged his ancient mentor upon his lap, cradling him in his massive arms. "He will die for this alone, I swear it, my friend, I swear it, by my mother's honor."

He leaned against the man's chest and could find no heartbeat. He would leave Mergwin now to rest in the glade, and if he could not bring him home to lie in Irish soil, then he would bring him to the water, cast him upon a bier with his runes and Celtic crosses, and send him off aflame, to blaze his very way to the halls of Valhalla. Every honor would be done him. And for his life Eric would remember him and miss him.

Suddenly Eric felt a rumbling within the frail chest. The wise gray eyes opened with a heavy effort and met his. "Take no more time with me, Prince of Dubhlain. I rest rather comfortably here in the forest. She knows that William is a traitor, and she will be slowing him down. Go quickly now. He is heading north along the cliffs and ridges. You will be at a grave disadvantage. Hurry. Leave me, and go quickly."

"I cannot leave you here to die!"

Mergwin smiled and beckoned Eric closer. He whispered to him and then fell back, exhausted.

"Rollo, come, take Mergwin. I charge you, bring him home with all the tender care of a babe."

"Then you ride on as three," Rollo protested.

"I've ridden alone against twenty," Eric reminded him dryly. "Take Mergwin. Jon and Edward have the death of a friend to settle with William, and I will have my wife and child. Go—quickly."

Rollo did as he was bidden. Eric remounted the white stallion, and he, Jon, and Edward started briskly through the woods once again.

19

It seemed to have grown so very late that Rhiannon
could not believe that they had not stopped for even
a moment. Garth had grown very restless, and his
crying had become so strident that she began to fear
William's reaction if she did not still him soon. She
had been forced to nurse him before William's gaze, a
gaze that chilled her to the marrow of her bones and
made her feel uneasy and shamed. She tried to ignore
him, then soon discovered that he was anxious only to
move as quickly as possible for as long as possible.

Mergwin had told her that Eric would come. If only
it would be so! Had they come to love each other so
very much, only to lose all to this treachery now? If
there was a God in heaven, it could not be so.

She tried to stall William and Allen frequently, telling them she had need of the woods, begging a drink,
complaining of thirst and hunger and exhaustion
again and again. But it seemed that William had a
destination in mind and that they were not going to
stop until they reached it.

They came to it very deep in the night, a cave upon
a high ridge with a narrow entry and a clear path
before it. Rhiannon quickly saw the wisdom of his

choice, for no one could come upon them without being seen.

William dismounted from his horse and came to Rhiannon's side. "I see you are aware of the advantage this cave affords, milady. The moment he comes near—if he should do so—I will know."

She cast her shimmering gaze upon him. "And what will that do? So you will see him coming. He will kill you, anyway. How will you stop him? Even if he comes alone, he will kill Allen, and then he will kill you very slowly."

"I think not."

"And why not?"

"Because he will know that if he comes near me, first the child, and then the bride, will go hurtling over the cliff to the rear. Now come down, Rhiannon."

He reached for her. She gripped Garth tightly against her, glad that he seemed to be sleeping peacefully at last. "I will come down myself," she said.

She dismounted easily enough with her son but was not able to avoid his touch. When her feet touched the ground, Allen caught hold of the mare and led her into the cave. William stood still, staring at Rhiannon. He touched his mustache and stroked his long beard, and then Allen reappeared.

"A fire is burning deep within. I've made a bed for the child and Rhiannon."

"Fine." William's eyes remained upon Rhiannon, his smile deepening. "Then you will take the first watch. Milady, you will come with me."

"I'll not—" she began, but William nodded to Allen, who caught her shoulders, and then William, himself, wrested Garth from her.

"He can go over the cliff right now, milady!" he warned her. "Walk with me and I will set him to sleep on his blanket. Walk with me now."

He would do it, she thought, torn, exhausted, fearing an onslaught of helpless hysteria. "Give him back to me. I will lay him down to sleep."

William shook his head and turned, walking into the cave. Desperate, Rhiannon followed him. "Please! Put him down, William, now."

He was doing so, setting the child down more gently than she had expected. Garth did not awaken, but his little body shook with a sigh, and his thumb climbed to his mouth. She stared with anguish at her son and then looked at the man before her.

"Time to pay, Rhiannon!" he told her softly.

"Pay for what?"

"Ah, for your pride and arrogance and insolence. You should have been mine from the beginning, and the land and the manor should have been mine. I was Alfred's man, loyal to the core. I watched you grow, and I went to the king and made it known that I should be the one to receive you and the land. But you were in love with Rowan, and the king was a fool for your desires until that bastard Viking entered the picture. I thought to dishonor you before the king when I had you fight the Viking. Alas, it all turned upon me. Again I thought that Ragwald could dispatch Eric the Wolf on his way to Valhalla, that invader could slay invader, but he failed me too. I had Rowan killed—"

"What?" she cried, feeling ill.

"Indeed, lady, 'tis easy to hire murderers. You would be amazed. A man's life is often worth a paltry amount in gold. And then again I tried to kill your husband and wrest you from him, but my dagger was deflected. If he does not know now that it was I who betrayed him, he will soon come to the realization. And so there is nothing left but you, and I will not let you go so easily."

"No," she whispered, backing away from him. "I loathe you. I despise you. The thought of you makes me ill. I shall never let you—" She broke off, frozen, as he drew a knife from a sheath at his calf. She thought he meant to toss it at her, and she thought that she would welcome death before his touch. But he turned suddenly and sent the blade hurtling toward the blanket where Garth slept. Rhiannon screamed, racing toward her infant. The knife had been well aimed. It did not strike the lad; it did not even awaken him. But it fell upon the blanket right beside the tiny golden head, and its warning was clear to Rhiannon.

She started to turn but it didn't matter. William was at her side, wrenching her to her feet and into his arms. "Lady, you will have me!" he insisted. His mouth came down hard upon hers, bruising her, causing her to taste blood. She fought him, fought his kiss, fought his hold. She kicked and pummeled and kneed him, and he swore, tossing her to the ground. And then he approached her with venom in his eyes, and before she could defend herself, he struck her hard across the face, then yanked her to her feet. His hands lit upon her bodice and she heard the rent and felt the fabric tear. He threw her then into the corner of the cave, and as she fell to the floor she was terribly afraid that she could fight no more, because a blackness was descending before her eyes.

God, don't let this happen! she prayed.

But she could still taste the blood.

The moon was high when Eric saw the cave gaping before them in the darkness. He lifted his hand, and behind him, Edward and Jon reined in their horses.

Neither Rhiannon nor the babe could be seen, nor William of Northumbria, nor the horses.

But Allen was there, seated at the opening of the cave, watching every movement about him.

Jon came up behind Eric. "I know this cave. There is an opening to the rear. Sheer cliffs lie below it. If we approach, William will threaten you with the lives of your wife and child."

Eric nodded. He had figured as much himself. But he could not wait. William was deep in the cliff, with Garth and Rhiannon. Rhiannon would not let him harm the babe.

And so he would harm her. . . .

He whirled about, his hand upon his sword hilt, and he heard the sound of horse's hooves behind them. Daria rode into view, and he swore vehemently. "I told you to stay home."

Daria dismounted, tossing back the hood of her mantle. "I thought that I could help—"

"Help!" Jon interrupted. "You should take a switch to her, Eric!"

Daria ignored him, walking toward the trees. "I *can* help!" she whispered. "Eric, please, I can! If you walk in, that man will sound an alarm. If I wander up, I may take him off-guard."

" 'Tis too risky," Eric began, but Daria smiled, and then flew past them all with such speed that they had no choice but to prepare to follow her with all haste.

Daria walked calmly toward the cave, calling out when she saw Allen at the entrance, "Dear sir! Could you help me, please? I am so afraid that I am endlessly lost in this forest." She continued to speak, but they could hear no more as she approached Allen. He stood there, clearly fascinated and perhaps mesmerized by her beauty. As she spoke, she moved and, in her movement, enchanted Allen from the entrance to the cave. "Now," Eric murmured. "By God, but she has given us a clear entry! Jon, see that he does not harm my sister. Edward, I implore you, see to my child."

Yet even as he started out across the clearing before the cave, Allen seemed to realize that something was afoot. "William!" he cried. "William, we've company!"

Eric straightened and started across the clearing, his sword drawn. Allen saw him and his eyes widened with alarm. He thrust Daria before him as a shield. "I'll kill her, Viking. So help me, I'll kill her." Daria kicked him with a vengeance, and he loosed his hold upon her, backing toward the cave.

"Daria, get out!" Eric warned. Jon, behind him, caught hold of Daria's arm and sent her whirling to safety behind them. Then they entered the cave.

Something had happened, something to save her, Rhiannon thought. Just as William had descended upon her, just as she screamed with horror as his fingers brushed her naked flesh, something happened. The world was still spinning, and she did not know what had occurred; she was only aware that William was rising, that he was racing forward.

Stunned, she clutched her tattered clothing to her, then thought to leap to her feet and go for Garth. But just as she came to her knees to do so, she saw that William had had the same idea. Her eyes met his across the earthen floor of the cave just as he reached for the babe. "Get behind me, lady, and stay there. We are ready to greet your husband."

Allen came rushing in upon them, his sword drawn. "He's here, the Viking is here!"

"Quit your quaking, you fool!" William advised him harshly. "Let him come."

And then Eric was standing in the entrance to the cave, towering there, his sword, his Vengeance, in his hands, his eyes a chilling blue fire against the shadows of the cave.

"You are a dead man, William," he said very quietly.

"Ah, but, Viking, you are missing the obvious. I hold your child in my arms. And a dagger as well. I hold your wife. If you wish them no harm, you will let me pass."

To Rhiannon's amazement Eric stepped back slightly and rubbed his chin, as if weighing the offer. "Give me the child. You can have the woman."

A gasp escaped her, but none of them seemed to notice her. "You will let me take Rhiannon? For the child?"

"Women are easy to come by. Healthy heirs are harder to achieve. Give me the child."

William did not answer. Then Daria burst through the men. Like a whirlwind, she came before William and snatched Garth cleanly away. William, amazed that he had allowed the girl to end the bargaining so quickly, backed toward Rhiannon, snatching her to him, setting his knife against her throat. "Let me pass now, unmolested, or I will kill her."

Eric sidestepped William while Allen went for their horses. Daria had disappeared with the babe, and Rhiannon's legs were weak, she was so grateful for his safety. But Eric could not mean to let her go now, surely he could not. . . .

And then she thought she knew his game. "Bastard Viking!" she called him. "So you would take my land and my child and be done with it?" As she spoke, she held still, then wrenched with all her might from William. "My lord!" she cried, "I am free!" But she was not. She could not pass before him, could only race into the depths of the cave.

She heard a sharp clash of steel and turned in time to see Allen attack her husband, then fall to the ground, dead. William cried out a hoarse, provoking war cry and challenged Eric: "Will the Wolf let others fight his battles? Come, milord Viking, the fight is between us."

And so he came onward into the cave. William's sword caught Eric's, and the clang and echo were terrible. Then Eric swung his great blade again and again, forcing William ever deeper into the cave and down upon the ground. William threw dirt into Eric's eyes and Rhiannon screamed, warning him of William's approach. Eric rolled just in time to avoid William's thundering blade. Rhiannon went deeper still, until she felt a cold breath of air and realized she had come to the northern entrance to the cave. Braced against the opening, she stared back in the semidarkness as the fight continued. Then she heard another clash and a thud, and there was a sudden, startling silence.

She clenched her fists and gritted her teeth, listening. She blinked against the darkness and realized that William was down upon the ground just inside the cave, and that Eric stood over him, his sword at his throat. "Rise, William. I will not murder you here. You must stand before the king."

"No!" William swore violently. "Kill me, Viking, my throat is before you!"

But Eric moved his sword away. "Get up. Your execution is the king's right."

Slowly William rose. But at the last he twisted away and came tearing toward the rear of the cliff. He saw Rhiannon there, and a horrible, harsh laughter came bubbling from him. He reached for her as he hurtled toward the opening . . . and the cliffs below.

Rhiannon screamed as his fingers fastened upon her. She fought him madly and freed her arms, but he caught hold of her foot and she felt an awful sensation as they started to fall together. They were going over the side of the cliffs.

"Rhiannon!" She heard her name on the night wind, heard it like a mighty roar from the darkness, heard it like the power of light and life itself. She clung hard to the scruffy bushes attached to the rocky ground of the cliff, but William had already fallen before her, his fingers wound tightly about her ankles, and he was pulling her ever downward. The pain was agonizing; she could no longer bear the torture upon her arms; she was slipping, slipping.

"Rhiannon!" Again he called her name, and then he was above her, his eyes crystal blue and commanding. His hands were wound around her wrists and he was pulling her upward. She could see the bulge and strain in his bronze muscles, and her pain increased and she cried out with it. "Hold!" he commanded. "Hold, I command you, I order you. Obey me, wife!"

Her fingers wound around his, and then suddenly she heard a long, drawn-out cry as William of Northumbria went pitching downward into the darkness below, into death.

But she was lifted into the cool night wind, lifted into her husband's arms . . .

And lifted into life.

She collapsed against him. He swept her up into his embrace, covering her with his own mantle, wrapping her in tenderness.

She remembered very little of the long ride that brought them from darkness into the light of day, and then into the coming dusk of darkness again.

Garth rode comfortably with Daria, who was tossing her elegant mane of hair about and—ever the princess—informing Jon of Wincester that she was her own woman, in charge of her own destiny, and that she had been every bit as helpful as any man.

Rhiannon listened to Daria and then laughed when Eric said that he was sure his father would be more than willing to entertain marriage offers on this youngest, most willful of his offspring. Jon warned Daria that she should be very careful—he just might make an offer to teach her what a woman's place should be.

Then Rhiannon and Eric heard no more, for Eric urged the white stallion forward and Rhiannon managed to open her eyes wide upon him and demand, "So women are easy to come by, milord?"

"Ah, my love, but I made no mention of women such as yourself. Women of courage and fire and beauty are rare. And the one that I hold within my arms is my very life." He shuddered as he held her. "My love, had he taken you over that cliff, my only desire would have been to follow!"

She shivered, then felt his arms tighten about her. She looked into his eyes once again. "Mergwin said that there would be peace, if we could weather the tempest. Oh, God, Eric! He gave his life to save me!"

"I saw him," Eric told her. "He has been taken home."

"He said that he would not see Ireland again," she whispered, and tears rose to her eyes.

"Hush, love, hush, rest easy. He has promised us peace, so peace shall be ours."

They spoke little throughout the rest of the journey. When they came home at last, Rhiannon had fallen asleep. Her exhaustion was so great that she did not waken when Eric carried her to her room, nor indeed until morning. And then Adela was in her room, telling her that a nice hot bath awaited her and that she would bring Garth soon afterward. Rhiannon rose and gladly stepped into the bath, wondering if she would ever wash away the repulsion that William's touch had aroused within her, then pausing as she closed her eyes and mourned anew for Mergwin. He had come to mean so much to her. But she was home and alive, and her son, too, was alive.

And Eric . . .

They had survived the tempest.

She rose and wrapped a linen towel about herself, and just then Eric came into the room. He, too, looked infinitely better than he had the night before. He had bathed away the dirt and blood, and he was as golden and regal and magnificent as she had ever seen him.

He came swiftly to her side and swept her, towel and dampness and all, into the fervor of his embrace. She clung to him, then felt the strength of his arms as he swept her up again, bearing her toward the bed. She met his kiss with a lusty fervor of her own, but when he peeled her towel away and his feverish lips kissed her passionately upon her breast, she pulled up, catching his golden head, protesting. "Eric, we mustn't! There's so much to do this morning!"

"Such as?" he demanded.

"Garth, milord. Surely he will be wanting me soon."

"Indeed . . . soon," Eric agreed. "Daria is caring for him, and he is sipping on a skin of goat's milk. She will bring him soon enough."

Still, Rhiannon shook her head. "Eric, we musn't!" Tears stung her eyes. "Remember Mergwin! There are prayers to be said, arrangements to be made. . . ."

"Ah, yes." Eric rolled to his side. "Mergwin." His eyes, carrying a light of wicked blue fire, fell challengingly upon hers. "There are no arrangements to be made."

"But—"

"Mergwin is alive and well and resting comfortably below. His only distress is that he did not correctly predict his own death. He has requested that my parents come immediately to visit us, since he is determined that he cannot set foot upon Irish soil. So, indeed, since I expect the King of Wolves and his lovely queen, my mother, any day, we will have preparations. But not, my love, this very moment."

"He—he—Mergwin is alive?" Rhiannon gasped.

Eric nodded. His smiled deepened as he ran a finger along her naked abdomen and said softly, "Truly he is alive, and he has taught me much of life, just as you have taught me everything of love. Our future was sorely imperiled last night! Indeed, our life together has been fraught with storms. So very often we have been parted—and swords have clashed between us and arrows have flown. But now we have this peaceful time together, and it is precious between us, just as all of our time, and all of our lives, must be from now on."

"Indeed, my love!" Rhiannon shivered and, catching his hand, kissed his fingers most tenderly.

He rose up against her and gently touched her lips with his own, his eyes still dancing. "Once upon a time, you see, when I was but moments old, Mergwin agreed that I was quite a Viking, quite a Wolf, just like my father. And he warned Olaf that I would go through tempest and travail and wander the world a-Viking, but then he said that a vixen would tame the wolf. And when that came about, I would seek adventure no more but find peace within the arms of my wild and courageous little fox."

Rhiannon nodded slowly, stretched out her arms, and wrapped them around him. "And am I such a vixen, then, milord?"

"Indeed you are. Willful, impetuous, fascinating, and very brave. Exactly the mate I might have desired. For life, my love, and beyond."

"Come then, my Viking, my Wolf. Breathe your sweet desire upon my lips, and I will seek to tame you if I may."

"With all my heart," he agreed, and his laughter was husky as he rolled her atop him, meeting the silvered beauty of her gaze once again. "You see, love, there's been another prophesy."

"Indeed?" she inquired warily.

"Mergwin has informed me that should we seize the moment, I shall soon be the father of a daughter to rival the beauty of the very gods—and that of her mother, of course."

Rhiannon laughed, but then her laughter faded as his lips descended upon hers and she was quickly swept into the fierce and tender passion of his kiss. The sweet heat of desire quickly engulfed her, and she yielded herself eagerly to the endless depths of her love.

It was later, much later, before she whispered beside him, "A daughter, my love?"

"A daughter," he agreed.

And she sighed, content, and curled comfortably into the great curve of his arms.

Mergwin was never, never wrong.

Outstanding historical romances by bestselling author

HEATHER GRAHAM

The American Woman Series

☐ **SWEET SAVAGE EDEN**   20235-3 $3.95

☐ **PIRATE'S PLEASURE**   20236-1 $3.95

☐ **LOVE NOT A REBEL**   20237-X $3.95

Other Titles You Will Enjoy

☐ **DEVIL'S MISTRESS**   11740-2 $3.95

☐ **EVERY TIME I LOVE YOU**   20087-3 $3.95

☐ **GOLDEN SURRENDER**   12973-7 $3.95

Reckless abandon.
Intrigue. And spirited
love. A magnificent array of
tempestuous, passionate historical
romances to capture your heart.